ARNETT HARTWELL

Deviant

Boudi-Ca Chronicles Book 1

To my loving wife with love

Author's Notes:

Thanks for reading my book. If you enjoyed this book, consider leaving a positive review at its source and reading on with the next volume. This is first book in a traditional trilogy (Boudi-Ca Chronicles, starting with Deviant), which required sacrifice and the best times of this author's life to write.Each manuscript was developed through hundreds of hours of effort and many revisions to deliver the finished, polished work. Any form of patronage is appreciated.

Preface

Deviant:

Dreams:

Deliver:

A Jinn:

*While Boudi-Ca A Jinn is meant to be read after the main Boudi-Ca Chronicles trilogy, or just independently, the events of the story occur chronologically between the second book Dreams, and the third book Deliver.

Chapter 1:

The stairway to Heaven ran perfectly straight from the lower realms to the Raqi'a Gates except at one place, where the steps bent and turned through the tumbled ruins of old Chickasaw. In the heart of those ruins, a seahorse statue curved over a crumbling pool. The bottom of the pool had been broken by the bombardments of Heaven's architects. The seahorse arched only over a hole with no water, just open sky below.

One sunny morning, a group of student Mimọs gathered at the seahorse statue. They were all handsome young males wearing skydiving trunks, except for one, a girl holding an umbrella. Boudi was half-pretty, but she was far from perfect. The standards were high in Heaven for mimọ girls.

Boudi's eyes were a fine shade of umber, but one was sometimes lazy. Her hair was ebony-colored and unruly instead of perfectly straight and blonde. Her halo floated slightly off to one side, no matter how she tilted her head to accommodate it. Boudi's imperfections made her a shy mimọ who liked to keep to herself, except when she went sky diving with her best friend, Tajee.

"So, are we going to dive, or not?" Boudi wrapped her gloved hands around the Platinum umbrella handle. Tajee fingered the umbrella spokes to make sure they were firm.

"I'm ready. You're in front."

Boudi stepped to the edge of the pool. She climbed onto the curved back of the seahorse statue. She balanced on her stockinged feet against the subtle air pressure. She prayed that the umbrella would hold the weight of two Mimos. Tajee's brown arms clasped her from behind. He pressed her towards the seahorse's slippery snout.

"Woo!" Hooted the onlooking boys. "Do it, Boudi! Do it!"

Boudi leaped forward, and then she was falling through the wide-open bottom of the broken pool with Tajee's arms wrapped around her. Far below them in the sky, the pale line of the stairway to Heaven tipped and spun vertiginously.

"Woo!" Hooted the boys from above. "Woo!"

The wind rushed. Boudi felt her skirt flutter above her waist. The dive-pleasure penetrated her shoes and stockings, starting with her toes and rising to her thighs. Tajee's hands grappled. Boudi gasped when his forearm levered roughly around her stomach. His fingers clutched the pleats of her dive skirt. A ripping sound crested the rush of the wind.

"Tajee!" She shouted. "Are you alright?"

He didn't answer. Boudi felt Tajee's chin digging for purchase at her rear end. He held his precarious position with his arms clamped around her thighs as they plummeted through the lowest stones of Chickasaw. The stairway to Heaven grew wider and wider in the sky. The trajectory resulted to be perfect. In two minutes, they tumbled together onto the wide sun-washed steps. Boudi disentangled herself with relief. Tajee's grin was bigger than she'd ever seen it.

"That was incredible, Boudi! Sorry about your skirt."

Boudi pivoted away from Tajee's low gaze. She'd spent three weeks working on her sinful skirt, hiding the thing in the closet of her Crystal College dormitory. After all that effort, her skirt was a disaster of torn fabric. She covered her exposed panties with her hand.

"Don't you dare look, Tajee!"

"I only slipped a little."

"Probably on purpose!"

Tajee didn't argue further with her. He only grinned as he always did, perhaps admitting his guilt, perhaps not. Tajee had a big, beautiful grin. His teeth were pearly white in contrast with his light brown skin. He rubbed his elbow and looked off the edge of the stairway as if that would assuage the awkward silence. "Ever wonder what's down there?"

"Earth of course—millions of souls living in material bodies and a lot of them forgetting all about Heaven."

"I heard some senior students talking about other places besides Heaven and Earth—dark places filled with hellions and evil creatures. If hellions go to Earth and try to seduce human souls, then they must live down there somewhere, right? I'd ask one of the professors, but I know they're forbidden to talk about such things."

Boudi sighed. "Yes, so why are we talking about them then?"

"I'm just glad there was no wind," Tajee continued. "I didn't want an accident to happen while we were doing the tandem dive together. You have to swear not to tell anyone, but William found a strange book while he was polishing the floor in Professor Elliott's office."

"What sort of book?"

Tajee's brown eyes turned mischievous. "It's a forbidden one—the kind they don't have in any of Heaven's libraries. It has a red Conclave censor stamp right on the front cover. The book is called Botany of the Yumboes Courts, whatever that is. It shows pictures of creatures covered with thorns and spines."

"I've never heard of the Yumboes Courts, but Botany is the study of plants, Tajee—how to identify different types, and how plants make babies with the blessings of our Lord. Elliott teaches Botany, but I'm shocked that she'd have a forbidden book in her office. Why would plants be forbidden?"

"The plants had little hellion eyes."

Boudi grimaced and tried to erase the horrid image from her brain. "Well, if the arch-Mimọs in their wisdom stamped the book as forbidden, then it's sinful, Tajee. You shouldn't have looked at it. Forbidden books make you think things a good mimọ shouldn't."

"You dive in the sky," Tajee countered. "You're a hypocrite sometimes."

"A lot of students dive in the sky during college, and they turn out just fine."

"Some even kiss."

"And they only kiss, because physical love is sinful." Boudi turned and shouldered her umbrella to defend against Tajee's warm proximity. "I need to do my homework for Earth History. If I keep slacking, my guardian won't be happy."

Tajee grinned. "Come to my dorm room and kiss with me instead. Rebels have to stick together."

"Maybe we're rebels, but that won't stop Professor Brown from failing me if I don't proofread. I already have to say three thousand prayers because Elliott saw you kiss me in the cloister hallway."

"I only got one thousand."

"That isn't fair. They always think it's the girl's fault."

"It is, especially when she's so pretty." Tajee's grin widened. "Let's do a tandem together again next time."

"I'm not sure there will be a next time." Boudi quickly climbed the stairs towards the white pediments of Heaven, which dwarfed the sunlit Olympic ruins underneath them. She suppressed a faint sin of anger. Tajee was a typical mimo male, possessed with brash masculine confidence. He always took charge, and he often tried to shock her with flattery and forbidden romance.

Everyone at Crystal College thought Tajee was her boyfriend. She wasn't so sure. Tajee's love was far from Mimoic or pure. Whenever he touched her or kissed her, she felt foggish and wrong. On that afternoon, she felt more wrong than ever before. Her new dive skirt was torn, and she'd done a tandem dive with a boy—something no proper mimo girl would even dream of.

~*~

That afternoon, Boudi sat at her desk in the back row of Earth History class. She struggled to focus on the tri-dimensional timeline on the chalkboard.

Professor Brown was nearing the end of another boring, forgettable lecture. Tajee sat in the second row. He was snoozing as usual.

Boudi nibbled on the end of her Platinum pen. The metal taste seemed unusually acute. Her legs tingled, and her chest felt warmer than normal in her over-hip corset. Her bruised thigh felt particularly queer where Tajee had handled her. Purply-pink tints were blooming on her skin beneath the prudent hemlines of her student robe.

She prayed that no one would notice. She'd dusted her face and neck with titanium powder before class, but not as carefully as she would have liked, since she'd been afraid to be late. She hoped the bruises would go away. She'd be humiliated if she had to see the school nurse. She'd have to tell the truth for her own good.

Boudi stacked her books so she could exit the classroom quickly. Earth History was almost over, and Tajee would surely ask her to go back to his dorm room for more illicit kissing. The more she gave in to Tajee's urgings, the further he wanted her to go. Tajee was out of control. Professor Brown raised his voice, interrupting her reverie.

"One final thing, class—an amazing opportunity has come to my attention. The Conclave of Deviant Operations—that's right, the CODO—is recruiting undergraduate Mimos for a special project."

Tajee roused from his customary slouch. Makeda Deen also perked up in the first row. Makeda raised her hand. "What's the project, professor? I thought the Conclave only took graduate students with the highest marks."

"The Conclave usually picks the best of the best, Makeda," Brown crooned at his favorite pupil. "In this case they've lowered the qualifications. The flyers are on my desk. Class dismissed."

Boudi grabbed her books and slipped in front of the crush of other students. She ducked into the stairs that led down to the privacy of the lower cloisters. She trotted the first flight of steps, but Tajee materialized directly in front of her on the narrow stone landing. The smell of smoke rose on the sanctified air.

"Tajee, you're not supposed to flash inside the Crystal College! With papers in your hand, you could set something on fire!"

"Look at this." Tajee held up a slightly smoking Conclave flyer.

WANTED: DANGER-SEEKING MIMOS

Do you have what it takes to join the Conclave of Deviant Operations? The CODO is recruiting undergraduate Mimos for a special top-secret project. Are you adventurous? Do you have acting skills? Are you committed to suppressing sin and corruption wherever they may be found? Standard entry requirements are waived for this once-in-a-soul-cycle opportunity. Get special operations training! No appointment necessary! Apply today!

Boudi shrugged. "The Conclave only accepts the best of the best, like Brown said. You're joking, right? You're only a sophomore. Makeda Deen is a senior, plus she gets perfect marks in everything."

"I know. Makeda and Ashanti almost beat me to the flyers." Tajee hefted the sheaf of hand-scribed flyers.

"You took them all?"

Tajee grinned. "Yep, but Brown already had one in his hand for Makeda. Imagine how amazing it would be to work at the CODO. Conclave agents fight every day against sin and corruption. Guardians go to Earth and defend people against evil. I couldn't be an inquisitor. My clairvoyance scores are too low."

"Tajee, the Conclave won't take you. You're great in Math class, but you're failing Earth History and school in general."

Tajee's enthusiasm drained from his face. "You're right, but I've always wanted to be an agent. I'd like to see the inside of the CODO building if nothing else."

"Sounds like fun until the Conclave locks you up for ignominiousness."

"You mean until they lock us both up. You're going with me."

Boudi blinked. "Are you crazy? I'm not going into the CODO unless they take me in handcuffs. Now you've done it. Brown is coming."

"Detention!" Boomed Brown. The professor descended the cloister stairs at a surprising speed for his oniony girth. "Hand over those flyers, Tajee.

Our good Lord says 'Thou shalt not steal.' You'll write those words five hundred times after the final period each day this week. A thousand for you, Miss Marcus."

"Why me? I didn't even—"

Brown wiggled his finger. "No backtalk, young lady. Girls are held to higher standards in a co-ed institution like this."

"Of course, sir. Thank you, sir."

Tajee surrendered the flyers to Brown's outstretched hand. "Boudi and I really wanted to apply for jobs at the Conclave, Professor. That's why I took the flyers. Do you think maybe our detention could be delayed —"?

"You two want to apply at the Conclave?" Brown laughed. "A Conclave interview would be a good lesson in humility, and I'm tired of babysitting a couple of failures. Fine. I'll want to see your rejection slips as proof that you went to the interviews. Otherwise, I'll file a complaint for theft and lying, and maybe you'll both get expelled from school."

~*~

Boudi fidgeted next to Tajee in the Conclave waiting room that afternoon. The Conclave of Deviant Operations was Heaven's intelligence agency. The CODO inquisitors could supposedly read the most impure thoughts of every mimo in Heaven. Bad Mimos were arrested and taken into the Conclave for reformation.

The CODO waiting room was crammed with job applicants, all sitting in uncomfortable metal chairs that were probably designed for sinners and delinquents instead of prospective employees. A group of scienticians was calling the student applicants to the front of the room. The applicants stepped into a scanning machine that beamed light over their bodies before they went deeper into the Conclave for interviews.

Makeda Deen and Ashanti had also arrived. They awaited their turns on the other side of the aisle. Makeda was beautifully prepared. A satin hair-band restrained her perfect blonde hair. Tapered white slippers with daring pink bows peeked from under the hem of Makeda's professional-looking robe.

Boudi shrank in her seat. Makeda made her queerly nervous—more nervous than an end-term math test or even the minds' scanner. She watched another student step into the scanning machine. She almost preferred expulsion over an interview at the Conclave, yet she had to give Tajee credit for his bravery. When Tajee wanted something, he went after it. She knew that only too well.

"I don't want to go into that thing, Tajee. It doesn't look good for bad Mimos like us."

A muscle in Tajee's neck twitched. "Just keep your mind blank. Don't think about kissing or anything sinful."

"I'm sorry, but I'm worried! Maybe if we tell them we changed our minds, they'd give us complementary rejection slips. It's better than getting arrested."

Tajee's face was resolute. "You can do this, Boudi. Trust me. Neither one of us is going to be arrested. I only wish I knew the right things to say so they'll take me. I'm so tired of going to that useless traditional school and listening to lectures from those professors. If the professors were any good at their subjects, they'd have better jobs in Heaven."

As if on cue, the bugle-phone crackled. "Tajee Al Adin," the metallic voice intoned.

Tajee stood up and smoothed his robe. "Here we go."

"Good luck, Tajee."

"There's no such thing as luck," Ashanti said from the other side of the aisle. "He'll need the blessing of our Lord, and he isn't going to get it. Hey Tajee, do you have an extra flyer, or did you use them all to write love letters to Boudi?" Makeda and Ashanti giggled.

Tajee ignored Ashanti and strode to the front of the room. A scientician motioned him into the scanner. A brilliant beam of light ran over his robed body from head to toe. The group of scienticians consulted the scanner controls. One of them leveled the same question that he'd asked the other applicants.

"Tajee Al Adin, have you dived illicitly, kissed, or engaged in any other ignominious or sinful activities?"

"No, sir."

"Tell the truth, please." The scientician tapped his pen on his clipboard.

"Um, yes," Tajee's voice cracked. "Just diving. Just once. A couple times."

"Interrogation room six." The scientician shook his head and made notes. Tajee slunk dejectedly towards the inner hallway.

"Next," burped the bugle-phone. "Boudilotta Marcus."

"You can do it, Boudi," Makeda drawled.

"Do it, Boudi. Do it," Ashanti echoed. Makeda covered her mouth quickly to contain the giggles. Boudi kept her eyes on the floor. The senior students weren't just making fun of her. They were mocking her reputation too. She stalked to the front of the room and took her place in the scanner. The scienticians worked the controls. Boudi closed her eyes against the brilliant light, but she was too late. The room disappeared in a sea of shimmering stars.

"Miss Marcus, have you dived illicitly, kissed, or engaged in any other ignominious activities?" The disembodied voice came from the void.

"Just diving. A little bit." Boudi blinked her eyes. The stars swam. She couldn't even see the scientician, who coughed audibly.

"Interrogation room eight."

Boudi groped her way out of the machine. She was halfway back to the crowded seating area before her vision resolved. She reversed and made a beeline towards the interrogation rooms. Hushed giggles erupted in the waiting area. Boudi looked over her shoulder. Makeda and Ashanti were pointing at her and laughing. Without thinking, she raised her hand and made a rude gesture.

The bugle-phone burped. "Stop, Miss Marcus."

Boudi froze. The scienticians clustered together, gesturing animatedly. Makeda and Ashanti were no longer laughing. Their faces were grave. A murmur of shocked whispers rushed through the waiting room. Boudi felt her legs go rubbery. She couldn't believe what she'd done in front of everyone. She'd never even made such a gesture before. She'd only seen Tajee do it once towards another boy who had insulted his diving technique.

The Conclave would probably just lock her up on the spot.

"Miss Marcus, interrogation room twenty-six."

Boudi walked down the long, dimly lit hallway. She felt feverish and thin as a pencil under her robe. Tears threatened to overwhelm her eyelids. She turned a bend at the end of the hallway and faced the foreboding silver digits. Twenty-six. She turned the cold round knob and entered a small, bright room. A white-robed arch-mimọ with a grey beard and a golden halo sat behind a semi-circular table, in front of which sat a folding chair.

"I'm Auditor Pasteur. You may sit."

"Yes, sir." Boudi sat primly. She pressed her legs together and lowered her chin with an attitude of virtuousness and humility that was proper for mimọ girls. Pasteur examined a worn silver clipboard.

"I see you were registered with Heaven as Charlene Boudilotta Marcus from Norfolk, England. Your earthly father and brother are bibliognost here, but your mother was an unrepentant agnostic and went the other way. Is that correct?"

"Yes, sir. I think so, sir."

"According to your Conclave records, you're a sophomore at the Crystal College of Sacred Moons. I see good marks for classes in acting, history, and English. In preparatory school, you placed first in a grade nine English contest, and in the same year you were elected to your class council."

"Yes, sir."

"In grades ten, eleven, and twelve, however, you served over twenty detentions for tardiness and skipping class. You were caught on four occasions kissing a boy, which resulted in an equal number of punishments and a formal warning."

"Yes, sir."

"For some reason we don't have your college records on file yet, but I doubt they are favorable. Do you Share the Conclave's dedication to fighting sin and corruption, Miss Marcus?"

"Yes, sir. Of course, sir."

"What other qualifications do you have besides your schoolwork?"

"None, sir."

Pasteur leaned back in his chair. "Your scan shows that you've been diving in the clouds below Heaven. That's the behavior of a bad mimǫ—a rule-breaker and a malcontent."

"Yes, sir."

"I was informed that you made an obscene gesture at some other applicants in the waiting room. Is this a joke, Miss Marcus? If you wanted the Conclave's attention, you've got it."

"I'm sorry, sir." Boudi felt her chin tremble. She didn't want to burst into tears in front of the cranky old arch-mimǫ, but she couldn't help herself. "I know anger is a sin. I only came to the Conclave because I wanted to support my friend, Tajee. He really wants to be a Conclave agent. I'm not qualified for this job. I'm not a good mimǫ girl."

The arch-mimǫ patted his forehead with a handkerchief. His grizzled moustache twitched. "So, you committed the sins of anger and pride, then, but in the context of love and charity. You were doing something you didn't want to do, but for the good of another."

"Yes, that's right, sir. School is boring for Tajee. He wants to work in the Conclave so he can go on adventures and actually do things."

"So, you're loyal to your fellow Mimǫs," the arch-mimǫ persisted. "You're willing to make sacrifices at your own personal risk. When your boyfriend wants a kiss, you let him have it despite the sin, and then you lie to protect yourself and him."

"I'm so sorry, sir. I'm weak, and I pray for forgiveness."

"Yes, of course. Of course." The arch-mimǫ nodded to himself, as if pondering. He tucked his handkerchief away and drummed his fingers on the table.

"May I go then, please?"

"Oh no, young lady. You'll be staying right here."

Boudi felt a chill run up her spine. So, she was doomed. She'd made too many stupid mistakes. She was a pathetic mimǫ girl failure. She'd never see Tajee or her classmates ever again. The only question was what painful reformations the CODO would use on her first. The arch-mimǫ's eyes looked haunted, as if seeing terrible things in a faraway place.

"This will be a very dangerous mission, Miss Marcus. This mission may involve a lot of kissing. You have more experience than most mimo girls with breaking the rules and indulging in sin, but nothing in Heaven can prepare you for the lust and corruption that you'll face down in the field."

"I… I don't understand, sir. What… what field?"

Auditor Pasteur rose up from the desk. His white robes gleamed, and his halo shimmered from on high. "I mean the field of battle between good and evil, of course. You'll start your training immediately, but first you need to sign some things—paperwork for risking your soul and notifying next of kin—all of the legalities. Congratulations. You've got the job."

The glorious light which permeated the mental realms illuminated the roofs of the Crystal College in tones of pale grey. A flock of harpy eagles swooped on the downdraft to scatter across the flagstones like papers in a swirling wind. The harpy eagles strutted back and forth, then flew again in unison. A few stayed to lodge in the shadows between the columns, where they fluttered, cooed, and fussed.

Boudi sat down on a bench with her Conclave manual lying on her lap. She was expecting Tajee, but she was no longer a student at Crystal College. She was not sure why the Conclave had hired her. Given the situation, she had been too afraid to complain. She'd signed all the complicated paperwork.

Even more unbelievably, after only six weeks of junior agent training, she was already working on her first Conclave mission—a secret mission so remarkable and startling that if Tajee knew, he would turn red with envy. The patter and slap of Tajee's sandals echoed across the flagstones. Boudi glanced at her Conclave wristwatch. As usual, Tajee was late.

"Hi, Boudi," Tajee said. He stopped in front of the bench and looked down at her. "Are you studying for the Conclave?"

"Yes. It is an advanced book on the seven deadly sins."

Tajee boggled at the heavy textbook on her lap. "You're learning all this new stuff. It's damned unfair. You did not want to set foot in the Conclave."

Boudi felt a faint warmth of pride, which she suppressed. According to her textbook, pride was the deadliest of sins. "You should work on your language, Tajee. Talking like that won't help you advance."

"Advance to what? With my marks, I'll be lucky to get a job scraping up dove gunk after I graduate."

"Maybe you should study harder."

"I like to have fun, and I don't plan to grow out of it. I like to have adventures too. They're the one thing I'm good at. That's why I wanted to work for the Conclave, but I know I'll never be qualified."

"Your marks aren't very good, but you're daring, clever, and good at figuring trajectories for umbrella jumps."

Tajee managed a half-grin. "Thanks for the kind words, Boudi."

"Kindness is an important mimo girl's virtue. I have to work hard on my virtues. That's why I'm reading this ridiculously enormous book."

"That's a fancy wristwatch Pasteur gave you. Does he ever punish you when you screw up? Does he ever take you into his office for a 'talking-to' like Professor Brown?"

Boudi felt heat rise to her cheeks. "That's none of your business."

Tajee shrugged. "Fine. So, are we going diving? I can't believe the Conclave lets you go down to the ruins of Chickasaw whenever you want. The ruins are supposed to be forbidden, except for historians and scholars with official conclave permits."

"I have a permit." Boudi smiled, but Tajee glowered at her like Brown.

"I don't know why you even signed up with the Conclave. You were perfectly happy going to Crystal College, and just because you get half-decent marks doesn't mean you'll be a good secret agent. You aren't adventurous or danger-seeking in the least."

"I can be adventurous."

Tajee looked skeptical. "When did you ever do anything adventurous when I didn't twist your arm to get you to do it? I'll bet you won't last. You won't even make it through your first mission."

"I'll bet I do."

"Fine. The bet is on. If I win, you must come to my dorm room and let me do whatever I want with you."

"That's disgusting, Tajee! You just don't get it. There's a vast prison in the Conclave, and most of the mimos are undergoing lust-reformation to purify their thought bodies. It's an epidemic. The prison is clearance level six, and the doors are double-reinforced with sin-preventative gold mesh. The inquisitors wear padded suits to protect against psycho-erotic contamination. Pasteur showed me his."

Tajee sighed. "I was joking, Boudi. You used to laugh at my jokes."

"The Conclave isn't a joke, Tajee. That's my point. There's pure divine love, and then there's physical amorous love. You're confused about the two types, and the Conclave tries to keep Heaven purified. That's what the inquisitors do—they observe Heaven on a psychic level and file arrest warrants when necessary."

"Maybe there are more types of love, and it isn't so black and white."

Boudi fidgeted. She'd heard of more types of love in ancient Greek history, but her Conclave textbook was clear on the issue. "No. It's black and white, just like good and evil."

"If I win the bet, I want a kiss for at least a minute. The Conclave says it's forbidden, but I'll never believe it's evil."

"Fine. And if I win, you have to admit you're wrong and apologize." Boudi stood up and pushed her textbook into her rucksack, wary of Tajee's hot gaze. "And I'm going to win because Pasteur already gave me my first mission."

"Well, what is it?"

"It's top secret."

Tajee palmed his forehead dramatically, as if afflicted with a painful headache. "Whatever. Meet me down at the Raqi'a Gates. I have to flashback to my dorm room to change into my dive suit. I'd invite you to come, but I know you don't want to." Tajee crinkled his nose and disappeared into his flash.

"Fine." Boudi buttoned up her rucksack and double-checked the secret bottle in the side pocket. She felt exasperated, even more than when Tajee had cornered her in the Crystal College scroll closet, and she'd clumsily knocked over a rack of holy scriptures with her backside. She wanted to tell Tajee about her mission in the ruins of Chickasaw, but any hints would depend on Tajee to put two and two together to make four. That would probably never happen.

Boudi shouldered her rucksack, grabbed her umbrella, and flashed to the lowest edge of Heaven. She stamped into the shelter of the open Raqi'a Gates, out of view of the spiraled watchtowers that guarded the stairway like beacons in the ethereal light. A pair of winged tenshiim circled above, but the protectors paid her no mind, and neither did the three mimọs who had arrived that morning with easels to paint skyscapes at Heaven's edge.

Within a few minutes, Tajee emerged from his flash with a residual smell of ozone. He wore his dive suit and carried his tabby cat in his hands. Boudi offered a conciliatory smile. She had to be nice. It was the virtuous mimọ girl thing to do.

"Hi, Tajee. Nice trick flashing with your cat. He doesn't catch fire?"

"Only sometimes. You still remember Coco, right?" Tajee dropped his grey tabby cat without looking at her.

"Why would I forget your cat? I've only been at the Conclave for six weeks. I haven't lost my memories. Are we even friends anymore, or are you too angry? It's not my fault that I'm working for the Conclave, so I can't kiss you. Is that why you want me to fail? So, we can be together again? That's selfish."

"Whatever makes you happy, Boudi."

Tajee turned and descended the stairway. Boudi hiked after him several hundred meters down to where the stairway to Heaven descended into the ruins of Chickasaw. She unfurled her umbrella and mini-jumped after Tajee from the left edge of the stair onto the older Olympic stones.

She followed over the sloping slabs that had once been the rooftops of forgotten, discredited Greek gods. They sundered the old marble from Heaven's bombardments, but it still hung in mid-sky as a testament to the power of magic in antiquity.

Tajee hopped across a broken pediment and then leaped down onto a perpendicular connecting section—a wide, flat marble block with green striations that gleamed dully. We dubbed the block the Upper Allyssia Platform—an ambitious diving spot that was little used due to a history of tragic accidents. A marble pylon stood with a red flag to warn adventurous mimos away.

"I'm going to wait here." Boudi blanked her face. She tried not to fidget or look suspicious. She didn't want Tajee to suspect anything. "Could you come and get me when you're finished? Where's your braking balloon?"

"Benjamin is bringing one for me." Tajee eyed her up and down. "You're not even wearing your suit under your robe, are you?"

"No. I got rid of my dive suit when I moved. I didn't dare take it into the Conclave."

"I'd do that as well. I'll see you in a few." Tajee scampered along the edge of a broken plinth block that led down to the lower platforms. Boudi felt a flicker of envy. She missed the thrill of diving, but she needed to focus on her mission.

When Tajee was gone, she walked to the end of the marble block and fished the Conclave message bottle from the pocket of her rucksack. It was an ordinary student ink bottle—small, round, with a sturdy base. She pressed the cork with her thumb to make sure it's sealed, and then she tossed the bottle over the edge of the marble, where it vanished quickly into the atmosphere. The sky seemed opaque that morning, greyer than normal, with clouds of moisture. The angles of the stairway to Heaven were barely visible in the mist.

Boudi opened her book and scratched a mark with her pen. She counted the marks. That bottle had been the sixth that she'd thrown. In the last three weeks, she had visited the ruins five times. She'd partly invited Tajee that morning because she was lonely. She hadn't made any friends at the Conclave. Pasteur had introduced her to Raphael and a few other important Conclave officials, but it only focused them on the progress of her mission.

Her mission seemed simple—to drop message bottles in the open sky below old Chickasaw. The messages declared in her own words that she was a rebel mimọ—a malcontent who wanted to leave Heaven. According to Pasteur, the messages were a ploy to lure a Jinn up to the ruins, where Conclave agents would be waiting to spring a trap and capture her.

According to Pasteur, a Jinn was a monster from the emotional realms that lured souls using the pleasures of her flesh, the better to trap her victims in cages and make them into her slaves. Pasteur had been sketchy on the unspeakable details, but he'd implied that nothing attracted a Jinn more than a chaste, innocent mimọ.

Boudi pushed the thoughts from her mind. She felt disturbed just thinking of such sinful things. She prayed that her mission would be a success. If she failed, she's out of the Conclave as Tajee predicted. If they did not hold her for reformation, then she'd have to go back to Crystal College in a cloud of shame. Makeda and Ashanti would laugh at her, and she'd never hear the end of it from Professor Brown.

No. Failing her first mission was not an option. Pasteur had advised her, "just be yourself". If a wicked Jinn manifested in response to the bottles, she was supposed to play the role of a rebellious mimọ until the Conclave watchers could arrive at the spot. Her acting role couldn't be that difficult. After all, she'd had plenty of practice.

The sky was thickening amidst the ruins. The pale colors of peach and pink were turning to purple and leaden grey. A flash lit up the atmosphere, and a low rumble of thunder rolled across the ancient stones. Boudi closed her Conclave book and tucked it back into her rucksack. She walked away from her exposed position towards the safety of the ruined pediments that led to the stairway.

A gust of wind buffeted her body, bringing dampness. She'd glimpsed storms before in the skies below Heaven, but never up among the broken blocks and columns of Chickasaw. She scanned the path leading down to the lower platforms. Surely Tajee would come back, and they'd make for the Raqi'a Gates as quickly as possible. Another boom of thunder echoed hollowly, followed by scratching sounds.

"Coco?" Boudi looked down the platform for Tajee's cat, but something larger loomed through the rain. The woman wore a red leather half-corset and a short russet skirt, an exotic ensemble that exposed her tanned, muscled midriff. Her thigh-high leather boots sported pointed brass toe protectors and polished buckles. The heels of the woman's boots clicked on the marble with her long, deliberate strides.

The woman stopped and peered from eye sockets that were precarious and gloomy under the overhangs of her wild chestnut mane. Her hair swam in the wind like a gaggle of serpents. Golden hoop earrings dangled from her earlobes—earrings of a sort that are instantly confiscated from any mimọ girl insane enough to wear them. The woman's lips were discolored with mottled bluish hues, as if from lip paint that had worn away. When she spoke, her voice was throaty, like a purr.

"Are you the mimọ named Boudi, I hope?"

"Yes. Who are you?"

"I'm Mistress Golda. Is this by chance yours?" The woman lifted an ink bottle between her fingertips. A small roll of parchment was just visible inside.

"It might be mine."

"Wonderful." Golda smiled. "I'll make this short, and hopefully your guardians won't show up and send me to the void before I finish. I am a Jinn of the New Order. I serve Lady Allyssia in the wilds of Meristyian. The nimfas found your message bottle on the beaches where the Styx flows into the Sea of Desire. The nimfas go to the beaches there to collect coins and things."

"I wouldn't know."

"I'll get to the point. We've come for you as you asked. My friend conjured this storm to hide us, but she can't hold it for long. Do you want to fall as your message said? Do you want to defect from Heaven? You'll have pleasures and freedoms beyond your wildest dreams if you join Lady Allyssia and the New Order Jinni. You'll have everything you ever desired. Our Ifreeta will make all of your fantasies real. That's what you want, yes? So, tell me."

"I, um—" Boudi worked her jaw. Her mind had frozen like her feet. A fast-developing panic attack had seized her.

"Say yes," Golda persisted. "Tell me you want to fall, and I'll take you down. You won't be punished anymore for being bad. You won't be alone. You'll be with the Lady and others like yourself. I wish I had more time to sell this, but I'm tired and in a dangerous situation this close to Heaven."

"I'm still not sure."

"Well, it's yes or no, and I'm expecting a yes because my friend and I have climbed half an eternity to get to you. Say yes, please, and say it now." Mistress Golda seemed taller and darker when she stepped closer. The wind whipped her red-brown hair, which made a sound like serpent hissing, but the hissing was the drops of rain, which hit harder on the marble with every passing second.

"Yes, fine. But I—"

"Fantastic," Golda interrupted. "Lady Allyssia has rules about free will, so I'm happy to have the agreement bit over with. Hold still."

Boudi glanced over her shoulder. Her chest felt heavy and hollow as a cathedral bell. Where were Pasteur and the Conclave agents to spring the trap? There were no Conclave mimos to be seen, and the Jinn are closing the distance quickly. Golda opened a leather pouch at her belt and withdrew a small bundle, which she unfolded into a queer-looking red hat. Boudi eyed the Platinum baubles, the small pink bow, and the abbreviated semi-circular brim.

"What's that?"

"They call it a Bliss-Trip Bonnet," Golda answered. "I don't know what it's for. I'm not savvy with the ways of dream magic."

Boudi edged back, but Golda reached and slipped the hat quickly over her head. The Jinn turned her around, pulled her hair through the loop in the back, and fastened the hat with a damp chin strap. Boudi shivered when Golda's hand gripped her forearm. The fingernails of the Jinn pricked oddly on her skin.

"I think we should talk more. I'm not ready yet."

"Whatever the hat is making you feel, it's normal," Golda said. "Or at least that's what I was told. Now we're going to jump. The trip down will be much faster than coming up. You're as light as a feather, mimọ. The philosophers say that a feather and a stone will fall at the same speed. I don't believe it. Please hold on tightly to me."

The sounds of male voices came through the rain. Boudi felt her heart leap until she realized it was only Tajee and his friends. They were running down the platform towards her. Their dive trunks clung wetly to their legs and waists, and splashes of rain flew from their feet. Tajee's mouth dropped open. All the boys gawked at the exotic interloper.

"Who are you?" Tajee said. "What are you doing with Boudi?"

"I'm taking her away," Golda answered. "Your friend isn't happy in Heaven. She wants to leave. I say she's made an excellent choice."

Tajee's brown eyes hardened. "What are you talking about? Boudi, who is this? She isn't a mimọ. She doesn't have a halo."

"Tajee, please go back up to Heaven. Just go away."

"I don't think so." Tajee took a step closer.

"Don't worry, Tajee," Golda said. "Your friend will be safe. Who knows—maybe if you're bad enough, I'll come back for you someday."

"Wait—" Boudi felt Golda's powerful arms wrap around her and yank. They tipped together off the edge of the platform. Boudi sucked her breath, expecting a crazy sustained plunge without a braking umbrella, but instead, she and Golda landed hard on the lip of another ledge several meters below the Upper Allyssia.

Boudi groaned when her sandals hit the stone. She felt like both of her ankles had snapped, but Golda had landed like a cat. The Jinn held onto her arm with a steel grip and twirled her back to her feet. The Conclave agents were still nowhere to be seen. Instead, a second Jinn was waiting. Golda's accomplice wore a faded black robe with a pinched waist and gold-embroidered lapels. Her long, jet-black hair blew in the wind. She held a wooden staff high and sang in a strange language.

"We've got her," Golda said. "Let's go, Mareinah. We'll leave the climbing ropes. Boudi, your backpack will be heavy. You should leave it unless it's really important."

"I want it. Please?"

"Oh, I like that attitude." Golda smiled, but the smile faded, and the silvery-blue eyes of the Jinn shimmered with concern. "You're trembling, mimọ. This is scary for me too, but don't be afraid. Have faith in the Lady. You're going to be safe."

Boudi trembled. The rain soaked her. Her head felt weird and heavy in the Bliss-Trip Bonnet. She worked her jaw against the damp chinstrap. A white light suddenly illuminated the scene. Thunder crack sounded with a hiss of steam and a smell of ozone. A team of Conclave agents had flashed directly onto the ledge.

"Jump!" shouted Mareinah. The black-robed Jinn brandished her staff. Boudi felt her heart leap with relief. She ran towards the nearest Conclave mimọ, but Golda grabbed her wrist and jerked her back, pulling her towards the edge of the marble and the end of any solidity under her sandals. Arcane spells etched the air. The Conclave Mimọs leveled short Platinum wands in the direction of the black-haired Jinn. White tendrils of magical power grabbed and squeezed. The Jinn shrieked.

Boudi gasped. Golda yanked her again, and then she was plummeting into the gloomy, rain-filled sky. Crashes of thunder sounded, followed by keening screeches that echoed through the atmosphere. The winged tenshi had been summoned to defend Heaven. Boudi prayed that a tenshi would snatch her away to safety, but the screeches drifted farther and farther away as she and Golda accelerated.

The familiar sensation of dive pleasure penetrated every inch of her body, going tenfold beyond anything that she'd ever known before. Her head began to buzz inside the Bliss-Trip Bonnet. She pressed into Golda's powerful arms for shelter against the battering wind. The Jinn smelled like leather, flowers, and sensual things from unheavenly places.

Wind frenzied and again rain. Boudi closed her eyes. She felt warm and hollow as its velocity increased the lightness within it ignited like a paper lantern, leaving only melted wax and ash adrift.

Chapter 3:

Boudi opened her eyes. A pale hand lay on the pillow next to her cheek. She willed the hand to move, and it did. She gazed at the solid, tapering fingers, the rosy whorled tips, and the translucent ovate nails. She bolted up on the bed and looked down at herself in shock. Her white robe was gone, along with her Mimoic under-trappings.

Her straight white corset had been replaced by an underwired black contraption that lifted her breasts in silk cups, displaying them instead of chastely compressing them. Her matching pleated skirt failed to cover even a third of her pale, naked thighs. Her braided hair flowed unrestrained by any proper clips, pins, or ribbons. Her hair fell loose over her shoulders with a pleasant, tickling sensation.

Boudi poked her thigh with her fingertip. Her touch echoed deep under her skin. She stroked, and she could feel the sensation in her bones. She was alone in a small room. The bed on which she sat was nestled in one corner. Cool air and light came from a high barred window opening. A tarnished Platinum chair dominated the polished stone floor. The arms of the chair ended in sculpted claws. Next to the chair stood a wooden table with an ink bottle sitting on it. The only exit was a silver door with thick bars and a floret lock in the center.

Shadowy figures lurked beyond the door. Low voices were having a conversation punctuated by faint clicks of heels on stones. A hand turned a key in the lock and pushed the door open. Mistress Golda ambled into the room and settled herself easily in the Platinum armchair. The door clanged closed behind her.

Golda had corralled her angoraic mane into a less menacing ponytail. The clip failed to contain Golda's wild red-brown hair, however. It flourished in unruly wisps over her freckled forehead. The corners of her mottled bluish lips turned into a slow smile.

"Congratulations, mimọ. You made it. I'm so happy you're awake. I went up to Allyssia's palace for a while, and I was worried about you the entire time. How are you feeling? You were unconscious for a night and a day."

Boudi sat on the edge of the bed to face the Jinn. She pressed her bare legs tightly together. Her limbs felt incredibly heavy. The floor was cold under her bare feet. She curled her toes so only the tips touched. "I'm feeling a lot of things, and I'm not used to feeling much at all. I'm embarrassed by what I'm wearing. May I have a robe, please?"

"You're a beautiful young woman," Golda countered. "Why would you want to hide yourself under a robe?"

Boudi felt a blush steal over her cheeks, and a warmth bloomed in her chest. She recognized the feeling as pride, but like every other feeling in the new world in which she found herself, the sin was ten times more intense than in Heaven.

"I need more clothes. Please."

"Why? Because you're cold?"

"No. Yes." Boudi took a deep breath and tried to collect herself. "I'm embarrassed to show so much skin. Don't you know anything about mimọ girl virtues?"

Golda relaxed deeper into the Platinum armchair and casually stretched her long, muscled legs. "What exactly did you do in Heaven, Boudi? Were you a student?"

"Yes. Not a great one."

"I'm curious why you questioned the Mimọic Hierarchy. If you'd never think of going without clothes, then what made you think of defecting from Heaven?"

Boudi avoided Golda's eyes. Of course, she couldn't tell the evil Jinn about her mission. She couldn't reveal that she was a secret agent, part of a Conclave plot to trick Golda and her witch friend like rats into a trap. No. She had to keep playing her role like the Conclave had told her—the role of an mimọ girl who had gone bad. She had to stick to Pasteur's instructions. She tried to remember the theatre class that she'd taken with Tajee. She needed to improvise.

"I got my rebellious ideas from my friend. He learned about this place in a forbidden Botany book. It sounded nice. I was tired of getting punished for my many failures."

Golda arched an eyebrow. "I can accept that. Do you remember anything of our trip here, then?"

"No. I don't."

"After we jumped, we fell into the Sea of Desire. By the grace of Lady Allyssia, I was able to swim you to the beach. Your robe and underthings were completely soaked with seawater, so I took them off of you. That's why you don't have your clothes."

"I liked my clothes."

"I'm sorry. You were wet and heavy, and I was worried about your guardians chasing me. I carried you in my arms across the jungles of Meristyian until I met up with a couple of friends. They escorted us here on horses."

"Where is here, exactly?"

Golda's brooding eyes brightened slightly, shimmering with a silvery light. "You're in the city of Lady Allyssia. We call it the Redoubt. It sits on the northern edge of the flowered fields of western Meristyian. Meristyian exists in vibration between Heaven and Earth. Walter Mosely called it the First Circle."

"So, I really am in the place that should not be named. I'm a fallen mimọ."

"Oh yes, you're fallen. You're still a mimọ, but a thicker, more sensual skin has densified around your soul. This is an emotional realm. It's a magical and beautiful place. It's different from the mental realm of Heaven and the material world of Earth."

"I just wanted to be sure."

"Cheer up. The Lady plans to fulfill your desire to join the New Order Jinni." Golda picked up the ink bottle from the small table and extracted the folded paper from the inside. "I'm told Mimǫs can be confused and forgetful when they fall into Meristyian. Have a look at your message. Maybe it will help."

Boudi took the Conclave note from Golda. She unfolded it, marveling at the crisp feel of the dry paper against her heavy fingertips.

To Whom It May Concern:

If you have found this message, whomsoever you are, I beg you. Please take this to Lady Allyssia. I'm an mimǫ in Heaven. I'm a rebel. I like to kiss boys, but I'm punished for it. I want to be free. I don't like rules. I'm a bad mimǫ, and they punish me. Please, Lady Allyssia. I leave Heaven many days to sit amongst the ruins of your old broken palace in Chickasaw, dreaming of a place where there are others like me. With all of my heart, I want to be yours. For the sake of Love, please save me from Heaven.

Yours truly, Boudi Marcus

Boudi felt her cheeks heat. She'd written the words, even though most of them weren't true. She'd protested to Auditor Pasteur, but he'd insisted that lies were perfectly fine if told for the greater good. Pasteur hadn't seemed happy with her hesitation. Golda didn't seem happy with her hesitation either.

"Yes. I...I wrote this."

"Your Mimǫic voice is beautiful. Has anyone ever told you?" Golda shifted forward to take the letter back. The Jinn folded it up in her long fingers.

"Maybe it's my choir training, but I'm not a great vocalist. In fact, I'm average or worse in every category by the highest standards in Heaven for mimo girls."

Golda shrugged. "That's silly. You should give yourself more credit. You don't fit Heaven's narrow-minded mold of what a woman can be."

Boudi felt another small wash of pride inside her. Golda's words made her feel good. The pride melted pleasantly in her belly like warm butter, sprinkled with cinnamon. "How did you even find me? How did you get up to Heaven?"

"I went up the stairway. The magic of stealth is my specialty. I'm a tracker—one of the best that Lady Allyssia has. When Mareinah and I reached the ruins, we hid with magic and waited until I sensed your presence in the tapestry."

"The tapestry?"

"It's like a weave—an invisible fate-woven matrix that runs through the realms. Unfortunately, the storm that Mareinah summoned to hide us didn't accomplish its job."

"What do you mean?"

"I mean Mareinah is gone." Golda's lower lip quivered. "She threw a spell to give me the moment I needed. She sacrificed her life to help you escape from your masters. I don't know if she's truly dead, but I hope so. If she's captured, it's much worse for her. The so-called forces of good enjoy torturing witches."

Boudi steadied herself on the edge of the bed. She looked at the floor and made her face a blank, but in her heart, she was thrilled. The Conclave had captured a Jinn then, or at least killed one, so her mission had been half a success. The only problem was her own horrible circumstances.

"I'm sorry for your friend, Mistress Golda, but do you think they could come here looking for me? Not that I want them to, of course."

"No," Golda replied. "Your guardians won't find you. Allyssia's redoubt is hidden by powerful magical dream-world veils that protect us from the eyes of our enemies, especially the Mimos. By our Lady's graces, you'll be safe, and you'll have what you desire—freedom to live and love how you want without judgment."

"I wrote those letters, and I meant what I said." Boudi felt another tingle of pride. She was surprised at how easily the lies came out of her mouth. Maybe the Conclave hadn't made a mistake in making her an agent, and maybe her theatre class had actually been good for something.

"Well, the last I heard, Allyssia plans to cast a spell to transform you. You're to become one of us—a fledgling Jinn. We didn't bring you down here just to serve us."

"Really? It's true that I'm a bad mimo, but this place is way more than I expected. I might have made a mistake."

"Nonsense. You were brave to rebel against Heaven. Mimos jump from Heaven to commit suicide every now and then, but no one has heard of an mimo sending a written message. You did very well to make those arrangements ahead of time, by the way. Most fallen Mimos aren't so clever, and they pay the price."

Boudi felt another wash of pride at Golda's little compliments. She knew pride was a dangerous sin because it led to self-delusion. She couldn't seem to fight the pride with her usual humble thoughts, however. The sin loosed from her mind and melted into the depths of her new thick body like a sweet, syrupy ichor. She fought to contain the emotion, but her frustration only melted in turn, chasing the pride downward into her physical heaviness.

"I'm sorry, Golda. I'm feeling so many things. I'm distracted, and I can't focus on what you're saying."

"Your new desire-body is starved for feelings. Here in the emotional realms, our bodies are composed of emotion. We feel, therefore we are. You need to let your emotions flow. Your feelings will heal you if you just let them breathe."

Boudi breathed and tried to calm herself—to ignore her feelings and focus on everything that Golda had told her. If the Jinn wanted her to surrender to her feelings, she needed to fight them tooth and nail. She needed to think like an agent—a tower of chastity and resistance like her Conclave textbook recommended. "Are there any other fallen Mimos here, Golda?"

"I myself went to Heaven for a few hours after my earthly death."

"I don't believe you."

"It's true. As an Egyptian noble in the first century, I advocated the free will of women in society. I was the wife of the Pharaoh Menes and the lover of Coptican, so I had that luxury. When I died and went to Heaven, my trip was just a formality."

"Free will is a gift from Lord Tuhan to all souls, unless they are bad."

Golda shook her head, and a stray lock of hair threw her face into shadow. "That's what the Mimoic Hierarchy leads you to believe—that the cosmic order moves through them. Free will is an inherent property of the soul, not a privilege awarded for proper behavior. I made a few mistakes on Earth, but I didn't deserve to be damned for them."

"Lord Tuhan doesn't damn souls. Souls damn themselves."

"That's what the Christians say on Earth to make you behave—think virtuous thoughts, obey your husband, and believe everything you're told. You must do everything Lord Tuhan commands, every word, or you'll suffer the torments of Hell forever. They even say that to little children." Golda's silvery eyes grew darker and gloomier, and she clutched the claw arms of the Platinum chair as if to prevent herself from springing up from it.

"Wicked souls go to Hell, don't they? So, it's true."

"It shouldn't be that way—Lord Tuhan and Lord Hades dividing up souls like sheep into two flocks, one white and one black. That's the point of this little city. Lady Allyssia is trying to make a beautiful place in between—a place of freedom and love independent from either of the two great patriarchs. The New Order welcomes everyone."

"I don't know if I'm right for this."

Golda nodded. "I understand your worries, and you probably feel pressure and a debt. The Lady sent me and Mareinah to try to save you from Heaven as you asked, and now Mareinah is dead. I hope that you have something to offer the New Order that will make up for that horrible tragedy."

"What if I don't?"

"First, we need to free your passion and allow you to feel the full power of your desires. Then we'll find out."

Boudi gripped the edge of the bed to steady herself. She felt flushed and dizzy. The walls of the stone cell seemed to close around her. "I wrote those letters, but I need time to adjust. I need to go slow. This is too much sin for me to cope with. I need clothes at least. Please."

Golda leaned forward. "Tell me what is wrong with freedom from the shame and guilt that were placed on you by the Mimoic Hierarchy. Your soul is free from Heaven, but your mind is still a prisoner."

Boudi met Golda's eyes. The intense presence of the Jinn was like a wave that crashed and filled the space between them. A rush of wings interrupted the silence. A grey dove darted through the narrow bars of the silver door, flapped twice through the air, and landed on Golda's shoulder. The bird pecked at her ear and disappeared. Golda rose to her feet. Her visage looked stormy again, as if the mysterious dove had flipped a switch.

"Wonderful," Golda muttered.

"What was that?"

"It was the Lady's messenger bird. She says there are more Mimos out in Meristyian. She wants to send a scouting party, and I have to go as the tracker."

Boudi felt her heart thump with sudden hope. Her heart had never thumped in Heaven, even when Tajee had slid his hand under her dive skirt in her dormitory, and she'd wrestled to get away from him. "Do you think they might be coming to rescue me? I hope they aren't, of course."

"I said you'd be safe here, didn't I?" Golda's brow furrowed, and then softened. "I'm sorry, Boudi. I'm upset about Mareinah, and I'm feeling my Hunger. Do you know about Jinn Hunger?"

"No."

"I have to go. If your mimo masters are trying to get you back, I'll do everything I can to make sure they fail. Your teacher will come and speak with you soon." Golda rose from the Platinum armchair and walked to the door. Boudi wrapped her arms protectively around her chest. She wondered what her teacher would teach her—about sinful things surely, and worse.

"Fine. I'll wait for him here then."

Golda belly-chuckled. "Your teacher is a Jinni, Boudi. The New Order is a matriarchal society of Jinni. Almost every male in this city is an Ahyehass—a devoted student who walks the divine path of love. Our Ahyehasi worship our Lady by celebrating love with their mistresses. We have a master or two living here if you happen to be interested—older men who are not Ahyehasi. They tend to be busy, but your Mimoic beauty might be enticing to them."

"Oh. That's nice."

Golda swung the cell door open. "Apparently no one believed that I'd bring you back, so no plans were made to take care of you. I'm sorry. Your teacher is preparing a room, and I'm sure she'll think of everything. She's a genius. She's very wealthy too. You'll have the best, and you deserve it with everything you're going through."

"Thank you, Golda. I'm sorry about all of this trouble."

"That's nice of you to say, Boudi. Now that I think about it, maybe the Mimos in Meristyian aren't your guardians after all. Mareinah conjured quite a storm over old Chickasaw." Golda closed the silver door behind her. The heels of her boots clicked down the hall, and then she was gone.

Boudi flopped onto her stomach and pressed her heated face into the linen pillow. Her situation was horrible, and if her deceptions were discovered, the consequences could be severe. She was indirectly responsible for the death of Golda's friend.

Despite her reservations and everything she knew about Jinni, she felt guilty. She'd just wanted to do well with her Conclave mission. She hadn't wanted to hurt anyone. On the other hand, Golda and the followers of the love Ifreeta deserved to be killed, or at least locked up and kept from spreading their lust and corruption.

She didn't want to discuss any of that with Golda. She needed to keep up her act. As long as the Jinni and their evil Ifreeta believed that she really wanted to join them, she'd be safe. She wouldn't be blamed for anything. Meanwhile, she had to look for a way to escape. Her very soul was at stake.

For the first time in her mimo life, she was alone. She didn't even have Tajee.

Chapter 4:

Tajee's eye itched. He brushed the sand from his cheek with his damp fingers. He was sitting on a beach. Foam-ruffled swells crested and ran across white sands that bordered a vast emerald green sea. Towering cumulonimbus clouds piled in the sky. Lightning played in atmospheres laced with faint crinolines of haze. In the distance, a rumble of thunder thumped.

Tajee shook his head to rouse himself. He squinted his bleary eyes away from the bright light and looked down at the beads of water that clung to his brown legs. His decision to jump was still crystallized in his mind. It had happened in a heart-stopping instant. He'd missed the stairway. He'd dropped at breathtaking speed with no umbrella or braking balloon. He'd been soaked with rain and turbulent emotions.

A green wave crashed and flattened across the beach. Tajee flinched when the cold water hit. The liquid inundated his buttocks and everywhere in between. Something caressed his leg as the water stalled and sucked back towards the sea. Tajee blinked with slow horror as he realized the beach was littered with millions of ancient bones. He wriggled to his feet, only to tip over as he reeled. His knee cracked against an eroded femur.

His body felt oddly heavy. His small damp wings tugged on his shoulder blades, sending aching sensations down his back. He churned his legs and clambered to the top of a nearby dune, where he planted himself again in a sitting position. His knee throbbed with dull pain. A skull with missing teeth winked at him with an eye socket full of sand. The skull was sitting atop the sand dune as if someone had placed it there.

Tajee shielded his eyes with his hand and scanned the serpentine shores from his new vantage point. He could see no people or civilization, only an endless beach blanketed with bones. He could see no trace of Heaven's gates above the clouds that crowned the vast sea, nor any stairway. Beyond the first dune rose a larger dune, and beyond the dunes a line of vegetation was visible—tall grasses and exotic trees with corrugated grey trunks and sprays of fronds at their tops. He saw no sign of Boudi.

Tajee avoided looking at the bones, and his horror lessened. He hadn't seen Boudi's face as she'd fallen, only the strange red hat encasing her head—a girly red-pink thing made bows, buckles, and straps. For a second, he'd met the queer silvery eyes of Boudi's kidnapper, then the beautiful woman had pulled Boudi over the edge.

The situation was surely related to Boudi's secret Conclave mission. His instinct was to stay clear, but Boudi had seemed to be in trouble. Her quavering voice had betrayed her real terror, just like the first time they'd gotten caught in a kiss, and she'd tried to fabricate an explanation for Professor Elliott. Boudi was no agent. She had no clue what she was doing. She didn't even know how much he loved her.

Tajee stood up and brushed sand from his dive trunks. He had no time to waste. The hellion woman was surely taking Boudi farther from him and any official rescue effort. His passage across the sand had left a track—an irregular swath of indentations that petered out amidst the old bones. Boudi should have landed nearby with her abductor, but no tracks were visible other than his.

Tajee felt a pain lance through the sole of his foot—a pain that wracked his leg and set his spine to quivering like a harp string. He'd stepped on something Sharp and pointy. The pain, disturbed him like the fin of some pricking terror that swam unseen beneath the green sea. Wherever he was, the physical sensations seemed magnified ten times beyond anything he'd ever felt in Heaven.

He walked up and down a large dune, and then another, doing his best to ignore the painful pokes of half-buried things. He went to where husks and other detritus had fallen from the spindly trees that lined the seashore. A maze of grasses began where the bone-strewn sands ended. The grasses gave way to different vegetation—tall, spindly plants that reached for the sky, squat thorny plants covered with purple pods, and fat spiked plants that spread their wobbly fronds to catch stipples of light. Little black insects meandered everywhere.

Tajee stared at the plants. They looked like the pictures in Professor Elliott's forbidden Botany book. Was that where he was—inside the dark world pictured in that book? If he was, he was in big trouble, which meant Boudi was too.

He scanned the shady, sandy paths between the plants. There were no more bones, and the air was warmer away from the wind and water. He crossed a low rise and pushed through a maze formed by thick stands of grasses that rose higher than his head. More fat wobble-fronded plants grew at the feet of the tall trees, and the pale sun returned from behind a cloud to cast shifting shadows over a loamy forest floor.

Tajee walked on. His progress was tedious, but the shelter of the forest beckoned him. Grains of sand itched inside his dive trunks, but he resisted the urge to take them off. Faint music floated to his ears, as if someone was playing a plaintive tune. As he approached the sounds, they receded. He trotted through twisty thickets until the music was gone, and he heard only the rustle of leaves again in the breeze.

He kept walking for what seemed like hours. Several times he saw sparkles and flitting shadows in the trees, but the things vanished before he could reach them. He kept stepping on twigs and flinty stones. Twice he stepped on thorns, and he had to stop and tug the little daggers from his tender skin. The thorns emerged with droplets of his red blood. He'd never bled in Heaven, nor felt such suffering.

He used the pain to fuel his anger, and he used his anger to keep moving forward. He imagined different ways that he could handle a confrontation with the evil redheaded demoness—how he might pummel her head with a rock or crush her neck with his hands. His violent thoughts disturbed him. The intense emotions twisted in his stomach and made him sick.

The trees were enormous in the depths of the jungle. Their grand branches swayed with the winds above the canopy, creating a multitude of shifting patterns like molten glass. Tracks appeared in the soft loam between the trees. They were here, there, and everywhere—scuffs, ruts, hoof prints and footprints of all sizes. Tajee examined the tracks as he passed.

Boudi had been wearing sandals, so he guessed her prints would look different from the rest. He found several footprints in the dirt, but they revealed the toes of bare feet like his own. He chose the freshest set of prints and tried to follow them. As he walked on, the light began to change and fail. The colors of the jungle simmered down to deeper shades. Lemon became mint, and lavender became eggplant. In the twilight, he finally heard a voice.

"Yassou, agori." A woman peeked from behind the massive trunk of a tree. A faint scent like herbs or flowers wafted from her. "Why you follow me? Are you lost?"

"Yes," Tajee answered warily. "I'm looking for a friend."

The woman emerged from behind the tree. Her eyes were dark brown. Her nose was oddly flattened, and her long dark hair felt tangled over her shoulders and back. Nipples like dark fingertips bobbed on the ends of her breasts. Below her smooth, caramel belly, an unruly thatch of brown hair drew attention to her womanhood. The woman was ogling him too. Her freckled lips curled into a grin. She advanced cautiously until she was only a few feet away. She held a bouquet of purple flowers that gave off a sweet smell.

"My name is Sekushi," the woman said softly. "You say my name like coochie. You have little wings, so you must be a mimọ. What is your name?"

"My name is Tajee."

"Well, I'm a nimfa. I live in a grotto with my sister and my master. You can visit us, yes? You come with?"

Tajee frowned. He wasn't convinced that he should go anywhere with Sekushi. He'd never heard of a nimfa. She was surely some sort of a hellion. Her nudity spoke volumes. The way she looked at him, however, with a wide-eyed beauty and a steady curiosity, weakened his will. He needed help, and Sekushi didn't seem to wish him ill.

"I might come, but have you seen an mimọ girl? She has braided hair with bangs and a red hat. She's pretty, and her halo floats a little off to one side—"

"No, but maybe my master sees her." Sekushi looked over her shoulder. "Master will be angry if I am in the forest after dark. You follow, Tajee. This forest is very dangerous for Mimọs. You are safer in the cave. Yes? We are safer."

The nimfa nodded as if an agreement had been reached. She padded away through the waning forest light. Tajee followed in turmoil. Why was the nimfa afraid of the forest after dark? What sort of sleeping arrangements would safe grotto offer him? High above the swaying leaves and twisted branches of the trees, darkness was consuming the remnants of twilight like black ink poured into a bowl of water.

Tajee followed the nimfa. He hoped a rescue party was formed in Heaven, but how would the Conclave agents even find him? He'd traveled far into the forest looking for Boudi. The nimfa glanced back and smiled in the half-light. Tajee felt a grin come unbidden to his lips, even as warmth of lust surged in his belly—the same sin that he'd always felt for Boudi, but much stronger. He slid his gaze down the sweep of Sekushi's sensuous long hair to her naked backside, which was much more sensual and womanlier than Boudi's girlish figure.

He'd always tried to fight his lust because he respected Boudi's chastity, but he hasn't always succeeded. For practical purposes, he preferred imperfect girls like Boudi. Makeda Deen was too perfect for him. Sekushi took his preference to the extreme. Her bare feet were dirty, and her thick hair was spangled with leaves and burs. The nimfa pranced back playfully and bumped into him, skin against skin. She grabbed his hand. Her hand was warm, and her fingers felt feminine when they entwined with his.

"We're almost there!" The nimfa giggled with her mood improved. Tajee caught Sekushi's earthy smell under the scent of the purple flowers that she held. The mingled scents made his nose tingle. Maybe the nimfa would do sinful things with him that Boudi had refused to consider. The nimfa thickened his lust like sweet honey in a beehive.

Tajee felt suddenly angry with himself. He had to keep his head straight. He had to resist temptation so he could focus on finding Boudi. The situation was the only chance he'd ever have to prove that he could be a hero despite getting bad grades at the Crystal College. If he could be a hero, he'd prove that he could do Conclave work.

The Conclave never made mistakes except by taking Boudi in the first place, so the situation was surely Boudi's fault. She'd screwed up her mission and caused something to go wrong. If he could fix Boudi's error by saving her, the Conclave might appreciate his courageous efforts. Maybe they'd even consider him to take Boudi's place. Boudi would be grateful too, and she'd have to admit that he was right. She was good with writing, art, and sewing, but she was hopeless as a Conclave agent.

On the other hand, if he couldn't find Boudi or the stairway to Heaven, they both could be trapped in the dark world of the Botany book forever. He'd questioned a few professors as to where fallen Mimos went. Professor Brown had only said that if fallen Mimos weren't rescued quickly, they were never seen again.

Chapter 5:

Boudi rubbed her eyes and sat up on the bed. The clack of heels outside the locked door had woken her. She resisted the urge to cover her naked legs. She'd passed several hours alone. Not long after Golda had left, the light had dimmed and turned dark outside the small high window. Eventually, she'd slept with a long dead sleep that had ended only when feeble light came through the window again.

She'd had time to think about escaping from her captors. Allyssia and the New Order Jinni didn't trust her yet, or else they wouldn't have locked her up. First, she needed to gain their trust. It had been far easier to skip classes at Crystal College when the professors had believed that she was a sweet mimo girl who would never intentionally do anything unruly. It was the same with the priestesses of lust. It would be easier to escape if they had full faith that she was a rotten mimo who wanted to stay. The problem was how to convince them while not drowning in sin.

A key turned in the floret lock, and the polished silver door swung open. The Jinn who entered was much older than Golda. Her dark grey-streaked hair was pulled back into a braid ornamented with three or four white pearls. Her silver-hazel eyes scanned the small stone room like a hawk as she strode to the high-backed Platinum chair.

The woman wore a burgundy long-sleeved bodice wrapped in a yellow leather corset. The intricately tooled corset drew her waist into a tight curve, and on the curve was strapped a sword in a leather case. The sword nestled down the folds of a burgundy skirt that flared widely at its owner's hips to form an hourglass figure that barely fit between the arms of the chair. The Jinn seated herself with a prim vertical posture—the complete opposite of Golda's easy slouch.

"It's a pleasure to meet you, mimọ. My name is Mistress Ayelet."

"Hello," Boudi said. "I'm Boudi."

"You truly look lovely in black lingerie."

"Excuse me, but do you usually begin conversations this way?"

Mistress Ayelet chuckled. "More often than you might think. I like to observe the facts, but some facts can only be judgments. For example, you need some new clothes to replace your old."

"I agree with you."

"You're smart too." Ayelet winked. Boudi shrugged nonchalantly. If the older Jinn thought she was smart, she wasn't going to argue. Mistress Ayelet spoke with a hint of an accent, enunciating her words with precision. Ayelet's face was roundish, pale, and plain—almost Mimọic except for a general cosmetic unkemptness. The older Jinn wore no titanium powder to cover her blemishes or any evidence of zealous waxing or eyebrow plucking. Her lips were bare and unpainted too, unlike Golda's faint mottled shades of blue.

"Golda said a teacher would come to see me. Is that you?"

"Indeed," Ayelet answered. "I'll be your guide to the ways of the New Order Jinni. You're to be my 'fledgling', and I'm to be your 'Mistress'. From now on, I'd like you to address me as 'Mistress', or 'Mistress Ayelet', and nothing much else."

"Sure. Whatever."

"It's a formality, but an important one. It creates a useful mental framework that we can discard later. You'll say 'yes, Mistress,' 'no, Mistress.' That bit. Later on, in our relationship, we can relax things if you wish."

"What is a 'Mistress' exactly?"

Ayelet nodded. "It's just another word for a female master or a teacher. In the case of a mistress and her Ahyehass, it implies a sort of belonging, but you're not my Ahyehass. You're my protégé. I'll be giving you wisdom, not orders."

"I was told that a Jinn seduces souls, keeps them in cages, and makes them into her slaves. Is an Ahyehass one of those souls?"

"It's a bit warm in here, don't you think?" Ayelet unbuttoned her bodice sleeves and rolled them up her forearms. "That's the way it works everywhere else in the Underworld—yes. Humans, fallen Mimọs, and less well-bred hellions are given slave papers and made to serve their owners until they've outlived their usefulness. That doesn't happen in our Lady's city. Our Ahyehasi has free will. Our Ahyehasi can refuse to serve if they wish. They can leave. We don't abuse our humans, whip them, or make them walk around in iron chains. This is the Lady's law. Love is the whole of the law."

"What happens to the humans if they stay?"

The goal of an Ahyehass is to unite with Love by submitting completely to us, the priestesses of our Ifreeta. Humans can't open themselves spiritually while their own egos are blocking the way. We Jinni are experts at dissolving those ego barriers, so it's perfect. We offer bliss to those who wish to serve Allyssia, and in return we take our sustenance from them. The goal is mutual celebration, not exploitation like elsewhere in the Underworld. The bonds are made of trust."

"You surely mean lust, and that's hardly comforting."

"The Lady wishes you to become more than a mere Ahyehass." Ayelet cleared her throat. "The social structure here, as on Earth and everywhere, is a manifestation of the Principle of Dominance. This principle is a subset of the greater aesthetic principle of asymmetry, which is a fundamental rule of nature, design, and beauty. Have you heard of Pythagoras' golden ratio?"

"Is that like the Golden Rule?"

"The Golden Rule is a fine rule, but no. Asymmetry is the law of nature. Dog chases cat. Cat snags mouse. Big fish gulps little fish, and so on. Our humans are accepting of their spiritual submission. It's better to serve freely here than to serve as a slave in the great societies of Hell's Court, the Seelie and Choshek Kishi courts, or even in Heaven, as you yourself have seen."

"You're showing your ignorance just like Golda. There aren't any slaves in Heaven." Boudi felt like she would faint. Her emotions were out of control. She hadn't planned to argue with her evil teacher, but her mouth kept opening, and the words kept coming out.

"Your superiors taught you obedience," Ayelet continued with an even tone. "You had to do everything you were told, and when you were bad, they punished you, did they not? You said so in your message. They crushed your self-esteem so you'd never leave their protection, but you still managed to escape. Congratulations. You should feel proud of yourself, but not too proud."

"That's silly. It wasn't exactly—"

"Yes, you were very much like a slave to the Mimoic Hierarchy. They just didn't call you that. They likened you to a yoked ox, or a sheep, or one of their flock of penguins, or whatever nonsense. From this day forward, I'll help you free your mind. You'll become one of us—a fierce and free-thinking Jinn."

Boudi suppressed a shudder. "That's what Golda said."

"Your ritual of transformation will be on the seventh night from tonight on the eve of the full moon. Don't be frightened, Boudi. You're going to be just fine."

"I'm not frightened." Boudi avoided Ayelet's eyes. In fact, the idea of participating in a dark Jinn ritual was a world beyond terrifying.

Ayelet smiled faintly. "After the ritual, it will be my task to teach you what you need to know in order to find a happy home here in the Lady's city. I'll help you to claim and grow your amazing inner gifts."

"I'm afraid I don't have any gifts."

"It's proper to address me as 'Mistress'. I didn't make the rules. It's been the tradition among the Jinni for these many thousands of years, and everyone properly abides. One more try?"

Boudi clenched the edge of the bed. Mistress Ayelet was starting to annoy her. "What kind of gifts do you think I have, Mistress Ayelet? You don't know me. You don't know Heaven. You're wrong about almost everything. I'm just an ordinary mimo girl. I sing in the choir. I pray to Lord Tuhan every day. I copy scriptures. Sometimes I get a math problem right if it's an easy one."

"You don't need to study math if you don't want to, despite my prior reference to Pythagoras. The Lady believes that you can do powerful magic."

"I'm afraid you're wrong about that too."

"Fear is weakness. That's one more thing we'll work on." Ayelet unwedged her unnaturally wide hips from the chair and stood up. "I'd like to try an experiment."

Boudi sighed. "What kind?"

"I understand that Mimos have an ability called 'flashing'. You have this ability, yes? You can flash from place to place?"

"Yes, but I can't here because everything is so different and heavy. I don't know this place. I wouldn't know where I'm going. I can't feel anything with my mind, and it's terrifying."

Ayelet nodded calmly. "Please try. Please flash across this room, for example."

"I'd never do that in Heaven."

"Well please do it here, if you can. Try moving a few meters as a test."

"Fine." Boudi reluctantly rose from the edge of the bed. Her cheeks heated when Ayelet's hawk-like eyes darted down her body. Ayelet's silver-hazels were even more intense than Golda's gloomy off-blues.

Boudi tried to compose herself mentally. She picked a spot at the far side of the little room. She scrunched her nose and focused. As she'd expected, nothing happened. She felt embarrassed and a little angry. She didn't have to prove anything to the uppity old Jinn, but she wanted to. Ayelet's greying left eyebrow arched with impending skepticism, much like Tajee's skepticism that an average mimo girl could ever be a Conclave agent.

Boudi squinted and stared at the spot on the far side of the room. She tried harder. She ferociously focused. Her anger grew and moved. She wasn't thinking, but desiring her way across the room. It hit her like a syrupy epiphany. She slipped into a dark grey space and skated along a black ribbon that twisted through the air. She ran down the ribbon, one step, two, and three, past Ayelet who was motionless as if frozen, until the ribbon ended, and she tipped forward into solidity.

Boudi slumped. She'd smacked headfirst into the hard stone wall. She'd managed to flash, although her nose felt broken, and her hair radiated heat around her ears, and her scalp burned hot and prickly. A bead of sweat tickled between her corseted breasts. Ayelet stepped forward quickly, blotting out the light from the high window. The concerned look on Ayelet's face deepened her eye wrinkles into crow's-foot furrows.

"Boudi? I'm so sorry! Are you alright?"

"I did it. In Heaven you just move, but here there was a delay. It felt like I was in a different world for a minute." Boudi felt a tear brim at her eyelid. She wiped it, and then she grabbed the warm wrist of the Jinn for support. Ayelet, who was just as supernaturally strong as Golda, lifted her like a doll back to her feet.

"In the emotional realms, only the gods, goddesses, and perhaps a few great sorcerers have powers like that—magic taken for granted in the mental realms. Allyssia says healing and telepathy are also potential gifts of Mimọs who fall into Meristyian. We hope you'll be able to do these things."

"I'm not so sure. I didn't do anything special in Heaven. I didn't have impressive abilities like the arch-Mimọs at the Conclave."

"Well, I'm sorry you got hurt. The Lady expressed a certain urgency—that is, if you didn't use your powers immediately, you could lose them. That's why you were wearing that enchanted hat. The Lady ensorcelled it with dream magic, so you could translate your abilities into the emotional world intact."

"Golda didn't mention that."

Ayelet nodded. "Let's get you out of this awful quarantine room. I'm taking you up to my Villa straight away. That's where you'll live, of course. So, let's get going."

"I can't go anywhere without clothes."

"Measurements were taken while you slept, and your clothes are being made. Until then, my dressing-girl will loan you some things. Undress is expected in the Lady's domain. This time of abrupt change is your chance to abandon attachments to your old ways of thinking. It's an advantage you have over Golda, who was my former student. We can progress you very fast if we can keep you from losing your sanity."

Boudi allowed Mistress Ayelet to escort her through the silver door. She was relieved to leave the cell and take steps towards freedom, even though she was shockingly exposed in her mini-skirt and corset. She walked with the elder Jinn up a hall and a narrow flight of stone stairs. They passed through a bright archway and emerged onto a cobblestoned city street.

Allyssia's city glowed with a rainbow of colors. Orange morning sunlight slanted at an angle over red-tiled rooftops from a pale indigo-blue sky above. The stones of the paved street were yellowed marble much like the ruins of Chickasaw, but with the addition of two varieties of green mosses growing in the cracks.

The architecture of the buildings also looked like Chickasaw, but the stone columns and facades were unbroken. Two-level homes bristled with balustraded balconies and columned porticos under wide corbelled overhangs. A breeze carried an earthen odor down the avenue. Dead leaves wafted from a nearby tree, spangling the street with reds, browns, and yellows.

An open carriage sat at the curb, harnessed to a pair of white horses with leather blinders and white decorative plumes. Ayelet gestured at the carriage with a flourish. "Hop in, fledgling. Don't be shy. It's mine, and yours when you start going places on your own."

Boudi climbed into the carriage. She scrunched to the side, but Ayelet's wide hip pressed against her leg anyway. Ayelet's hourglass figure was apparently formed by an antique framework under her burgundy skirt. Ayelet applied the whip, and the horses jolted forward to pull the carriage down the street, through an intersection, and up an incline on the far side.

The heart of the Lady's city was a maze of quaint streets punctuated by plazas with statuary, greenery, and trees that gifted a panoply of natural colors and organic shapes to the hard lines of the buildings and their deep eaves. A myriad of smells drifted in the air. Incense and soap mingled with more exotic odors of flowers and wood smoke.

A dark-haired girl in a boyish tunic ducked from an ivied hedge into a fieldstone outbuilding with an armload of chopped kindling. A brown horse stretched its tether to sniff grasses growing by a stone sundial. A tawny housecat crouched on top of a white-painted fence, watching a pack of birds playing in a tree.

Boudi felt a growing sense of dread as the very unheavenly world unfolded around her. How would the Conclave ever find her in such a big, exotic place? To add to her nervousness, Ayelet kept looking over at her while driving the carriage.

"Are you feeling uncomfortable, mimọ? Those pointy trees are called alpine cypresses. I have some at my Villa. That's where we're going."

"I'm sorry, Mistress Ayelet. I know I wrote those messages saying that I wanted to come here, but I don't think I made the right decision. Maybe I should go home."

"You and Golda already discussed that."

Boudi blinked. "How did you know?"

"Mistress Ivanka, who is our most powerful resident witch, has a magical obsidian ball that allows for remote viewing. Some of the mistresses had a get-together to see you chatting with Golda." Ayelet clucked and snapped the reins. The horses veered onto a narrow, shady street that ran upwards and diagonal to the others.

"I wish I'd known I was being watched."

Ayelet smiled. "We were fighting over the viewing ball. I felt like I should have been front and center since you're to be my fledgling, and I said as much. There was a bit of a tussle over looking at you. It was fun."

"I hope I didn't say anything too stupid."

"No one is judging you, mimọ. It's obvious that you're in a state of complete shock. The controversy was more about Golda."

"Why?"

"Golda said that she hoped you had valuable gifts to offer the New Order Jinni to compensate for the loss of Mareinah at the hands of the Hierarchy. The Lady's decision was a dangerous gambit with possible consequences, and you shouldn't feel responsible. Golda was expressing her own frustrations. She's out of sorts. I'd be upset too if my lover died right in front of me."

"Lover? What do you mean?"

"I mean until last week Mareinah and Golda lived together. They slept together. You didn't understand that? Golda enjoys men, but she also goes with women. We celebrate all forms of love in the Lady's city. What sorts of love do you like, Boudi? Golda didn't quite probe that question directly. Are you attracted to the sensuality of women?"

Boudi swallowed. "Is that what Jinni do with each other?"

"No. We, New Order are rebels just like you. We believe in Allyssia's ideal of loving whoever we want, and that's why we came here. Most Jinni love men only. We call those Jinni the Old Order. They serve Lord Hades and Lady Allyssia, the king and queen of the Underworld. The Old Order are required by divine law to marry Djinnus husbands. They serve their husbands for eternity and can't ever divorce unless their husbands file the papers for them in Hell's Court."

"A Jinn shouldn't get married anyway. Marriage is a sacrament of Lord Tuhan."

"Lord Tuhan doesn't own marriage just because He wrote it so, just like Lord Hades doesn't own love just because he wrote that two Jinni can't love each other. Nonetheless, lesbians are arrested every day by the devils of Hell's Court. The punishment is reformation or death, and this is what makes our Lady's society special. The New Order accepts love that is punished everywhere else. Love is the law, so no form of love should be controlled by laws, whether those laws are written by gods or arrogant political men."

"If you say so."

Ayelet lapsed into an uneasy silence. The horses pulled the carriage up a steep street. The peaks of stony mountains appeared over the rooftops.

The city of Allyssia lay in a mountain valley with tiers of houses climbing each side, and Ayelet's carriage was rolling through the center, up a wide thoroughfare lined with trees. They arrived at another junction of stone-paved streets. Two Jinni idled on the backs of sturdy horses in the center of the plaza. Ayelet brought the carriage to a halt and raised her hand to greet her comrades.

"Good morning, Golden Gorila. How are you, Jade Turtle? It's a pleasant fall morning, is it not?"

"She's the mimọ?" The short, stocky Jinn named Golden Gorila gawked. Golden Gorila wore a silver-grey robe with a white sash that matched the white powder on her face. The thin lines of Golden Gorila's black-painted eyebrows twisted like little lizardlings on her forehead as she urged her horse closer. "She's pretty enough. I've rarely seen such a beautiful, fine-boned creature outside of the Kishi courts or the high-class slave shows in Haawiyah."

The lanky younger Jinn named Jade Turtle had a powdered face to match the older mistress, but she wore boyish short-cropped hair instead of a coif. Boudi scrunched into the carriage seat even as a surge of panic overwhelmed her abdomen. She could feel Jade Turtle's silvery gaze lingering on her half-exposed breasts, and she crossed her arms quickly to cover them.

Golden Gorila smirked. "The little bird is trembling like a leaf. One of her umber eyes is odd too. It looks off to the side."

"Only when she's nervous," Ayelet said. Golden Gorila guffawed.

"First you train an ex-slave to become a Jinn, and now you're training a meek mimọ girl with a lazy eye. Who will be your next project, Ayelet? An ambitious nimfa? A field badger with a gift for combat strategy?"

"I'm sure Boudi will be just fine," Ayelet replied evenly. "The Lady wishes to make her into one of us. That should be enough to put any skepticism to rest."

"Ludicrous," snorted Golden Gorila. "I'm sorry, Ayelet—of course I respect the Lady's will in this, but I live among the New Order for my freedoms, and that includes the freedom to speak freely."

"Indeed. Well, you two have a good day."

Mistress Ayelet flicked her whip, and the carriage horses strained in their harnesses. The horses surged past fledgling Jade Turtle and churned towards a steep hill. Boudi dropped her arms and allowed the cool air to wash over her heated chest. She didn't care if her silken Jinn corset was thrusting her scant mimọ girl assets into the faces of lusty onlookers. She felt hot from embarrassment—so hot she might faint.

"I don't know if I can do this, Mistress Ayelet."

"Have courage, Boudi. You desired to serve the Lady, and here you are. You can do it. We have faith in you."

Boudi admonished herself. In a way, the wicked old Jinn was right. Her goal was to convince the New Order Jinni that she was a sinful, danger-seeking rebel mimọ, not a weak, insecure girl. She could imagine Tajee laughing at her failure as a secret agent. Tajee probably would have liked riding with the Jinn. Even though Ayelet was older and greying, she exuded the intense physical presence of a well-developed sexuality.

"I guess I'm worried, that's all."

Ayelet smiled. "Did you see Jade Turtle? She couldn't take her eyes off of you. Turtle only goes with women and never men. She thought you were beautiful."

"I didn't notice." Boudi felt a flush of mingled emotions. She was acutely aware that Ayelet was watching her face more closely than the road.

"It makes you feel good, doesn't it? You'll get used to it."

"Beauty isn't one of my strong points. In Heaven I was plain compared to the others, even on a good day."

"I was speaking of your pride. It's strong in you, although you're constantly undermining it. The strongest Jinni use pride as the source of their ambition to power. In that aspect at least you show a lot of promise."

Boudi shivered. "It's a horrible sin, and I can't seem to stop it."

"Then let it grow. We need to get rid of your humility. I plan to dispel your negative self-image like a bad habit, because it is."

"Is that what you're planning to do with me, Mistress Ayelet? You'll keep praising me and making me feel more and more sin? If I feel any more sin today, I'll explode."

Ayelet chuckled. "Do me a favor and don't explode, Boudi. Pride doesn't mean to hold yourself above others or divorced from the divine. True pride is to understand that spirit and love are gifts that are already within us, and those things are much bigger than us. Knowing that, we are already humbly whole. We can accept ourselves as we are, which means we can't be manipulated by enemies who try to bring us down. We can't be swayed by the lies and illusions that others try to force upon us."

"You told me that I'm beautiful. Isn't beauty an illusion?"

"There are many Jinn, including some in this city, who devote themselves day and night to beauty and the arts of inspiring desire. That's not what I'll be teaching you in the coming moons. I'm a rather skilled and infamous sword master. I'll be training you in the art of blades."

Boudi looked askance at Ayelet's sword, flared burgundy skirts, and leather corset. "I'm sorry to be skeptical, Mistress Ayelet, but fighting is for men. That's why Lord Tuhan made men so much stronger than women, so they can protect us."

"Muscles don't count for much in the desire realm. In this place, our passion is our strength. Have you heard of Queen Mab? She's the fairy queen of the Choshek Court on the far side of Meristyian. She's a highly skilled assassin, and she's no bigger than a pumpkin. She kills her enemies in a blur, straight to the point using a wicked bodkin that weighs half as much as she does. In this world you need passion guided by will, speed, and accuracy. I'll teach you these things."

"Why would I want to learn?"

"Allyssia has enemies. She rejected the established political order to found this free rebel society of Jinni here in Meristyian. She is a true daughter of the original Titans, just like Lord Tuhan and Lord Hades, but her brothers selfishly divided rulership of the realms between themselves. Lord Hades and your Lord Tuhan both know that love is the most powerful and dangerous force that exists, so naturally they both would like to control Her. That means our New Order needs to be strong. Have you ever used a sword, Boudi?"

"That's very funny. No. There are no swords in Heaven. Mimọs pray, sing, and read scriptures. We don't go and kill things."

Ayelet's face darkened. "Oh, yes you do, chérie. The Mimọs wage wars against those who won't conform to the written laws of Lord Tuhan. The Mimọs are greatly motivated by a desire to eradicate evil things with sword and flame."

The carriage had reached the top of a hill that rose on one side of Allyssia's city. The bulk of a palace came into view at the head of the mountain valley. Five crystal spires crowned the palace like the fingers of a protective hand. Ayelet pulled the reins, and the horses came to a halt on the gravelly hillside road amidst a flurry of leaping grasshoppers. Ayelet gestured at the view. "The Lady dwells high in her palace bower and dreams this city, Boudi. Look behind us and you'll see a beautiful view of the Isandlwana Fields."

Boudi twisted in the carriage seat to look in the other direction over a roadside railing. A vast plain stretched to the horizon—a swath of intense blue under towering peach-colored cumulonimbus clouds that piled one on top of the other across a wide-open sky.

"Can I get out and look?"

"Yes, but I'd like to be home soon."

Boudi slipped out of the carriage. She winced and tiptoed quickly across the hard stones of the road. The hill overlook was adjacent to the edge of the Lady's city. Not far below the tarnished railing, down a rocky slope studded with clumps of tall grass, ran a high stone wall. The top of the wall formed a long stair-stepped path that circled the outer perimeter of the city, which nestled in a shallow valley amidst immense mountainsides. Mistress Ayelet sidled up to the railing alongside her.

"What say you, Boudi?" Ayelet smiled. "Is Meristyian big enough for a bold mimọ girl like you?"

"It's big. I admit it's beautiful, too."

"The Isandlwana Fields are straight ahead, and the Heartland forest is to the west. Beyond the Heartland stretches the flower-spangled meadow-realm of Asphodel. If you had a good spyglass on a clear day, you might see the Blessed Isles of the Seelie Kishi across the straits of the Sea of Desire.

Beyond the Alpacian Mountains to the east are the steppes of Eastern Meristyian, and farther still are the beginnings of the Acheron and Styx rivers. The vampires and werewolves bicker over the deserts there. Behind us are the mountains that divide northern Meristyian from the howling plains of Erebus, where the cities of Pythia, Judecca, and Vegasis offer safe haven. Those cities are ruled by the cruel Furies, and their vintners and florists export fine wines, nectars, perfumes, peppers, and honey to all of the Underworld. Far beyond Erebus stretch the dark vastness's of Haawiyah, where Allyssia and Hades rule as Queen and King from the capital city of Mer."

"I've heard of Haawiyah. Is it a place of damnation?"

"The Hell's Court devils there oversee millions of human souls who dig in the Great Blue Hole mines, yet there is beauty even in Haawiyah," Ayelet answered. "The Gypsies hold ancestral domains in the grand black Haawiyah forests. Aside from the Ahyehasi in this city and the most favored human servants in the Kishi courts, the Gypsies are the only free humans in the Underworld. In eastern Haawiyah, the titanic husk of Kronos is still chained in the icy heights of Cocytus, where the titaness Oya births her scaly broods from the womb of her avatar Echidna, mother of monsters, using the seed of Typhon. Oya also makes the Underworld's most potent poisons, which are controlled and distributed through a Hell's army fortress in Judecca. Someday when you're capable, fledgling, maybe you can see those places."

"Everything here is so colorful. Heaven is all white and grey. Darkness hides evil, and too much color is sinful, of course." Boudi eyed the old silver bench that sat near the railing. Her heavy legs felt rubbery again.

"The lower wilds of Meristyian are ever summer-green, but the tree leaves are falling in our city, and soon everything will be snowy with the winds of our mountain winter. The Underworld's days and seasons arise from the same solar fluxes as on Earth, but borne on lower-level energies that penetrate through the planes of vibration."

"What are planes of vibration?"

Mistress Ayelet eased her leather gloves off of her fingers. "Good question. They're layers of density of some sort. I try to stay apprised of the latest advances in science, but most Jinni couldn't care less. In Haawiyah, when the weather turns tempestuous with spring heat, they just say Lady Allyssia is bedding the King. Maybe sex is the point where the physical realm allows magic to take over. I don't know. Would you like to sit and look at Meristyian?"

"You said we needed to go."

Ayelet's lips turned into a small smile. "I'd like to. You can walk down here later if you want, or any time. The Villa is only a few minutes up the hill."

Boudi looked once more over the railing, gauging the distance to the thick outer wall of the city, which was the closest thing to a potential escape route that she'd yet glimpsed. She wasn't going anywhere without sandals or clothes. She followed Ayelet back to the carriage and climbed in. The horses struggled farther up the road until the carriage topped a steep hill. Ayelet drove the horses through a gate in yet another stone wall, which gave onto a semicircular gravel drive. The drive fronted a sprawling Villa perched on the flat hilltop.

Ayelet's home was multi-storied with narrow glass-paned windows. The slanting tile roofs cut the vertical lines of the cypresses and tapering brick chimneys. The carriage rolled to a halt at the beginning of a stone walk that meandered left across the lawn. Boudi hopped out of the carriage, following Ayelet's lead. The elder Jinn led the way along the curving walkway past shrubbery and a garden full of sweet-smelling flowers, and then under an overhang to an old oak door.

Ayelet pushed the door open. Boudi followed into a modest bedroom that smelled of mastic incense. A comfortable-looking bed stood against one wall. Next to it sat a low table with a stack of leather-bound books. A candle on a writing desk afforded the only light in the room except for the outside light that came from the doorway and a shuttered window over the head of the bed. Ayelet went to the bed, pulled back the wool blanket, and fluffed the pillow.

"This was Golda's room when she was my fledgling. She slept in this bed. My Ahyehasi replaced the linens this morning, of course. I have four Ahyehasi currently living here with me. You'll meet Yenta, Herzl, Anders, and Bola soon. You have a wardrobe, a vanity, and a full-length mirror. Down the hall through the inner door, you'll find a courtyard with a hot spring-fed bathing pool. The outer door opens to the gardens, of course."

"It's nicer than my dormitorium in Heaven."

Ayelet smiled. "We will get your fitted clothes for you. Mistress Gallinah is quick with her sewing, and I don't think she ever sleeps. I've decided to leave you alone for the rest of the morning so you can bathe in the inner courtyard, get dressed, and explore the gardens if you wish."

"You want me to take a bath?"

Ayelet shrugged. "I imagine in Heaven you had to do everything you were told. Your classrooms were assigned seating. You raised your hand to ask permission to sneeze. Things around here aren't so strict—far from it."

"I'm not the perfect mimo girl that you may think I am, Mistress Ayelet. I'm used to breaking the rules."

"Well, good. In the moons to come, I'll instruct you in the ways of the Jinni. I'm ready for a new pupil, having just graduated Golda a few years back. I hope you're ready for me too."

"I'm ready." Boudi avoided Ayelet's silvery eyes. She wasn't ready at all, but she felt ashamed to keep complaining. She wasn't just an mimo girl. She was a Conclave agent.

"The gardens are well past their summer bloom, but they're still beautiful," Ayelet said airily. "Watch out for the chasm bats. They fly up into the city to eat the insects. Try not to let moths in. They occasionally nest in our wardrobes. I'll send my dressing-girl down in a few minutes to help with your situation. Herzl is close to your size, and she's very devoted. She can unlace your corset for you, and then sponge you in the bath and give you a rub to help you relax. I'll come down and check on you around noon."

"Thank you for—" Boudi stiffened. Ayelet leaned and pressed a warm shocking kiss on each of her cheeks.

"Expect my dressing-girl. She's young and Ukraine. Some don't care for her, but I love her." Ayelet turned on her heels and swept out of the room. The tip of Ayelet's sword scabbard bumped hollowly against the doorframe. Her greying pearled braid swung as she closed the oak door behind her.

Boudi listened to the boot heels click away down the walkway outside. The clicks faded until they were fainter than the sound of her pounding heart. She made her way to the bed and collapsed. The bed had a sensual smell to it, probably because it formerly belonged to Golda, who had no doubt slept with her ample breasts and other parts unrestrained, the better to commit sinful acts with both women and men.

Boudi felt another queer surge of emotion curl like smoke through her body. She needed keep ahold of herself. She needed to keep her mind from spiraling out of control. She was a somewhat-trained Conclave agent inside the fortress of the enemy.

The creeping darkness of the bedroom pressed against her for several minutes like an echo of Ayelet's kisses until the candle on the desk brightened. Molten wax spilled from a gap in the candle's lip and ran down to congeal in the silver shell-shaped holder. Shuffles and thumping sounds came from outside, and a knock sounded on the door.

"Boudi-Ca? Bonjour. I am Herzl." The door pushed open. A mousy dark-haired girl entered, allowing a flood of warm daylight into the darkened bedchamber. The girl scraped a pink-striped, gold-cornered trunk across the wooden floor.

"Yes. Please come right in." Boudi sighed and looked skeptically at the odd, gaudy clothes trunk. She knew she couldn't hope for proper clothes from her hosts. Mistress Ayelet was wearing a corset as outerwear, and Herzl wore no corset at all—only a black form-fitting strapless dress that fell to her mid-thigh, revealing bare shoulders, pale legs, and sandal-less feet. The slender young Ahyehass had dirty knees. Herzl's black dress matched the black leather collar around her pale doll-like neck.

The girl's brown eyes were lined with kohl. A silver clip glinted in her dark hair. The clip was a beetle with ruby eyes and silver wings. Herzl could have been a senior student at the Crystal Academy Of Sacred Moons, but she was the opposite of any mimo. Herzl dripped with a long history of lust. Her sinfully painted lips formed a slow smirk like a little unfolding rose bud.

"You are so beautiful, yes? Please sit to unlace your corset. We have a bath for you, and then we dress?"

Herzl's accent was thicker than Ayelet's. The girl gestured towards the chair at the desk. Boudi felt her cheeks heat yet again at the thought of going nude in front of Herzl. She scoured her mind for a non-insulting explanation of why she didn't want the dirty girl's hands on her, but she couldn't find one. Worse yet, unlike her mimo underthings in Heaven, her Jinn corset was back-laced. She could hardly remove it herself even if she wanted to.

"Fine." Boudi felt dizzy when she rose up from the bed. She was on the verge of a panic attack. Where was the damned Conclave? Where was Pasteur? He was supposed to be her new guardian. Golda had said there were more Mimọs out in Meristyian. Surely the Conclave was staging a rescue to save their missing junior agent.

Chapter 6:

Masad padded across the beach, placing his paws with care. He flicked seawater from his ears. The rolling waves of the Sea of Desire gleamed yellow-green in the glow of morning. The waves crashed onto the sands and died with little whispers amidst the billions of human bones.

After fifteen hundred years, Vilks the boatman was still following orders to drown all human souls and send them onwards into the unknown void, unless they were hand-picked by the devils to dig the Great Blue Hole mines or serve as slaves. Only pureblood covenanted Gypsies were exempted from those two ordained fates.

The Underworld was no longer a seething madhouse. The serpent Queen had changed everything. She'd seduced the dark-eyed, closed-fisted brother. The titanic establishment had formed sides, and the Olympians had split like the Kishi before them. The humans had been forced to pledge their souls to Lord Tuhan or Lord Hades, or else their desire-bones would most rot forever on god-forsaken shores. The Underworld had become a well-pruned dark paradise under Allyssia's influence, a twisted mirror image of exclusive Heaven.

The emotional realms still seethed with restlessness, however. To the far east over the thorny jungle trees, angry clouds met the implacable granitespackled swells of the Alpacian mountains where they tumbled towards the sea. To the west, beyond many kilometers of Kishi-wild terrain, began the vast Asphodel meadows and the steamy valleys of the river Bourbon, which snaked and boiled from the lava-oozing headwalls of monolithic Mount Purgatory.

Masad could see all of it with his inner tracking senses, not with his feline eyes. He glanced up at the sky over his furred shoulder. The mimọ 'rescue party' was camped in the clouds above the Sea of Desire, safe in a mental way-station. The agents of Lord Tuhan were waiting to siphon the souls of their fallen students back to Heaven where they belonged. The Mimọs couldn't descend properly without their thought-bodies densifying in the emotional thickness of Meristyian.

Masad sniffed the air. He twitched his whiskers. By his reckoning, the blown-down Mimọs had been in Meristyian for at least three days. The Mimọic Hierarchy had delayed and debated before Pasteur had summoned him. *There is dirty work to do, and dirty work is best done by a hellion. The pay will be the usual.*

Masad trotted along the first mimọ boy's track. He enjoyed possessing a feline. The grey tabby cat that he'd found skulking forlornly in the ruins of Chickasaw was an excellent host. The animal's hunting instincts smoothed the channeling of his own skills in Meristyian. Cats were trackers, after all, like him.

He could see the stale threads from atop a dune—shimmering ribbons that shouldn't exist in the desire-world tapestry. Only two of the mimọ boys could be recovered—an expected percentage. The third was far away—likely netted by lucky hunters. Mimọs were the Underworld's most desired slaves. The boy was destined for Hell's Court papers, followed by an auction for at least a hundred gold coins, and then a chained existence of endless pleasure or suffering depending on the species and needs of his owner. Masad frowned and focused. Strangely, he could see a fourth thread. Four Mimọs had fallen into Meristyian recently, not three.

Three Mimọs, oh venerable possessor, oh illustrious hellion prince, oh wise and sapient one. Pasteur had addressed him using the proper tone of respect for hellion princes, plus the usual touch of added sarcasm. Their names are Tajee, Benjamin, and Kale. Find them in that order if you can. Pasteur had either lied, or he hadn't counted his Mimọs right, and the Mimọic Hierarchy was always right when it came to the counting.

Say you three, but four fallen, Pasteur. Think me so blind?

The fourth thread, the pink one, tapered to a frayed end. Masad focused, sending his sensitivity across the leagues to the place of the irregularity. He could barely see the blur left by great magic, a blur recognizable by a master of both the weave and the arcane, which he was. The fourth mimọ hadn't gone to the void. Her thread had been snipped on purpose, but by whom, and why?

The Mimọic Hierarchy was hiding something, and the delay in sending a rescue party spoke of something important. Masad bristled. It irked him when the Mimọs withheld things. Hierarchy secrets were worth far more than fallen Mimọs to interested parties, even if the fallen Mimọs were beautiful and nubile.

Masad broke into a bouncing lope over the sand, out of the dunes and into the Isandlwana jungle. The nearest mimọ boy's track resolved into a loopy, directionless blue-white thread. Masad ran fast in the cat body for an hour, then two. He slowed when he heard the music. The aperture of a cave opened at the bottom of a rocky embankment. A chuckling rivulet ran out, adding a gentle counterpoint to the melody being played.

A shaggy rake lounged by a boulder in the grotto, blowing a tune on his flute. The mimọ boy was dancing in the nude. Two nimfas danced with him. The boy was lithe and brown, on the cusp of mature masculinity. His arms were strong-willed but thin with his youth. Dark hair fell over well-proportioned shoulders.

Handsome chit he is. Makes the Mimọs proud, his phallus.

The nimfas teased the mimọ boy as they danced, caressing his slender buttocks lightly and brushing as if by chance against his manhood. The boy made a joke, and one of the nimfas chortled his name—Tajee.

Masad stalked from rock to rock. The grotto offered little cover suitable for the physical form of the cat. He followed the shadows between the patches where the morning sunlight fell through the forest. A quiet scamper placed him within pouncing distance. The song ended. The rake spoke to the nimfas. Masad listened. A skilled possessor could elucidate the basic voice of his chosen host from its vocal cords, but the proper usage—the words chosen and the inflections employed—required a master actor.

The two nimfas gathered with the bearded half-man. They wanted to show Tajee the flowery Meristyian plateau. The rake wanted morning sex. The nimfa named Sekushi playfully grappled with the rake, only to be lifted off her feet and spun end-over-end until her buttocks were up in the air. The nimfa named Kan'nō-tekina joined in the fray, reaching low between the rake's legs to grab his massive phallus, then dancing back, only to have her wrist trapped by the rake's hairy hand. Kan'nō-tekina tugged, Sekushi squirmed, and the two fell in a jumble at Tajee's feet.

The mimo stepped back, but a female hand tripped him. Sekushi crawled onto the boy, who accepted the nimfa's overture. Kan'nō-tekina freed herself from the rake with a peal of laughter, but the master rose on massive legs and collared her. He bent her double with his hairy hand. The nimfa's laughter changed to a moan when the rake speared her. Masad crept closer. Animal sounds rose on the morning air as the rake worked Kan'nō-tekina on her knees. The way was clear. He bounded across the space and leapt onto the rake's back. The creature flinched at the impact and reared.

"Coco?"

Masad heard the mimo boy's hesitant voice at the moment of transference. He slid out of the feline and between the rake's second and third cervical vertebrae. The rake was weak of will. Masad flowed into his cranium and gained hold, beating the rake's soul into the lower portions of its own brain, there to remain subjugated.

Mine you are, beast, for a time.

Masad braced against the intense pleasure. He became aware of the Rake's desire, the rump of the nimfa against his hairy lap, and the length of the engorged phallus in Kan'nō-tekina's wet sex. He could see, hear, and taste through the rake's senses. He laved his tongue over big flat teeth. A bird in the forest was chirruping.

"Master, is there something wrong?"

Masad focused the rake's eyes on Kan'nō-tekina's supple back. He moved his desires down the arms of his host and into the hirsute digits that gripped the nimfa's narrow waist. He had no time for idle pleasure. He quickly renewed the rake's thrusts, and the nimfa responded with a new zeal. Her fingers clutched at the dirt. Masad found the floodgates of the rake's anatomy and disabled them, allowing the animal seed to run free.

"Meow. Meow." The grey tabby cat, released from control, skulked nearby. Masad let go of the nimfa and stretched upright on his two hooves. He savored the lust that coursed through the rake's thumping veins.

Know you I am here, little kitty. Feel no bad feeling, little friend. Stay and be happy. Need you I might again.

Tajee and Sekushi were watching raptly, entangled with each other like resting kittens. Masad shifted his gaze to the exposed phallus resting dark and heavy between the mimọ boy's legs. Long had it been since he'd enjoyed a boy. Sekushi untangled herself from Tajee and rose to her feet.

"Can we go now, Master?" lilted the nimfa.

"No," Masad grunted. "Do work, we must." Masad stepped towards Tajee. Tajee hopped to his feet and walked towards the skittish cat.

Sekushi pouted. "Master? Are we going to the flowers now?"

"Time for Tajee to go home. Take him to the sea I will, there to release. Flies he back to Heaven. Stay you here, nimfas."

"Master, no!"

"No, Master!"

"Come." Masad snatched the mimọ boy's brown bicep with the rake's huge hand. The mimọ boy mumbled something nervous, unintelligible. Tajee had managed to grab the tabby cat. He held it against his bare chest.

"Master, you always keep your promises!" Kan'nō-tekina persisted.

"No, no." Masad shook his head. He preferred not to arrive at the beach with two nimfas in full bloom. He'd done it once before when he'd delivered a missing mimọ, and the Mimọic Hierarchy hadn't appreciated it. The nimfas hadn't appreciated what happened next—the bloody separation of the mimọ from his newly densified flesh, allowing the rescue party to siphon up his soul. Masad scanned the grotto for a useful tool. He saw no forged metal edges. The rake's hands were strong, but a snapped neck was less reliable than a severed head.

"Take us to the flowers, Master!" Kan'nō-tekina persisted. Both nimfas stood with arms akimbo, looking as indignant as nimfas could look.

"Go to the sea first we," Masad said. "Then pick flowers. Promise I. Follow if you must, but stay—"

"Master, you said—" Sekushi interrupted.

"Enough!" Masad boomed. The nimfas stared wide-eyed at each other. Masad led the small procession out of the grotto. He charged through the forest back towards the sea. He escorted Tajee for almost two hours, scolding the nimfas when their will to walk flagged. They neared the beach. The trees drew farther apart. The sunlight fell in broader swaths across the forest.

Masad paused before navigating the bank of a trickling, leafy creek. He was suddenly aware that he was being followed. He wasn't the only tracker in western Meristyian on that ever-summer afternoon. He opened his senses as wide as they would go. It was a distinct feeling being tracked, one that he hadn't felt in a while. He was always the tracker—the one unseen and unexpected.

Still, two midnight blue skeins were converging fast with his thread in the fabric of the tapestry. They were either patrolling Seelie Kishi wardens on horseback, or they were slave hunters coming with ropes, cuffs, and collars. The hunters would kill the rake to score a pretty mimọ boy, regardless of how the Seelie Kishi felt about poaching in their forests. Masad grimaced. He could make his own thread disappear in the tapestry, but he couldn't conceal the threads of the nimfas and Tajee. His true skills lay in the realm of the dead, divination, and makumbacy. Grand alteration magic had always eluded him.

"Stay, nimfas." He raised his hand and gestured for them to wait.

"Master no!" they exclaimed in chorus.

"Wait here! Stay!" Masad snatched Tajee up in his arms and began a strenuous trot with the mildly protesting mimọ and his cat, leaving the nimfas to weep quietly behind him. He launched himself across sand and gravel, running the sinuous course of the creek towards the sea. Soon he was splashing through deep rivulets of water. The rake's body was strong and agile. He moved with speed for several more minutes, even as he watched the threads close in on him. The decaying leaves and round rocks in the creek's bed gave over to littoral sand and old bones. He'd almost reached the beach when he rounded a bend and saw the two interlopers. They'd caught him more quickly than he'd anticipated.

Two sweaty horses bounded down the stream bank. Two women rode astride with swords strapped to their hips. One was a sandy blonde riding a white horse. She hefted a Platinum-plated long gun. The woman in front was taller with wild reddish hair and bluish lips. Her linen shirt was half-unbuttoned to ease her impressive cleavage. Neither Jinn wore any insignia of Hell's army or the Smokeless Flames. The women were quite possibly the rarest of Isandlwana inhabitants—New Order Jinni, rebel followers of Allyssia.

"Hail, Rake," the redheaded Jinn spoke. "My name is Mistress Golda. This is Mistress Cybelah. We mean you no harm."

Masad bowed slightly, allowing no trace of reaction on his face. His acting skills might fool the dumb nimfas, but the priestesses of the love Ifreeta were cunning and capable.

"We're looking for Mimọs," Golda continued. "Oh! What do you have there? You found one!" The Jinn enunciated each word clearly. Since he hadn't responded, Masad guessed, the Jinn assumed he was stupid, if not mute. What now, Masad?

"This one," he said gruffly. "I return him to the sea."

"Give him to me, and I'll take him for you," Golda said. "There are angry Mimọs at the beach. The angry Mimọs are bad."

"Go mimọ home. He be safe." Masad tried to gauge the mood of the Jinn and how much she wanted the boy. It couldn't hurt to buy time to consider his options, up to a point.

"Allyssia rules this forest, rake," Golda continued. "She has joined with the Seelie Kishi to protect western Meristyian, and in return, she demands your respect. Give that mimọ to me. I'll take care of him."

"Put me down." Tajee struggled suddenly. "I want to go with her."

Masad wrestled with the mimọ boy. The chit was no match for the rake's burly arms. The Jinn was a more capable adversary. Golda's gloved hand slid to the worn hilt of the blade at her belt. Masad restrained the mimọ boy with a choke hold. His choices seemed clear. He could possess one of the Jinni—a dicey strategy—or surrender the mimọ boy within a half-league of the beach. Neither option was appealing. Golda kicked the flank of her horse. The horse left the bank, the sword left its sheath, and Golda's blade was at the rake's face in the space of a second. The Jinn with the gun circled slowly to the left.

A remembrance, Masad. Have satyrs poor reflexes.

"Let go of that boy," Golda warned, her voice throaty and threatening. "If you hurt him, I'll have your head."

"Take him. He's too much trouble." Masad loosened his grip on the mimọ and edged away from the blade. He wasn't sure if he could follow the riders while possessing the rake or even the quick but short-legged tabby cat. Any attempt to possess Tajee would cause him intense pain. He'd tried that trick before. Mimọs remained holy ground even in their densified emotional forms. Worse yet, leaving the rake's body would cause more complications. The beast would regain his senses and surely have something to say.

Not if the rake is dead, Masad. Show some backbone. Spill some guts already. You are soft. Soft as an mimọ boy's bottom.

"Help me, rake. Lift him." Golda kept her blade poised.

"Aye," Masad grunted. "His name is Tajee." He reluctantly hoisted Tajee up onto the horse. He helped the redheaded Jinn to position the boy in front of her in the saddle.

"Ow!" Tajee yelped. The tabby cat shot from his arms over the head of the horse. The feline bounced out of a rivulet and dashed wetly into the cover of the forest.

"Are you injured, mimọ?" Golda tugged at her reins to steady her mount, which was skittish and struggling with the treacherous streambed.

Masad slipped the wavering blade, grabbed Golda's arm, and yanked.

The Jinn, surprised, tipped off and bore them both into the stream with a heavy splash. Masad wrestled, but Mistress Golda was predictably strong. Her knee landed squarely in the rake's midsection. She crushed the rake's throat with her corded forearm and wrenched her sword back.

Masad slid downward to gather himself inside the darkness of the rake's chest. He could no longer see from the rake's eyes, but he could feel the impact of the blade. The rake shuddered viscerally in the rushing water. Masad slipped away from the intense flood of pain, across the gap and into Golda's groin.

He pressed through her perineum and forced his will up into her throat. He felt the Jinn thrust with the blade again. So sensitive were the tissues of Golda's neck that he could feel the spray of the rake's warm blood and the trickle on her skin. Masad slipped further upwards, where he began the battle for control of Golda's body.

A tremendous force fought him back—a brick wall of intense passions. The Jinn was strong with love, lust, envy, pleasure, pain, and above all, addiction. Recent use of purple nectar buttered her blood. Deep down lay the twisted scars of black nectar, centuries old.

Older you are than you look, Jinn. Feel I like I should know you. Strong your vices have made you against me.

Masad eased his force. Psychic injury to his hosts was against his personal code. Golda could no doubt feel him inside her. Her muscles were rigid, and her heart raced. She rose to her feet and staggered back. She stepped wetly into her stirrup and raised herself back into her saddle where Tajee still sat.

"Are you alright, Golda?" said the second Jinn. Masad heard the voice faintly at a distance, not through any sense of hearing, but through his inner tracking senses, combined with the extraordinary sensitivity of Golda's skin.

"I don't know," Golda replied. Her voice resonated in her throat. Masad pressed back down through heated tingle of lust in Golda's easier underbelly and through the leather saddle into the vertebrae of the horse underneath. He shot up the spinal cord and occupied its brain in scant seconds. The quadruped was nervous and offered little resistance. Masad reached for the sensory centers, and then took over muscular control. He could hear the Jinni clearly.

"Did you just kill that rake?"

"He attacked me!" Golda answered.

"Why in the name of the Lady would he have done that? He must have felt threatened. You were very aggressive."

"The rake was hurting Tajee. I'm shaken up, Cybelah. I'm not feeling right. I feel bad for the rake, but he shouldn't have grabbed me."

"The Kishi won't appreciate this. Should we try to bury him?"

"No. We should go."

Masad winced when Golda's boot heels kicked the horse's lower ribs. He struggled to spring forward. He felt ungainly, but he managed to get up the bank. The horse was frightened inside, at war with its own training. Masad eased back and allowed the horse more reflexive control. The animal bolted forward. Golda kicked harder, and the horse surged through the forest. The horse's heart thundered in its barrel chest.

Easy, hairy one. Just a friendly hellion along for a ride.

Masad pondered as the horse made its way towards an unknown destination. He hadn't yet collected a bounty, but he'd found one fallen mimọ. If he was lucky, the New Order Jinni would lead him straight to another—the fourth fallen mimọ, the mysterious severed pink thread.

Chapter 7:

Golda rode through the last stretch of forest into the camp—a sheltered valley nestled on the upslopes that led to the northern flowery plateau. She held Tajee close in the saddle in front of her. He'd barely stirred or struggled, which was a good thing, but also a bad thing. He likely wasn't in his right mind.

She was exhausted. Her arms felt like lead, and so did her Hunger. She desperately wanted to feed again. Her emptiness was affecting her. The scuffle with the rake had been unnerving. The creature hadn't fought when she'd fallen on him. She'd killed him on instinct—a reflex from countless sword lessons with Ayelet. She imagined after-echoes of the rake's thread flickering through the tapestry at odd angles. The thread couldn't be real. The rake's lifeblood was running down a stream towards the sea.

In the bottom of the valley, Mistress Ivanka and fledgling Herpessenia sat at a smoldering fire in front of the tents. Ivanka was hard to miss. The witch's olive skin was stark black like the coat of her ebony Hell horse, which was tethered to a nearby tree. The Hell horse expelled a sulfuric stench that filtered through the forest.

Golda closed her olfactory senses against the acrid smell, but not before she caught the sweet scent of Herpessenia's perfume. Ivanka's blonde fledgling sat cross-legged next to her elder mentor, nursing her nectar habit with a field-concocted flower ale that she'd mixed in a clay mug. Golda dismounted and helped Tajee to the ground.

"Hail, Golda," Ivanka said. "I see you found another mimo."

"Yes, by the grace of the Fates. A rake had him."

"Lucky boy." Herpessenia grinned impishly over the rim of her mug. "It must have been exquisite to be broken by such a well-endowed beast."

Golda squeezed the mimo boy's shoulder. "I don't think he was touched. His name is Tajee. He must have blown down in that storm that Mareinah conjured. I feel responsible for him."

Herpessenia ogled Tajee. "Would you consider selling him or making a trade?"

"This is no time for such nonsense, Herpessenia-Ca," Ivanka interjected. "It was foolish of you to snatch that fallen mimo boy, Golda, unless you wanted to interrogate him. This is a scouting party, not a slave raid."

Golda felt her heat rise. Too often she found herself at odds with the abrasive black witch, who seemed to enjoy needling her. She always tried to hold her tongue. Ivanka was a legendary sorceress and a key ally of Allyssia.

"Of course this isn't a slave raid, Ivanka. How could it be? The New Order doesn't have slaves anymore like the Old Order. We have Ahyehasi, and many Ahyehasi in our city happen to be boys who enjoy serving."

Ivanka guffawed. "We're far from the Lady's well-meaning city, which makes those politically correct words even more pointless. Your trip to Heaven was itself a bold raid to steal the mimo girl. It doesn't matter if Boudi wished it. The Lady has revealed herself as a hypocrite."

"I couldn't just let the rake take the boy, could I?"

"Of course you couldn't. You saved him," Cybelah said quickly. Cybelah shouldered her gun. "We should leave this place. A few Mimos fell in Mareinah's storm, but I see no real threat. Perhaps the faster their Mimos disappear, the faster the Mimoic Hierarchy will leave Meristyian in peace."

"And not come back," added Herpessenia. "So we're going home?"

"Yes," Ivanka rasped. "Pack the tents."

"No." Golda cleared her throat. "I really need to feed. Cybelah and I have been going all day. I'm not getting back on my horse this minute. I just came home from a trip to Heaven. I'm too tired for this."

Ivanka uncoiled her bent black form from the forest floor. "Take the time you need, if you're too weak. I'll collect herbs and keep watch. Talk to the boy, Golda. Ask him what he knows. Make sure he understands his difficult situation."

Herpessenia grinned. "I'd love to show him the 'ins and outs' of how mimọ boys are expected to behave in this place."

"You'll do no such thing, Herpessenia-Ca," Cybelah said.

"Tajee should rightfully belong to Golda," Ivanka said. "By the old rules, of course. It isn't clear that the boy has any desire to serve of his own free will in the Lady's city. Golda, take the boy to your tent and rub him with oil. It will help hold him together."

"Who are you people?" Tajee muttered. "Are you hellions?"

Ivanka glared pointedly at the boy. "Stay silent and learn your place. Golda will speak with you when she's ready."

"This way, Tajee. Let's rest. You look as haggard as I am." Golda gently guided the boy towards her tent. She winked over her shoulder at Herpessenia. The spoiled blonde daughter of Allyssia blew a kiss and stroked her clay mug suggestively. Golda turned away. Was Herpessenia really flirting with her? In her fatigue and grief over the death of Mareinah, flirting was the last thing on her mind. The mimọ was looking over his shoulder at Herpessenia too.

"She's really pretty," Tajee murmured.

"Herpessenia-Ca is too much for you." Golda chuckled despite her gloomy mood. She took Tajee's hand and led him into her low, cozy tent. She gestured at her travel bed, which scarcely accommodated one person, much less two. Tajee flopped onto his stomach and made a sigh that sounded almost like a groan.

Golda settled next to the boy. She dared to brush her fingers gently over Tajee's feathered wings. Small and pale white, they folded against his brown shoulder blades. She bent further and grazed her fingertips down Tajee's muscled back and over the dimples above the curves of his near-perfect ass. She withdrew, pleased that he'd let her touch him without protest. The mimo's halo was just visible as a golden glow in the gloom. He was breathing quietly.

Golda felt a small rush of pride warm her belly. If Ivanka was right and Tajee could be hers, she'd be the envy of the other Jinni. Fallen Mimos were rare and coveted things in the Underworld—expensive status symbols owned by only the very wealthy who could afford them. She'd hoped for favor from the Lady for attempting the trip to Heaven, and the outcome had exceeded all of her expectations, despite Mareinah's horrible death.

She'd emerged from the Sea of Desire with Boudi, much to the shock of everyone. She'd succeeded in bringing the girl back per the Lady's bold plan, equipped with the magical hat. She was about to go home with Tajee, but unlike Boudi, Tajee could actually be hers. She just needed to convince him of what she had to offer. Allyssia allowed no Ahyehasi to live in Her city against their will.

"How do you feel, beautiful one?"

Tajee stirred. "Mmh. I feel so tired. So sleepy."

"You've been out here a while. The jungles of Meristyian are known to drive fallen Mimos to madness. It looks like you've been afflicted, but when we get back to the city, I expect you'll feel better. I remember you from the ruins of Chickasaw. Did you fall in the storm? Did a gust of wind send you over the edge? I'm sure you feel afraid, but you're in a much more wonderful place."

"I jumped to save Boudi. So are you some sort of hellion?"

"No. Demons are born when divines have sex with animals, or when divines have sex with women while in animal form. I used to be a human. I was a noblewoman in Egypt centuries ago. I served as a slave in Vegasis for a while after I died, and now I'm a jinni by the grace of Allyssia. She transformed me. I'm going to take you to Her hidden city, Tajee. I'm doing you a favor. It's too dangerous for you to be out here. I'm going to oil you too. The oil will hold your energy and help you feel better."

Tajee frowned. "What do you mean?"

"Olive oil." Golda snapped her fingers. "Wake up, Tajee."

"I'm trying to stay awake. I'm so sleepy."

Golda extracted her herbal oil flask from her leather travel pack. She poured a dollop of oil onto Tajee's back and smoothed it up to his neck. In the short term, the oil would help the boy's desire-body to solidify, or so she'd been told. She hadn't laid oiled hands on Boudi while the girl was sleeping, although Ivanka had recommended it. She'd felt guilty enough over stripping the mimọ naked and hauling her across Meristyian, among other things. The girl had no idea what she'd agreed to. The life of a jinni was not to be taken lightly, yet Allyssia had determined Boudi's fate without even giving the mimọ time for reflection.

Golda felt the ache of her Hunger rise, and she pushed aside her concerns. She and Tajee had pressed against each other in the saddle for half the afternoon. She was familiar with the reservoir of pent-up lust just under his skin. She continued rubbing the oil into Tajee's lower back, and then moved down to his legs, where she cleaned his dirty feet, poking her finger into the crevices between his brown toes.

"Now I'll do your front side, Tajee. Turn."

The boy flipped over. His nervous chocolate eyes flicked over her, expressive and sensual. Golda rubbed the olive oil gently across Tajee's temples, then down to his neck, his collarbone, and his chest. She grazed over Tajee's nipple. The boy twitched, even as his eyes lingered and settled on her chest.

Golda felt her Hunger surge. She wanted to pinch. She wanted to make Tajee gasp with the pleasure and pain. She wanted him to say her name. No. Tajee wasn't ready for any of those ridiculous Hunger-fueled urges. The boy's dark eyebrows squirreled to a frown.

"You have Boudi, right? You're keeping her somewhere?"

"Lady Allyssia has her. Boudi isn't mine to have." Golda poured more oil from the flask. She worked it into Tajee's chest and ferried it down to his stomach. She attempted to calm him there, but Tajee's muscles were knotting again with his every breath.

"Why did you bring her here?"

"Boudi is fine. She's in the city. We have a hard ride back across Meristyian ahead of us. You don't need to worry, Tajee. Right now you should focus on yourself."

"What have you done with her? I need to see her when we get there. Please. I need to make sure she's alright."

"Calm down. Let's talk while I oil you." Golda stroked slow circles over Tajee's chest to soothe his thumping heart. "So you're in love with your female friend?"

"How did you know?"

"I'm a Jinni. It's not so obvious that Boudi loves you back, though."

Tajee hesitated. "Deep down, I think she does."

Golda nodded. She didn't want to upset the boy more, but she could feel Tajee's weakness. It was a bad moment, but it was a natural opening. Her Hunger urged her to exploit it. Tajee's body as a whole was beginning to relax. The oil was doing its work, soothing him.

"If I remember correctly, Boudi said she wanted to go with me. She made a decision to leave Heaven. She didn't want you to interfere, much less come here. She told you to go away."

"Boudi is a bad liar."

"You might be right, but it still sounds like the feelings aren't mutual, even if there are feelings like you think."

Tajee's jaw clenched. "Boudi kissed me, so she must love me deep down."

"That doesn't make sense. If she loves you, then why did she want to leave you? Why did she write a letter to Allyssia and throw it down into Meristyian, asking to be rescued from Heaven?"

Tajee frowned. "What letter? I don't know anything about a letter. It's probably her damned Conclave mission. I wish I'd never picked up those stupid flyers!"

"What are you talking about?"

"I'm talking about the Conclave of Deviant Operations. They took Boudi for a secret mission. Boudi never wanted to do this. She's just a girl. She does her homework. She says her prayers. I'm the one who should be an agent! She shouldn't even be here!"

"Tajee, calm down. I'm sorry you're upset."

"No, I'm sorry! I'm sorry this ever happened!"

Tajee's eyes had gone wild. Golda held him down with one hand on his stomach. He gripped her wrist. She held his bare shoulder firmly with her other hand, aware that the conversation out by the fire had gone silent. Golda looked deeply into the boy's brown eyes.

"Breathe. And be quieter, please."

"I'm sorry."

Golda nodded. She'd formed a link with Tajee through his sudden outburst. An emotional bridge had formed between them. She needed to weigh her next words carefully, even as she eased her grip. "Thank you so much for confiding in me, Tajee. I do like you. You seem to be a wonderful, handsome young man."

"Thanks. I guess."

"I see you looking at me. You think I'm beautiful?"

Tajee took a deep breath. "Are you kidding?"

"So that's a yes?"

"mimọ girls try to hide their breasts instead of showing them off. No mimọ girl has red hair either that I know of. There might be some though, because a lot cover their hair up completely. Your purple lip paint is pretty. mimọ girls aren't allowed to use much color—even too much pink is considered sinful."

"My lips aren't painted. They're stained. Sometimes I paint my eyelids to match. How do I explain? I'm a flower-eater, and so is Herpessenia-Ca, that pretty blonde out there. The nectar from the Isandlwana flowers stains my mouth. It's considered a bad habit in the New Order, a bad habit more for Ahyehasi than Jinni. That's one reason why I'm kind of a rebel among the others."

"I was a rebel in Heaven. I got in trouble a lot."

"Were you a naughty boy?"

A tense grin edged Tajee's lips. "Yes."

"That's wonderful. We have something in common then, don't we? Perhaps I can encourage your bad habits and show you a few more. How would you like that?"

"What do you mean, exactly?"

Golda tilted her head and caressed Tajee's chest again slowly, lingering with her fingertips, teasing around his nipple. The mimo was staring up at her, not fully comprehending but nonetheless wanting her to continue. "I'm a real woman. I have a lot more to offer than your little friend from Heaven. How would you like to stay down here with me? How would you like to be mine and play with me for a time?"

"No."

"I know you want me, Tajee. Don't lie. I can feel it."

"I know you're evil, and you're doing something with Boudi, but I keep thinking about you in other ways. I know it's horribly sinful."

"Focus on it. Don't deny yourself, Tajee. I know what you want. You were so deprived of pleasure in Heaven. You had no outlet for that wonderful lust inside of you. Tell me you'd like to stay here with me. Tell me you don't want to go back to Heaven, because if you don't decide to stay, that's probably where you're going."

Tajee blinked. "I can go back? How would I do that?"

"Well, you'd use the stairway. I got up there, didn't I? I'd have to show you where to climb it, though."

"Is it close?"

"No. The stairway rises diagonally over Meristyian, but the bottom steps aren't close. The Trivium is a meeting of roads on the eastern slopes of Mount Purgatory, which you'd then have to climb for a good long while."

"I've heard of Purgatory."

"The old material stairway to Heaven starts at the top of that mountain, but you don't want that, Tajee. Stay down here with me for at least a few weeks. Play with me. At least then you'll know what you'll be missing when you leave."

"I'd be lying if I said I wasn't tempted."

"So that's a yes? If you said yes, that would officially save everyone a lot of trouble. You don't want to go back yet. You're a boy who likes an adventure, right?"

Tajee's burning anger was muddled with lust. Desire shone in his deep brown eyes. Golda leaned close, allowing him to smell her scent. She subtly pressed her corseted breast against Tajee's arm. The mimọ boy didn't pull away.

"How do I know I can trust you?"

"You don't. Most of Hell's citizens make a habit of lying, but we New Order Jinni aren't the lying types. That includes me. I keep my promises, and I believe in the truth. Speaking of the truth, did you and Boudi get naughty in Heaven? You know how she is. She was too shy to admit it."

Tajee grimaced. "I kissed her sometimes. Boudi isn't the best mimọ girl, but she's still a girl. She's proper and takes her virtues seriously. She'd never do anything too bad, and I'd never take advantage of her even if she caved in and let me. I wouldn't want to get her in real trouble with the Conclave."

"You're badder than she is, aren't you Tajee? I'll let you do everything you ever wanted to do with Boudi, and then I'll want you to do a lot more."

"I don't think so."

"You don't have to answer now. You can think about it tonight while you're sleeping by my side and over the next few days while we ride. When we get to the city though, you'll have to decide whether you want to go back to Heaven or let me show you pleasure."

"What about Boudi?"

"She's staying with us. The only question is whether you're staying too."

Tajee stifled a sudden yawn. "I have to see Boudi before I answer. Why am I so damned tired? I just want to sleep for a long time."

"I promise you'll see your friend. You have my word."

"I only came here for Boudi, but I'll think about your offer, Golda." Tajee's voice was quiet. The boy's eyes fluttered and closed. He could no longer keep them open.

Golda swept her hair over her shoulder and looked towards the door of the tent. Her Hunger was overwhelming her. She needed to sate the monster before losing control. She could barely restrain herself from straddling Tajee and taking him right then and there.

"Stay here until I come back, Tajee. Sleep. Let me know if there is anything else you need. I hope you won't mind sleeping beside me tonight? Our sleeping arrangements are a little tight."

"I might sleep under a tree." Tajee's voice cracked. "I really need some clean clothes."

"You've been nice. You can look through my pack for something of mine." Golda crawled out through the tent door. If Tajee dared to wear her clothes to satisfy his modesty, her scent would get into his head. She felt a twinge of guilt amidst the moil of her other emotions. The mimo boy loved his sweet girlfriend, not his girlfriend's Jinn abductor.

Cybelah and Herpessenia-Ca were smoking herbs by the fire and speaking in low tones.

Golda strode over to the Ahyehass tent, ignoring the curious gazes. She was glad that she'd spoken and hadn't let Ivanka push her into leaving immediately.

The sun was sinking over the Isandlwana jungle, and the evening promised to be cool and peaceful. She'd keep her tracking senses open to the tapestry. She'd know if any Mimos were approaching to save their wayward little soldier.

The two travel-Ahyehasi were dirty from three days of forest living and over-used moreover, but they folded their playing cards and arranged themselves dutifully on their beds when she entered. They were two of Allyssia's city servants, borrowed ad hoc on the way out of the stables. The boy was a farrier's assistant. The girl was an attractive redhead from Britannia, a favorite in the Lady's city. Claire was a lazy street sweeper, but she did wonderful work in a bed.

Golda pressed the Ahyehass with the force of her Hunger, dominating Claire on the thin bedroll. Claire wore no underthings under her linen skirt and bodice. The girl butterflied to accept intimate attentions. Golda locked lips and began a slow suck on Claire's mouth, engaging the mystical vacuum that would consume the girl's life-giving love energy—that sweet cream that was already rising ahead of her orgasm.

Claire had a shy tongue, and she was a little drunk. Her skin smelled like

Cybelah's perfume, and her sour mouth offered traces of Herpessenia's nectar ale.

Chapter 8:

Boudi sat on the bench at the southern end of Ayelet's gardens. The sensitivity of her new skin was shocking. The wrought iron felt chilly against her back and buttocks, even through her too-prickly wool coat. It was early evening in the city of the love Ifreeta. The sun was dipping over the mountainside, and the last rays of light were fading from the red-orange roof tiles of Ayelet's Villa.

Mistress Ayelet paced back and forth in her flower beds, directing her gardener's work. Ayelet pointed her finger with an order. Her voice was muted at the distance by the whisper of the evening wind across the lawn grasses. The bearded, big-nosed gardener nodded emphatically as he collected the leaves at Ayelet's feet. The gardener's name was Anders. He lived in a small cottage on the north side of the gardens where he worked. Like the dressing-girl Herzl, Anders had once been a human on Earth. Ayelet had seduced him through the dream-world, and he'd chosen to serve his Jinni mistress forever in death.

A pair of chasm bats, as Ayelet called them, flitted over the gardens, swooping to eat the glowing fire beetles. The bats were just visible against the darkening sky. They were toothy-ish and dangerous like everything in Meristyian. Boudi scrunched deeper into her coat. She felt conscious of the sensitive exposed skin of her neck. At least she was wearing clothes.

Her first seven days in the city of Allyssia actually hadn't been that bad. The week had passed like a dream that she couldn't wake up from. Each evening she went to bed early and slept deeply for at least ten hours. According to Ayelet, her new desire-body needed lots of rest to properly densify.

She'd received several deliveries of clothing to fill her oversexed Jinni wardrobe, including four revealing dresses to replace the one that Herzl had loaned her. Her new corsets were dark and heavy with black ribbons and steel fastenings—completely unlike her delicate white underthings in Heaven, yet still fitted to accommodate her body. She'd also acquired several pairs of stockings, three robes, and leather shoes with three-inch heels. All of the clothes had been hand-designed for her small, wiry frame by Mistress Gallinah, an affable, rotund Jinni who managed the city workshops.

Boudi subtly stretched. Her feet fit well in her beautiful leather shoes, and her lace-topped burgundy stockings caressed her skin pleasantly from her toes to her upper thighs. She felt elegant even though the clothes were incredibly sinful. None of her dresses covered even two-thirds of her modest breasts, much less her neck. She'd begged Ayelet for a scarf, but nothing had manifested. Instead, she'd taken to wearing her winter coat during most hours, even indoors.

Ayelet had taken her in the carriage on a few tours around the streets of the Redoubt. They'd looked at Allyssia's palace with its impressive marble façades, its wide front steps that led up to the sculpted palace doors, and its high crystal spires that shimmered in the sunlight. They'd explored the palace interior with its many marble statues and oil paintings that told a magical story from the old days of antiquity. They'd met several Ahyehasi and the palace steward, Master Priapus, but Allyssia herself hadn't descended from Her bowers to welcome them as Ayelet had hoped.

They'd visited the Divinity District on a nearby hill, where they'd abandoned the carriage to hike a steep, zigzagging street of extravagant three-story homes that belonged, Ayelet had said, to elder mistresses and the family of Allyssia. At the top of the Divinity District, they'd sat for hours and talked while looking at the mountain scenery beyond the city walls.

The city of the love Ifreeta, for all its intimate grandeur, was smaller than it had first appeared. The trips around the streets had been lengthy only because Ayelet had stopped to speak on points of interest and greet every passer-by.

Boudi feigned a smile and waved. Ayelet was looking across the garden at her. Ayelet had introduced her to many of the city's Jinni, Jinn fledglings, and resident Ahyehasi. The embarrassing conversations had focused on her future among the New Order. All the while, she'd done her best to play the role of a rebellious mimo girl who was inexplicably thrilled by the great opportunity to become a wicked Jinn consumed with lust.

Each afternoon, Mistress Ayelet had sat her down on the bench in the garden, in the sunlight, and they'd drunk tea and chatted for hours. Ayelet had asked her about her life in Heaven, about her professors and guardians, and about her classes at the Crystal College. Ayelet had questioned her on what she thought about almost everything—the nature of the soul and the organization of the universe; her preferences in music and paintings; her knowledge of Earth religions and political systems; her tastes in footwear and hair styles; her personal philosophies and interpretations of the scriptures of Lord Tuhan; and many other things, including things that she'd never thought about.

Earlier that very afternoon, Mistress Ayelet had pressed her with an uncomfortable battery of questions about Tajee and her former relationship with him. She'd tried to answer honestly, but the questions had left her feeling depressed. The more she and Ayelet had talked of her "old life", the farther away Heaven seemed to be. She'd been too busy at the Conclave to miss spending time with Tajee, but when she'd slept alone each night in her dark room in Ayelet's Villa, she'd wanted nothing more than to see his smiling face again.

Ayelet took leave of the hard-working gardener and strode across the lawn in the gathering gloom. Boudi sat up straight and smoothed her skirt.

Even after a week, she'd decided that she couldn't give up on the Conclave. She had to have patience and wait. She had to have faith that Pasteur and the Conclave would save her. She had to preserve her chastity and humility while continuing to act her role as a rebel mimọ.

She'd had chances during the previous week to return alone to the railing down the hill—the only real avenue of escape that she'd yet seen. She was too terrified to flash to her freedom. She was deathly afraid of being caught as a fake—a secret Conclave agent who had tried to lure Golda to her doom. If she fled from the city over the wall, the game was over. She'd be lost and alone in the vast wilderness of Meristyian, and she wouldn't know where to go.

The days had passed one by one, and each day she'd decided to wait and maybe escape on the next day. Her effort had never happened. Instead, she'd prayed fervently in secret for the Conclave to save her. She'd been a coward and a failure as an agent. Soon it would be too late. The full moon was rising. Her transformation was supposed to happen that night, despite her attempts to request a delay.

"The fire beetles are eating my flowers." Ayelet sighed. "I suppose if I can consume the love energy of my Ahyehasi, the beetles are allowed to consume my flowers. The bats eat the beetles, thankfully. Shall we, chérie? It's time to go inside."

"Yes, Mistress." Boudi rose from the bench and walked with the elder Jinni towards the Villa front door. Apparently chérie was Ayelet's pet name for her. She had worse things to worry about. Ayelet had promised a celebratory soirée before the mid-night ritual. Boudi shivered. She hadn't asked exactly what a soirée entailed, but it was surely sinful.

Ayelet led her through the front door and into the Villa entry hall, where twin marble columns supported a vaulted ceiling. Bola stood at attention next to the buffet table. Bola was a big olive-skinned Ahyehass who went nude except for black silk pantaloons and a smattering of gold ornaments on his wrists, fingers, and earlobes. Bola was a musician and a handyman. In the morning, the sound of his hammer would often knock across the Villa lawns, to be replaced by the tinkle of the piano in the evening. Ayelet stepped past Bola and headed for the staircase, patting the black man's arm in passing.

"Bring the crushes that we discussed?"

"Yes, Mistress," the male replied with his rumbling voice.

Boudi wondered what a 'crush' was, but she didn't have to time to think on it for long. Ayelet beckoned her with a crooked finger from the foot of the darkened foyer stairs. The elder Jinni took off her coat and leather gloves as she climbed. Ayelet raised her hand and snapped her fingers. A glowing ball of magical light sprang from Ayelet's hand to hover above her head. The tenebris lux spell sent a blue-violet glow across the plaster walls.

Boudi followed Ayelet up the stairway from the entry foyer, around a long curving hall, and up to the lamplit second floor. Yenta lurked in the opening of her bedchamber doorway. Yenta was Ayelet's house-girl. The pretty, full-bodied Ahyehass wore a maid's uniform as usual. She had dark bangs, liquid black eyes behind long lashes, and a solid nose that almost rivaled Anders's. As with Herzl, a leather collar encircled Yenta's neck.

Ayelet led the way through an oak door into her bedchamber, which was high and round with coved crown moldings. The walls entire were hung with tapestries on curved, gilded rods. The tapestries depicted lavishly embroidered hunting scenes. Candlelight spilled over a floor covered with burgundy carpets. The square carpets left patterns of bare wood floor around the circular perimeter, from which sprouted ornate cabinets and side chairs. Every wood surface glistened with polish. Ayelet ran her fingers over the armrest of a chair with a padded red cloth seat.

"These are Shulamit XIV replicas made for me in the city workshops. That's my favorite piece." Ayelet pointed at the enormous four-posted bed that dominated the center of her bedchamber. "It's identical to the one I possessed during my last Earth life in France, except it's oak and not mahogany. Those were hard times for me, but I survived. You still haven't told me much about your own Earth life, Boudi."

Boudi shrugged. "It's hard for Mimos to remember the material world, the same as humans have trouble remembering Heaven. I lived in Norfolk, England. My father was very religious. We fell on hard times after my mother left. I went to the convent when I was of age, and my father raised my brother. I became sick when I began my religious studies, and thankfully they took me into Heaven. Golda was telling me about her Earth life too. Is that important?"

"Ah, yes—Golda, the seducer of popes and the mother of the Pornocracy. Golda had a difficult path to become a Jinni. I don't blame her for her need to prove herself to people." Ayelet seated herself on a chair and began to unlace her leather boots. "Golda is an old soul, almost as old as me. Her suffering has scarred her deeply, though. Many Jinni in the Redoubt don't appreciate her. She was an important Egyptian woman on Earth before dying into the life of a slave, only to be noticed and saved by the Lady."

"So someone owned Golda?"

"Yes. When she died and arrived in the Underworld, the devils took her and auctioned her in the capital city of Mer, where she was purchased by the cat goddess, Basteh. Golda helped the Lady during the schism of the Jinni orders, and the Lady transformed Golda into a Jinni as a reward. Now the Lady is going even further to transform you, Boudi. This surely takes the Lady's magic a big step further, but Lady is always experimenting with love, and we need more Jinni."

Boudi felt her stomach turn. It all felt like an awful dream that she couldn't wake up from. "That's good, because I want to be bad, Mistress Ayelet."

Ayelet glanced up from where she sat. Her face was expressionless. Ayelet had removed her boots. Instead of normal feet with toes, a pair of slender cloven hooves emerged to rest on the carpet under the hem of Ayelet's dress. "I imagine everything must be overwhelming for you, Boudi, even frightening. Don't fight it, chérie. Just relax and let things happen. The Hierarchy trained you to deny yourself pleasure. You need to relax into this different level of existence, and you will with my help."

"If you think so."

"Herzl!" Ayelet raised her voice towards the door. "Undress Boudi, please." The mousy dressing-girl, who had been waiting outside, appeared with a flurry of bare feet. Boudi stood still while the skilled fingers of the dressing girl flew over her body, first removing her coat and lifting her dress over her head, and then unfastening her slip and pulling it off, followed by her stockings, leaving her clad once again only in a corset in front of Ayelet.

"What do you want her to do now, Mistress?" Herzl's red-petal lips curled into her characteristic little smirk.

"She can get in bed."

Boudi lifted herself dutifully onto the bed past the massive bedpost, conscious of Herzl watching her every move. Ayelet's bed reminded her of the body scanner at her Conclave interview, but instead of standing up, she was horizontal. She imagined a brilliant beam of red light shining down over Ayelet's sex-worn sheets, probing her body for unwanted virtues instead of unwanted vices.

Boudi turned on her front side to hide herself. Ayelet loosed her grey-streaked hair from the pearl pins that restrained it, and then teased her braid apart with long fingers. Ayelet brushed her hair out with a mother-of-pearl comb before exchanging the brush for a crystal flask from the bedside drawer. The elder Jinni approached the bed, still clad in her corset and skirt.

"Flip onto your back, Boudi."

Boudi took a deep breath and did so, horribly embarrassed but resisting the urge to cover herself up. Ayelet settled next to her on the bed and poured warm oil into the hollow of her collarbone. Boudi tried desperately to calm herself. With slow sweeps, Ayelet worked the oil upwards over her shoulders, and then down onto the slopes of her breasts above the rim of her corset. Boudi clutched the bedcovers with both fists, but she could feel herself relaxing. Ayelet's fingers felt incredibly good.

Ayelet caressed back up to the angles of her neck, and then downward, wiping the last dampness of oil onto the tops of each of her thighs before setting aside the flask to answer a rap at the door. The knock was from Bola, who handed Ayelet a Platinum tray that bore a pair of goblets. Ayelet transferred the tray to the side table.

Boudi closed her eyes as Ayelet settled down onto the bed again. Ayelet's strong fingers continued, pushing oil around her ears, down the muscles under her jaw, then pressing again into her sternum to ferry more excess oil to the tops of her sensitive breasts. Ayelet's fingers lingered on her breasts to press and wedge under the rim of the corset. Then Ayelet's fingers moved away, slipping down to pinch her hip.

"Back onto your stomach, darling mimọ."

Boudi was happy to roll over onto her stomach and press her oiled breasts into the red sheet, thereby to hide her vulnerable front side from more agonizing attention. She tried to think of chaste thoughts. Prayers. Saints. Scriptures. Makeda Deen.

Boudi groaned. Ayelet's powerful fingers had begun on her body again, first at her hairline at the top of her neck, and then down her spine, skipping past her corseted wings and testing slightly into the crease of her buttocks, where Ayelet's fingernails produced little scrapes and thrills. The bed shifted, and Ayelet unexpectedly left.

Boudi pressed her sweaty forehead to the pillow. She had no control. She had no poise. Even as the emotions and sin arose in her body and overwhelmed her, they diffused into slow, wonderful pleasure. The oil that Ayelet had spread on her skin rendered her still more relaxed and sensual. A torpor stole over her.

Ayelet faced the bed while Herzl helped her undo her voluminous skirt, and then the dressing-girl unfastened the pair of antique wooden frameworks on Ayelet's hips. Ayelet's hourglass figure of impossible hips and narrow waist was an illusion. "My corset too, Herzl."

"Oui, Mistress."

"Pull the laces completely. They need to be replaced." Ayelet undid her necklace clasp and drew her greying hair over her shoulder. She turned to allow the dressing-girl access to her back. Herzl leaned to pull the corset laces free with her teeth. The dressing-girl's head darted back and forth. Herzl finished the laces within a minute. The silk-lined leather shell fell away. Ayelet swiveled to the serving tray and grabbed a goblet.

"Drink, Boudi."

"What is it?" Boudi eyed the goblet warily. She didn't move.

"It's a poppy crush—purple poppy mixed with lemon and pomegranate in fresh Isandlwana water. Sit up. You need to drink it."

Boudi sat up and took the goblet. She was wary of the purply-pink drink, but it would soothe the cottony-panicky dryness in her mouth. The fruity draught was bittersweet. It warmed her throat and made her tongue tingle. While she sipped, she continued to gaze over the rim of the goblet at Ayelet.

Ayelet's arms were chiseled like her stomach, and her breasts were modest without her padded corset—between sagging and pert. Teardrop amber beads dangled from her smallish nipples. Ayelet's long grey-streaked hair fell loose over her shoulders to cast shadows across her face. A thatch of matching hair tufted the lowest expanse of her taut belly. Without her elaborate antique apparel, Ayelet was a plainer, less shapely woman.

"Drink it all, darling Boudi. You need it for our journey."

"Our journey?" Boudi drained the remainder of the crush. The cool drink inundated her throat with fruity pleasure. Ayelet took the empty cup from her fingers.

"Yes. Tonight we'll sleep and cross over into the dream-world, where Lady Allyssia will work her magic on you. Before we sleep, I need to feed."

Ayelet drained her own goblet and picked up a pair of wooden batons from the side table. She made a loud tock. Bola re-entered the bedroom within seconds. Boudi crossed her legs in the center of the bed and hugged herself. Despite the many candles, the room was cool. The drink pushed a drowsy effect over her, joining with the sleepy feeling of the oil.

Bola stripped his pantaloons. The dressing-girl Herzl knelt on the carpet and employed her flower bud mouth until the big black man's phallus grew to three times its resting size. Ayelet faced an armchair, bent at the waist, and spread her legs. Bola stepped forward and slid his phallus slowly into Ayelet's feminine cleft. The male Ahyehass began a steady rhythm with the strong muscles of his buttocks flexing.

Ayelet tossed her long greying hair into the seat of chair. She was closed-eyed and focused. Boudi forced her gaze away, but the sounds of sex still badgered at her ears. The male began to grunt with his thrusts. The slurp of wetness added to the slapping. After only a few minutes, Bola groaned.

Boudi jumped when the bed shivered. Ayelet plopped next to her on the bedsheet, half-obscuring Herzl's attentions to Bola's appendage with her quick pink tongue, spidery fingers, and handkerchief.

"Did you like watching us couple, Boudi?" Ayelet murmured sensually. "We have places to go, so I ended it quickly. A strong Jinni has a bit of skill."

"It was, um—"

"Bola was feeding me. A Jinni must feed, and it's perfectly natural. We consume the love energy of others and convert it into our personal energy, just like humans consume their food. In the morning you'll know the Hunger too. It's a terrible gift, but a beautiful one. You'll celebrate love every night, and you'll serve Allyssia with your endless desire."

"I suppose." Boudi bit her lip. Her words came like a whisper and a croak, and she hated herself yet again for being too afraid to flee over the stone wall alone. She hadn't been sure of what her transformation would entail, and Ayelet had glossed over the facts until that moment. Bola strode from the room. Herzl approached to hover quietly behind Ayelet.

"Open yourself to your feelings of desire, Boudi," Ayelet persisted. "Let your feelings flow from within you. Your pleasure is yours—the gift of the Ifreeta to you. Don't let the Mimoic Hierarchy take that from you. You're a rebel. You're one of us."

"Yes." Boudi felt a tendril of pride rise like smoke inside the moil of her fears—that deadliest of sins coiling deep in her chest. Somehow Ayelet made her feel like she mattered, like she belonged. None of her professors in Heaven made her feel like that. The oil on her skin trapped her emotions and sent them to her head, which felt more and more leaden. She was too tired to fight any more. Ayelet's fingers lifted her chin.

"Boudi, we are the female nobility here in the lower realms. When you wake up tomorrow, you'll be a proud huntress of women, men, and whatever you wish. In the moons and years to come, you'll learn magic and the art of the blade. You'll become an independent woman instead of a humble, subservient mimo girl. The millions of humans in the Underworld will live to kneel at your feet. One day you'll appreciate this, even if you don't realize it."

"Yes, Mistress."

The Platinum shimmer in Ayelet's hazel eyes was bright in the low light. Boudi tried to focus, but she was so sleepy. She stretched her legs, and her thighs rubbed pleasantly against one another, greased with the warm oil with which Ayelet had slicked them.

"You're exquisite, Boudi. Your golden halo looks beautiful in this darkened room. You won't have it after your mid-night ritual, I think. Instead, you'll have the moon-silver in your eyes like mine."

"I feel so lost and fallen."

"Sleep now, chérie. Dream your last mimọ dream. Tonight you'll meet Lady Allyssia, and you'll feel better and differently."

Ayelet's smile was shadowed. Herzl tiptoed around the room and extinguished the candles. The light in the bedchamber dimmed. Boudi nestled her head into the pillow and looked at the last flickering candle that was burning on the side table. The sinful scene had left her drifting on a sense of inner devastation. The oak door to the bedchamber closed with a thump, like a final seal on her deathbed of purity and virtue. Ayelet's bedchamber was her mimọ girl tomb. She slipped into a drifting oblivion.

Chapter 9:

Golda drew her chestnut mare up to the hitching post in front of Mareinah's dark two-story house. She counted the faint clock chimes coming from inside of Hatshepseh's house across the street. The chimes marked the eighth hour, and then fell silent. The autumn night was cold, and the Redoubt smelled homey with odors of wood smoke. Golda dismounted, tied the mare, and helped Tajee down from the saddle.

The trip with Mareinah to Heaven's gates marked a bitter end to the best time of her life. With Mareinah either captured or sent to the void by the Mimoic Hierarchy, the Lady had ruled that the house and all of Mareinah's assets would fall to her. She'd taken Tajee to the palace to meet the Lady, and the mimo boy had been predictably awestruck. He'd pledged with little hesitation to stay in the Lady's city and serve as an Ahyehass. He wouldn't go back to Heaven, at least not yet.

Golda helped Tajee up the worn steps. He shuffled comically. She'd dressed him in her spare riding pants, which were a little too big for him. She'd never before had her own Ahyehass, and now she was going to have three. She'd never seduced or trained an Ahyehass either, although she vaguely knew the ways.

As a former slave herself, the idea of training brought up disturbing memories of when she'd served as a sex toy for coins, stoked by the heartless whips and addictions of the cat goddess Basteh. She was resolved to train Tajee properly.

Tajee would serve her and do as she bid, or he would leave the city. The boy certainly needed attention. Evidently Boudi cared more for the virtue of chastity than for charity. Golda pushed open the front door and guided Tajee inside. Her arrival back home had magnified Mareinah's death in her mind. She needed to unwind and feed so she could attend Boudi's midnight ritual, one that promised to be very interesting. First she needed to handle Tajee's living situation.

Mareinah's split-level was modest. The vaulted, wood-floored foyer gave onto three staircases. A narrow stone stair led down to a single-room cellar, while a wider wooden staircase led up to the second level, which in turn featured a hall, a master bedroom, and a bath. Adjacent to the foyer, a storage room gave access to a third stair to the sunken stable in back, which formed a mirror-image of the cellar in the front half of the lower level, but with space for horses instead of Ahyehasi, as well as double doors that led up to the adjacent alleyway.

"This is my home, Tajee."

Tajee sniffed. "It's not bad. I'll have a bed, right?"

"You might sleep upstairs with me some nights, but for now you'll sleep downstairs with Phylicia. She's our dressing-girl."

Tajee's brown eyes turned owl-like. Golda chuckled. The mimọ boy was a bright spot in her dark mood. She wanted to take Tajee up to the bedchamber, but she hungered too much again to trust herself to do things properly. She lit one of the candles that sat in a neat row on the hall table, placed it in a silver holder, and led Tajee down the stone steps into the front half of the lower level.

Mareinah's cellar was a subterranean chamber with a beamed ceiling. Small barred windows high on the plastered west wall offered feeble moonlight from window wells behind the hibiscuses along the cobbled city street outside. A fire-blackened hearth punctured the wall between the windows. A stack of cut wood and kindling sat beside the stone-and-mortar surround. A mess of glowing coals in the fireplace crackled and spit flames that radiated warmth. Trace, the handsome male Ahyehass, had built a fire against the cool autumn evening in the Lady's domain.

A row of three spacious silvered cages dominated the far end of the room. Adjacent to the cages, a chair sat with a smooth leather seat and a high ribbed back. Mareinah's rack of bondage and discipline equipment hung behind the chair on the wall. Golda held the candle aloft with one hand and tugged Tajee across the room with the other. Phylicia was sleeping as usual on her bed in the far-left cage. The girl stirred into a sitting position as they approached. Golda led Tajee to the cage in the opposite corner from Phylicia.

"You'll be good to sleep in here, Tajee. Rest to your heart's content. I'll come for you in the morning, and then we'll get to know each other better."

Tajee examined his cage with skepticism. He pointed at the straw pallet in the corner with its simple linen pillow. "I have to sleep there? Is that even a bed?"

"I can't have you wandering. Half the Jinni in this city would love to get their hands on you, and you're very naïve about how we do things. It's best if you stayed safe."

"I didn't agree to this."

"An Ahyehass must be obedient and respect the wishes of his mistress, Tajee. That mat is more comfortable than it looks. I've slept there myself a few times, and that's where I want you tonight. Mareinah liked the old-fashioned slave cages because they reminded her of the old days, but maybe I'll get rid of them. These things don't really belong in this city."

Tajee shrugged. "Whatever."

"Just sleep like I know you need to, and you'll be fine. Everything will be fine. How are your thighs? Are they chafed from the ride?"

"Is Boudi fine? When can I see her?

"I promised you'd see her, but the time isn't right. You promised to serve me first anyway, remember? You're so close. I hope you haven't changed your mind?" Golda gave her best seductive smile. Tajee's eyes dodged down to her breasts, which were illuminated by the light of the candle.

"No," Tajee finally answered with a note of protest.

"That makes me happy, Tajee," Golda purred. "Good night. Phylicia will keep you company."

"Sleep well, Mistress," Phylicia said quickly.

"Please talk with Tajee, Phylicia. Tell him anything he wants to know." Golda pushed Tajee gently into the silver cage, swung the heavy door shut, and locked it. She went to the fireplace and banked the glowing coals to last until morning. The coals cast a low red glow to help Tajee get situated.

She left the room, aware of Tajee's simmering eyes on her backside. She jingled the cage keys and worked her hips and ass as she climbed the stairs without looking back. She continued through the foyer into the storage area, where a lantern light flickered. Mareinah's boy was oiling leathers at a long wooden bench.

Trace was strong and wiry with sensuous lips and limpid lover's eyes over distinctive cheekbones. He wore a pony tail that had pleased Mareinah, along with a simple tunic and pants representative of a previous century in his Earth life. Trace was a devilishly handsome Italian—a decade older-looking and more mature than Tajee, but in one way less of a man.

"Good evening, Trace."

"Mistress," Trace replied shortly. He kept a steady rhythm with his oilcloth and didn't look up at her.

"How are you tonight? I know Phylicia won't cope well with the death of her Mistress, but I'm even more worried about you. You loved her very much, and I didn't have time to talk with you before the Lady sent me out scouting. I'm sorry Mareinah is gone. There was nothing I could do. The Hierarchy jumped us just after we found the rebel mimo. I barely escaped."

"I can't believe I'll never see her again." Trace's jaw worked. "I doubt I'll ever love another mistress as much."

"I don't expect you to, but Allyssia has given you a new mistress. I want you to go up to the Divinity District tonight after we're done and buy me a hundred drams of fresh purple nectar from fledgling Herpessenia-Ca. I already arranged it with her. I'll give you some gold coins."

Trace nodded nonchalantly. "Yes, Mistress."

"Tomorrow you can clean up Mareinah's horse, saddle, packs, and blankets. I want to sell it all. Of course we should remember her, but I don't want her things around to remind me. I'll be out tomorrow morning for another meeting with the Lady, and then I'll come back and get you and Phylicia for Mareinah's funeral ceremony tomorrow afternoon."

"Thank you, Mistress."

"Are you and Phylicia going often to the Pandocheion?"

"Yes. We can still go, right?"

"Of course, but not tonight. It's good for the Ahyehasi in the city to have a special place of their own where they can play, dance, and drink. The Lady has given you that privilege. I just don't want my new mimo boy going. He's not ready for a wild Veneralia, and I think the Lady will agree with me. I don't want you to mention Pandocheion privileges to the new Ahyehass either. In fact, I want the front door always locked, and I want you to watch the stables. Tajee isn't to leave this house unless I allow it."

"Yes, Mistress. As you wish."

"I'm going to bed now. Make yourself presentable. I want you in fifteen minutes." Golda walked out of the storage area and up the staircase to the second level. The sounds of her boot heels on the wood floor were hollow like her heart. She entered the master bedchamber, which was designed in the type of sixteenth-century decor that Mareinah had liked, offering polished plaster walls, heavy oak furnishings, and a high raftered ceiling. She placed the candle on the side table and removed her boots, which she tossed at her personal armoire—the smaller of the two in the room.

Mareinah's armoire stood open with her three favorite dresses hanging on one of the doors, having been cleaned in her absence. They were heavy winter dresses. Mareinah had prided herself on her weather witchery. Mareinah had predicted the Lady's withdrawn mood to usher seasonal weather into the city soon. She'd had been right.

Golda sighed. Mareinah's jewelry mingled with hers on the long antique vanity, which accommodated two chairs side by side. Necklaces, bracelets, and bangles lay everywhere. A turtle-shaped ceramic bowl contained several earrings that had lost their mates. Between the two of them, they'd never kept everything straight. Golda felt a sudden surge of hate for Lord Tuhan and the Mimoic Hierarchy.

She was too damned tired to box Mareinah's belongings. She'd sleep that night in a bedchamber shrouded with loneliness and death, and then she'd deal with everything in the morning. In the moons to come, she'd try to find peace beneath another poured layer of remorse on her soul.

Golda threw her body onto the bed. It creaked and shivered underneath her. She slithered over the quilt and rubbed her cheek on a silk pillow that still breathed with Mareinah's magical scent. The bed was big and beautiful with seven-foot posts at the corners, two of which came within inches of the slanting rafters. The posts held aloft a faded black canopy embroidered with stars. The fabric was Kishi-woven, an imported piece of art from the Blessed Isles. Mareinah had loved her magical bed canopy.

Golda gazed up at the canopy. She was scheduled to attend a second meeting at the palace without Tajee, where she planned to inform Allyssia and the elder mistresses of everything that Tajee and Boudi had individually told her. She'd already surrendered Boudi's wrist-watch and rucksack to Mistress Ivanka for examination.

Tajee's story was worrying. According to him, Boudi was involved in a secret mission given to her by Heaven's intelligence agency. Golda closed her eyes and relaxed her limbs. She'd intuited that Boudi was telling half-truths. She hoped the Lady wasn't making a mistake by making Boudi into a Jinni in a dream-world ritual that very night. She hoped that she herself hadn't made a mistake by seducing Tajee so aggressively.

Mistress Ivanka had counseled her on how to handle the boy—how to win his trust from his innocence. Tajee was handsome, sweet, and virginal. He would be her first, just as she would his. Males were dominant in the Mimoic Hierarchy by the design of Lord Tuhan. According to Ivanka, even while male Mimos preached to turn the other cheek, they were rarely submissive until made to submit.

Golda felt her Hunger rising. Sometimes her Hunger was beautiful, but at that moment she was sick of it—that endless emptiness that would lead to paralysis and death if left unchecked. She already wished that she'd brought Tajee up to her bed. His lust would fill her need like sweet honey. That was exactly why she hadn't. She knew herself too well.

She'd informed Ayelet of Tajee's presence via messenger bird that morning, but she needed to meet with Ayelet personally. The matter of Tajee's love for his mimọ girl needed to be resolved. For the moment, Boudi had more important things to deal with in her life than the infatuation of a young male.

Golda rolled over to the side table and opened the drawer to reveal the silver box that contained her nectar. Mareinah would have wanted her happy that night, not sad. She tapped the box on its corner to fill the small silver spoon with the remnants of the purple powder. She lifted the spoon and heated the contents in the flickering candle flame. Her nectar box, as usual, seemed emptier than when she'd left.

Trace had been stealing her nectar for several moons, and without Mareinah around, she planned to do something about it. The spoonful of nectar sizzled at the edges, and then slowly liquefied. Her hand trembled. She turned on her back and slipped the spoon between her legs to nudge the lips of her pumpum.

Golda slipped the spoon deep inside. She stretched with the hot pain and pleasure that inundated her depths and pushed glorious flowery warmth through her core. She let go of the spoon handle and gripped it instead with the muscles of her pumpum. She rolled across the bed, allowing the pleasure to spread through her abdomen. Her tangled hair wrapped her face. She nipped and bit.

The nectar was still fresh enough to be effective and felt all the better after so many days without it. The nectar embraced her like her own personal flower Ifreeta. Golda squeezed her inner muscles to suck pleasure until her muscles went numb. She lay still, allowing the pleasure to warm every inch of her skin. The handle of the spoon tickled gently between her thighs from random contractions. Trace knocked on the door. Golda rolled onto her back and let gravity pull her legs apart. She pushed her fingers through her nether hair, pulled the spoon, licked it clean, and placed it on the side table.

"Come in, houseboy."

Trace entered the bedchamber with his eyes lowered. He unbuttoned his shirt and approached Mareinah's bed without much eagerness. The phallus of the well-trained Ahyehass was nonetheless pressing acceptably against his pants.

Golda gazed up at the flickering shadows on the bed canopy as Trace climbed onto the quilt with her. She would miss Mareinah. She'd mourn, and then she'd spend the dark moons of winter searching for another lover who could respect her, love her, and accept her. It seemed unlikely, but she had to try. The thought of sleeping alone again for years, with only the Ahyehasi for company, made her want to cry.

Chapter 10:

Tajee awoke into darkness. He'd tried to stay awake, but he'd dozed off. The two barred windows high on the wall gave dim moonlight into the room, and a faint red glow sketched the rectangular opening of the fireplace. Phylicia snored softly in the subterranean silence.

Phylicia had asked him questions after Golda had left. He'd told her the story of how he'd fallen, and how he was looking for Boudi. Phylicia hadn't seen Boudi, and she'd quickly seemed disinterested. She'd told him her own story instead—of how she'd married a Catholic man in Valencia, a reserved man who had failed to satisfy her desires.

Mistress Mareinah had found her in the moons after her wedding, attracted by the intensity of her unfulfilled yearnings and loneliness. The Jinn had urged her into new pleasurable ways to masturbate, and had driven her to distraction with bisexual fantasies. Mareinah had persuaded her to leave her husband and forsake the company of males.

After many years living as a poor hermit, satisfied only by self-pleasure and visits with Mareinah in her dreams, Phylicia had died of a fever, and her body had become young again. Her Jinni mistress had taken her via a dream-carriage to an afterlife of lust in Meristyian. Strangely, Phylicia seemed fine with her bizarre life inside a Jinni cage, as if it were somehow desirable. The Ahyehass had ignored the question of whether she ever felt sinful, or if she regretted not going to Heaven.

A thump sounded on the basement stairway, and a light entered the room, accompanied by footsteps. The light moved, and so did the vertical shadows cast by the cage bars. The light came from a candle held by a handsome man. The man was of average height, youthful but not young, with shapely lips and a cut, smooth-shaven chin, a well-groomed ponytail, and a tunic open to show his corded throat and hairy chest. Phylicia stirred.

"Trace," the Ahyehass murmured. "You finally came. Have you seen Tajee yet? He's in the third cage."

"I saw him in the foyer when they came in. He's the mimo that Mistress Mareinah went to Heaven for? I thought they were going for a girl. I was looking forward to another girl around here."

"They went for a girl mimo, and they got her," Phylicia said in a low voice. "Tajee is her friend. He jumped from Heaven to rescue her. Isn't that nice of him? He met a nimfa out in Meristyian, who led him to a rake. Golda killed the rake and brought Tajee back here."

"He really met a nimfa in Meristyian?" Trace chuckled. "That's lucky. I'd screw a wild nimfa any day of the week and twice on Sunday."

"You'd screw a horse if it had a pretty tail. You always smell like the stables."

"I clean the stables, Phylicia," Trace said. "I'm a hard worker, unlike you. I was late because Golda sent me to do things for her."

"I'll bet she did. You're her bitch now. I can't believe our Mistress tried to steal an mimo from Heaven. I think she only went because the Lady commanded her. I knew it was a horrible idea, but I didn't say anything."

Phylicia's dour visage was visible in the flickering light of the candle. The pretty Ahyehass wore only a saffron wrap around her ample hips. She had full bared breasts that rivaled Golda's, but on a shorter, plumper body instead of a long statuesque one. A silver clip glinted at the gather of Phylicia's thick, shoulder-length dark hair. Her sensual black-lined eyes glistened in the candlelight. Trace stepped closer to the row of cages. He peered inside.

"I can't see him too well, but his halo is brilliant."

Phylicia snuffled. "I can't believe Golda survived and Mareinah didn't. Golda probably ran away and left Mareinah to fight the Mimos alone and die."

Trace shrugged. "Golda is our new mistress."

"She's hardly a mistress. Golda used to be a slave. How many times did Mareinah lock her up in that cage, like it was some sort of slave game? How many times did Mareinah make Golda worship her right there at the throne where we did the same? I don't know if I can accept being owned by her."

Trace shrugged. "The Lady has given us Golda, so if you don't accept it, you'll have to petition. I like Golda in bed. I like the nectar. She needs to bathe more. That's my only complaint at the moment."

"You're just horny, Trace. You like horses and stinky low-class tramps."

"Right." Trace sighed. "That's why I like you. I brought you some nectar, but first I get mine, and I don't want the new guy watching."

Trace licked his fingers and pinched out the candle. Scuffles sounded in the darkness. Phylicia whispered and moaned. A soft smacking sound came from her cage. The rhythm continued for some time, interspersed with animal panting. Tajee lay back on his sleeping palette and fixed his eyes on the faint rectangles of moonlight that came from the high window openings. A mix of lust and disgust warmed his loins. The thought of Boudi in a Jinni cage like Phylicia made his stomach turn over. Worse yet, Golda had suggested that Boudi actually wanted such a thing, which was surely a lie.

Wherever Boudi was, he had to find her and get her away from the Jinni. Boudi was a pushover. She was no doubt afraid and doing everything she was told. A rescue by the Conclave seemed more and more unlikely, so he needed to be the hero. If he and Boudi could escape the city, they could find the stairway together. Golda had told him where it was—the Esplanade Road west to the Trivium for three days, and then to the top of Mount Purgatory and the beginning of the stairway. He needed to keep the directions etched in his brain along with his many questions.

Where was Boudi in the city? Why had the Jinni taken her in the first place? What was Boudi's secret mission? What was the Conclave's role in everything? He had no answers, and Golda was being catty. Despite his attempts to get an explanation, Golda hadn't really told him anything. She'd made sultry promises that he could see Boudi, and then she'd locked him in a cage.

Tajee took a deep breath to clear his head. Phylicia's sounds of pleasure stoked his lust, and his lust burned far stronger in Meristyian than in Heaven. He had intense conflicting urges to throw himself on Golda and run as far away as possible. He'd slept next to her in a tent for three nights with her long nude body alongside his. She hadn't kissed him or touched him intimately, but her warmth and scent were so feminine, a sensuality beyond any chaste mimọ girl.

Lady Allyssia was even more radiant than Golda. The Ifreeta had awed him even with Her face hidden behind a mask. She'd spoken to him in full nude beauty, looking down from Her golden throne. In Her presence, he'd felt happier, calmer, and more loved than he'd ever felt in even his most religious moments. When the Lady had asked his intentions in Her city, he'd pledged to stay and serve as Golda had coached him, although he hadn't made his decision until that moment.

The Ifreeta had twisted the situation into a gift—a sacred opportunity for his happiness and spiritual advancement. He hadn't asked about Boudi. Lady Allyssia had dictated the conversation, not him. He'd sealed his deal with Golda, and then the Jinni had taken him home and locked him in a cage. It was enough to drive him insane.

Suddenly, a bright flare of light illuminated the room. Tajee squinted through the bars. He could see the form of Phylicia in Sharp relief. She was on her knees with her heavy buttocks to her cage door. Trace knelt behind her, pressed against her rump. Golda stood behind Trace with her arms crossed. A ball of brilliant blue light shimmered above her head, casting a lurid glow over her nude form.

"As I suspected," Golda growled.

"It's Trace's fault." Phylicia's voice was loud. "He made me."

"Be quiet, lying little kitten. I know you've got him wrapped around your finger."

"Yes, Mistress," Phylicia answered feebly.

"I've been looking forward to this for a long time. It's my first night alone in the house and you two are already at it, and worse yet stealing my nectar for your fun. Mareinah put up with it, but I've had enough."

Trace coughed. "Phylicia asked me to steal the nectar, Mistress."

"Eso no pasó," Phylicia said. "Bastardo."

"Then what happened?" Golda countered. She knelt and fished in Trace's clothes, which lay on the floor. She lifted a small box. The box glinted in the light of the queer magical glow above her head. "Here's the nectar—the evidence of the theft. You two think I never noticed?"

"He loves me, Mistress," Phylicia said. "It's not his fault."

"Ever since I came to live here, you two have been at it, and Trace has been stealing my nectar to feed your habit. I never said anything out of respect for Mareinah, but now things are going to change. You both know this is forbidden. Ahyehasi do not steal. Ahyehasi do not fuck each other without the permission of their Mistress. You save your lust. It's not just a rule for the Ahyehasi in this city—it's a rule for all humans who live with Djinnus and Jinni in the Underworld. Go stoke the fire, Trace. It's cold."

"Yes, Mistress." Trace crabbed to the low stone opening of the fireplace, where he raked out the glowing coals. The basement room brightened with a ruddy red glow, and the strange magical light above Golda's head faded away. Trace shuffled kindling and wood from the stacks into the fireplace opening. The fire caught. The wood flamed. Tajee sat up straight. Golda was approaching his cage.

"This doesn't concern you, Tajee. I'm taking care of a few things tonight so we have a household where everyone knows the rules. I can't have my houseboy stealing my things, and I can't have him spending his love energy on Phylicia."

"He could withdraw." Phylicia's voice was barely audible.

"Over to the chair, Trace." Golda's voice was commanding.

Trace crawled to the great silver chair, where Golda met him. She slid her hand under his throat and clipped his collar to the base of the seat so that his chin rested on the polished leather lip. She stood over him for long moments before she spoke.

"You can smell Mareinah's scent, can't you?"

"Yes, Mistress." Trace's voice was strained.

Golda paced to the wall, snatched a strap from the implements that hung there, and folded it in her hand. She swung at Trace's bare back. The Ahyehass flinched. Golda ran the strap through her fingers. "I'm sorry Tajee has to witness this, but maybe it will be good for him."

Golda swung the strap again, and then again, pausing between strokes to pace back and forth behind Trace's exposed buttocks. Tajee didn't watch Trace. His eyes were riveted on the sight of Golda's furry sex at the joining of her thighs. Tajee felt his phallus stirring yet again with a desire that sickened him. His body responded to Golda's presence. He couldn't help himself. He'd almost been at the point of accepting Golda's seduction of him for what it was, but her cruelty was too much. The Jinni had swayed his mind with her sweet words and promises of lust, but he'd been stupid to allow the woman to make him her prisoner. The Jinni paused mid-swing.

"How many is that, Trace?"

"Ten I think, Mistress."

"Enough. I loathe this, and until now I've never given a punishment to an Ahyehass." Golda paced back to Phylicia's cage and pointed at her with the leather strap. "I'm disappointed in you too."

"Yes, Mistress."

"I know what nectar can do to your mind. I used to be much worse than you, and I can sympathize." Golda produced her key ring and turned it in the cage lock. "You can have your powder now, but you can get it from me, not from him. Come out."

Phylicia crawled forward on her hands and knees. Golda moved towards the hearth alongside the female Ahyehass and seated herself on the flat stones by the fire. She retrieved the small box that she'd taken from Trace's clothes. She produced a small spoon from a chink in the hearthstones. She dipped the spoon into the small box and held it near the flames.

After a minute, Golda withdrew the spoon from the hearth and reached down. The spoon clinked on the floor in front of her feet. Phylicia crawled across the floor to the spoon where it glinted in the flickering shadow cast across the floor by Golda's frame. The Ahyehass leaned close.

"Good girl," Golda said softly.

"Thank you, Mistress." Phylicia's voice was oddly querulous. Her head bobbed over the spoon. The basement room dissolved into silence, interrupted only by the occasional crackle of the fire and the clinking of the spoon from Phylicia's licks. Golda rose and loomed at full height over the girl.

"I heard those things you said about me earlier, Phylicia. I was listening from the hall. I'm quiet like that. You'll never know how hard I've worked to become what I am. I was on my knees for uncounted years down in Erebus. I cleaned Basteh's fur from head to toe with my tongue to earn my daily nectar plates. My mistress whored me night and day for coins to the Djinnus and hellion businessmen in Vegasis. I even took Gypsies. I was abused in every conceivable way by thousands of the worst men, and now I'm sitting here as a fully-fledged Jinni mistress. I have my own home. I have my own clothes, horses, jewelry, and Ahyehasi. You think I'm a joke?"

"No, Mistress. I'm sorry."

Golda crouched close to whisper in Phylicia's ear. Golda's long muscled back, wild hair, and heavy pendulous breasts glowed in the firelight. She ran her hand down between Phylicia's legs and slowly stroked. Phylicia moaned. Tajee tore his eyes away. He couldn't look at such sinfulness. The redheaded Jinni soon re-entered his field of vision, however. She'd left Phylicia to cross the room again, where she bent and unclipped Trace from the high-backed chair.

"Trace, you can sleep in the center cage tonight so you can remember that your position of houseboy is a privilege."

"Yes, Mistress."

"I've decided to be rid of you at the end of winter during the Spring Festival. Tomorrow I want you to start training Tajee with the skills he needs to replace you. Tajee has more of what I need from a male that serves me. I'm told that mimọ boys have virtues and morality. He won't lie to me. He won't steal. He won't let Phylicia seduce him. He's beautiful."

"Yes, Mistress." Trace's voice was strained.

Tajee blinked. He felt a twinge of bizarre pride at Golda's compliments—a coil of a different sin within his inundation of lust. Golda looked over at him with her sultry smile—that smile that made him so weak. Tajee tore his eyes away from her gaze. He had to resist Golda if he wanted to save Boudi. He had to fight the distractions from his quest. Golda seemed to believe he was more trustworthy than he really was. Perhaps he could use that to his advantage.

"Are you doing alright, Tajee?" Golda was looking down at him. She'd approached his cage without him noticing. Golda moved with surprising speed and silence. "There are consequences to breaking the rules here, just like in Heaven. Do Mimọs steal in Heaven, Tajee? Do the boys and girls get together in secret and have sex after saying prayers?"

"No. They'd be arrested and taken for reformation by the Conclave."

Tajee shuddered when Golda drew away from him. His heart felt hard, but his mind was melting with an urge to be against her again. Golda pointed at Phylicia's cage. The female Ahyehass crawled inside obediently. The Jinni re-locked the cage doors one by one. Golda waved as she walked away. "Goodnight, my beautiful Ahyehasi. I'd like to stay, but I'm late for a mid-night ritual. This one I can't miss."

Chapter 11:

Boudi woke to a hand shaking her shoulder. The lone candle still guttered on the side table next to the bed, silhouetting the form of Ayelet leaning over her. Ayelet was dressed in a grey evening gown with matching pearl earrings. Boudi took the offered hand hesitantly and rose from the bed. A copy of her body remained on the red sheet with her head nestled against the angular collarbone of Ayelet, whose body also still lay on the bed as if comatose.

"What's happening, Mistress Ayelet?"

"We're dreaming," Ayelet answered. "Our souls have entered the dream-world. Do you see my tapestry?" Ayelet pointed to one of her bed-chamber wall tapestries, where a huntsman and his hounds had disappeared to form a black hole. The embroidered pine forest had yielded to a deeper, deciduous canopy with an extra dimension.

A rich starry night intruded into the room. A path of liquid darkness melted and oozed across the floor, thickening the air with odors of fungus and decay. Boudi felt Ayelet's hand clasp hers. The elder Jinni pulled her across the room and through the hole into the cool air of the night. Her bare feet pressed into the moss that covered a damp bank.

Heartbeat.

Stars glimmered on a lake. Frogs croaked and crickets chirruped. A skiff was moored with a rope to a thick wood post. Ayelet untied the rope and climbed into the boat. Boudi climbed in after. She realized she was wearing a simple white dress, almost identical to her mimọ robe in Heaven and tied with an ordinary white sash. The dream-world lake changed into a maze of weedy canals while Ayelet rowed.

Ayelet guided the skiff around silent facades, piers, and other moored boats. The moonlight rippled across the surface of the water. The canals opened onto another dark lake. Ayelet navigated the boat to the center of the lake, where an edifice loomed. The cathedral rose from a low rocky island in the middle of the dark waters. Its facade was illuminated by feeble torchlight. Five spires and a golden dome jutted up against the starry sky.

Heartbeat.

"We've arrived at Allyssia's palace." Ayelet stepped out of the boat and onto the island. The silver-hazel eyes of the Jinni appeared oversized like a frog for a moment. Ayelet extended her hand. Boudi hesitated.

"I don't like this."

"Don't be afraid, chérie. I'm with you all the way. Remember that our minds see the dream-world with our own personal imagery, so you might see things differently. I don't know what you'll see. If you start to panic, please tell me."

Boudi took Ayelet's hand and allowed herself to be pulled forward. The croaking of the frogs had grown louder on the night air. The cathedral seemed to grow smaller and darker as they approached its narrow portico, until it was hardly larger than a shack. Twisted, treelike columns framed the old wooden door. A small, distorted window of stained glass was the only ornament of the façade. The glass glowed softly with muted amber as if lit from within.

Heartbeat.

The immense weight of the tiny cathedral seemed incongruous on the little island. The building was sunken, as if mired deep in rotten muck and god-touched clay. Ayelet pressed against the portal, which swung open at her touch. Boudi followed Ayelet into a short nave that gave into a vaulted apse. The interior of the cathedral was gigantic, entirely out of scale with the exterior. Fluted columns rimmed the walls, each bearing a golden candelabrum that illuminated the great room.

Ayelet's high heels clicked with a metallic sound as she paced forwards. The bottom hem of her pearled gown made uncanny whispering sounds as it brushed and skittered the floor. Illegible names were inscribed in gold on the square stones from which the smooth floor had been fashioned.

Heartbeat.

Beyond the slabs of names, a beveled ring of marble rose in the center of the floor. The raised stone ring contained a perfectly still reflecting pool. Ayelet gestured. "Come here and strip please."

Boudi crossed her arms and fidgeted. Mistress Ayelet kept pushing her deeper into the new worlds in which she found herself. She didn't like it, but at the same time, she couldn't summon the nerve to back out. She was supposed to be playing the role of a bad mimo, wasn't she?

Heartbeat.

Maybe she was bad. Maybe she couldn't blame Ayelet and the Jinni. They'd only shown her the truth. Pasteur had called her a team player, but they'd really just needed a failure of an mimo to throw those messages down and be convincing about it. Thinking objectively, she'd served a lot of detention compared to every other mimo girl she knew. She'd thought that she was pretending to be bad to fool the Jinni, but maybe she was only fooling herself. Maybe the messages she'd written were just as much truth as lies.

Heartbeat.

Tajee would have wanted her robe off. He'd always wanted to see her in the complete nude. Boudi shivered. Ayelet was staring her down with her wide hazel eyes, as if frozen in time, waiting for her to disrobe.

"You can do it, Boudi," Ayelet said distantly.

"You're right. I can do this." Boudi bit her lip. How long had she been standing there, debating with herself? It seemed like forever. She looked down and found the knot of her sash. She tried to insinuate her fingertips into the pretzeled bindings in the eddy of white fabric. The knot of her sash was very tight. Finally, she got a finger into the knot and pulled, and a great weight seemed to lift from her tense body when her robe slipped off.

Heartbeat.

Ayelet was smiling with a glimmer of triumph, as if something had been accomplished. The elder Jinni held a long, tightly wrapped bundle of what appeared to be dead dry roses with withered petals. Ayelet pointed with the bunch of them. "Now stand at the edge of that altar so you directly straddle that brazier. Good. Place your hands on the top and bend over so your elbows form a triangle. Keep your legs wide with your feet flat on the first step."

Heartbeat.

Boudi could see her own reflection in the waters of the pool—a silhouette rimmed by sparks of pale gold where the light from the candelabra caught her hair. When she adjusted her grip on the rim of the pool, her fingertip grazed the surface of the water, sending ripples across her reflection. The hot smoke from the brazier curled across her stomach and naked hips. She heard a distant drumming and a hiss of rattles. She tried to look at the reflection of her face, but she couldn't recognize herself. She looked older and heavier, like someone else.

Heartbeat.

Ayelet's bundle of roses snapped suddenly across her buttocks. The roses snapped again and again. Boudi shrank and flexed under the ache and pain. Small showers of rose petals wafted over her back and onto the waters of the pool with every stroke, accompanied by Sharp shards of pain shooting down her legs. She held fast to the edge of the pool. She was floating, drifting in and out of consciousness as Ayelet rained the blows down in a regular rhythm. She was bad. She was a bad mimo.

Heartbeat.

The petals continued to fly, whisking as if in slow motion across the pool and spattering coolly on her back and her head. Ayelet whipped her and whipped her with the roses, until each stroke sent a sting not just through her backside, but through her entire being. At last, when her arms were trembling, and she felt like she was going to fall unconscious, and she had conceded inwardly that she was the most wicked mimo girl in the world, the whipping stopped.

Heartbeat.

Boudi held fast to the pool, even as her arms trembled from the weight of everything. She didn't have to pretend. She was bad, and Ayelet had showed her just how bad she really was. The word was no longer an adjective. It was her.

"She is ready." A female voice boomed in the expanded space. The interior of the cathedral changed dramatically. The magnificent space quadrupled yet again in size. The light brightened, and the little pool became an ancient stone altar.

Heartbeat.

Boudi raised her head. A hundred silvery-eyed Jinni were gathered and chanting a song that she couldn't understand. Golda stood at one end of the throng. Golda was in the nude with her red hair glowing above and below. At the head of the room, a throne rose in golden splendor. A Ifreeta with golden brown skin sat on the throne. She was nude like Golda except for gold bracelets and a necklace of gold and purple stones.

Heartbeat.

The face of the Ifreeta was hidden by an ivory mask that gave her a magical appearance of perfection. The darkened eye slits and smiling red-painted mouth radiated a presence both terrible and wonderful. Everything that existed in the space seemed to flex around the presence of the Ifreeta Allyssia, who rose from the throne and closed the distance across the floor, drifting perfectly on her magnificent golden-brown feet.

Heartbeat.

Boudi felt a torrent of heat course unbidden through her sex, and then a hardness pushed slowly inwards. A pressure moved her insides. She groaned when her resistance gave in. The hardness began a slow rhythm in pace with the drums, and each thrust was like a roll of thunder. She went light-headed. She was drifting, weightless. An unbearable pleasure began to build in her core.

Heartbeat.

Boudi blinked. The Ifreeta of Love had moved position quickly. Allyssia loomed directly in her field of vision. As the hardness continued its rhythm into her very being, Boudi craned her neck to stare up at the shining mask of the Lady.

Heartbeat.

The seductive sashay of Her hips, the graceful movement of Her hands—everything served to enchant. The rest of the room and even the pleasure and pain fell away into the dream space, leaving only a core of arresting reality.

Heartbeat.

"You are ready for my gift." The Lady's voice was melodic like a bell that harmonized with the sounds of the drums and rattles. "My gift." The voice accelerated into a chiming sound that echoed and resonated. "My gift. My gift."

Heartbeat.

Boudi gasped. Her heart leapt with inexplicable joy as the silken touch of Allyssia's hand flowed like a forest river over the apple of her left cheek. She stared up into the inscrutable mask while the Lady's fingers ran in odd patterns over her forehead.

Heartbeat.

She felt happiness flowing through her, and then the Lady's fingers were tracing circles, repeating three times, nine, and a bright light exploded in her consciousness. The top of her head felt searing hot.

Heartbeat.

The room started spinning, and then the spin slowed, and time itself seemed to stop before the room righted and began to spin in the opposite direction. The voice of the Lady came again, but it was too fast to understand, and backwards.

Heartbeat.

Boudi hitched. Allyssia's exquisite fingers had pinched her chin. Just when she thought she couldn't take any more, another sensual aperture opened—her nose. Boudi felt her mouth drop open as her nostrils flared.

Heartbeat.

The palm of the Ifreeta gave off a scent unlike anything she'd ever smelled. The scent filled her head with animals and plants… petals opening… sepals splaying… horns clashing… hooves pounding… thick fur bristling and warm in a winter wind…

Heartbeat.

She was frozen in the moment, suspended in the air, floating between the hand of the Ifreeta and her badgered sex, a primary axis that kept her from spinning into infinity. The chanting voices re-exploded into her head and accelerated to a fast, high babble.

Heartbeat.

The Lady's hand released her, and then she swirled away to take her appointed position among the stars, her place in the vast and infinite universe, and then she was losing her place, a star falling head over heels, trapped and predestined by an inexorable heaviness, a gravity in heat.

Heartbeat.

Heartbeat.

Heartbeat.

Chapter 12:

Masad crept along the roof of the Villa, pausing with each step to assure the purchase of his small cat claws on the steep clay tiles. He was so distracted that he failed to notice the harpy eagles sleeping quietly on the rim of the skylight. The birds shattered into the low darkness of the Isandlwana night.

Playing are you a dangerous game, Masad.

He'd successfully ridden into the hidden city inside Mistress Golda's horse. In the stables, he'd slipped out of the horse into a more mobile host—another domesticated feline. He'd pawed freely about the small city of the Love Ifreeta the entire day, and he'd even been greeted amiably by a few Jinni.

After sunset, he'd grown bolder in his explorations. He'd pinpointed Tajee's location in a small house past the smells of metal, leather, and clay that came from the city workshops, and then he'd set out to follow a second faint mimọ track to the dark Villa that perched high on the eastern edge of the city.

It was difficult to decipher the tapestry inside the confines of Allyssia's domain, but the second track was different and unique enough to barely perceive amidst the ever-shifting probabilities within the proprietary weave. Masad could see the mimọ girl through the skylight with both his inner and borrowed eyes. The track that the Mimoic Hierarchy hadn't wanted him to follow ended there. It was the fourth thread—the frayed dead end that wasn't dead. A female mimo lay on a magnificent bed.

The mimo was beautiful. Her pale skin was stretched over a lithe framework of birdlike bones. The hollow of her cheek was shadowed in the dying light of a single flickering candle. Her shoulder-length ebony hair mingled on the pillow with the longer, darker, grey-streaked strands of the elder Jinni who lay on the bed next to her.

Masad bristled his whiskers. Both women were asleep. They were there, but they weren't there. He could scarcely feel the waking presence of a New Order Jinni in the entire city. They'd all crossed into the dream-world, and the mimo was with them.

He could see the dream portal down in the bedchamber with his inner eyes. It was a dark stain that dripped from the tapestries. If he could get inside the Villa, he could enter the door in demonic form, but he wasn't sure if he should dare. If all the Jinni in the city were on the other side, he figured, there could be more than a hundred, and the Lady herself had to be lurking somewhere.

Who are you?

The lilting voice came unbidden to his mind. Masad crouched on his paws. He saw no one except a single dove that still sat on the brim of the nearby chimney. The bird hadn't flown with the others. It ruffled its feathers and tilted its head sideways to look at him in the starlight. The bird repeated its question.

Who are you?

No one am I to be trifled with. Answer you the question first.

The dove bobbed its head, as if amused.

Here am I. I am here, and I am everywhere. You are inside me. Prince Masad? Is that really you?

Masad heard laughter like faint chimes in the wind. He'd accepted the risk and eventuality of discovery by the Ifreeta Allyssia. He'd hoped to go undetected for longer, however, and the event couldn't have happened at a more difficult moment. He bowed as best he could on his four cat legs.

Yes, milady. Just looking I for a few lost Mimos. Seems found I another one.

These Mimos are turning into quite the conundrum.

Sent me the Mimoic Hierarchy after them. There is no problem. Go can I. Forget can I this place. Or perhaps can I not.

Let's go somewhere more comfortable and discuss. Wait for me. I'll be coming.

The rooftop whirled and disappeared. Masad found himself moving through a dream tunnel, a sudden shortcut in the weave. His cat body came to rest in a large room that was dimly lit by lamplight. A row of silver cages lined one wall. A long table equipped with manacles stood against another wall. A rack of torture implements hung above it. A massive door banded with iron barred egress. Masad sniffed. The room smelled faintly of pain and blood, reminding him of the devil pits in the capital city of Mer.

Well done, Masad. A prisoner are you in the dungeon of Love.

He wasn't alone in the room. A lanky male figure slumped in one of the heavy silver cages. His face was wrinkled, giving every evidence of decrepitude. His body nonetheless appeared corded and whip-like under worn leather pants and a bloody evening shirt. The creature slowly opened its beady eyes.

"Here, kitty-kitty. I won't bite."

Bite you will, vampire.

Masad scanned the room mechanically for exits. Not that he would try to escape from the Lady before business could be discussed, but it was instinct. The vampire stirred further in his cage. "Here, kitty-kitty."

Footsteps sounded on the stair. A key turned in the lock of the door. Allyssia entered the room. She was no longer in the form of a bird. The foam-borne daughter of the titan Uranus was breathtaking in her near-nude beauty.

Allyssia wore only an expressionless ivory mask with her fabled gold cestus slung low over her glistening hips—that bejeweled girdle soul-forged from the love of her ugly ex-husband, Haephestus. The polished golden beads of the artifact rubbed over the Lady's precious thighs. The curve of the cestus formed a grand archway over the shimmering apex of the Lady's infinitely attractive femininity.

Masad felt a magical force pulling his cat eyeballs—an attraction no male or female could resist, or so said the myths. The Lady was stronger than he remembered, and worse yet he was affected by the weaknesses of his feline host. His cat brain went drunk and happy in his skull. A distracting purr vibrated unbidden in his throat. He devoted a portion of his willpower to resisting the urge to scurry forward and rub his fur against the divine leg of Love.

"Lady Allyssia," the vampire said from his cage. "You're lucky you showed up. I was about to have your cat for a snack."

"I know you hunger, Huesca," Allyssia said without looking at her prisoner. "You'll find Golden Gorila's cat to be more than your match. I'm pleased he hasn't eaten you instead, at least not yet."

"A Ifreeta with a sense of humor. So when can we have neck sex? I'm pathetic. I'm begging. What sort of love Ifreeta deprives a man for months? Give me a slave girl to play with at least. Please. Have mercy on me."

Masad. It's been a long time since I saw you in Haawiyah. How is your father Hades? Have you been to Hell's Court lately?

Masad collected his senses to focus on Allyssia's voice. The conversation wasn't starting on a pleasant note. The Mimọs had bounties on their heads from Heaven, while he had one from Hell's Court. The Lady knew this. She was looking to negotiate.

Seen my father have I not for ages. Wanted have I not to see him.

I'm sorry about the surroundings. I'm sure you imagined something more extravagant. Until I understand your intentions, however, I have to take precautions.

Came I for an mimọ. Sorry am I for your cat. Met him I in the stables and seemed he friendly.

Allyssia chuckled, a sound like chimes.

Golden Gorila's cat does like to frequent the city stables. There is much coming and going there. It's amusing, don't you find, for a spy to possess another spy?

No spy am I, my Lady, but a rescuer and righter for hire.

A spy is one who infiltrates, sees things, and reports to others what he has seen. You've found my hidden city and seen things. I know that you're working for the Mimoic Hierarchy, and Lord Tuhan and his arch-Mimos are persuasive in the ways they extract information. I also know that you've a side business in ferreting secrets and selling them to the highest bidder.

Wanted I only to know what the Hierarchy was hiding. Information is power long before used it is. Think I not so far into the future.

Foresight is survival. Free will is a difficult thing to predict. It was my desire to try for Boudi, but I didn't expect success. Golda wanted to help with the mimo, and her wild energy can be a changer of fates.

Who is Boudi?

Don't play games with me, Masad. I'm not in the mood.

I am not here for the girl, if that is what mean you. I am here for the boy Tajee. Told me the Hierarchy not to save the girl. Only the boys.

Not save Boudi? Why not?

Not say, they. Not ask, I.

Of course. Perhaps my Jinni did not fail because the Hierarchy let them succeed. Something has been wrong with Boudi since the beginning, but I took the risk. I wanted this mimo. Yet we are all governed by the Fates, and playing with their will is like pulling the Gordian knot. It will recoil in your fingers.

Stole you the girl from Heaven and gave her the Mimos did?

If you truly do not know the answer to that question, Masad, then I may place myself in your debt yet.

A humble hellion prince am I. Try I only to do my job.

Masad, you've always impressed me with your stoicism.

"So are you going to stand there all night and stare at your cat, or torture me like Mistress Ivanka?" The vampire prisoner laughed dully. "I need to feed so much. I need to fuck. How long can this go on? I thought you were the Ifreeta of love, not the Ifreeta of suffering."

A friend of yours, milady?

No. The mimo business aside, I have a vampire problem. Mistress Freyah killed the other two that we found out in Meristyian, but she spared Huesca for questioning. Now I've got an issue with the Hierarchy, or so it appears. The Mimọs are great reformers. They don't cast down their own unless the situation is grave. Is Boudi such a bad mimọ?

Not want I to know, milady.

It's too late, Masad. You do know.

Tell me you this why?

Why are you working for the Hierarchy?

Masad twitched his whiskers. Have I my reasons.

Which are?

Good pay and other things. Mainly, not care I for being a pawn for my father. Left I the insanity of Mer and Haawiyah before you, if recall you, and at the time, were not many options. Spent I some time in the east, got trouble, struck a deal with my father's brother.

I always liked you, Masad. So unlike your father. But to ally yourself with Lord Tuhan? I never saw that coming.

Said I the pay is well for me, and protection.

I have no intention of handing either of my Mimọs back to Lord Tuhan. Tajee is here of his own free will, such as it is. Boudi is now a Jinni. She's one of us. You might think me cruel and capricious, but I have my reasons that are important to me.

Lead you an innocent mimọ into lust and darkness.

Only so she can show my Jinni the light. My city is still ever-darkened by Allyssia's cruel old ways. My New Order Jinni struggle to discover love. Boudi was an epiphany for me. Perhaps a few Mimọs can balance my equation and save this place.

What of Mistress Golda? Changed you her into a Jinni too? She is different. A slave she used to be?

Your guesses are accurate, Masad. She is talented, but the pain that her old mistress inflicted on her pushes her to impulses of cruelty. She's a part of the problems in my paradise, not the solution. She isn't well-liked among the others.

Like her I.

You have things in common, but Golda is valuable to me. I'd appreciate it if you didn't make a gesture of your affection.

So leaves this me where?

I'd like you to work for me when you're finished this business with the Mimos, Masad. The Fates may have shown me the way. Perhaps your appearance isn't mere coincidence. I can make it worth your time.

Consider the offer I will. Of course, will cost you, think I.

I may be able to pay, depending. You weren't meant to be a lackey for Lord Tuhan and the Mimos. You disappoint me, son of Lord Hades.

Then I am sorry, milady.

Out the door and go down the hallway. Please tell no one what you've seen here unless you want another goddess angry at you. Know that I can make it worth your while if you want to work. Otherwise, I don't want to see you again soon.

Always to the point.

Count on it. Especially when someone has me at a disadvantage. Now please go and leave my Mimos alone. Release Golden Gorila's cat at your earliest convenience.

Masad bowed on his paws and padded to where Allyssia pointed with her infinitely beautiful finger. The Ifreeta had won the negotiation such as it was, and there was no point in that moment to bargain for more. The corridor was dimly lit beyond the dungeon door. A stair led upwards.

Masad pricked his ears. He was somewhere deep beneath the city. He could feel the weight of it—an ascendant complexity of creation over the darkness of the under-halls. The force of Allyssia's divine magic lifted him again suddenly. The world whirled, and his paws landed on dirt and gravel.

He was back under the night sky at the limit of the Lady's private tapestry. The Isandlwana forests unfolded before him in his mind. The open weave was relieving to the claustrophobia that he'd felt in the city. There was no visible sign of civilization behind him. An eroded track vanished at the brink of a fog-shrouded chasm. A black mountain range blotted out the stars on the far side. A small moonlit obelisk stood inconspicuously on a mossy bank.

Masad noted the location for future reference as he paced into the endless expanse of the Isandlwana Heartland. He had another mimọ boy to track. He had no time to waste, and he struggled to push Allyssia from his mind. He wouldn't soon forget Her divine beauty. He was still happy and purring.

The self-exiled Ifreeta had no army of soldiers like Lord Tuhan or Lord Hades, but she was still formidable. Her hidden city in Meristyian was apparently some sort of experiment in worship—an equation of Love contained by lofty mountain surroundings.

Chapter 13:

Boudi shot through the atmospheres like a pinwheel rocket. She twirled so high that she could see the zigzag lines of a glorious white stairway gleaming in the sky like a solemn promise. Then she fell, mauled by the indecorous arms of gravity, into a dark plain under the Isandlwana sky.

Across the plain stretched fields of purple poppies. The night-tightened buds of the flowers stirred in the cool morning air as they awaited the warm light of Dawn. To the east the light limned vast cumulonimbus clouds in pale shades of peach. To the west, the deep purple field was still one with the waning night—an impenetrable wall of stars and darkness.

Boudi bounded at furious speed across the yielding tips of the highest buds. She looked over her shoulder. The wind stripped her diaphanous robe into a pale streak of light that trailed in her wake. The streak faded behind her like a pale comet trail. She was faster than the light of Dawn that rose over the plain in chase. Dawn's light slowed as it crashed across the vast undulations of flowers, pausing to set aglow millions of hungry petals.

Boudi-Ca. A voice whispered.

Boudi accelerated towards a full moon that gleamed like a beacon over a distant jumble of mountainsides. She was an unimaginable distance from the towering white confines of cold Heaven. The Conclave Mimos would never come to her rescue.

Boudi-Ca.

An irresistible force pulled her. She flashed along a rutted track. She flew past a stone obelisk. Allyssia's city shimmered into view where it cozied up with the mountain slopes. Onwards she flowed, over the bridge and into the city, up a dozen steep streets. A narrow road curved around a hillside and gave into the gates of a sprawling estate. Boudi tried to halt her motion and gaze for a moment at the spiderweb of tiled rooftops below, but she was drawn inexorably towards the nearby Villa, across the flower gardens and under a shadowed overhang.

She slipped liked a bird through the slit above her shuttered window and into the cool darkness of her room. Her body lay on the bed. Her face looked peaceful on the pillow beneath a splay of her honey-ebony hair. Mistress Ayelet sat on the edge of the bed. The elder Jinni pulled back the quilt to reveal a pale neck and bare breasts. Boudi snapped downwards into her comfortable enclosure of flesh. She opened her eyes. Ayelet's warm hand was kneading her tender neck, probing into the hollows above her collarbone.

"Welcome home, chérie."

"I had a dream. I was flying."

Ayelet smiled faintly. "After we returned last night from your ritual of transformation, your soul left your body again of its own accord. You traveled through Meristyian's tapestry and out of the Redoubt. It was a powerful after-effect of the poppy crush. I gave you too much. I had to be certain that it would work."

"How did I get down from your bedroom to mine?"

"Herzl and I carried you. You were unconscious, and I was a bit fatigued and wanted to feed my Hunger again. I've checked in on you from time to time, and I'm sure the Lady is watching over you too."

"The ritual is over?"

"Yes. You're one of us now. Your new name will be Boudi-Ca. The -Ca suffix denotes a fledgling among the Jinni, whereas an -ah or -eh honorific denotes a fully-fledged mistress. How do you feel, fledgling?"

Boudi-Ca frowned. "I feel really different, I think."

"Like a different person?"

"Yes." Boudi-Ca looked up into Ayelet's silver-hazel eyes. The events of the night before replayed in her mind—the touching, the whipping, and the ritual. She felt a profound connection with Ayelet that she hadn't felt before. Her stomach quivered. "I feel good. I do. I feel kind of bad too. Like I'm hollow. Or full of sin. I don't know. Probably both."

"The good thing that you feel is your first glow of the power that is now yours as a Jinni." Ayelet's voice took a motherly tone. "The bad thing that you feel is the Hunger, the handmaiden of all Jinni. From this time on, you must feed to sustain and grow your new capacity for strength and magical energy."

"What if I don't?"

"If you don't, then you will die. You've been expanded and restructured inside. If you do not feed yourself, your desire-body will collapse into your inner emptiness. You'll separate into the void, ceasing to exist in this world as we know it."

"That sounds horrible."

"Then feed." Ayelet patted her arm softly. "And feed again. Your Hunger will make you want to. There are always sacrifices to be made to gain power. If not, we would all be goddesses like Allyssia."

Boudi-Ca licked her lips. Her mouth had gone suddenly dry. "I don't know how to feed."

"It will come to you naturally. It's simpler than it sounds. The Ahyehasi accumulate love energy in their desire-structures. We harvest the love mystically through sexual release. It's the way of things. For now, until you learn all of this, I have something else."

"What?"

Ayelet held up a small red-pink fruit in her hand. "It's a pink knuckle-bark pomegranate. These are mostly grown in Pan's domain down on the plains of Erebus. They are potent. They are also difficult to import to this city. Certain plants in the Underworld absorb energy that we can feed from, although they are less effective than sex. For now, I'll feed you one pink knuckle-bark each morning while you're learning to take your love. The pomegranates can fatten a Jinn who eats too many, but a few won't hurt you. You're too skinny, and I received Allyssia's approval for you eating these."

Boudi-Ca struggled into a cross-legged position on the warm bed. Her back ached. She flexed against the discomfort. Her mimo wings, despite their small size, were heavier in Meristyian than in Heaven. The muscles on either side of her spine felt sore from bearing their unusual weight for a week. She blinked and looked down at herself. She hadn't realized until that moment that she was completely nude. The corset that she'd worn the night before was missing.

She didn't mind the missing corset. Her nudity was a relief. She could breathe, and Ayelet had already seen everything of her body. She felt her stomach quiver again with a definite ache—an emptiness. She reached to pry the fruit from Ayelet's fingers, but the mistress held it fast.

"Can I have it?"

"Not yet," Ayelet answered. "I'll cut it for you."

Boudi-Ca reluctantly yielded the pomegranate. She pushed a stray strand of hair behind her ear. The Hunger, as she felt it, was an uncomfortable drum like stretchiness in the depths of her body from her chest to her hips. The ache pooled in her nether places, but she could somehow feel it everywhere, even in her feet.

She watched Ayelet place the pomegranate on a round silver tray on the side table. The mistress removed a slender folding blade and a small silver spoon from her pocket. The misshapen fruit squatted on the plate. The cool light that spilled from the window purpled the pomegranate's red-pink skin. Ayelet paused to roll back her sleeves, and then bent over the tray and worked the knife, peeling the fruit and slicing the flesh into slivers. Rich burgundy ichor sluiced through the silver filigree of the tray. Ayelet daintily excavated wet flesh and seeds.

"Your last delivery of clothes is coming this morning, fledgling," Ayelet murmured. "Mistress Gallinah and the city seamstresses are keeping busy.

You'll have a robe for your blades training. You'll have riding clothes so you can learn to ride a horse, and two more corsets with matching stockings."

"Thank you, Mistress."

"You'll have a beautiful ball gown too for dances at Allyssia's palace. It's very cute and fanciful. It's bright purple."

"Bright purple? That's too much color. I don't want to draw any attention to myself. I have no plans to dance, anyway."

"Boudi-Ca, chérie—" Ayelet smiled as she worked. "You may have been an ordinary wallflower among the Mimọs in Heaven—"

"In Heaven I was very average."

"Yet here you're an exotic young newcomer, the talk of the city. I couldn't know what you were like in Heaven compared to the other mimọ girls, but in this world you're perfectly exquisite, I assure you. Beauty is simply what it is, and to me it's not a contest."

Boudi-Ca felt a small flush of pride warm her belly. "Even though mimọ girls are supposed to be chaste and humble, beauty is important. The prettiest mimọ girls get the most special attention from professors, and it seems like they always get picked to sing in the choir."

Ayelet smiled. "Are you calling the Mimọs out for hypocrisy, Boudi-Ca? If so, I'm glad that I've been able to talk some sense into you. Did you get any special treatment yourself?"

"Only if extra punishment counts. I'm a bad mimọ girl, Mistress Ayelet. I think I secretly like getting into trouble. Good girls like Makeda Deen don't think that way."

Ayelet scraped the pomegranate seeds nonchalantly into a small pile with her knife. "Trouble is good for you. You're with the New Order Jinni now, so you have all the trouble you could want."

"You're a good teacher, Mistress Ayelet. You teach me, and I don't even know it. You're better than preachy Professor Brown by far." Boudi-Ca stared boldly at Ayelet, who stared back at her in turn.

"You try to flatter me, fledgling? Yes, you're lucky to be here, but you're not yet as wise as you might think. Like I said, there are prices to pay for everything." Ayelet scooped a dollop of pomegranate into the silver spoon.

She lifted the spoon up in a smooth motion. It was laden with kernels of fruit. "Open, s'il vous plait."

Boudi-Ca leaned forward and opened her mouth. Ayelet slipped the spoon quickly inside and upended the wet lump of pink knuckle-bark on her tongue. Boudi-Ca chewed. The juice burst into her throat. She swallowed the seeds and shuddered involuntarily. The sweet fruit trickled down into her stomach. The sensation was queer. She'd never eaten anything in Heaven. Ayelet lifted the spoon to her lips again. Boudi-Ca chewed briefly and swallowed. Her stomach felt warm and heavy. A tingling sensation pulsed between her legs.

"It's nice, don't you find?" Ayelet watched her impassively. "Three more spoonfuls. Can you do it? It's good for you. Think of it as medicine for a newborn young Jinn."

"Mmmh." Boudi-Ca held onto the edge of the bed to steady herself. Another spoonful came to her lips.

"Open."

Boudi-Ca swallowed the seeds. Ayelet lifted yet another spoonful of pomegranate to her mouth. Boudi-Ca opened. Her stomach felt swollen instead of empty. The seeds radiated a torrid heat. The warmth percolated gently through her folded legs.

"Mmmmmph."

"One more. Open."

Boudi-Ca took the last big spoonful in a single gulp. The heat continued to spread inside of her. Her toes tingled. The lumps of the seeds felt like a slender silk rope drawn in knots down through the core of her body, starting at the base of her throat. Ayelet lifted a linen serviette. Boudi-Ca leaned forward to allow the mistress to pat her juice-wet lips. Ayelet folded the silver spoon inside the cloth and slipped the bundle into her skirt pocket.

"How do you feel, chérie? Do you like your first pomegranate?"

"I don't know yet. I think so." Boudi-Ca lay back on the bed. The heat from the seeds was rapidly turning into a delicious pleasure that pulsed in her limbs, burned in her cheeks, circled her eye sockets, and tickled the roots of her hair. Ayelet kneaded the soft skin around the base of her throat, and then caressed her chest down to her breasts.

"It's taking to you well."

"Mmhmph," Boudi-Ca said. She stretched on the bed and clutched a pillow to her stomach. Every inch of her body was abuzz.

"I need to take care of some business now," Ayelet said abruptly. "I'll return in a bit. Is there anything else you need?"

"Yes. There was something, but I don't remember what it was." Boudi-Ca frowned. Her body was light, bobbing on waves of gentle pleasure like a small boat on the rumpled pool of her bedclothes. She couldn't concentrate.

"Perhaps you'll remember later. Stay in bed and rest. There are worlds spread out before you now—places and adventures that you've never imagined. This is only the beginning. You'll need to work. The outcome is far from certain."

"What kind of work?" Boudi-Ca looked askance at Ayelet, but Ayelet was already gone, and the question was lost in the rustle of petticoats and the thump of the door. Boudi-Ca sighed as the boot-clicks of the Mistress faded down the walkway outside the bedroom window. The sounds of the boots faded, replaced by the chitter of the birds and the clunks of Anders working outside with his tools and wheelbarrow.

Boudi-Ca curled on her side away from the light that seeped through the window shutters. The edge was fading from the sensations of the seeds, but she could still feel them melting into soft ribbons in her body, ribbons that went low and pooled, forming delicious warmth where her legs came together. She placed one hand between her legs and nestled her other against her forehead. She stretched her legs and clamped her thighs around her wrist.

She arched her back so her hand pressed more deeply against her heated nethers. When she turned her head to hide from the light, she could feel her eyelashes tickling against the linen, such was her sensitivity in Meristyian. She closed her eyes, turned on her bare belly, and bent her wrist again into her gap against the warm dampness. Slowly she began to move her buttocks up and down, back and forth. The silken knots of the seeds stretched inside her as she flexed, stimulating her. She bucked faster against them in a rhythm.

She kicked at the bed quilt. It rustled as it slid off of the bed. She closed her eyes and lay on her stomach on the sheet, grinding for slow moments, savoring the feel of her naked skin. Finally, she widened her thighs and palmed her damp mound. She pressed her fingers against her furrow and moved them up and down, experimenting. She quickened her fingers insistently, pushing through her fear, washing away the sinfulness with ripples of pleasure.

She knew what she sought when she found it. The wave crashed through her, and she shuddered as she tumbled in it. She tore away her hand from her wetness and flailed, clutching at her pillow with both hands as the passion subsided in stages. She buried her head in the pillow and wriggled this way and that, reveling in the sensations until her hair was strewn across her eyes and through her mouth.

Boudi-Ca lay perfectly still in her new Jinni body. A final little thrill ran from the beginning of her buttocks to the furrow of her sex. The pomegranate seeds slowly settled again inside her. When she lay still, their hold upon her lessened. She kissed the pillow with her tingling lips. She felt almost relieved to finally embrace her nature as a bad mimo.

For the first time since she'd left Heaven, she was without fear or regrets. A little voice in her head whispered a warning, but she ignored it. She'd experienced the forbidden, and she'd conquered it. A tickle and wetness on her hand distracted her. She peered through the strands of her tousled hair, surprised by the red liquid running down her wrist.

She thrust herself up from the bed.

The bed sheet was wet with a deep pink stain. Her pillow was stained by burgundy blotches where her hand had settled. Boudi-Ca felt a dread creep through her chest. Her hand and wrist were sticky with red-pink ichor. She slid from the bed, leaving burgundy stains on the sheet as she went.

She scampered stiffly down the hall and through her inner bedchamber door, moaning as the pomegranate seeds inside her danced. They admonished her Sharply, beckoning her back to the bed with promises of more sinful pleasure. The bathing pool in the inner Villa courtyard burbled softly, welcoming her into a dark, cleansing embrace.

Boudi-Ca slipped over the marble lip and into the water that flowed hotly up from somewhere deep in the sulfurous bedrock of the Underworld. The pool soothed her, but also heated the seeds. They danced in her belly. She felt dizzy and delirious.

What in the name of Lord Tuhan was she doing? What had she done? What had she become? First Ayelet had given her the poppy crush, and then the pomegranate. The one had been bitter and the other sweet. Ayelet was feeding her things to influence her thinking. Boudi-Ca gripped the mossy stone edge of the pool. Her mimo-girl-self had come back to her mind suddenly, like waking from a long, terrifying trance.

The Conclave wasn't coming for her. She was on her own, and she had to find a way to get out of that evil city and go home. In the meantime, she had to keep fighting Ayelet and the sin, all while still pretending to be a willing young Jinni and playing her role. She couldn't let herself forget again. If Ayelet tried to make her consume anything else, she needed to find an excuse to refuse.

"Boudi-Ca?"

Boudi-Ca opened her eyes at the touch of the hand on her shoulder. She'd almost dozed off. Mistress Ayelet knelt over her at the edge of the pool.

"Fledgling, are you alright? Perhaps I shouldn't have left you. Speak to me, please."

"Yes, Mistress. I'll be fine." Boudi-Ca tongued the lingering taste of the pomegranate from her teeth. "Sorry about the sheets."

"Yenta will change them. I'm so sorry. When a Jinni eats a pomegranate, the nutritional effect can induce desire. Your goal was to resist and hold that concentrated energy, absorbing it to feed yourself. I just assumed that you would, but I'm even happier that you managed to let yourself have pleasure. It's healthy every now and then."

"I don't like the pomegranate. I don't want another one."

Ayelet cleared her throat. "Can I get in the pool with you?"

"No. I'd like to be alone."

"I don't think being alone is good for you right now, chérie. We've learned that much at least. Make some room for me, please."

"Fine." Boudi-Ca felt the urge to cry, but she blinked away the tears. She felt an odd connection to Ayelet again while in her presence, and with it came a disturbing sense of sisterhood that she'd never felt with her female teachers in Heaven. She really wanted to trust Ayelet. She watched as Ayelet shed her shirt, skirt, and hip frameworks until she was wearing only her under-bust corset around her hard, svelte body. Ayelet looked older and paler in the outdoor light of the courtyard than in the warm candlelight of her tapestried bedroom. Her long-braided hair looked greyer and still less well-kempt.

Horizontal wrinkles wrapped the base of Ayelet's neck and the undersides of her breasts. Her amber nipple piercings swayed as she lowered herself deep into the heated pool, hooves first. Boudi-Ca shrank to give Ayelet as much space as possible. Under the water, she felt a hoof slide and come to rest against her hip.

"I like when you look at me, Boudi-Ca," Ayelet murmured. "I hope you don't find me too old and repulsive."

"Do all Jinni have hooves? Does Golda? I didn't notice."

"No. Golda is an old soul, but she's still young in her Jinni life. Jinni only get hooves when we get old. It's a change that we go through. Someday, many centuries from now when you're older and wiser like I am, you'll get them too. Or maybe not. I'm not sure in your case."

"Does it hurt?"

"Yes, but there are medicines. My own transformation was difficult because I had to re-balance myself as a blade mistress and re-learn my fighting stances. The adjustments took me many years and specially designed footwear, but I think I'm even better now for the effort than I ever was. I'm not so quick with mobility like you can be."

"Mistress Ayelet, just so I know—could I ever still change my mind? Could I ever go home now that I've been through that ritual?"

Ayelet looked down into the water. "The Mimǫic Hierarchy has a history of capturing Jinni to imprison them, torture them, and who knows what else. You likely could go, but I wouldn't recommend it. I know that Allyssia doesn't want you to go home. She wanted you in Her city for a reason."

"Why?"

"Maybe because she needs you, chérie. She needs all of us. The Lady is weak, and her brothers Tuhan and Hades would like nothing more than to control her. They don't like they she dares to defy the great patriarchies and create a new society, a beautiful place that is neither dark nor light. I don't believe we've spoken much of the politics between the divines. We can do it another time."

"This place is horribly sinful, but I have to admit that it's beautiful."

"You're a perfect symbol of the Lady's New Order, fledgling. We embrace everyone, including Golda and you. The only law is Love above all. Nothing is more precious than Love, not even gold coins." Ayelet lowered herself deeper into the pool until the water lapped against her chin. "I've raised five fledglings, and you might be my favorite already, Boudi-Ca."

"I doubt if that's true, but it's nice of you to say so."

"Don't say such things. Don't deny yourself happiness, mimǫ. Don't deny yourself pride. Perhaps your masters in Heaven wouldn't let you be who you are, but here you can be everything you want to be. Here you can find others who truly love you. I'd be sad if you wanted to go back. Just relax and enjoy life without shame. In fact, that reminds me. You had a rucksack of some sort when you fell. I've been told you can have it back."

Boudi-Ca frowned. "I wonder why Golda didn't mention it. I thought she left my mimǫ things behind because they were too wet and heavy."

"Golda is kinder than she's willing to admit. She craves respect, and part of achieving that is by showing toughness. Among the Jinni, charity is a suspicious sentiment."

"It was nice of her to save my bag for me."

"Indeed. Your school books were ruined by your fall into the Sea of Desire, but a few silver pens and glass bottles might be serviceable. Perhaps they'll comfort you in your new life as souvenirs of your old one."

"I just remembered what I wanted a little while ago, Mistress Ayelet. I wanted some paper. I want to write a diary like I wrote in Heaven."

Ayelet lifted her hand from the water and flicked her wrist. A magical yellow bird, perfect and alive, sprang into being on her dripping fingertips. The bird flitted away over the rooftops of the courtyard.

"I sent a message to Gallinah. You'll have something by tonight."

"Will I be able to do magic like that?"

Ayelet smiled and winked. "Absolutely. I just now spoke with Mistress Ivanka about setting up regular lessons. She'll teach you your personal messenger bird first. That way I can communicate quickly with you when I need to. After that, you'll learn a few spells common to most Jinni, like the desirous and hateful kin-hexes."

"Is that witchcraft?"

"No. It's better. As soon as possible also, I'll teach you to feed. I think Yenta would be perfect for you to experiment with. She's easy. You'll see what I mean."

Boudi-Ca felt her cheeks heat. "I'm going to kiss a girl?"

"Yenta is intrigued by you, chérie. She even dared to tell me so. Yes, I think you'll feed from her. You can even sleep with her if you want to. Normally that wouldn't be preferable, but I can sense the loneliness in you."

"I like sleeping by myself."

"Just so you know, you won't sleep again with me unless we're traveling in the dream-world. Some mistresses in this city plumb the watery depths with their fledglings. I keep a strict ship. It's best for you to be independent. If you ever feel the need to discuss sensual feelings towards me, please say so. Don't be ashamed."

"I don't think you need to worry. I mean, it's nothing personal. You're pretty enough and everything."

"You'll still be visiting my bedroom, however. Many lessons for a young Jinn are best learned when they are demonstrated, and you need a lot of lessons."

"Right." Boudi-Ca felt her heart pound suddenly in her chest. Mistress Ayelet was already setting forth an unspeakable plan to bury her neck deep in sin, and her inner mimọ girl was already registering an inner protest. She was still a Conclave agent. She was going to stay that way if she had anything to say about it. She looked down at her sinuous reflection in the warm roiling water. Ayelet's voice interrupted her thoughts.

"Boudi-Ca, remember that your mind is still a prisoner of your Mimọic conditioning. You have to let go of the very concept of sin just to let yourself live. There is desire. There is reaching for that desire. There is fulfillment. Such is the way of our Lady. She will help. She is a great transformer, just like her brothers. You'll see. You'll need to live this life. It won't be enough to simply stop denying it."

"Right."

Ayelet smiled widely. "The moon-silver is striking in your pale umber eyes, chérie. Look at yourself in a mirror when you have the chance. The Fates have truly blessed you in this world with youth and beauty."

Boudi-Ca sank deeper in pool until the heated water lapped at her mouth. She closed her eyes. The smell of the scourging sulfur was intermittently acrid in her nostrils—an olfactory counterpoint to the drafts of cool mountain air that swirled into the Villa courtyard over the rooftops, stirring dry fall leaves along the walkways under the deep eaves. The eaves reminded her of the courtyard at the Crystal College.

It was strange to think that her whole situation was Tajee's fault. If Tajee hadn't stolen the Conclave flyers and made the deal with Professor Brown, she'd still be a chaste and ordinary mimọ. Tajee added two more reasons why she had to get back to Heaven—firstly so she could prove to him that her first Conclave mission had been a success and he'd lost his crude bet against her, and secondly so she could walk right into Brown's history class and smack him.

Chapter 14:

Boudi-Ca shut her bedroom door and paced the stone walkway around the outside of Ayelet's Villa. The glass windows of the training hall glowed like a yellow beacon across the evening-darkened rear lawn. She was excited. Ayelet had promised something special that night—a sparring match with another fledgling for the first time.

Winter in the Lady's domain was already waning. The moon on the last day of February shone over Allyssia's city like a mother-of-pearl button on a black bodice, bestowing a gentle nacreous glow upon the snow-dusted cypresses. A sweet scent of wood smoke rose from Anders's shed. The gardener was burning pine that night, not oak.

Boudi-Ca sniffed the cold air. In the night, when everything in her Jinni life was beautiful and the moon and stars were shining, and the cold air smelled like smoke, she almost wanted to remain a Jinn and never return to Heaven. Every day and every night in Allyssia's Redoubt was a little bit different. Every plant, bird, cloud, frog, and raindrop seemed to breathe with a mysterious inner magic. Every moon was different too, and she'd lived in the city for four of them.

Under Ayelet's tutelage, she'd learned much about life as a Jinn. She'd reluctantly learned the rudiments of magic from the black witch, Mistress

Ivanka—how to throw a desirous kin-hex to pull something to her, how to cast a glowing tenebris lux over her head, and how to summon and send her own magical messenger bird.

She'd learned the basics of sword-fighting styles from Ayelet—the Long Foot stance, the Strong Blade stance, and the difficult Serpent Stance, among others. According to tradition, Jinn fledglings were required to master at least one art form, and only then could they graduate to become a fully-fledged mistress. Ayelet's art was sword fighting, and Ayelet was one of the best in all of the Underworld.

Boudi-Ca quickened her pace towards the training hall. She was late, and Ayelet didn't like to be kept waiting. For the most part, she liked learning from Ayelet. Ayelet scolded her occasionally, but never made her do detention or say thousands of prayers, and never gave her bad marks that made her feel like a failure. Ayelet encouraged her to be assertive and independent instead of meek and obedient. Ayelet stoked her Jinni desires and urged her to explore new things.

It was at that point, when Ayelet tried to push her deeper into sin, that her inner resistance would protest. Ayelet was always convincing her to go further, and the persistence of the Mistress almost always prevailed, much to the dismay of her mimo girl self. Through the long frigidity of the city's winter, she'd fought against Ayelet to retain the remaining shreds of her purity and chastity.

Her main success was that she hadn't yet been with any male. Despite Ayelet's mild prodding, she refused to be with any male whatsoever, especially huge Bola. She'd sinned horribly with Yenta every night—giving the Ahyehass pleasure and draining love from the Greek girl's body in the Jinni way. At least she'd preserved her own personal virginity. No one, as of yet, had taken her.

Her restraint had been difficult, but she was proud of it. Her Jinni Hunger badgered her constantly to ignore her inner Mimoic resistance. Her Jinni Hunger was a beast that she could resist, if not tame, until she could find a way to escape. She hadn't given up, even after four months, on the idea of an escape when the weather turned warmer.

She'd snuck on several occasions down to the overlook on the steep hill road. She'd gazed for hours beyond the old railing over the stone city wall. Unfortunately, the mountain outside the city had turned forbidding shortly after her ritual, and had remained blanketed with snow and ice. Worse yet, she'd learned that a great natural chasm separated the Lady's city from Meristyian, with steep cliffs and precipices that formed a natural defense.

The only realistic way of escape was through the city front gates, which offered a crossing bridge into Meristyian. That possibility seemed better than flashing over the perimeter wall, trying to navigate the wild mountainside and chasm, risking a fall or getting lost. Ayelet had promised that if she did well with her blades training, she could go on horse riding trips into Meristyian in the spring. According to Ayelet, she needed to be able to defend herself first. Meristyian was sometimes traveled by vampires, slave hunters, and other dangerous things that hunted Mimos as prey.

She needed to excel in her first real sparring match that night, and thereby earn a horse and permission to leave the city. She needed to win, and win convincingly. Ayelet's training hall was a detached building on the lawn behind her Villa, medieval in style like a shrine to armed combat. Boudi-Ca hurried down the last stretch of snowy walkway and pushed through the massive wooden doors. Ayelet was waiting in the warm torchlit interior with arms akimbo.

"You're late again, fledgling."

"Sorry, Mistress."

"I've invited a guest to spar with you tonight, as promised. His name is Zissu. He belongs to Mistress Freyah. He should be around your level."

Boudi-Ca eyed the tall male that approached her. Zissu wore a grey tunic and a silver coil collar at his throat. He challenged her with his eyes instead of looking down at the floor as was proper for a human Ahyehass in the Lady's city. Boudi-Ca frowned. "But he's just an Ahyehass, Mistress. I thought I was going to fight another fledgling."

"You've made amazing progress, Boudi-Ca, but your techniques are limited, and your exceptional speed can only make up for so much. I changed my mind about letting you fight another fledgling. Jade Turtle would defeat you easily."

"She can't flash like I can."

"Yes, but Turtle is strong as an ox, and she's trained in blades for many years under Golden Gorila. I've watched Zissu in the past, and I'm familiar with his abilities. This little skirmish will help me see where you stand at this point in your training without discouraging you too much. Let's waste no more time. Begin."

"Wait. I need to get a blade."

"You shouldn't have arrived late. Attack her, Zissu. Now."

Zissu dropped his cloak to the floor, revealing a pair of practice swords resting in a wide leather belt above a patterned kilt that was his only clothing. He drew the twin blades and moved to cut off the angle to the far wall and the weapon racks. Boudi-Ca felt a burn of fury. She'd looked forward to sparring with another fledgling. A victory would have gone far in proving to Ayelet that she was ready for adventures in the wilderness. She'd worked hard all winter, and Ayelet's lack of faith in her made her angry.

She feinted towards the weapon racks. Zissu swung zealously, overextending. She slid under his swing, gripped the human's wrist and closed against him, blocking him to her right and rendering his swords useless. She dodged left, keeping him locked, but he anticipated the move, swinging away in a twirl in the opposite direction.

Boudi-Ca dropped to her back on the floor mat as the blunt edges whipped past her head. She rolled quickly away towards Ayelet, who was watching closely. The Ahyehass turned his blades to prepare another strike. She'd thrown Zissu off balance for a moment, but he'd recovered quickly.

He waited for her to rise before approaching again. He seemed more confident. He was actually smiling at her just like Tajee used to smile when he said she was just a girl. She quickly undid her sash. Zissu attacked again with a predictable sideways slash. She swung her sash and caught the blade in the heavy cloth. With a wrench she unbalanced Zissu and sprinted past him.

"Well done, fledgling!"

Boudi-Ca gasped. Zissu caught her ankle with a trip. She felt flat on her face and rolled to the side just as Zissu's practice sword thudded to the mat. She skipped to her feet and threw herself out of another broad arc of the blade. The Ahyehass really wanted to beat her. He was attacking like a madman. She focused and flashed. Time stopped in the training hall. Ayelet and the Ahyehass froze in place. The little ribbon uncoiled through the dark grey space.

Boudi-Ca tiptoed quickly along the ribbon to the weapon rack. She emerged from her flash, seized a blunt scimitar, and whirled to face the startled Ahyehass, who approached her again with his eyes wide. Boudi-Ca pressed forward. She thrust, spun, and slashed with as much force as she could muster with the sword, but the Ahyehass easily parried and redoubled his efforts on the offensive. She fought her way to the nearest pillar and danced around it. If the Ahyehass followed her, she thought, she could flash to his flank. Zissu stopped, however. The boy looked more confident, as if he thought her move to the pillar was a retreat and not a tactic.

Boudi-Ca slipped around the pillar on the attack, surging forward and whipping her scimitar down at the male's head in an overhead smash that he barely parried off his guard. He quickly swung sidearm with his second blade. Boudi-Ca dodged backwards away from the slash that grazed her abdomen. Ayelet clapped.

"Good counter, Zissu. A point."

Boudi-Ca growled. The Ahyehass attacked her again while she was off-balance. She parried, and then counterattacked. Zissu slipped her attack, caught her blade between his pair, and twisted triumphantly. Boudi-Ca felt her sword wrench from her fingers. She grabbed at air and circled behind the pillar, weaponless again. Zissu moved warily, feinting to the left, then the right. Finally he dove for her, and she dove to the other side of the pillar. She sprinted for her fallen sword.

Zissu's lunge was only another trick and a twirl. She dropped backwards to the floor again, and Zissu's sword flashed a hair's breadth from her face. The Ahyehass was almost as fast as she was. This time she didn't roll away from under him. Zissu's wild attack had thrown him off balance. Boudi-Ca summoned energy and threw a desirous kin-hex at the boy's feet. Her desire flowed through her, out of her hands and across the short space. The spell caught the Ahyehass under the knee. His feet jerked forward, just enough to tip him backwards onto the mat.

She leapt onto the Ahyehass and grabbed his sword arm. He tried to pull away, but her Jinni strength was more than a match for his thick biceps. He underestimated her grip and succeeded only in yanking her fully on top of him. She grabbed his throat and pinned him. Zissu dropped his sword and lay limply underneath her, admitting defeat. Boudi-Ca felt a faint heat of embarrassment in her cheeks. Zissu's phallus was swelling under her leg.

"I yield," the boy said with a proper tone of deference.

Boudi-Ca released the male, who groaned softly and massaged his throat. She pushed herself up and went to retrieve her sash. She fanned her corset free chest and breathed to diffuse the last warmth of her anger. Ayelet stood looking at her with arms crossed, ready to pass judgment.

"You carry yourself as if you won the combat, fledgling, yet you were not the better fighter."

"I won, didn't I? So I must have been the better fighter."

"You were connected emotionally to the outcome of the fight, not the fight itself. Your mind was here, but your heart was in turmoil. In my judgment, your attachments made you unbalanced, so naturally you ended up falling on the floor. A warrior must be fully in the present moment. You were lucky to win."

"I did what I needed to do and used every skill I had. A good fighter creates her own luck. You told me that."

Ayelet chuckled. "So I did. I just want you to succeed, Boudi-Ca, so I have to pick at your weaknesses. Your success is my success, and I insist on succeeding. You can be ten times better than Golda if you realize your full potential."

"What does Golda have to do with my training? And why do you always talk like she's a failure?"

"Golda has no trouble with keeping her heart in the moment. She has a lot of trouble with her heart being scarred and broken. I haven't said that my former fledgling was a failure. I've only said that she disappoints me. I had hoped for more."

"Well, then that's your problem, isn't it? I'm doing the best I can. I'm sure Golda does the best she can too."

Ayelet stared at her with a look of shock. The wrinkles deepened around Ayelet's wise silver-hazel eyes. "You're absolutely right, fledgling, except our best is not a fixed quantity. In a few moons, I'll expect your best will be better if you put forward the effort to listen to me and meditate on your lessons. It's your choice. Is something bothering you?"

"No."

"Let's quit early tonight. You're irritable because you haven't fed. Go to your bath, and then come up to my bedchamber. I took both my housemaid and my dressing-girl for myself just a few hours ago. I want you to have Bola. I'll prepare you. I'll give you a poppy crush to relax you. He's handsome and gentle. You'll love it."

"No. Absolutely not, Mistress."

"Bola will give you pleasure, fledgling. You aren't feeding well from Yenta. That isn't your fault. Taking love from women is difficult due to their natural yin polarity. We are made to take, not give. You need some variety in your Jinni diet. You really don't like Bola?"

"No."

Ayelet arched her eyebrow. "Your skills in the bedchamber should be as diverse as your skills with a blade. Come upstairs in half an hour."

"I wanted to write in my diary tonight."

"I thought you wrote already. Isn't that why you were late?"

"I was thinking about what I wanted to write, and that took more time and effort than anyone would ever imagine. Then I sort of fell asleep."

"Go back to your bedchamber. I'll send you a bird when I'm ready for the evening feeding. Feeding is a top priority for a young Jinn." Ayelet smiled wryly. "I'll speak with Zissu now. He deserves a critique since he was trying so hard to impress me."

"Fine, but I'm not having Bola." Boudi-Ca stalked from the training hall with her sash in hand. She could feel Zissu ogling her ass with his stupid phallus still half-swollen under his kilt. She paced back down the walkway to her bedchamber. The snowflakes were falling in thick flurries over the gardens outside. Once again, Ayelet was trying to push her further into sin and onto a cock, despoiling her on a whole new level. Boudi-Ca felt a warmth of anger, but also pride that she'd held fast. It wasn't like Ayelet could force her to take a male.

The fire that she'd built earlier in her bedchamber still smoldered. The warmth felt good on her cold sweaty skin. She added a few more logs from the stack. She shed her training robe, tossed it on the hearth, and sat down at her writing desk. Her room was warm enough for nudity. She picked up one of the two silver quill pens that she'd salvaged from her old college rucksack.

Boudi-Ca held the pen near the ink bottle, but she didn't dip it. She wanted to write about her pride in her resistance against Ayelet, but she didn't want to get in trouble. She had many private thoughts that she didn't write for fear that Ayelet or Yenta would snoop and read them. She hadn't written a word about the Conclave or the lies in her letters to Lady Allyssia, of course. She seemed to be accepted by the New Order Jinn society after four months, but her Conclave mission had still caused the death of Golda's friend.

Boudi-Ca frowned and nibbled on the end of the pen, trying to decide what else to write. To her surprise, the pen fell apart. One half of the thin silver cylinder remained trapped between her lips, and the other stayed between her fingers. She removed the piece from her mouth and examined them both. A tiny rolled piece of paper poked from one half of the pen. She pulled it out and unfurled it on the desk with her fingertips. She bent to read the tiny writing in the firelight.

This pen is the property of the Conclave of Deviant Operations or one of its employees. Any unauthorized mimo found in possession of this pen will be subject to punishment in accordance with the Hierarchical Code section

402 governing the correct use of writing implements, article 32,926-F. If you have found this pen, return it immediately to the nearest Conclave agency.

Boudi-Ca stared at the small rectangle of paper and read the message over and over again while memories of Heaven flitted through her head. The Conclave's presence in her Jinn bedroom strangely unnerved her. Finally, she heard a scratching sound at the little bird slit above her shuttered window. Ayelet's magical yellow messenger bird swooped and landed on her shoulder.

It's time.

Boudi-Ca waved her hand and conjured her return bird.

"I'm coming." She said the message aloud. She hadn't learned Ayelet's trick of sending a bird silently. She pictured Ayelet, and the bird flitted from her fingers and out of the bird slit. According to Mistress Ivanka, the personal bird of every Jinn was a different species and size. Her own blue finch was the smallest of any that she'd seen.

Boudi-Ca rose from her desk, slipped her diary and the pen pieces into the desk drawer, and threw on a sack dress with no panties or slip. She made her way around the Villa and through the rear door to the kitchen, then up the back stairs to the second level. Ayelet's bedchamber door was open. The circular tapestried room was warm and candlelit.

Boudi-Ca sighed with relief. Apparently, she'd have no further confrontation with Ayelet over Bola. The huge black man lay on his back on Ayelet's bed. Ayelet straddled him with her legs wide and her hooves pressed along the sides of his massive black thighs. The Mistress rode slowly. Her buttocks flexed as she worked to suck the wellspring of the man's love into herself.

Yenta was waiting in the nude as usual, relaxing in a nearby armchair. The girl smiled coquettishly. Boudi-Ca felt her Hunger quiver. It was a quiver both physical and psychic. Her pangs of Jinn Hunger weren't just in her sex or in her stomach. They were full-body feelings of need. She embraced Yenta with a kiss. She rubbed against the house-girl. She knew the body of the Ahyehass well. She knew what to do to make Yenta's thick sex wetter and surrender. It wasn't hard. Yenta, as Ayelet had intimated, was easy.

Boudi-Ca guided Yenta over to the armchair and bore her back, asserting her control, nipping and licking with quick and unpredictable kisses. She pressed skin against skin and let her hair fall across Yenta's face so the house-girl could smell her scent. She looked deeply, purposefully, and desiring into Yenta's eyes, all as Ayelet had taught her.

She insinuated her hand under Yenta and found the girl's vulva with her fingers. She moved her head up to Yenta's neck and kissed the underside of the girl's chin. She nuzzled, licked, and nipped at the tender stretches under Yenta's chin and jaw. The Ahyehass smelled faintly of a perfume that she'd applied earlier that day.

Boudi-Ca brought her body to bear on top. The Greek Ahyehass was a little bigger than she was, but she'd learned how to compensate—to lever her own body in ways to make her seem more in control. The Ahyehass responded to the dominance with a soft moan.

Boudi-Ca pressed the advantage, pushing into Yenta's well-used pink with two insistent fingers. She began a steady practiced rhythm. She could feel the Ahyehass straining inside, attempting to release and please her. She could also feel the emptiness in Yenta as Mistress Ayelet had intimated in the training hall—that lack of love energy inside a recently-taken human soul.

Boudi-Ca slid up further, sealed her mouth over Yenta's lips and began her suction anyway, drawing with her Jinn Hunger and tugging on the remnants of the girl's love. Yenta moaned into her mouth. Boudi-Ca worked harder with her fingers—deeper and quicker. She worked for long minutes to get Yenta's love energy to break open and flow.

Still Yenta wouldn't release. Slaps suddenly sounded, and Yenta flinched. Boudi-Ca looked over her shoulder. Ayelet had left the bed to join the fray. The Mistress was holding Yenta's foot. She snapped it with a little cane. Every snap sent a miniscule shiver through the pretty housemaid.

Boudi-Ca felt her Hunger jump, and with it her Jinn sensitivity. She could feel Yenta. She could feel the slaps loosening Yenta's hold on her composure. Still Yenta wouldn't release. Ayelet knelt close.

"A powerful Jinn would take it from her anyway, fledgling, but you don't yet possess the strength. I'll help you. Yenta, get down here on the floor. Boudi-Ca needs to feed."

"But Mistress, you took me yourself earlier, and you took everything. I'm empty, obviously!"

"I've never taught you the true meaning," Ayelet countered. "But I've taught you not to argue with me. I think you need to be punished. Get on your back on the carpet in front of Boudi-Ca. Fledgling, take this cane. Hold it like so."

"Then what?" Boudi-Ca took the cane hesitantly from Ayelet. It was a slim, flexible wand, two or three feet in length. She looked down at Yenta, who lay mutely and waited. Sparks of lust and veiled indignation were evident on Yenta's face. Boudi-Ca felt the pride inside her ignite. The sin rushed to her head and colored her thinking in shades of red.

She recognized that familiar feeling from Ayelet's many lessons. Ayelet had tested her defenses that evening, only to retreat and attack her from a different wicked angle. Once again, Ayelet was using a silent compromise as a way to push her deeper into Jinn sin. Ayelet produced a length of woven cord from a nearby drawer. The elder Jinn pushed Yenta on her side and lashed together her limp wrists. Ayelet spoke as she worked.

"Only when a Jinn wraps a human soul fully in her hands can a special and deep connection form. Bondage is at the heart of traditional dominance. I'm going to give you a lesson, fledgling. Are you ready?"

"Yes, Mistress."

"Bondage can involve physical restraints, but these are just tools that happen to work with Yenta. The best forms of bondage are invisible conditionings of desire that form in the mind. If these conditionings and controls are imposed on an Ahyehass, they can create strong emotional bonds that will persist long after the ropes and cords are put away."

Chapter 15:

Tajee lay nude on Golda's bed, covered to his waist by a warm wool blanket. He nestled his head between two silk-cased pillows and stared at the faint bands of light and dark on the bed canopy. He was alone, as usual, waiting for the Mistress. He was bored, although Mistress Golda had only been gone for a few hours.

Time passed quickly in Meristyian. In Heaven, the clocks had measured a metronymic life planned by the arch-Mimos. In Mistress Golda's bedchamber, he could only tell time by the presence and non-presence of the Mistress and the sunlight outside the bath window at the end of her upstairs hallway.

In Heaven, the light had been everywhere. In Golda's bedchamber, darkness ruled, except for the candles burning on the side table, shedding a warm light that reflected a thousand times in the manifold bangles that littered her mirrored vanity. In Golda's bedchamber, in the measureless time of worshiping every inch of her sensuous body again and again, he'd become hers. She'd made him hers just as she'd promised, in ways that he'd never imagined when she'd first offered him a life of sin.

When she spoke to him, his body answered. He couldn't help himself, yet a part of him continued to resist. When Golda left, that resistance would be relieved to be free, if only for a few hours, to think virtuous thoughts of rebellion and plan an imminent escape from evil. Slowly, his lust-filled body would long for Golda's return. When Golda came home, he would hear her boots on the stair, and his body would surge with a curious happiness that he could neither suppress nor deny.

Sometimes when Golda returned, she smelled as she'd left—of perfume, bath salts, or the sweet-smelling blue nectar that she often consumed. Other times Golda smelled of foreign things—of horses, smoke, cinnamon, grasses and leaves, or of perfume that wasn't hers. Sometimes Golda would pass by the bedroom door and go to the bath. He would go back to the bed then, for he knew that he'd have to wait for another hour while the Mistress bathed with Phylicia.

On those occasions, he would often hear Phylicia's moans from beyond the bath door. He hadn't asked Golda what she did with Phylicia or how the Jinn had sex with another girl. He would think of Boudi-Ca then, and his heart would darken with anger.

Golda always knew when he was in an angry mood. Her voice would soften, and she'd speak to him sweetly with reassuring words. She would press against him in her bed, and the part inside him that still resisted her would melt. The Mistress would envelop him in her incredible warmth. She would slide against him with her breasts and kiss him with her silken purple-stained lips.

She would pull him down, and he would press his nose and tongue into that lower manifestation of her glorious mane. He would lap at her pumpum and savor her taste. Golda made him venerate her there in infinite ways—with his tongue, his fingers, his phallus, and even his feet. As much time as he had spent between Golda's strong legs, her pumpum had become synonymous with her power and his weakness.

Despite Golda's power, however, his inner resistance to her would inevitably return. He welcomed that resistance when it came, and he kept it in a secret place where he kept all of his innermost thoughts. His resistance told him Golda was evil. His resistance told him that despite her honeyed words, Golda wanted nothing more from him than to consume his lust. For that, as he'd learned from Trace, was what Jinni did with humans and Mimos who they seduced into serving them.

Due to his near-constant arousal in the presence of Golda, he'd developed insomnia. He would often lie awake and watch the Mistress sleep through the night until the candles died. In the morning, if he'd managed to sleep, the strike of a match would stir him. He would rise to brush Golda's hair and lace her corset when she chose to wear one. He would tie her boots, and he would catch up on his sleep, or he would help Trace with chores around Golda's cozy home while Golda supervised.

The Mistress sometimes took him down the hall to bathe. On those occasions he'd see Phylicia, who worked the water pump and prepared Golda's towels, soaps, and herbs. Sometimes in the bath, if Golda was in a good mood, the Mistress would seat herself at the low vanity and allow him to rub her shoulders or put herbal unguent on cuts and scratches that mysteriously appeared on her forearms.

Then she would turn the tables and brush his hair, which had gone long and uncut over the winter months. She'd clean his ears and pluck his eyebrows. At first he'd found it embarrassing, but Golda had insisted. His new desire-world body had queerly grown hairier than his heavenly one. Despite the pain that Golda gave him with her little tweezers, he didn't mind the grooming.

Golda would look at him in the mirror as she worked on him. Her silvery blue eyes would sparkle. It was those times, when Golda was most happy and loving towards him, that he would dare to mention Boudi-Ca and Golda's promise to let him see her.

Golda would always make one excuse. Boudi-Ca wasn't ready. There was nothing she could do, but soon. It was in those moments, when he loved Golda most, that he most hated her. He'd tried to sneak out of the house a number of times during the winter when Golda was out, but the complicated locks on the front door seemed to need a key, even from the inside.

Trace was almost always working in the stable or the stable access room, and neither the cellar windows nor the window in the bath were available avenues of secret egress. The winter snows and ice over the city had added an extra barrier to an exploratory exit since he owned no shoes.

He could still see Boudi-Ca in his mind's eye—her smiling face, her virtuous umber eyes, her beautiful dive-suit, and her white headband. It was like a nightmare. The Jinni had surely made Boudi-Ca into a whore like Phylicia. He imagined all sorts of horrible things happening. He wondered if Boudi-Ca made animal noises like Phylicia. It was enough to make him want to throw up.

He'd made one bit of progress. He'd thoroughly searched every nook and cranny of Golda's bedroom and bathroom. In the bottom of a drawer he'd discovered a number of geographical maps depicting regions of the Underworld. He'd studied the maps carefully while Golda was away. One of maps, the most worn and dog-eared one, clearly indicated Mount Purgatory and the Trivium that Golda had spoken of.

He was convinced that he could get to the stairway to Heaven. He'd located a compass too, and a Sharp hunting knife that Golda apparently never used. He just had to find Boudi-Ca and strategize a way for them to escape. Tajee stirred. A Sharp rap on the bedroom door disturbed the quietude of Golda's bedchamber.

"Tajee?" Trace called from the hall. "Come to the stable. Put on your coat."

"Coming," Tajee answered. He slid from the bed, drew his hair into a ponytail, and clipped it. He slipped into his linen drawstring pants and fetched his coat where it was hanging behind the bedroom door. He wondered what Trace was going to teach him that day. He enjoyed his Ahyehass lessons, but the timing was strange. Trace gave him lessons every day, but always in the afternoon and rarely while Golda was away.

Tajee padded out of Golda's bedroom into the upstairs hall. The hall was empty. Golda said that she was selling Trace at the upcoming Spring Festival, whereupon he himself would become the new houseboy. The Jinn trusted him more and more, and becoming her houseboy would give him better opportunities to look for Boudi. He assumed that he'd have full access to the house keys as well as the stable exit, just like Trace.

He descended the stairs to the first-floor foyer and peeked into the storage room. The stable access door was cracked open, emitting a cold draft. He passed the storage room workbench and Trace's small bed and clothes trunk, then on through the access door and down the steps into the spacious underground room. Harsh sunlight streamed through the half-open double stable doors, which gave onto a sloping alley that led up to the street. Tajee clenched his toes. The floor was ice cold under his bare feet. Trace was busy brushing the mane of Golda's chestnut mare.

"Are you going to work, or not?" Trace indicated a wire brush on a hook. "Brush her hindquarters. Long, easy strokes. She won't kick, but it's good practice to stay away from her legs. While you're working, watch what I do with her mane, then we'll clean some more leather like we did yesterday. You need more practice with that."

"How hard are horses to ride?"

"They're easy if they're trained," Trace answered. "This mare here has some spirit, but she's real gentle once when she's saddled up."

"Could I learn how to ride a horse, do you think?"

"What for? Ahyehasi walk or drive a carriage if our mistress wishes it. Horses are for nobility. That's them, not us, or at least not me. You're a damned handsome mimọ, so who knows. You could ask Golda if she'd let you ride her horse."

"I guess." Tajee took the brush and began to work. The idea of riding a horse out of the city seemed unlikely, but he had to explore every possibility. He stroked the mare's hindquarters. The horse's tail flicked, and he glimpsed the long slit of the animal's sex. He tore his eyes away. Images of Golda's pumpum flickered into his mind's eye as seen from behind. Tajee felt his phallus harden slightly. Out of the corner of his eye he saw Trace smirking.

"So did Golda let you see her yet?"

"Who?"

"Your mimọ girl. The one you've been asking about. Phylicia says she heard you and Golda talking about it in the bath. Did Golda make you some kind of deal, and now she won't follow through with it? Phylicia wants to know the whole story."

Tajee frowned. "I tried to tell Phylicia my story when I first came here, but she didn't seem interested. She just wanted to talk about herself."

"Mate, that's what girls do."

"Boudi-Ca sort of does that too." Tajee ran the brush down the haunch of the horse. He'd never talked about Boudi-Ca with the older boy, who according to Golda was a liar and a thief. Trace stopped working and rubbed the stubble on his face. The Ahyehass wore a pensive look.

"So you say her name is Boudi?"

"Yes."

Trace sidled along the horse. He spoke in a conspiratorial tone. "I spoke with fledgling Herpessenia down at the workshops recently. Herpessenia was talking to Mistress Gallinah about a girl named Boudi."

"Really? What did they say about her?"

"I didn't hear everything, but they said who her mistress is—Ayelet. I happen to know where Ayelet lives. Maybe I could take you up there to visit if Golda won't."

Tajee fidgeted. He didn't like Trace having any involvement with his quest to find Boudi, but he'd be a fool not to accept help if Trace knew where to find her.

"Do you really think we could do it? The Mistress ordered me not to leave the bedroom unless you're giving me a lesson. I don't care anymore. I have to see Boudi, and Golda isn't going to let me."

Trace grinned. "You really like this girl, don't you? I don't blame you. They say fallen mimọ girls are sweet, innocent, and eager to please with a little motivation. I've never seen one, and I've lived here for a couple hundred years. Well, first we'll have to wait until Golda is gone for quite a while, preferably at night."

Tajee gritted his teeth. "Fine."

"Your mimọ friend isn't that far away up the east hill, but it's not that close, either. It's about half the distance to the Lady's palace, maybe a fifteen-minute fast walk."

"Why are you helping me? You don't even like me that much."

Trace snorted. "I'm doing this to spite Golda, of course. I'm glad Golda is dismissing me at the Spring Festival, but it's kind of insulting at the same time, mate. I still want something from you in exchange."

"What do you want? I don't have anything."

"You're really beautiful, mate. Herpessenia was talking about you too."

"What did she say?"

"She told Mistress Gallinah that you're the most beautiful boy in the whole city, and she wished she could get her hands on you. See, I mentioned to Herpessenia that Golda was letting me go at the Spring Festival next week, so I'm going to need a new mistress. She laughed at me and said it was no surprise. That's how we got on the topic. Well, I need to think about my future. It would help my reputation in the city if I could say I was with you."

"What do you mean?"

"You know. You've probably never done it before, right? If you like it, maybe I could do you too." Trace unbuttoned his pants and pulled out his phallus. Trace's phallus was semi-turgid and ample. Trace massaged it slowly in his fingers. Tajee felt his stomach clutch.

"No way."

"Come on."

"Hell no. I've already sinned enough with Golda. I don't want to do anything worse, and that's the worst of the worst."

Trace smirked. "Do you want to see your girlfriend, or not? I don't really care. It's your choice."

"What if Golda comes in and catches me?"

"Fledgling Herpessenia picked her up in Herpessenia's carriage. With the stable doors open, we'll hear it coming to the house." A faint rumble and clop of hooves sounded outside the house even as Trace spoke the words.

"I hear one coming now."

"That one has wooden wheels. It's probably Mistress Hatshepseh from across the road. Herpessenia's carriage is nicer since she's Allyssia's daughter. She has iron-studded wheels. You can hear the difference in the sounds the wheels make when they roll over the stones. So is it a deal, or not? If you've got something else to offer, I'm willing to listen."

Tajee took a deep breath. In truth, he was at the point where he didn't care how he got to Boudi. He was desperate to see her, and the bastard Trace knew it. "Fine. What do you want me to do?"

Trace stepped forward and offered his phallus. Tajee reached out and took it in his fingers. Trace's phallus was soft and silken. He began to stroke it lightly.

"Get down and put it in your mouth."

Tajee knelt. Trace's hand steadied his shoulder. The Ahyehass thrust with his phallus. Tajee took it into his mouth. Trace's phallus tasted salty. Trace's hand found the back of his head and began to thrust.

"Mmmh." Tajee sucked softly, trying to avoid biting the thing with his teeth. Trace's phallus twitched and stiffened further.

"Oh, yeah Tajee," Trace laughed. "Keep it up. With a little practice, you can be as good as Phylicia. So the stories are true. Mimos are really pushovers."

Tajee yanked his head back. "No. No more."

"Mate, come on. Don't leave me like this."

"Go to hell, Trace. Oh, I forgot. You're already in it." Tajee pushed Trace with all his strength. Trace staggered. The Ahyehass shoved him back. Tajee tottered. On his knees, he was at a disadvantage. The older boy was on top of him quickly, pinning him with his superior strength and weight. Trace grinned at him.

"I could fuck your pretty ass right now, Tajee."

"I'm not a damned girl."

"Aye, you are! Golda's turning you into her little bitch. Look at your long pretty hair and manicure. You smell girly too since you're always in Golda's bed."

"Get off of me!"

Trace let him go and stood up. "Damn, Tajee. You didn't have to do it, mate. I was just messing with you. I was going to help you anyway because you're a fellow Ahyehass."

"I'd be stupid if I believed you."

"You'd be thick not to. We Ahyehasi have a code. Never betray another

Ahyehass. Always help a fellow. I'll help you."

Tajee gritted his teeth. "You're not just trying to trick me again?"

"Nay. My word is good. I won't tell Golda if you don't. We just have to wait until the Mistress is gone for a long time at night. That's the problem. I don't know when that'll be. I'll have to come and get you from the bedroom, and we'll sneak out quiet-like."

"What will happen if Golda finds out I left the house?"

"Are you really that afraid of the Mistress? She's sad and lonely because she lost Mareinah, and you're her little pet. You sleep with her every night in her bed. No Ahyehass sleeps with his mistress like that. Damn it. I hear another carriage coming."

"Is it her?"

"The wheels are ironclad. Go back to the bedroom and pretend you're asleep or something. If Golda is gone on a night before she dismisses me, I'll come get you and take you to your girl. That's a promise from one Ahyehass to another."

"Fine." Tajee heard the sound of the metal-studded carriage wheels. They clinked on the uneven street stones, and they stopped in front of the house. He hurried up the stable stairs, pausing only to wipe his feet on the wool mat just inside the access door. He was up the stairs to the second level and back into the bedchamber by the time the front door of the house creaked open and thumped shut.

Boot steps sounded on the stairs and then the hall floorboards, but there were two pairs of boots, not one. The door opened, and Golda entered the bedroom. She approached the bed, carrying with her the scent of leather. Tajee yawned. He sat up in the bed mock-drowsy as if he'd been sleeping. Golda bent at the side table and lit a second candle. A shapely blonde Jinn stood behind her. Golda's silvery eyes shone with an extra-intense sparkle in the half-light.

"Hello, my wonderful Tajee. I want to introduce you to a friend of mine." Golda bent and kissed him on the lips. Tajee accepted the kiss, distracted by the guest. His heart was suddenly pounding with the prospects of Golda's intention. Golda frowned, and then she kissed him again. Her thick tongue probed into his mouth. Tajee felt his tongue tingle. Golda tasted nectared, which explained her elevated mood. When Golda stood up, however, she had a scowl on her face. "What have you been doing, Tajee?"

"Nothing. Just sleeping." Tajee kept his face a blank, trying to look innocent. Golda gazed down at him in amazement, and then looked over her shoulder at her friend.

"I think my boy just lied to me for the first time."

The blonde Jinn smiled wickedly. "Your sweet, innocent mimọ boy just lied? Delightful. We should have some fun with him. Misbehaving slaves are the most excitement one can find in this city."

Golda stalked from the bedchamber and stormed down the stairs to the foyer. Her voice boomed through the house. "Trace!"

Tajee pivoted and settled on the edge of the bed. He had a feeling Golda wasn't done speaking with him. She'd left him alone with the blonde Jinn, who appeared somewhat younger than Golda, with a doll-like oval face and an arrogant arch to her high, plucked white eyebrows. Her skin was ghostly pale, almost as white as her hair, and her dress was transparent. He could see almost everything through it. She winked down at him.

"Hello, Tajee. How have you been?" The Jinn sidled close and caressed his shoulder. Her voice was high-pitched and girly, and she smelled faintly like flowers.

"I'm sorry. Have we met?"

"You're such a beautiful boy. Yes, we've met. I was with Golda in Meristyian when she picked you up from that rake. I'm Herpessenia-Ca, Mistress Ivanka's fledgling. You might not remember me."

"Not quite."

"Well, you should. I'm a daughter of Allyssia herself."

"It's a pleasure to meet you then, Mistress."

"The pleasure is mine, mimọ, but you haven't been well-trained. You shouldn't look me straight in the eyes." Herpessenia took his chin in her fingers. Her lips descended in a kiss. Tajee raised his lips to receive it. Herpessenia's kiss was different than Golda's. Her mouth was oddly cool, not warm, and her tongue was slender and furtive instead of thick and insistent. Herpessenia pulled away and licked her lips. "I think know what Golda was talking about. Were you a bad boy this morning, Tajee?"

"Yes. I guess I was."

"Who were you bad with?"

"Trace. He put his cock in my mouth for a minute. That's all."

Herpessenia grinned. Her white teeth were strangely small, pointy, and straight. "I like a nice cock in my mouth too, Tajee. It's nothing to be ashamed of. Did you know that when my mother moved here to Meristyian during the Jinn schism and founded the New Order Jinni, there were hardly any cocks in this little city at all?"

"No. I haven't heard that."

"At first my mother forbade the presence of all males except for Master Priapus, Master Hermaphroditus, and Master Cupid. The Gypsy craftsmen worked like bees for over a century to build everything, but they were made to sleep in their camp outside the gates. Exceptions were quickly made because the mistresses complained that we needed more Ahyehasi, and many of us wanted quality cocks too. Gypsy men ended up in beds. Some unmarried Gypsy males were allowed to stay amongst us, and today there are even male Ahyehasi in the Lady's palace. My mother makes them dress in skirts as a compromise with her original rules. Would you wear a skirt, Tajee, if Mistress Golda asked you?"

"I suppose I'd do whatever she wanted."

Herpessenia's eyes were hooded. "That's the right answer, but I'm disappointed. I was hoping you had more spirit." She reached down and pinched his cheek with a bored look. "At least you like a cock in your mouth. I suppose that's something."

Tajee felt anger spark in his chest. "I didn't say I liked having a cock in my mouth. I just said Trace put it there."

Herpessenia's lips curled again into a smile. "Oh, now that's a bit better. Perhaps you just redeemed yourself. Would you like some advice?"

"Sure."

"An Ahyehass who always does as he's told is as boring as a frog on a log. I'm going to go now and see what my lover is up to. I've been trying to convince Golda to let me play with you, but she's being stubborn. Hopefully I'll be back for some fun. If not, it was lovely."

"Wait."

Herpessenia blinked. "Wait? Did you say wait? Tajee, your impertinence is incredible. You need some serious behavior modifications."

"Did you just say Golda is your lover? You have sex together?"

"Oh. I see. I can feel your envy, mimọ boy. It's delicious, but it's weak—very weak. Work on that and get back to me after I've fucked and humiliated your Mistress some more."

Tajee clenched his fists on the edge of the bed. "Fine. I'll do that."

"Actually, you should work on your anger instead. It has much more potential. By the way, you've got bits of stable straw all over your pants, Ahyehass. Poor show. Clean yourself up quickly before your mistress gets back." Herpessenia turned on her heel and strode into the hallway. Tajee rose from the bed, hurried to the bath, found an old hairbrush, and brushed his pants. He felt hot from head to toe from Herpessenia's scolding.

He could faintly hear Golda's raised voice through the bath floorboards. Trace's answers were inaudible. Tajee licked his lips. He couldn't taste Trace's phallus in his mouth, but he wasn't surprised the Jinni had detected it. He hoped that he wasn't in trouble with Mistress Golda. He prayed that Trace wouldn't reveal his promise to help him see Boudi. Somehow he felt like he could trust Trace to keep a secret.

Chapter 16:

Lady Allyssia's palace was a magnificent marble edifice—a multi-winged panoply of arches, windows, columns, parapets and cornices. Ravens fluttered and cooed in window openings and out-of-the-way corners. Five crystal bowers of various sizes crowned the palace. The tallest two bowers towered like giant fingers to touch the sky.

Boudi-Ca sat next to Ayelet on the top palace step, which offered an elevated view of the crowded palace plaza. Snowflakes grazed her cheek and fell on the sleeves of her coat. The full moon intermittently glowed through threatening clouds that night. A light breeze blew. A purple stripe in the sky marked the last vestiges of sunset over distant Meristyian—a fading line broken by the twin spires of the city gatehouse. A slow drum throbbed with a rhythm inside Allyssia's palace. Boudi-Ca could feel the drumbeat in the stone under her buttocks.

It had been four days since Ayelet had taught her to use the discipline cane on Yenta. Under Ayelet's supervision, she'd caned Yenta's feet, thighs, and breasts, all while the mistress had kept the Ahyehass tied up and stimulated. When she'd finally drunk Yenta's lust, the girl's lips had been quivering with the desperate effort of her orgasm. Yenta's lust had tasted different than normal—thin and bitter.

Boudi-Ca wrapped her arms around herself to ward off the evening chill. After the instructional episode, Ayelet had put away the cane as if nothing special had happened. Ayelet had complimented her on how well she'd done with her sparring, suggested a few improvements on her blade's technique, kissed her cheek, and told her to go to bed. She hadn't slept. She'd stayed awake half the night, praying and pleading forgiveness from her inner mimọ self. The sin that she'd felt from punishing Yenta had been extra-intense because she'd secretly loved it. Her inner mimọ girl had insisted that she deprive herself completely of feeding to fight the sin.

She hadn't fed her Hunger in four days. She'd only pretended, taking Yenta to the privacy of her bedchamber, and then not taking her. At first her inner mimọ had been happy, but then it had grown faint. It was her Hunger's turn to complain. She'd doggedly resisted her Hunger, trying to hold onto the last empty shreds of her Mimọic chastity. What would happen if she stopped feeding sexually? Ayelet had painted a dire picture.

It was the first week of March in the Lady's domain, and Ayelet had taken her to the opening evening of the Spring Festival. The wide plaza in front of Allyssia's grand palace bustled with activity. Torches and lamps shed warm light through the busy chaotic scene. The Gypsies had set up their stalls around the perimeter of the palace plaza for the sale of oils, leathers, metals, textiles, horses, and more exotic animals from elsewhere in the Underworld. One great beast stomped and tossed its tusks where it was tied to a marble column. The Nokian Oliphant stood nearly the height of three men.

At the bottom of the palace steps, a long platform had been erected. Ahyehasi would be sold there in the Night Auction, which would mark the end of the spring celebration. A small crowd gathered at the end of the platform to watch a procession of humans being previewed.

The buyers and sellers in the plaza were a bizarre assemblage. Boudi-Ca recognized some of the Jinni and fledglings, but most she'd never seen before. The tanned visitors in outlandish patchwork garb were the Gypsy merchants. A pair of slender Kishi men wore purple robes. Another woman had leafy skin, a tattooed face, and waist-length brown hair. A coiled whip hung at her waist, and on her shoulder sat a second miniature female. A sinuous tail swung from the tiny creature's bare buttocks. Its small head darted, and its tongue flicked in and out.

"There are more Choshek Kishi at the festival this year," Ayelet said idly. "I think Queen Mab has lessened her objections about this city. The Kishi need to trade like everyone else, and several Gypsy caravans don't take the dangerous road to the Choshek Court. The New Order is rich by Isandlwana standards. Most of us came from Hell's capital city, which is a very wealthy city. We sold everything to join the Lady, and we remain quite wealthy here because the Lady provides everything. Meanwhile, our artisans like Mistress Isabellah work hard with the stuff of Meristyian to sell their products for an influx of precious coins."

"I don't understand."

Ayelet arched her eyebrow. "You don't understand what, fledgling? I imagine material wealth is not important in Heaven. Hell has used the old Egyptian coinages for centuries—the gold aureus and the silver denarius."

"I thought this was a society of freedom from the rules and laws of Lord Hades and Lord Tuhan, but those humans at the auction aren't free. Most of them are wearing collars like Yenta and Herzl, and they are slaves, not Ahyehasi. They keep their heads humble and low. Their Kishi mistresses are using whips to control them. I thought such things were against the Lady's rules."

"Yes. We allow coins to be exchanged for humans at the Night Auction because we have buyers visiting from other places in the Underworld. Everyone considers human souls as possessions to be bought and sold—everyone except the New Order in this city and the Gypsies who are our allies. We have to break our own rules in order to do business with the Kishi, the vampires, and the others. It's a necessary evil, and the Lady makes an exception. For example, if I liked a human male down there, I could buy him and free him."

"It's still evil."

"Why? The Lady will occasionally sell Ahyehasi, but only because they misbehaved. The Lady's rules leave them no choice but to accept slavery or be exiled into Meristyian alone. You don't yet realize how well our Ahyehasi are treated, fledgling. In the capital city, the devils love to pierce the flesh of their slaves, even their faces. A devil procurer will pierce a slave's face to show the boy or girl is available for public use and abuse. The numbers on the coins are the prices. A coin piercing in the septum indicates anal, for example, and coins on a slave's left cheek mean availability for oral."

"That's horrible. Please don't say any more. I don't like having your Ahyehasi serve me like slaves. I don't like giving them orders."

"It's natural for the weak to serve the strong, chérie," Ayelet said evenly. "You used to be one of the weak, but now you're one of the strong. You do enjoy it, which is why you're trying to soothe your guilt. Your Jinn desires will trouble your soul for a long time." Ayelet drummed her fingers on her sword hilt. "These souls are all slaves to their own desires, chérie, and we Jinni are the mistresses of that desire. We are the nobility of lust. Collars and locks exist in nature, so naturally agents are needed to turn the keys. We only honor the power the Fates and the Lady gave us."

"So the Fates give us power over these human souls?"

"Not directly. Humans seek comfort and wisdom from powers greater than themselves. They pray to the gods for protection. It's natural for them. Humans also seek sex, which leads them into relationships with Djinnus and Jinni. Elder Jinni in ancient times sometimes proclaimed themselves goddesses in order to trick the stupid humans into worshiping them as such. At least the New Order gives humans a choice to follow their own path. We try to lead those souls to the love of Lady Allyssia, and we recognize our roles as priestesses in the sacred way of things. If the humans don't like this path, they can leave."

"We're still all equal souls. It isn't right for some to serve others. It's not like we're doing them a great favor. We're using them like horses."

"As I said, they volunteer to be used. Like pieces of a child's puzzle, Boudi-Ca, the bonds that bind souls are inscrutable, and if you try to define their contours, you will go around in circles. Would you call Herzl or Bola an animal? Or our housemaid Yenta, or Anders? I take good care of them.

They are happy and lucky to be living with me in their death. I give them joy and pleasure. There are far crueler mistresses in the Underworld—the Old Order Jinni down in Haawiyah, the pain-loving devil matrons in Hell's Court, and the twisted, madding Kishi royalty of the Choshek. If a vampire owned Yenta, she'd surrender her skin every night and bleed. Humans must earn their keep. They are an inferior and overpopulated species."

Boudi-Ca sighed. As usual, Ayelet was talking circles around her points. "You're insulting them by saying that."

"It's a simple fact. We discussed this. I mentioned the Golden Ratio, the Principle of Dominance, and the aesthetics of asymmetry. Hawks and cats. Cats and mice. Mice and whatever mice pounce on and eat. Cheese."

"That idea makes us all animals, then. Or cheese."

"Do animals think about this issue, Boudi-Ca? Do they understand it? No. We have reason. Unlike the Mimoic Hierarchy, we have reason without denying what is obvious and natural. The delusions of self-righteousness and spiritual materialism are the most hopeless forms of bondage. The truth, on the other hand, cuts through lies. It's time. We should go inside."

The drum beat had changed its cadence, and the crowds at the foot of the steps were dispersing and starting up the stairs to the entrance of Allyssia's Palace. Boudi-Ca rose and walked alongside Ayelet with the flow of the crowd through the palace portico into the warm incensed air. The mother-of-pearl doors were wide open and inviting that night.

Past the massive palace doors, a short vestibule gave into a vast round hall. Hundreds of people—well-dressed Jinni, foreign guests, bare-chested male Ahyehasi, and dolled female Ahyehasi alike—thronged the palace floor or looked down over the railings of the surrounding galleries. The galleries ascended in several balustraded levels towards a crystalline ceiling high above, which reflected the brilliant glow of a golden chandelier of a size that rivaled that of the Nokian Oliphant outside.

Boudi-Ca craned her neck, but it was difficult to see anything over the taller Jinni. She could glimpse the masked face and tawny body of Allyssia, who was seated in an enormous high-backed throne on a dais. The avatar of the Lady was flanked by a small number of Jinni and attendants. Her son, ivory-masked Cupid, was standing silently beside her.

Boudi-Ca held onto Ayelet's arm. She felt faint, and all the more so after the philosophical debate. She'd awoken exhausted that morning from her long practice the night before, and then she'd been absorbed in writing in her diary all day. She'd practiced at blades yet again that evening. Ayelet was surely aware of her weakness from lack of feeding, but hadn't issued a stern reprimand—at least not yet.

"Hades and Persephoneh will come out first, fledgling." Ayelet said, just loud enough to be heard over the buzz of the crowd. "Lord Hades is just an actor, of course. Allyssia would never allow the king of the Underworld himself into Her city, at least not willingly."

"Why not?"

"That's complicated and political. Ask me tomorrow, and let's just enjoy the festivities. Ah, the sistrums. Do you hear them? They are ancient musical instruments using in many Ifreeta rituals."

A rattling hiss filled the hall over the noise of the crowd. The sistrums were held by rows of Ahyehasi who leaned over the second-floor balustrades. A procession filed out of an archway. Boudi-Ca stood on tiptoe. She could barely see past the bald head of a short Gypsy merchant. The procession mounted the steps to Allyssia's throne. A dark man wearing an animal mask led a young woman who wore a bridal veil. An older woman in a flowing brown and gold robe descended the steps and embraced the bride.

"The older woman is Demetriah," Ayelet said. "Demetriah is another avatar, Allyssia's first form—the first avatar that she wore when she was born from the titaness Rhea. The young woman is Persephoneh, Allyssia's divine daughter by her brother, your own Lord Tuhan. The man is meant to be Lord Hades, but it's a political mockery for him to wear a donkey head instead of a horned goat. Now watch closely."

The young woman bowed before the animal-headed man, who shoved a red-purple object to her lips. Boudi-Ca squinted. From the distance, the fruit looked like a pink knuckle-bark pomegranate. The white veil fell away from the bride. A warm wind began to blow in the room. Persephoneh kneeled before the man. The wind whipped at the wedding dress of the young goddess until it parted from her body.

The gown rose several feet above the crowd before it ripped apart into small fragments that metamorphosed into harpy eagles, which in turn flew upwards in tight spirals towards the chandelier above. A shriek sounded. The brown form of Demetriah folded in upon itself and disintegrated into a cloud of swirling leaves that floated upwards to follow the harpy eagles. A cheer erupted from the crowd, and the drums began a lively tune, accompanied anew by the sistrums.

Boudi-Ca smiled. Her heart leapt in happy sympathy with the collective mood in the grand room. The wind strengthened and continued to collect the brown leaves into a rising, twisting column that followed the harpy eagles upwards until finally the leaves burst into flaming ashes, which drifted down over the assembly.

The air in the hall turned warm, and some of the guests tossed their coats and danced to the beat of the drums. Boudi-Ca blinked. With the change in temperature, her head was suddenly swimming. She stumbled when someone jostled her in the crush of people. A stranger's hand cupped the curve of her ass. Her cheeks and sex instantly heated. Her Hunger surprised her in that moment, jumping up and seizing her throat, constricting it mercilessly with its psychic claws. Her inner beast attacked her at the worst possible moment. She couldn't breathe.

Ayelet caught her mid-fall. The face of the Mistress was indistinct and shifting. Boudi-Ca shook her head, but she couldn't clear the cobwebs. She gasped when Ayelet lifted her bodily into the air. The elder Jinn conveyed her through the crowd into a shadowed side gallery.

"I've taken a new strategy, Boudi-Ca, to motivate you to embrace your new nature and leave your mimǫ girl behind. This is what happens when you refuse to feed. You get sick. I thought if I let you get sick, you might learn something from your suffering and make the proper effort to avoid it."

"I'm sorry Mistress," Boudi-Ca managed feebly. "I didn't have time to feed."

"Nonsense. Don't lie to me."

A battle-Ahyehass dressed in full armor guarded a massive wooden door in the side corridor. The guard held up her gloved hand, indicating for them to stop while she examined a piece of parchment. The Ahyehass shook her head. "The parade starts in a few minutes, but I don't see your name on the official list, Mistress Ayelet."

"It isn't," Ayelet said Sharply. "I declined to strut my new fledgling in front of everyone, but she's desperate to feed. You'll let me into the rear staging area immediately."

The Ahyehass bowed shortly with her eyes lowered. "Of course, Mistress Ayelet. My apologies. I was just doing my duty."

Boudi-Ca rode limply in Ayelet's powerful arms. She closed her eyes and focused on the motion of the air over her body as Ayelet bore her through the doorway and onwards. She opened her eyes when Ayelet stopped again. They'd entered a large, dimly lit chamber adjacent to the main palace hall. Scents of perfume and incense were thick on the air.

The expansive room was crowded. Ahyehasi and Jinni primped and preened around mirrored columns. In one corner, a gyrating belly dancer kept time with finger cymbals. Red velvet divans lined the walls. Ayelet moved to an empty one. Boudi-Ca winced when Ayelet deposited her unceremoniously. She watched Ayelet converse with a tall Jinn who she'd never seen before. The Jinn shook her head in the negative. Her words were just audible over the hubbub.

"The parade is about to start, and what mistress wants her empty, just-taken Ahyehass dragging across the platform?"

"Yes, I understand," Ayelet said.

Boudi-Ca slumped on the velvet divan. She hardly had the strength to sit up, much less arrange the skirts of her dress. She folded her arms limply over her stomach instead. On the adjacent divan, a slender blonde Jinn with her hair braided high in extravagant hoops was kissing her Ahyehass—a handsome male. His mistress reached between his legs and touched his phallus, the impressive length of which was imprisoned in a leather thong that dripped with pearls.

Boudi-Ca swept the room again with her gaze. She suddenly realized that everyone in her proximity was looking straight at her. In fact, a small crowd was gathering around her feet. One of the Jinni was speaking with Ayelet.

"This is Boudi-Ca? I missed her mid-night transformation ritual, and for some reason I've never seen her."

"Yes, this is she, Mistress Freyah," Ayelet replied. She's feeling faint. It's my fault. I worked her too hard at blades in the last few days."

Mistress Freyah laughed heartily. She was a blonde Jinn wearing gold armor. Her flattish forehead was framed by tufts of blonde hair that swept into a thick mane at the back of her neck. "I've worn out a few fledglings myself over the years."

"Do you think if it isn't too much trouble—?"

"Of course. Zissu is here. He told me that your fledgling bested him in their sparring match. He spoke of Boudi-Ca in elevated terms, in fact. He'll give himself to her. It would be fitting for him to submit to her again."

Ayelet smiled. "That will serve nicely, Freyah."

Boudi-Ca bit her lip. The crowd was continuing to thicken around the divan on which she sat. Everyone was staring down at her. She was surrounded by a sea of lusty and silvery Jinn eyes. She felt herself blushing, and the heat of the blush made her feel even fainter than before.

"I also offer the services of my Ahyehass." The speaker was the blonde mistress who had been primping her boy at the adjacent divan. He stood just behind his mistress, looking curiously over her shoulder.

"Thank you, Mistress Cybelah," Ayelet said with a nod.

"My Ahyehass would also be honored to serve Boudi-Ca." Another mistress nearby came forward and spoke.

"Mistress Ayelet, you've started a mutiny!" The rotund Mistress Gallinah bustled forward through the crush, looking exasperated.

Ayelet smiled widely. "I'm very sorry, Gallinah."

Gallinah raised her plump arm along with her voice. "The ceremony can't be delayed even to ogle the beautiful Boudi-Ca! Everyone who is scheduled to be in the parade, please form the customary line now at the front of the room! Prepare to present yourselves to the Lady and the Festival goers!"

Boudi-Ca turned her face into the comforting dark fabric of Ayelet's dress. Ayelet had seated herself on the divan and was reaching over her. Ayelet helped her remove her coat, and then reached low. Boudi-Ca took a deep breath as Ayelet lifted her skirts in front of everyone. The close warm air of the room washed over her bare thighs. She heard murmurs of approval from the crowd, and then Ayelet's hand moved over her chest and forehead as if to comfort her.

Boudi-Ca slid down deeper into her bunched-up dress until she was flat on the divan with her legs and buttocks splayed indecorously off the edge. She raised her hands and wedged them into the velvet pillows above her head to stabilize herself. To her mimo girl's horror, her Hunger was in full control of her actions at that moment. She was moving her limbs mechanically, like some sort of doll or automaton. She intended to satisfy her Jinn Hunger right then and there with whatever Ahyehass she could get.

"Here is Zissu at the service of the young fledgling Boudi-Ca," Freyah said loudly with a hand raised to the crowd. "He will graciously surrender to her as he did in his sparring match." Freyah lifted a horn and put it to her lips for a long drink.

Boudi-Ca felt her pink heat fiercely when the strong and handsome male bent over her. She caught a glimpse of Zissu's solid cock before he gripped her pliant thighs and pressed himself between them. With a last effort she arched her back to receive Zissu's phallus. She groaned. A pain splintered through her sex and her abdomen, and then it was gone, and pleasure slowly rose. Her inner muscles clutched and quivered in symphony with Zissu's slow rhythm.

Her Hunger drew on the phallus with a suck that quickly turned into a feverish vacuum, an instinctive pull of need that was so powerful that it tore at her inner moorings. Her Hunger wanted all of Zissu's love. The male's rhythm broke into an uncoordinated shudder shortly after it began. Boudi-Ca felt life and warmth flow into her, coursing upward through her heart and downward toward her feet in a gentle, life-giving cascade through her body. Her Hunger retreated momentarily like a tide to assimilate what it had taken. Zissu stood up and withdrew feebly into the crowd.

"What kind of pathetic public performance was that?" growled Freyah. The armored mistress raised her drinking horn again to take a swig, and then wiped her lips.

"We have a few more," Ayelet said to the crowd.

"Thank you Zissu," Boudi-Ca murmured. Her Hunger, as always, rewarded her for feeding. She felt much better from the flush of Zissu's love. The next Ahyehass was waiting. Ayelet was plying her with another male. Boudi-Ca felt her inner mimọ girl awaking to register a timely protest. There were female Ahyehasi in the room. Why males? The Ahyehass ogled her with his phallus fully erect. He pressed between her legs, gripped her thighs, and fitted himself with a casual deftness, as if he were thumbing open a book to read. Boudi-Ca felt queasy. Her Hunger was creeping like a beast in her belly, collecting itself to pounce and devour.

Her Jinn Hunger didn't distinguish between genders. Her Hunger filled her with lust, possessing her to take the love of others, indiscriminate of whether she even liked them. It was her Hunger that made her arch her back and spread her legs shamelessly in expectation of getting filled again.

The Ahyehass speared into her vigorously, sending wave after little wave of pleasure into her lower belly. After a few minutes the Ahyehass spasmed. Boudi-Ca sighed as more love rushed through her body, washing away her muddy Mimọic resentment. The second Ahyehass had sated her, yet her Hunger wanted still more. The next Ahyehass in line smiled as his blonde mistress knelt and worked at the complicated locking ring that imprisoned his thick phallus. The mistress pulled the male's ring away with a flourish. The Ahyehass was ready. The audience applauded. Everyone around was watching. Boudi-Ca rose from where she lay pressed against Ayelet.

"That's enough, Mistress."

Ayelet gripped her arm. "No. These kind mistresses offered their Ahyehasi to you, Boudi-Ca, so you'll be polite and take them. If you're embarrassed, so much the better for your lesson. You need to stand up and take the reins of your fledgling life or someone else will take them for you."

Ayelet's words were frigid. Boudi-Ca felt anger spark in her chest, but she allowed Ayelet's firm hand to press her back down on the divan.

"Fine. You win this time."

Ayelet beckoned to the third Ahyehass. His phallus lurched through the air. Boudi-Ca gritted her teeth. At least the man was handsome. His thick reddish hair reminded her of Golda's wild mane. He entered and began a rhythm. He was better than the others. He caressed her legs with gentle, attentive fingers. He looked into her eyes with pleasure and wonderment. He leaned and kissed her neck and breasts while his blonde mistress looked on.

Boudi-Ca closed her eyes, self-conscious again. She tried to focus on the pleasure, but she felt nothing of the candlelit magic that she felt with Yenta in the privacy of her bedchamber. Something was missing, and for the first time as a young Jinn, she recognized a difference between love and lust. She felt an inner strength, and a calm came over her like the wind stilling over Ayelet's gardens. She had intuitions that Ayelet didn't. She wanted love, not lust.

Chapter 17:

Golda lurked alone at the end of the line. As a tracker, she had a gift for going unnoticed, and she was employing it. She wasn't in the mood for answering nosey questions from Gallinah about her progress with Tajee. At least thirty other Jinni and their Ahyehasi were among the invitees to the parade. They were waiting to present themselves in front of the Lady and the assembled guests at the start of the Spring Festival. Thankfully, none of them paid her any mind.

She was watching Boudi. The mimo girl was taking her third male Ahyehass. Boudi's face, framed by her ebony bangs and peeking over the folds of her raised dress, glowed gloriously with restrained Mimoic pleasure as the Ahyehass thrust into her. Boudi-Ca possessed the remarkable quality of showing every nuance of her emotions, not only in her face and expression, but in every youthful gesture of her limbs. Boudi-Ca was evidently unashamed to fuck in public. Ayelet was making a lot of progress with her new pupil.

Golda licked her dry lips. She still felt guilty for keeping Tajee away from his mimo girl, but it wasn't her fault. She'd spoken at length with Ayelet after the two Mimos had arrived the previous fall. Ayelet had insisted that Boudi-Ca shouldn't know about Tajee. Boudi-Ca needed to be completely immersed in her new fledgling Jinn life. She couldn't handle distractions. An old friend from Heaven would only cause problems for Boudi's adjustment to her new life.

The Ahyehass between Boudi's legs was taking his time. Ayelet presided over the proceedings with her usual control. Golda turned away. She wondered if Ayelet was taking things too far, but what could she do besides file a mild complaint? Ayelet was Boudi's appointed mistress. If Allyssia wasn't going to do anything, then on what grounds should anything change?

Unfortunately, her lack of argument with Ayelet made her complicit. She hadn't pushed to fulfill her promise to Tajee partly for her own selfish benefit. She'd pacified him all winter, deflecting his questions about his friend. She always trusted her feelings, and nothing grated on her nerves more than when Ayelet told her to ignore them.

She'd resolved to take the opening night of the Spring Festival as another opportunity to broach the topic of Tajee with her old teacher. If she could corner Ayelet and Boudi-Ca together, perhaps it would go better. She'd never disrespect Ayelet by outright telling Boudi, but perhaps she could let something slip by accident. The mimọ girl was innocent, but she wasn't an idiot.

Unfortunately, Ayelet and Boudi-Ca were occupied. Golda sighed. She hoped Herpessenia was available. She didn't want to go home alone that night. Watching beautiful Boudi-Ca had heated coals in her that Herpessenia could fan into flames.

The line for the parade was moving. Golda stepped forward with relief. There were too many presences in the Lady's palace—too many threads running everywhere, and she was too sensitive. Even with her tracking senses closed down, she felt a headache. The line finally accelerated, snaking forward through the open door into the great hall, which was still semi-full after the opening celebration. The Jinni and guests were drinking, dancing, and watching the pageantry.

Like every year, the guests were mostly business people—Gypsy caravaners, a few Choshek Kishi, and other friends of the Lady from distant places—friends willing to risk the political incorrectness, to say the least, of visiting and trading with the New Order. Fortunately, not everyone in the Underworld toed the prejudiced, male chauvinist lines drawn by the Hell's Court devils.

Lady Allyssia was seated in Her radiant glory on Her throne, masked as always. Her son Cupid stood semi-nude at Her shoulder. The chief of arms of the Redoubt, Mistress Freyah, had also joined the assembly on the dais, standing bright in her golden armor. Freyah passed her drinking horn to the favorite Ahyehass of the Ifreeta, Her shepherd boy, fair Ankhises. The handsome Ahyehass wore a skirt like all of the males in the Lady's palace.

Herpessenia was there too. She stood behind Cupid with her pale, bored face and white-blonde hair half-obscured by the feathered shafts that protruded from the young love god's fateful quiver. Herpessenia wore a snow-white gown for the occasion, symbolic of the purity of Persephoneh's rebirth. Golda smiled to herself. The gown was symbolism and irony at the same time. Herpessenia was possibly the most perverse of Allyssia's daughters.

Golda felt herself warm just thinking of Herpessenia. After knowing only the stories of Herpessenia's exploits, she'd finally experienced the divine fledgling firsthand. The flirtation had begun on the trip into Meristyian when she'd captured Tajee, and it had grown over the long winter months into something more. Could Herpessenia be Mareinah's replacement? Herpessenia was holding her at arm's length emotionally. Their relationship was uncommitted and non-public.

Golda watched the second-to-last group make its way across the dais in front of the throne and the divines. It was her turn. All eyes in the hall turned to her. As always, the presence of Allyssia took her breath away. The Lady's glistening form was more perfect than a living statue. Her tiara and mask hid Her visage entirely. The wisps of sparking, flowing hair at the Lady's temples were indistinct and seemed to melt into a diaphanous golden glow of raw power. The physical form of the Lady was supposedly only an avatar—a mere projection into the reality of the Redoubt from other dimensions in which the Ifreeta lived—but the tangible, invigorating presence seemed to cast doubt on such a concept.

Golda bowed to Freyah and Cupid, and then knelt in front of the Lady. Allyssia tilted her head in recognizance and waved a silver scepter. Golda felt a thrill run through her body. She was no longer jittery. A cloud of glittering light precipitated to her shoulders, where it coalesced into a soft grey cloak that fastened magically around her neck. Golda clasped her hands together in silent thanks as Mistress Freyah addressed the assembly.

"Our Lady Allyssia specially honors Mistress Golda with this gift of a magical moon cloak, which will help her do her duties for the New Order. Mistress Isabellah and Ivanka made the cloak. It required two moons to do the weaving and another moon to do the spell. Golda is our newest fully fledged mistress, graduated the summer before last from the guidance of our great teacher, Mistress Ayelet. Ayelet unfortunately is not here due to her faithful devotion to her new fledgling, the oft-spoken-of Boudi-Ca." The crowd responded with applause. Golda stifled a wry smile. The crowd had clapped for Boudi-Ca and not for her. Freyah continued her speech.

"Mistress Golda has already distinguished herself by her excellent service as a tracker who ventured to the very gates of Heaven. She returned not only with Boudi-Ca, but also with an mimọ boy who will go unnamed. Golda took the boy as her First and stowed him away in her bedchamber. If the rumors of the mimọ boy's great beauty are true, then she's wise to keep him hidden from the rest of us." Freyah belly-laughed and raised her drinking horn. "That's all for the parade. Blessed be our guests, and welcome to the Spring Festival in the Lady's city. Remember—no violence or rape will be tolerated. Respect the New Order and honor the Lady with libations, or else skulls will be cracked open."

Applause filled the great hall. Golda rose from her kneeling position and waved to the crowd, which began to disperse. She inclined her head once more to the Lady, who nodded back, and then she made her way down the steps on the far side of the dais. The palace drums struck up a lively beat—the signal that the Spring Festival had officially begun. Ahyehasi, Jinni, and visitors to the redoubt crowded around to socialize with the parade presentees.

"Move back, please!" Mistress Gallinah said loudly to no one in particular.

"Here, kitty." Herpessenia's voice was clear like a chime over the din. Golda pivoted. The divine daughter of Allyssia had followed her down the steps.

"Herpessenia-Ca." Golda carefully kept the formal -Ca suffix on Herpessenia's fledgling name as was proper in public. Social status was important to Herpessenia, and at every step of their dance of intimacy through the winter, she'd followed Herpessenia's lead.

"Congratulations, Golda." Herpessenia smiled seductively. "Come see me at my home in the Divinity District in a bit. There's a party tonight, and I want you to go with me."

"I'd love to go. Do you know if Mistress Ayelet was invited to the party, though? I was wanting to—"

"I have no idea, but I'm going to change out of this ceremonial robe. It makes me uncomfortable, you know, wearing so many clothes. Follow me at your leisure, but don't make me wait." Herpessenia kissed her on the corner of her lips, smiled faintly, and drifted away.

Golda let her tension ease, to be replaced with a flush of happiness and triumph. She'd been honored by the Lady that night in front of all of the Jinni, and she'd been given a public gift of recognition for her service. Freyah had trumped up Tajee to the benefit of her reputation. Best of all, Herpessenia had invited her to an afterparty and had given her a public kiss.

"Congratulations, Golda," Mistress Gallinah said in passing. "Well done."

"Thank you," Golda answered. Perhaps she needed to change her priorities that night. A party sounded nice, and no one else stepped up to congratulate her, not surprisingly. She would have expected Ayelet and Cybelah to say something, but neither was anywhere to be seen. She watched Herpessenia walking out of the palace. Herpessenia was ghostly in her white dress. Her colorless hair flowed loose behind her as she strode on an undeviating path out of the open palace doors. Even the drunkest Gypsies had the sense to clear a path for Herpessenia's self-important, silver-heeled glory.

Golda headed alone out of the palace in Herpessenia's wake. She passed through the open bivalves of the doors and down the steps to her horse where she'd tied it at the posts in front of the stables. She unhitched the horse and mounted while Herpessenia was pulling away from the palace curb into the chilly night.

The Divinity District, where Herpessenia lived, was secured by high marble walls and a dedicated set of silver gates that separated it from the palace plaza and the rest of the Redoubt. The District was more intimate in its grandeur than the less wealthy areas of the city. A twisting street ran up through steep, difficult terrain on the high mountainside adjacent to the palace, where the street gave birth to a handful of cliffside dead-ends that sheltered a dozen or so homes in which dwelled the few and exclusive divines and their secrets.

Golda urged her horse through the District gates and up the steep deserted street. She visited the District far more often than most thanks to her nectar habit. Herpessenia had been her supplier for years, although before the previous winter, the divine daughter had never so much as invited her inside, much less to her bedroom. Herpessenia lived halfway up the ridge, just before Ivanka's dark landmark tower. Golda turned into a small cul-de-sac and rode into a shadowed courtyard between Herpessenia's matching pair of marble medusas. The snake-haired women's mouths were frozen open, silently screaming in the moonlight.

Golda dismounted and tethered her horse. She sat on a bench and waited for several minutes in the deeply shadowed portico before she finally rose and rapped on Herpessenia's silver portcullis with its heavy knocker, unleashing a succession of metallic echoes. Soon Herpessenia's voice called out from a balcony above.

"Give me a few more minutes, my kitten."

Golda felt a slow wash of contentment from the prospects of pleasure. She'd been upset and had stormed out of a party weeks earlier when Herpessenia had first hurt her while flirting. Of the many Jinni she'd fucked during her years of living in the Redoubt, Mareinah alone had truly understood her needs as a former slave of the cruel cat goddess, Basteh. Cruelty was what she needed, what her lost lover Mareinah had done for her.

She'd sent Herpessenia a pair of messenger birds the next day to explain, and the fledgling had accepted her apology. They'd talked again, and during their subsequent meetings, she and Herpessenia had Shared more of their harsh mutual desires. The bolt of Herpessenia's front door clunked and the pale white-blonde divine stepped out. Herpessenia wore a thinner, simpler, nearly transparent dress that was tied under her breasts in the Greek manner. Diamond earrings glinted in the moonlight, and so did a diamond-studded silver handbag. Herpessenia struck a pose.

"What do you think, Golda?"

"Lovely, but you seem a little tense. What is it?"

"Mother ignores me. She cares nothing for her younger daughter."

"I'm sorry." Golda caressed the divine fledgling's shoulder. Herpessenia looked tired, as if she'd been doing nectar all afternoon. Her white-blonde hair fell loose over her shapely shoulders, and the hollows of her eyes were bruised, not just from kohl. The divine daughter silently reached down to adjust the ankle strap of her silvered sandal.

Golda steadied Herpessenia with a hand on her lower back. She loved the delicate recurve of Herpessenia's youthful yet womanly hips. Whenever she was in the presence of a divine, she marveled at the magic that made them beautiful beyond normal beings in a way that was impossible to define. As the Jinn daughter of the Ifreeta of Love, Herpessenia possessed an ample abundance of that special quality.

Golda wanted to crush herself against Herpessenia that very instant, but she resisted. The pale fledgling's perfume was red nectar-based, expensive, exotic, and intoxicating. Golda breathed it in. The perfume made her feel simultaneously strong with desire but weak from desiring. Herpessenia finished with her shoe, stood up straight, and stretched.

"Let's go to the party, Golda. You had a good show at the parade, didn't you? Freyah made a good point though. You should think about sharing Tajee, preferably with me. How is he, your beautiful boy?"

"Fine. Months of veneration have done wonders for his attitude."

"Did you punish him for that thing with Trace?"

"No. I punished Trace with twenty lashes on his ass. I asked him if he knew of another mistress he wanted to be with, and he mentioned you."

"I saw him at the workshops weeks ago. He described the situation, but he didn't beg and grovel nearly as much as I would have liked. I might be interested, but he's a little boring. I know he wants my nectar. You should have punished Tajee. Your mimọ boy isn't disciplined."

"How so?"

"He looked right into my eyes, and on top of that, he had the audacity to judge me with them. Is it true that Tajee knew fledgling Boudi-Ca in Heaven, and that he's in love with her?"

"Who told you that?"

"Mistress Ivanka did," Herpessenia said nonchalantly. "Relax, my kitten. It's just gossip."

"I told the Lady and the elder mistresses everything that Tajee said about Heaven and his relationship with Boudi-Ca. It wasn't much, but I didn't expect it to be common knowledge."

"I'm the Lady's daughter and Ivanka's fledgling. Is that common?"

"No, of course not. I didn't mean it like that."

Herpessenia snorted. "Everyone knows about the situation with Boudi-Ca and your Tajee except Boudi-Ca and Tajee, just like everyone knows about you and me already. You can't keep secrets for long in this city, not with Gallinah chattering over every fence post."

"Tajee loves his girl, which is unfortunate. I expect he'll be devastated when he learns what the Lady did to her."

"Delightful." Herpessenia grinned, revealing her pointy little teeth. "He's an angry boy, your Tajee, isn't he? I guess it makes sense with your history that you like to drink your passion from the dark side. I completely understand."

"No. That isn't the path I want for Tajee. I don't like the anger and bitterness in him. It's just a side effect from the situation."

"Really? I was hoping you and Ayelet were doing a classic goad technique on him—using Boudi-Ca to stoke the Tajee's emotions so you can make him more intense and bitter to feed from. What a perfect situation for it, don't you think?"

"No. Drinking anger is for Old Order Jinni, not the New. I don't want it from my Ahyehasi, and neither does Ayelet. Tajee is a free-willed young man with a beautiful soul. He's not a slave to be manipulated and stoked for more intense emotions."

"If you think so, Golda. I'd say why waste such a powerful passion in Tajee, even if it's anger. Variety is good for the Jinn diet."

They began to walk, ascending the winding street through the Divinity District towards its end, where it turned into little more than a gravel track that switch backed up the hillside, abandoning any pretense of being passable by anything other than feet, nimble hooves, or wings. Herpessenia summoned a tenebris lux as they walked. The light took the form of a white rabbit that jumped in the air above them. Golda smiled.

"Show-off."

Herpessenia smirked. "You should have studied with Ivanka instead of wasting your time at swords with old Ayelet."

"Ayelet and I have had our differences, but I didn't waste my time. Ayelet is one of the greatest blade mistresses in existence."

"Is she so great anymore? It's been a long time since the legendary Butcher of Mer has actually butchered anyone. Ivanka says our resident murderess has gone soft."

"Ayelet is a criminal in the eyes of the Old Order and Hell's Court, but not in mine, nor the Lady's."

Herpessenia sighed. "So how did it feel to be favored by my mother tonight, Golda? She likes you just as much as she likes Ayelet. She hardly even notices me anymore."

"How can I describe the Lady's generosity?"

"My mother needs you," Herpessenia drawled. "You're a tracker."

"It's nice that the Lady appreciates me. Your witch Mistress doesn't."

"Ivanka respects you more than you might think. If she didn't, she wouldn't have helped make that cloak for you. She's just hard to understand. And please don't call her a witch."

Golda cleared her throat. "Why not?"

"It isn't flattering to be the fledgling of a ratty old witch, now is it?"

"My dead ex-girlfriend was a witch. The word 'witch' isn't derogatory."

"Nothing personal, Golda, but you sound like Ayelet sometimes with all of those big words." Herpessenia walked ahead towards the end of the District in silent darkness. Candles lit a narrow-stepped walkway that ran between hedges to the entry of a residence. Golda followed Herpessenia. Herpessenia had a reputation for being moody and unpredictable—it was another thing that she and Herpessenia had in common.

They topped the steps and turned into a wide, high courtyard that was ringed with burning torches. The heavy door of the residence stood open. They walked under the low arch, eyed silently from above by a coven of stone gargoyles, and then on into the gloomy interior of a gothic residence. Several winter cloaks adorned a wide row of hooks made of spiraled mountain goat horns in a vaulted vestibule.

Music floated on the air in the populated courtyard past the entryway. Several masked and costumed Jinni socialized by a stone railing. A female Ahyehass waited with a tray of various intoxicants. In the center of the graveled inner courtyard, dimly lit by torchlight, stood a silver stool. A female Ahyehass perched on the stool, singing softly in an ethereal voice. Her legs were splayed to the stool legs, where her feet were strapped into silver stirrups.

The top of the singer's mechanical stool, in profile, was tilted at an angle. She was mounted, rather than seated, on the top. Her thighs appeared strained, and her pumpum appeared stimulated by a curved flange, which in turn surely sprouted a hidden phallic device.

Golda followed Herpessenia, who was leading the way along a side gallery. They passed down a short flight of stairs into a low passage, where they left the music and guests behind. They stopped at a tall, iron-bound door. Herpessenia pushed it open to reveal a steeper stairway. The fledgling led the way down into the cold dank air that wafted from the sublevel.

"Make a light for us, Golda," Herpessenia breathed. Herpessenia walked quickly down the steps into the darkness. Golda followed, summoning a small tenebris lux as she went. The lux bounced to and fro like a blue will-o-wisp down the ceiling. At the bottom of the steps, the passage flared into a low hall skirted with caryatid columns. Between each sculpted ceiling support was an arched door opening. Golda sniffed the rich odors of earth and stone.

"Where are we going?"

Herpessenia didn't answer. She passed through the nearest opening and entered a long low room with a coffered ceiling. The subterranean chamber smelled like musk, death, and chemicals. Several rows of motionless bodies were laid out on dozens of stone slabs. The underground air was cold. Soft blue light emanated from a crystalline partition across the far end.

Herpessenia gestured grandly with her pale hand. "They're all slaves."

"There are no slaves in the Lady's city."

Herpessenia shrugged. "I disagree like Ivanka does. We Jinni bind humans to us with invisible chains that they will never break. They're weak. They let us use them, and they can't help themselves. It's pointless to think the Ahyehasi in this city will ever be more than our slaves. I haven't yet gotten in trouble from my mother for calling them slaves, and I don't think I will. She knows there's no difference."

Golda gritted her teeth. She felt tension flow into her limbs. "There is a difference if we have the right attitude. The Lady is trying to make a better society, a noble place that sets us apart from both Heaven and Hell. I believe in it. I used to be a slave until your mother saved me from my fate. Did you forget?"

"Look around you, Golda. My mother allowed Persephoneh to do this to all of these humans. Did they suffer? Yes. Did they wish it? No. My mother is a hypocrite."

"Your mother is Love, and less of a hypocrite than Heaven. If this room is Her will, then She must have a good reason."

Herpessenia shrugged and wandered among the desiccated human forms. Some of the bodies were male and others were female. All were completely nude and lay on their backs, where they were bolted and bound securely to the stone slabs by thick leather bindings around their wrists, necks, and ankles.

Golda stopped next to Herpessenia and looked down at one of them. It was a male with a withered appendage like a dried-out sausage that was curved and pinched at its end. The boy's lips had dried and retracted, revealing twin rows of yellowed teeth between the sunken hollows of his cheeks. His nose was only a thin ridge of parchment-skinned cartilage. The pits of his wide nostrils were skull-like. Golda crinkled her nose. The smell of death in the room was overwhelming. She felt Herpessenia next to her and turned, surprised by the cool kiss on her cheek.

"Come look at this." Herpessenia took her hand and advanced towards the glowing crystalline partition at the far end of the low, slab-filled room. A long glass box sat on a wood table that was eerily illuminated in the magical light that emanated from the crystalline partition. "Do you know what these are, Golda?"

The glass box resembled a coffin in size and shape. A pair of ornamental tree branches arched in the box over arrangements of dried grasses and flowers. Faint flitting forms zipped around inside. One of the forms landed on the glass. Golda bent to examine it closely. It was an insect with wings that beat slowly with life. Its translucent body formed a shell for a dense interior circuitry of fine, glowing pink lines. Feelers protruded from its head. The feelers were curved and pointed like little fishhooks.

"I might have seen these in the Isandlwana Fields."

"Not likely," Herpessenia said. "They're Haawiyah moths. They're very rare. This is a mating pair. They belong to my sister, Persephoneh. She gets them from a merchant at the Spring Festival each year, but she absolutely refuses to tell me which one. My older sister, in case you didn't know it, is a bitch."

"This is Persephoneh's home, correct?"

"During three seasons it is. Persephoneh winters in the palace until the start of the Spring Festival. This party is actually a house-warming since my sister will move back in here tomorrow. I can see why she likes to live in Mother's palace for the winter months with the warmth and the swimming pools, but I prefer my personal privacy away from prying eyes. It's easier to sell nectar from my place."

"Speaking of private, is it fine for us to be down here? I had no idea Persephoneh did anything like this."

"Just don't tell anyone that I showed you. This is Persephoneh's secret hobby. The slaves on the slabs are where the moths lay their eggs. These humans once lived and served with so-called free will in this city. Now they serve my mother here."

Golda stared at the desiccated bodies on the stone slabs. "I can hardly believe this. It would be hard to find so many disposable Ahyehasi. I wonder if I'd recognize some of them if they weren't so dried out."

"I'm sure you would. One is an Ahyehass that belonged to me, actually. Persephoneh stole her. Did you see that female Ahyehass up in the courtyard singing? That's Persephoneh's pick for this year. The girl doesn't know it yet, but in a few days Persephoneh will lay her out on one of these slabs and strap her down. It's a real pity. She's a beautiful singer."

Golda frowned. "What exactly will happen to her then?"

"Persephoneh described it to me once when I kept pestering her. It's hard to forget. Are you sure you want to know?"

"Yes. I think so."

Herpessenia licked her lips. "Fine then. That pretty Ahyehass will drink a purple nectar crush, and then she'll swallow this pair of Haawiyah moths through a funnel while her throat is numb. The moths will crawl down her gullet and feast on the nectar in her stomach. They'll feed until they are full, and then they'll make a little nest inside of her."

Golda nodded. Herpessenia moved towards her and pressed against her gently. Golda caressed Herpessenia's shoulder. They were so close that she could feel Herpessenia's cool breath on her cheek. She felt her pumpum respond. Herpessenia's hand dipped between her legs and pushed under the fabric of her dress. Golda caressed Herpessenia's arm, and then over her shoulder to stroke her pale neck.

"And what then?"

The moon-silver in Herpessenia's eyes shone bright in the half-light. "The Haawiyah moths will die, but not before they mate. The female will lay thousands of eggs in the walls of the girl's stomach. The eggs will hatch within days. The baby worms will be hungry."

Golda bent and roughly kissed Herpessenia's neck. "And then?"

"The baby worms will eat the slave's body from the inside out. She'll enter a state of shock, but she won't die. The suffering is not enough."

Golda drank in the scent of Herpessenia's blonde hair. She moved her hand down to stroke the divine's lissome back and soft buttocks through her tissue-thin dress. She felt Herpessenia's hand working between her legs. Herpessenia's fingertips pinched wickedly at the lips of her pumpum. Golda moaned. The mingled pain and pleasure trickled through the old familiar cracks in her desire channels. Herpessenia pinched hard again, and again, and again, until the divine fledgling's fingers went slippery with wetness.

Golda leaned back against the crystalline partition wall next to the moth cage and drew Herpessenia's lithe body against her. Herpessenia's arm levered deeper under her dress. Golda spread her legs apart pliantly, sighing when Herpessenia's fingers finally slipped up into her pumpum. She involuntarily shivered when her shoulder blades rubbed against the crystal partition wall. The wall was not just magically lit—it was magically frigid.

"Go on. What happens then?"

"The worms will consume the girl's moisture from within," Herpessenia continued throatily. "They will grow and fill up her innards, leaving only a protective husk of skin, muscle, and bone. Her body will be dead, but her soul will not leave and go to the void. The worms will get their little hooks into her soul, feeding on her energy while preventing her freedom. The true habitat of the moths down in Haawiyah is neither the dead nor the living."

"What is it then?"

"It's the undead, Golda. Haawiyah moths feed on the undead. When a mating pair can't find an undead to lay their eggs in, they become more aggressive. They try to make a nest by turning a living body into an undead instead."

Golda sighed and moved her hips to the rhythm of Herpessenia's insistent fingers. Her pleasure was pooling heavily in her belly, bringing her ever closer towards her much-needed release. She gazed at Herpessenia's pallid face, which had turned bluish like everything else in the cool light of crystal wall. Herpessenia's eyes had turned silver-black with her passion.

"And then? Tell me more, Herpessenia."

"The worms will weave thousands of cocoons throughout the girl's inner cavities. They will slowly metamorphose into moths. They won't hatch without the warmth of Haawiyah, so Persephoneh keeps her collection cold. My sister says the humans in this room are home to a hundred thousand Haawiyah moths just waiting to be born."

Golda groaned. Herpessenia continued to work her powerful hand, digging ever deeper into her pumpum with cool skilled fingers. Golda quivered. She was going to come. She could feel her wetness sluice down the inside of her thigh.

"Kiss me, Herpessenia. Please?"

"You can't come yet. I want you to venerate me," Herpessenia whispered. "Get down on the floor. Tonight, I want you to start being my bitch."

"No. I don't think so."

"Get on the floor. That's an order!"

"Fuck you, Herpessenia."

"You're the one getting fucked. Open your fucking legs wider! Open them! I want that cunt open, slut!"

Golda groaned and opened until her inner thighs ached. Herpessenia's blonde head bobbed hard to her chest. Herpessenia ripped through her dress and bit. Herpessenia worried the sensitive flesh with primordial pointy teeth that were more fishlike than human. Golda felt tears coming to her eyes, and she allowed herself to surrender to the ecstasy. The left hand of the young divine reached behind her head and wrenched her by her hair.

Golda slid down the end of the crystal partition towards the smooth marble floor, pushing with her feet to wedge her head under the shelter of the moth cage, thereby keeping her mouth away from a wicked facesitting. She didn't want to venerate the divine fledgling. She didn't want to become enthralled to Herpessenia through ingestion of her fluids. She wasn't ready for Herpessenia to hold such addictive control over her emotions. She'd been Mareinah's bitch for two years, but she didn't trust Herpessenia so much. She felt a Sharp stab of pain as Herpessenia pressed hard to enter her entirely with her hand, tightly spitting her liquid surge to the wrist.

"I love you," Golda grunted. Her thighs were trembling. She wanted Herpessenia deeper. She wanted Herpessenia to reach so deep, deep enough to hold her beating heart. With that thought, her belly fluttered. Herpessenia pushed forward hungrily, sensing the impending orgasm. The fledgling slid her head into the intimate space under the moth cage for the kiss. Golda opened her mouth to receive it. She opened herself inwardly to the desire that rushed up inside of her to fill Herpessenia's Hunger.

Herpessenia's wrist hooked firmly over her mons, keeping her hips in check as she bucked violently, pressing for every bit of extra pleasure. Herpessenia locked lips and applied the pressure. The love-energy reversed itself, and Herpessenia hungrily drained the rising orgasmic waves.

Chapter 18:

Boudi-Ca blinked her eyes open. The warm silken bed sheets wrapped her body almost like Golda's arms. It was the third time that she'd dreamt of Golda. She'd re-experienced for a few delirious moments the feeling of falling again. Boudi-Ca sat up in her bed. Her legs were stiff and ached a little bit. Ayelet had taken her all over the city to see the festival arts exhibitions and music performances. They'd walked for hours, including through the labyrinthine polished precincts of Allyssia's palace.

She'd seen exhibits of beautiful sculptures in plaster and bronze made by the mistresses and fledglings who worked in the workshop district. She'd seen beautiful tapestries made by Isabellah, a mistress artisan who she hadn't met. She'd admired fine drawings and paintings of Isandlwana landscapes by Mistress Cybelah and Mistress Colleteh.

Boudi-Ca gazed out of the window. The view outside her room looked subtly different. Tiny buds had formed on the brown stems of the bushes. She reached down and caressed her lower belly. Like the garden and the seasons, she was changing too. She ran her fingertips through the wisp of honey hair on her mons that seemed thicker with each passing moon.

Her body seemed even more different since the opening night of the Spring Festival, when Ayelet had made her take three cocks in quick succession. She'd felt full after taking the love of the second Ahyehass, but the third had broken something open. Her inner space had seemed to expand, and since then, she'd fed her Jinn Hunger from Yenta like never before.

Her inner mimọ girl had wept silently for an entire day because of what Ayelet had done to her in public. Her mimọ girl sadness had eventually given way to rage. She hated Ayelet for manipulating her, pushing her deeper into sin, and taking her treasured virginity so casually.

Her Jinn-self, on the other hand, wasn't particularly angry at what had happened because Ayelet, as always, had made a very rational point. Ayelet had only made her take the Ahyehasi because she'd refused to feed for four entire days. It was her mimọ self's silly rebelliousness that had led to her fainting spell.

She'd tried to put the episode at the palace behind her, but she was growing tired of listening to her inner mimọ. It was a torment being torn between two worlds, and she felt pulled apart. She'd been transformed into a Jinn, and the Conclave wasn't coming. What did her mimọ self want? Her mimọ self wanted her to remember her vows to resist the Jinni and try to escape. Heels clicked on the walkway outside, softly at first then louder as they approached. A shadow crossed the window, and a familiar knock sounded at the door.

"Come in, Mistress."

Ayelet opened the door and strode into the bedchamber. Ayelet wasn't wearing her normal skirt that morning. She wore flared black riding pants strapped to her pannier-less hips with a black leather belt. Her white linen shirt with flounced sleeves and ruffled collar almost gave her the silhouette of a man. Ayelet's greying eyebrows were furrowed with a look of concern.

"Good morning fledgling. I trust you slept well?"

"Yes, Mistress. What's wrong?"

Ayelet smiled faintly. "We have a small problem. A late-arriving Gypsy caravan for the Spring Festival was attacked in Meristyian in the dead of last night. From what the messenger said, the culprits were vampires."

"You mean the kind that bite?"

"Precisely. Those kind. Here in Meristyian we have the ascended ones—those that have crossed over purposefully from Earth to live in the Underworld. Meristyian has always been a vampire playground and neutral meeting place, but their hunting grounds are usually far in the east. Lately they've been scouting here in the west, however, including the hills just outside the city."

"Why are they coming here?"

"We don't know, but they're back again, and the Lady would like someone to go and investigate. Freyah is occupied with city security for the festival and Artemisiah isn't in the city at all, so it seems that I've been chosen to go. I want you to go with me, fledgling. Get up and put on your riding clothes. Herzl will help you. I'd like to be outside the Redoubt within the half hour."

Boudi-Ca blinked. "We're leaving the city?"

"Yes. You haven't been out since you arrived, and you're ready to see some of the Lady's domain. Get dressed and meet me at the stables." Ayelet turned on her heel and left. Herzl poked her head through the open doorway that the Mistress had vacated.

"Fledgling? You are ready to dress, yes?" Herzl went to the wardrobe and produced the necessary clothes. Boudi-Ca stepped first into her brown riding pants, and then slipped into a loose riding corset that supported her breasts without squeezing her stomach too much. Herzl pulled the laces and tied them, then followed with a flounced long-sleeve riding shirt.

Boudi-Ca flexed her fingers. Her nerves were on high alert, but not at the thought of chasing after dangerous vampires. For the first time since she'd arrived in the city of the love Ifreeta as a virtual prisoner, the gates would open and let her leave. Could she somehow get away from Ayelet on horseback and flee into the forest? It was terrifying, but it was the golden opportunity that she'd been waiting for.

If she could slip away from Ayelet, she could ride far from the Lady's city and never return. She could pray fervently to Lord Tuhan and the arch-Mimos. Perhaps they would hear her in distant Heaven. While she waited, she could search for the stairway.

Boudi-Ca felt her heart pound harder in her chest. A good Conclave agent would try to escape. If she didn't at least try, she would be a real failure. A new worry was at the forefront of her mind, however. How would she feed her Jinn Hunger without the help of an Ahyehass? If she was unable to find any sexual sustenance or any way to reach Heaven within four days, she could faint, fall off of her horse, and never awake.

She sat at her desk and laced her riding boots while Herzl's nimble fingers wound her hair into a bun. When the dressing-girl was done, Boudi-Ca exited the bedchamber. She walked around the Villa and into the sunlight, up the drive to the stables, where Ayelet was already waiting. Bola was there too, holding the reins of a pair of saddled horses. Ayelet held a weapon in her outstretched hand—a medium-length straight blade with a polished leather belt and a matching sheath with floral designs down the seams.

"This is for you, fledgling. It's a gift. You can wear it."

Boudi-Ca took the offered blade. The belt was clearly new, but the sheath and the leather wrappings of the sword were worn. She pulled the sword halfway from its scabbard. The blade felt heavy. A large citrine adorned the heart of the steel flower bulb that formed the pommel. Two more citrines glinted from the hearts of the designs on the guard, which were shaped like two curved metal claws of a predatory bird.

"Thank you, Mistress. It's beautiful."

"It's an Oya-blade. It's enchanted with dream magic, which makes it particularly effective against opponents that have psychic anchors in the dream-world, like vampires. When you learn to travel in the dream-world, you can even carry this sword with you there. It was forged for Oya by Master Muramasa, a legendary bladesmith who lives in the capital city of Mer. It's a very special gift."

"Who is Oya, again?"

"Oya is the Nanka-Mother who dwells in the icy aeries of Cocytus, from which the headwaters of the Acheron flow. Oya is a divine dragon-kind who breeds the Nanka used as mounts by Hell's army. She also watches over the prison-tomb of the titan Kronos with the help of three Jinn high priestesses. Those women were given these blades as weapons. I killed one of them and took her sword. My sense of honor prevents me from using it myself, so I always meant to give it to a student. I think that student is you."

"Thank you, Mistress. I don't know what to say."

Ayelet nodded. "I'm not much for giving gifts, but this is one of my most treasured possessions. Ivanka gave me the idea that you should have it. She thought it could be of special use to you if you develop your flashing potential. Right now it could be of use against the vampires outside the Redoubt."

Boudi-Ca wrapped the leather sword belt around her waist and fastened the clasp. "I'm not sure I'm ready to fight a vampire even with this sword."

"Nonsense, fledgling. Another young Jinn might practice on her own for years and not be as good as you are now with only a few months of my daily instruction. Vampires are rarely very good with blades anyway. To them, a cut is a waste of blood."

"If they don't use swords then what do they fight with, Mistress?"

"Magic and teeth. Actually vampires can be fine with blades. I once knew an Auerbach ambassador who hid a hundred-centimetre rapier in his overcoat when he went about his business. I imagine he opened difficult negotiations with a good puncture wound. Now mount up, and let's ride, fledgling. Don't be frightened, but this is for real."

Boudi-Ca approached Bola, who held the stirrup for her. She climbed onto a horse that was as high as her head, pausing to adjust her sword so it didn't catch against her hip. She rode side by side with Ayelet at a canter down the hill road, through the workshop district, and onto the marble-paved central streets towards the front gates of the Redoubt.

The entry plaza was filled with colorful Gypsy tents. The tents were most dense in front of the three-story stone facade of the Pandocheion, which according to Ayelet offered pleasant repose for Ahyehasi and visitors to the city. Boudi-Ca followed Ayelet at a trot around the edge of the festivities, then out of the plaza and under a portcullis that was suspended between the twin towers of the city gatehouse. A massive stone bridge spanned a chasm, and at the far end they entered Meristyian. A rutted road led to the right. They turned over a low hill into a vineyard and past a small grove of olive trees.

Boudi-Ca looked over her shoulder. The Lady's city and the crossing bridge disappeared behind them, transforming into an illusion of a wild mountainside that blended seamlessly with the surrounding terrain. Gouts of steam drifted in midair from the chasm. The summery Isandlwana forest was much warmer and wetter than the spring weather in the Lady's private domain.

Boudi-Ca urged her horse to catch up with Ayelet, who had accelerated to a fast canter. Boudi-Ca grabbed for the pommel when she almost tipped off backwards. Ayelet had given her only a handful of riding lessons in the previous months. It didn't help that her horse was excited. It forged forward of its own accord, breaking into a gallop to draw almost even with Ayelet, who was riding quickly.

"We're nearing Esplanade, the closest village to the Redoubt," Ayelet called over the sounds of the hooves. "The souls here are simple farmers. They were devoted to the Lady while they lived on Earth, and thus were rewarded with a home here in Meristyian. The bounty of the desire-realm is endless. The humans harvest it for us—olive oil, plant materials, and parchment as well as stone and ore from local quarries. The Lady relies on the work of these worshipers to collect the coalesced energy forms that we use to build and maintain Her city."

"The people in Meristyian are servants of the Lady too?"

"You could see it that way. Or you could say these farmers are freemen who work the land of the Lady in exchange for living in this paradise. It's a model for the earthly feudal system. As above so below. It's an example of how important worshipers can be to the power of any god or goddess."

"Do any of these humans worship Lord Tuhan?"

"No. By treaty, this is supposed to be a de-militarized zone. Lord Hades considers Meristyian to be his, and so do Lord Tuhan and the Mimos, who renamed this place Purgatory to fit their view of things. If either side builds outposts in Meristyian, that could restart the great war."

They crested a low rise. A cluster of wooden buildings came into view with high thatched roofs that caught the morning sunlight. Ayelet kicked her great brown stallion and surged again into a gallop. They descended a slope into the village proper, where women and children scurried to get out of the way.

Boudi-Ca followed. Her horse again matched Ayelet's pace of its own accord. She smelled grass, sawdust, animals, and baking bread. She heard the rhythmic ring of a blacksmith's anvil above the sounds of the hooves. A few of the simple souls of Meristyian emerged from homes and hovels to watch them ride past.

A peasant woman made signs over her breast. Another woman hid a small boy behind her skirt. The boy peeked out rebelliously with his eyes wide. Another woman with patchwork clothes and a row of kids pushed her girls into the street as quickly as she could. At the end of the village they passed a number of carts, where a merchant and a handful of men hastened to move out of the way. A few knelt, while others stood stock still with their faces frozen.

Praise the Lady," cried out one man, and then the town fell behind them, and they rode into the countryside again. Ayelet slowed slightly. Boudi-Ca drew alongside. She raised her voice to be heard over the pounding hooves.

"Do those humans know who we are?"

"Yes, those men understand," Ayelet answered. "They work for us, as I said. Sometimes when a Jinn needs a new Ahyehass she can find one in an Isandlwana village, but they make very poor servants. They're too ingrained in their simple daily existences, and their desires are too weak and limited to give a Jinn much sustenance."

"Where do we get our Ahyehasi, then?"

"Most come directly from Earth, where the sufferings of the flesh can stoke the passions of a soul. Fallen Mimos are passionate in even deeper ways. A hellion can make a good Ahyehass if their divine parent sells them instead of allowing them an independent life, but hellions are lazy and never as loyal as humans can be. Look there, fledgling. It's a roadside shrine for Mistress Demetriah. Do you remember her from the festival ceremony?"

Ayelet slowed the pace further to a trot and pointed with her gloved hand at a statue poised over a low, brick-lined pool of stagnant water. Piles of herbs and grain offerings lay alongside the pool.

"It's pretty."

"Those shrines were abundant on Earth during Egyptian times, but Lord Tuhan and the Mimoic Hierarchy systematically destroyed them, determined to remove the devotion to the old gods from human minds. Without devotees, divines become weak."

"Can divines die?"

Ayelet slowed her horse further. "I'm not sure. Divines can move throughout the universe. They aren't discrete beings like us. They interact with this world and the Earth magically through living avatars. They can sever those avatars from themselves to form independent children, like Allyssia created fledgling Herpessenia, or they can sever avatars from themselves like a dead branch, solely to keep the tree healthy and conserve their energy. Do you remember Mistress Freyah? She is one such severed avatar. The titanic goddess that was Freyah left this world centuries ago to travel to a more fruitful one. Freyah today is but a dying, abandoned shell of her old self. Like other divine avatars, she uses the Jinn arts to survive."

"Does the Lady make these avatars from herself, then?"

"Yes. The Lady has a few live avatars in our little city, although their identities are a secret. If someone wished to harm the Lady, they would strike first at Her avatars."

Ayelet grew silent and led the way along a winding forest edge, following a wide, hardened track. They were passing through the foothills of the mountains, weaving through hills that swelled down from steeper terrain. They turned left onto a wider road. Ayelet again eased the pace. They'd ridden through the last of the olive orchards and into rougher terrain. The road was muddy, and the tumbled rocks that skirted it were wet. The sky was grey, and cool mists drifted down deep fissures in the looming mountainsides. Ayelet rode primly in silence, gazing straight ahead. The mistress fingered the hilt of her sword.

Boudi-Ca touched the pommel of the Oya-blade, reassuring herself that it was still firmly fastened at her belt. She hadn't yet had any chance to separate herself from Ayelet. She wondered if Ayelet would notice if she lagged far enough behind to escape into the depths of the forbidding forest. The terrain amidst the trees appeared treacherous. She doubted her ability to out-run the Mistress through the trees and thorny underbrush.

"Why did the vampires attack the Gypsy caravan, Mistress?"

"I don't know," Ayelet answered in an odd tone. "This particular caravan was attacked as it was coming up from the lower regions of the Underworld. I believe it was bringing rare gold thread for Mistress Isabellah and exotic herbs for Demetriah. Those are difficult things to get up here so far from Mer. Mer is the capital city, of course, the home of Lord Hades, Hell's Court, and the Old Order Jinni. Patriarch Reik caravan is coming."

Boudi-Ca listened and peered ahead, but she saw and heard nothing. They were riding along foothills that were shrouded in mist from a recent rain. Finally a handful of dark riders appeared, coalescing into grim solidity. Behind the dark riders rolled the first horse-drawn wagon of what appeared to be several in a line. Each massive wagon had a roof, appearing almost like a miniature house rolling on giant wheels.

The advance riders brought their horses to a halt in front of Ayelet. They were tall, powerful men in dark armor that gleamed greenish in the forest light. A few of the riders seemed wounded, with blood-soaked bandages on their arms and necks. One man, burly and bearded, rode at the forefront. The man's voice was hoarse and challenging.

"Hail, Jinni. I am Boris, captain of the guard for the Reik family."

Ayelet raised her hand in greeting. "I'm Mistress Ayelet, and this is my fledgling, Boudi-Ca. We welcome you to Meristyian on behalf of the Lady Allyssia. We heard word that you were attacked."

"Yes. I'm glad the rider got through. The caravan was attacked by a large group of vampires last night. We were finally able to turn them away from our camp, but we had several casualties. They stole some of our horses."

Ayelet pursed her lips. "What kind of vampire were they, and where?"

"They were Egyptian types." Boris looked over his shoulder and gestured vaguely. "They hit us a distance back up the road towards the Trivium. It's daytime now, so they've gone into hiding. Last night was a terrible night."

Ayelet shifted in her saddle and seemed to consider the warrior's words. "My fledgling and I will investigate the incident. Continue and know that the road ahead is safe to get you to the Lady's Redoubt before sunset."

Boris nodded with respect. "Thank you, Jinn. May the might of the Lady ride with you into the Isandlwana Heartland."

The man gave a signal to his men, and the company rode on, followed by the line of Gypsy wagons. Ayelet nudged her horse to the side. Boudi-Ca followed suit, riding slowly behind Ayelet along the muddy edge of the road until the last of the wagons had passed. She used the break to lift her feet from the stirrups and stretch her legs.

When the men had passed, she followed Ayelet onwards. The damp forest air warmed further. The pressure of the late morning sun steadily dispersed the mist. They rode for another hour while the sun rose through the towering trees until they rounded a bend in the road and faced a scene of carnage. A score of dead bodies lay strewn around an open flat. The only movement was a trail of smoke from a circle of stones by the road.

Ayelet reined in. "Here we are, fledgling. We need to be cautious. Many types of vampires aren't bound by the night in Meristyian. The night is much more comfortable for them, but the sunlight here is different from Earth and won't really set fire to their skin."

Boudi-Ca held tight to her reins. Her well-behaved horse had gone skittish, as if reluctant approach the bodies. A few of the dead were slumped against trees as if they were sitting there when their throats were torn open. Their heads hung limply at the neck. Others had clearly died fighting. The silence of Meristyian was suddenly oppressive. The birds had stopped chirruping. The only sounds were the wind in the trees, the low clomp of hooves, the clink of the bits, and the creak of the leather saddles. Ayelet sat motionless on her horse as she studied the scene.

"What do you see, fledgling?"

"Some of them still have their weapons sheathed. That one there appears to have been thrown against that tree. And that one is withered, like he's been dead forever."

"He was completely drained by a powerful vampire. We should be thankful that our Ahyehasi don't look like that after we take them. Can you imagine? Let's get off of the road. I need to send a messenger bird. This is a larger problem than the Lady expected, and we are in real danger."

A line of intense light curled from Ayelet's fingertips and coalesced into her glowing yellow messenger bird. The Mistress held the bird close to her lips and spoke silently for a moment, and then the bird took flight, darting at dizzying speed towards the Redoubt.

"What did you say, Mistress?"

"I asked the Lady for Golda and more good sword arms. Golda is a great tracker. She'll help us find the vampires so we can learn what they're up to."

Boudi-Ca nodded. She'd completely forgotten that Golda was a tracker. "Golda can find anyone, anytime?"

"She can find almost anyone. Golda is the second-best tracker the Lady has. Mistress Artemisiah, the divine huntress and ally of the Lady, is the best, but she roams alone to places far, and is only available when the Lady calls. Golda is our most dependable for practical purposes."

"She found me in the ruins of Chickasaw, so she must be good." Boudi-Ca followed Ayelet off the road through the forest until they reached a rocky clearing, where broad patches of Isandlwana sunlight glowed down through the trees. The bloody evidence of the rampaging vampires made her happy that she was with Mistress Ayelet. An attempted escape was clearly a bad idea. Even if she managed to fool Ayelet and get a head start, she'd be in the forest alone with the vampires, and Golda would be able to track her down.

"Let's find someplace to get comfortable, fledgling. We'll be waiting a while for Golda. Perhaps we should spar a bit so you can use your new Oya-blade."

"I don't understand how you can speak so highly of Golda sometimes, Mistress Ayelet, and other times you say that she's a horrible disappointment."

Ayelet dismounted. "She isn't the master of her passions, fledgling. She is deeply scarred. She has problems with controlling her emotions and making good decisions. Long ago in Haawiyah she was a slave."

"I know. So?"

"Little Dora, as Golda was called then, was the favorite kitten of her cat goddess mistress. Golda was a human sex toy—a redheaded Egyptian princess with nothing of the Jinn stature that she has today. She cleaned her mistress with her tongue, crawled everywhere on her knees, and licked up platefuls of nectar every day. As a reward for her dedication, the cat goddess bestowed upon Golda a gift. Most would call it a curse."

"Golda doesn't seem cursed to me. She's fierce and independent. She's beautiful and smart, and you said she's a great tracker."

Ayelet smiled. "I suppose the cat goddess Basteh gave her all of that in a way, but those things are just a part of her wild heart. When Golda wants, and often when she doesn't, she can transform into a giant cat."

"That's hard to believe."

"It's true, chérie. Intense passion in this realm can work amazing magic. The Lady wondered if Golda's difficult trip up the stairway to Heaven might purge her curse, but it didn't work."

Chapter 19:

"I'm leaving, Phylicia!" Golda paced into the storage room past Trace's low bed, through the access door, and down the stone stairs into the cool, damp air of the stable. She'd received a messenger bird from Mistress Freyah. Ayelet needed help with tracking the vampires that had attacked the Gypsy caravan.

Her sturdy chestnut mare was hitched, groomed, and waiting for her, but the horse wasn't saddled. Another horse stood outside the stable doors—a grey and white dappled stallion. Herpessenia's steed shied away at the sight of her. A silver crossbow glinted in the sunlight where it was secured to the saddle. Herpessenia's perfume rose over the odors of straw and dung. The divine fledging leaned over Trace in the last stall with her left hand clutching his pony tail and her right hand smacking his backside. Herpessenia looked over her shoulder.

"Hello, Golda. I was just amusing myself with your Ahyehass while I waited. I hope you don't mind."

"My saddle isn't ready, Trace. Get up and finish your work." Golda leveled her best stern look at the veteran Ahyehass, but Trace was in no hurry. He rose to his feet and brushed the dirt and straw from his pants and shirt.

"Faster, Ahyehass," Herpessenia snapped. "Your mistress told you to prepare her horse, not to stop and groom yourself. You're almost as hopeless as Tajee."

Trace strode quickly to the mare and hefted the saddle onto its back. Golda stifled a smile. She liked how Herpessenia had handled that, although she didn't care so much for another insult to Tajee's training. "How are you, Herpessenia-Ca?"

Herpessenia shrugged nonchalantly. "I've been well. You're looking exquisite as always. Your new moon cloak looks flattering on you."

"Thanks. Are you going for a ride?"

"Of course. I'm coming on the vampire hunt."

Golda embraced Herpessenia. She licked the divine's soft neck, and then drew back for a kiss and a tongue. Herpessenia's mouth tasted cool and nectary as usual. "Wonderful. Then we'll have another adventure together."

Golda straightened her cloak on her shoulder and turned to examine Trace's work, hiding her look of concern. Vampires were truly dangerous, and she didn't believe Herpessenia had any real combat abilities aside from a crossbow, a few spells, and a talent for summoning lux bunnies, the latter of which could only fend off a vampire by making him laugh. She wondered why the young divine had been invited. Herpessenia poked her playfully in the shoulder.

"I've missed you since the other night, Golda. Really I have."

Golda smiled and flashed her bedchamber eyes. Herpessenia had taken her twice that night in Persephoneh's grim insectarium. After that evening, she'd been two days in bed taking Tajee and Phylicia to recover from her emptiness. The ache from such a fisting still hadn't completely gone away. The ache was lesbian-decadent. She was considering asking Herpessenia to come stay with her on a trial basis.

Was she crazy? Completely. She intended to offer the idea as a first bid, only so Herpessenia could counter with an invitation to live together in the Divinity District. Golda licked her lips. She'd get a steep discount on Herpessenia's nectar then, and she loved the prospect of endless lazy days without worries for expenses. Trace had saddled the chestnut mare in record time. Golda frowned silently and tightened the weakly cinched girth.

"Thank you, Trace. Close the doors behind us and get some rest. Be certain to throw the wards on all the doors when I'm gone. I expect to be gone for the rest of the day and possibly overnight. Don't you dare touch Tajee. You're done giving him lessons, too. In four days' time, you'll either pledge to another mistress, or the Lady will put you up on the Night Auction at the end of the festival."

"Yes, Mistress," Trace said with his voice obedient and his eyes properly downcast. "Thank you, Mistress."

Herpessenia sidled out of the stable to her stallion and mounted. She unfurled her reins with her leather-gloved hands. "So when can I play with your mimọ boy, Golda?"

Golda mounted her mare alongside Herpessenia. The divine fledgling looked striking on her horse with her shell-white hair struck by the sunlight that streamed down the alleyway. Herpessenia wore russet leather riding pants that rode low on her hips with a matching long-sleeve half-top that exposed both her navel and the cleft of her moon-pale breasts. Golda felt an ember of lust burn harder into her high-energy mood. If Herpessenia wanted Tajee so much, then Tajee was a bargaining chip.

"Let's talk about that on our trip. I think Boudi-Ca is with Ayelet though, and remember the mimọ girl still doesn't know that I have her boyfriend sleeping with me."

"I'll try to be discrete, my kitten."

They rode out at a canter, side by side. Within minutes they approached the front gate. Golda slowed her horse to a walk at the entry plaza, which was full of festival guests and activity. It was so crowded that she was afraid of running over someone. The festival visitors were mostly Gypsies who relaxed on hammocks and bedrolls under the awnings of their merchant tents.

The morning traffic was over, and the festival goers were resting in the afternoon before the evening revelries. The colorful flags flying over the nearby amphitheaters hung limp in the stillness that echoed a feeling of spent dancing legs and shopping desires. A hundred horses or more milled in temporary pens near the city gatehouse. They were mostly draft horses—hardy pullers of the massive Gypsy wagons.

Golda navigated her horse through the pedestrians. She veered around a pair of drunken Erebus mercenaries comparing the lengths of their longswords. She detoured around the fledgling Henne-Ca, who was in discussion with well-dressed Seelie Kishi—probably a merchant placing orders for products made by Isabellah, Apolloniah, Gallinah, and the other resident artisans.

Golda glanced back at Herpessenia. Herpessenia was surveying the entry plaza with a haughty curl on her divine lips. Golda smiled. She could hardly remember her earth life as an Egyptian empress, yet she'd always wished to re-assume the stature she imagined she'd once commanded. Herpessenia held a convincing air of superiority that could only be achieved by royalty.

Could it work? Could they live together as lovers and Share Tajee and nectar? Golda prodded her chestnut mare through the cool valley of shadow between the twin towers of the massive gatehouse. A rider in black was waiting for them on the crossing bridge into Meristyian. The rider was Mistress Ivanka, which explained Herpessenia's unlikely invitation.

The old black-skinned witch sat astride her Hell horse, which stood a hand higher than even Herpessenia's mighty white stallion. The Hell horse pranced forward, exhaling a puff of smoke. Ivanka looked even more shrunken than usual on the back of the great equine beast.

The witch rode bare-breasted, wearing only a short black leather skirt that rode so high on her dark hips that her old shrunken pumpum was surely in contact with the black leather saddle. Ivanka eschewed boots as well as underthings, fitting her ebon hooves firmly into her stirrups. Ivanka's greying hair was pulled tightly into a bun. A curved blade with a jeweled pommel swung at her belt. Gold rings glistened on her fingers when she raised her hand in greeting.

"Good afternoon Jinni," Ivanka rasped. "Are you ready for the hunt?"

Golda nodded, even as she tried to hide her disappointment. She wasn't eager to ride with Ivanka again. "I thought Freyah was going."

"Freyah's battle-Ahyehasi protect the Redoubt," Herpessenia said from just behind. "Mistress Freyah is too busy watching the Gypsies and the outsiders in the city."

Golda fingered her pommel. "I doubt if we'll need your magical help, Mistress Ivanka. Ayelet and I should be able to track down and handle a few vampires."

Ivanka laughed darkly. "Your bravura is admirable, cat. You underestimate the vampires, and you underestimate Ayelet. If she thought she needed Freyah, then she must have a good reason."

"I suppose you're right."

"Of course I'm right. You're the tracker, so let's be going."

Golda shrugged. She didn't care so much. The more hands they had at the task, the better. She kicked her mare, and the horse clattered down the crossing bridge. Herpessenia and Ivanka followed her apace. She led the way across the bridge, which shimmered and disappeared along with the Redoubt when they arrived at the far side, leaving only a gaping chasm and a mountainside. Allyssia had tightened the illusions that hid the city.

Golda opened her senses to Meristyian and quickly picked up Ayelet's track, which led along the Esplanade road towards the misty southern skirts of the mountains. Another thread ran alongside Ayelet's. Boudi's pink streak was remarkably prominent in the Isandlwana tapestry. Golda led a fast pace down the road. It was best to go as far as possible while the sun still shone. The vampires would have an advantage at night, or so she imagined. She'd seen faint vampire tracks occasionally in Meristyian, but she'd never met one of the bloodsuckers face-to-face. Her growing excitement, coupled by the danger, made her as edgy as she'd been before her trip to Heaven.

She quickly encountered the Gypsy wagons that had been attacked. Patriarch Reik grim guards saluted as they passed. The fields around the village of Esplanade offered a shortcut before rejoining the main road, which rose slowly upwards through the foothills over the course of an hour, then two, until it forged through the great maples and towering ash and oak trees of the Isandlwana Heartland. The late afternoon sun slanted at a low angle through the budding boughs that brushed blue-violet skies.

Golda slowed to a trot when she neared the ends of the tapestry threads. She sensed Ayelet's presence. She urged her mare around a wide bend and down a slope to a flat—a level area just before a low stone bridge where a creek cut the old road. Ivanka and Herpessenia closed the gap behind her. Golda reined in and pointed.

"Here."

A litter of dead bodies was strewn through a clearing that had been used the night before as a camp. Everywhere there were signs of struggle. The bodies already stank with decay as the weave of Meristyian assimilated them. The smell of fresh overturned earth wafted from downslope. More blood. Worms and roots. A few of the bodies had been hastily buried.

Over the smells of earth and acrid blood, the bittersweet scent of sap wafted from a stray cut in a maple. Faint odors of dried sweat, leather, and oiled armor mingled with the rest. Golda turned her horse and caught Ayelet's thread again. The elder mistress was only a few hundred yards away. Golda spurred off the road and up the slope, followed by the others. She could hear Ayelet's voice through the oaks.

"…the emotional energy of the male Ahyehass has more of a tendency to anger and negativity. The energy of the female is often healthier, but is more difficult to feed from because of the natural yin polarity. You see, fledgling…"

Golda smiled. Mistress Ayelet was giving her poor fledgling one of her endless lectures. Ayelet and Boudi-Ca were just ahead on a small knoll. The top of the knoll was rocky and bald. Boudi-Ca sat on a boulder listening to Ayelet. Their untethered horses idled nearby.

"…but Djinnus, on the other hand, are our opposite and some would say our complement. Just as we have to feed, they have to release. Luckily for the Old Order Jinni in Haawiyah who are required to marry Djinnus husbands—"

"We're here," Golda called, hailing them with a wave of her hand. Ayelet waved back and rose to her feet. Ivanka and Herpessenia ascended the rocky slope and closed ranks. Ayelet arched an eyebrow.

"It appears we have an interesting hunting party."

"Yes," Ivanka said, spurring her Hell horse to the fore. "Freyah is busy with the arrangements for the festival, so I came in her stead."

"Indeed. Well, that will have to serve." Ayelet moved to her horse, clearly disenchanted by the witch's presence. Ivanka looked down with her own brand of skepticism at Boudi, who had clambered from the rocks and was brushing flakes of lichen from the backside of her dark brown riding pants.

"I see you have your newest protégée with you, Ayelet," the witch said. "She's wearing your Oya-blade. Is she ready for the hunt?"

"She shows much promise with her blades, Ivanka," answered Ayelet shortly. "I wouldn't underestimate her."

"Oh I won't, I assure you," Ivanka murmured, her tone slippery with sarcasm. "Mount then, and let's be off."

Golda watched Boudi, as did everyone else, as the mimọ silently approached her horse. Boudi's tight riding clothes offered a different and lovely view of her exquisite figure than she'd revealed on the red divan in the low light of the parade staging room. Boudi's transformation and four-month stay in Meristyian had changed the mimọ. Her girlish breasts were slightly fuller, and her buttocks were a bit less boyish.

Every part of Boudi-Ca was beautiful—even the small uneven white wings that protruded from hemmed slits in the back of her flounced long-sleeve white shirt. Boudi-Ca paused by her horse to put on her leather riding gloves. She started to awkwardly mount, and then stalled. She doubled over to re-tie the lace of her boot with her ass towards the black witch.

"I think she likes you, Mistress," Herpessenia said with a smirk. Ivanka guffawed. Golda felt a chuckle in her belly, but she suppressed it. Boudi-Ca didn't comprehend the comment. The mimọ looked over her shoulder with her umber eyes questioning. One of Boudi's eyes was oddly off center, and the girl shrank visibly from all of the gazes. Golda had the urge to come to Boudi's defense, but she kept silent. Boudi-Ca needed to learn to fend for herself.

"We have a small problem," Ayelet said in an annoyed tone, hopping onto her horse and indicating brusquely for Boudi-Ca to do the same. "Patriarch Reik caravan was attacked by more than just the few passing vampires."

"Obviously," Ivanka said. "They were probably using illusion magic to hide their numbers. A lord was with them, perhaps a prince. Probably not a sorceress. She would have burned the caravan and left swaths of fire damage in the forest. Why were the vampires this far west across the Isandlwana Fields?"

"Good question," Ayelet said. "We need to determine who is responsible for this, where they are, and whether they pose any more danger to the Redoubt and the Spring Festival. I assume the Reik caravan made it safely to the gates?"

Golda nodded. "They were close to the bridge when we passed them."

"I can't think of a reason for a group of vampires to be here," Ivanka said. "Unless they were headed through the Trivium into Erebus or Vegasis for some reason and needed to feed, but there are faster routes down through the mountains to the lower regions—more direct roads and passages from the vampire lands in the east."

Ayelet pursed her lips. "What about the vampire that Freyah captured last year and locked in the palace dungeon? Huesca was his name. Was anything ever learned from his interrogation?"

"Nothing of use," Ivanka said dismissively. "He was a wormy Disciple of Set—a misbegotten toady of Lord Hades."

"Well, whatever the Disciples are doing in the Lady's lands, with Golda's help we'll track them. Shall we?"

Golda wordlessly turned her horse towards the downslope. She spurred her horse from the knoll and back to the road. She sensed the others falling into a file behind her. Once she was at the road, she opened her senses as wide as they would go.

She focused and tried to unravel the passage of the large group of vampires. They appeared as faint red threads through the tapestry, gathering together like a river from the bloodshed. They appeared to be using magic to hide, but their magic wasn't strong enough to blind her. She aligned herself with the threads and followed the sickly wash of violence coursing through the forest, through the trees, and down a slope studded with oaks.

The others followed closely behind. Herpessenia's musical chortle echoed through the forest. The divine daughter was laughing at something Ivanka had said. Golda glanced back, annoyed. Tracking the vampires was a serious affair. A force that could kill all of those armored human warriors could easily take down Jinni.

Golda felt Ayelet's eyes on her back, however, and she felt comforted. Many times her teacher had tested her, praised her when she had succeeded, and corrected her when she had failed. In the time since she'd become fully fledged and had gone to live with Mareinah, she'd tried to separate herself from Ayelet, but she felt safer going after the vampires with the legendary blade mistress at her back.

Evidently Herpessenia felt safe too in the escort of Ivanka and the Butcher of Mer. The divine fledgling was amusing herself by trying to engage the mimọ fledgling in idle banter. Golda sighed. If her old lover were on the ride, Mareinah would have been silently riding up front alongside her partner, reverent and respectful of the tracking arts.

Golda crinkled her nose, keeping her senses open to the red threads in the tapestry. She nudged her hardy chestnut mare to a brief canter to gain distance over the group. The tangled odors of the others, particularly the scent of Herpessenia's perfume, were clouding her senses. Even at thirty paces she could smell the sulfur exhaled by Ivanka's horse, Sharp over the rich odors of turned loam.

The vampires numbered at least ten. They were moving slowly. The vampires were likely unfamiliar with the Isandlwana Heartland, so far from their eastern lairs. Golda led the party onward for hours until the sun tipped over the western hills and folded into the edge of Meristyian, leaving behind a darkening violet sky. After nearly another hour, when the Isandlwana sun was all but gone, she knew they were close to their quarry. She could see the threads ending and converging. She slowed her horse until the others were almost abreast.

"There's something ahead. There's a whole mess of tangled tracks, but I don't sense the vampires."

"Lead on," Ayelet said from behind. "It could be a trap. Ivanka, watch Golda closely. I'll cover the rear with Boudi-Ca."

"Shouldn't the blade mistress be in front to deflect a frontal assault away from our sorceresses?" Ivanka rasped. "And since when were you giving the orders, Ayelet? I'm the senior here."

"The Lady sent me on this mission. We're all working together."

"Then let's get to work." Ivanka spurred her black horse ahead and drew her curved blade, which glowed magically in the darkness to light the gnarled boles of the oaks with a pale violet glow. Ayelet also drew her blade and Boudi-Ca followed suit, riding tensely in her saddle. "Mind your fledgling, Ayelet," added Ivanka. "She looks like she might faint."

"Everything will be fine, Boudi-Ca," Ayelet said quietly.

"Maybe Boudi-Ca needs a quick sparring practice before the battle?" Herpessenia said from behind.

"Boudi-Ca can beat you at blades with one hand tied behind her back, young divine, and you've been pretending to practice at them for several hundred years," Ayelet countered.

"I'm a magic mistress," Herpessenia retorted weakly. "Blades are no match for a ball of fire or a crossbow bolt through the chest."

"Point that thing away from me."

Golda smiled. Ayelet had scored points in the skirmish of words. Allyssia's children, especially Herpessenia, were notoriously lazy, preferring to live their lives indulging in endless pleasure rather than working to better themselves.

The forest track had opened onto a clearing that stank of death and the undead. Golda focused to hold the visions of both worlds simultaneously in her head. She could see the tapestry threads of the vampires everywhere through the forest like a tangled mess in a kitten-mauled sewing box. She prodded her mare slowly forward. Two bodies were lying dead on the ground, sprawled at awkward angles.

Ivanka muttered a spell. A strong tenebris lux glowed in the air, casting brilliant blue light over the scene. Stones ringed a fire pit in the center of a small glade. In a wide circle around the fire pit, strange sigils were drawn on the ground with powdered chalk.

Golda edged forward further. She couldn't sense anything dangerous in the scene. The lithe brown bodies were two dead women. Even from several paces, it was clear that their throats had been torn out. Their mouths were frozen open in silent screams like Herpessenia's medusa statues.

"This is not good," Ivanka muttered.

Golda urged her mare closer to the bodies. "Who are they? Their belts and hand wraps are strange. I've never seen anything like them."

Ayelet handed Boudi-Ca the reins of her horse and dismounted. A gilded weapon lay on the ground nearby—a bloody long-hafted polearm with a crescent blade at one end. The women had apparently made a stand. Ayelet knelt next to one of them.

"You're right, Ivanka," Ayelet said quietly. "This indeed is not good. Look at the tattoos. They were both high priestesses."

"We should report this to the Lady." Ivanka waved her hand, which produced a large crow. The bird shot off into the dark forest with a rush of wings.

"Who are these women?" Golda repeated. "Ayelet?"

Ayelet knelt at the bodies and rifled through their belts. The clothes appeared similar in style to Old Order trappings, but the brown-skinned women weren't Jinni from Haawiyah. Haawiyah was hot, yet the haze, pollution, and gas clouds weren't conducive to a deep, weathered tan. Thin ribbed skirts with woven gold borders draped the thighs of the women, and they were naked from the waist up, with the exception of one, who wore golden nipple shields.

Ayelet shook her head. "Vampires do not make fires. This was the camp of these women. The runes—"

"Were a warding spell against the vampires," Ivanka finished. "The vampires broke through and had these fine ladies for a meal. The deaths don't look recent, either. Maybe the vampires hit them a few days ago and came back the same way."

Golda grimaced. "For the third time, who are they?"

Ayelet looked up. "These are Eastern Order Jinni, Golda. I didn't believe they still existed."

"For a long time, the Eastern Order has been lost and forgotten," Ivanka added. "They were always hermetic Jinni, isolated and hidden, much like Allyssia should have been instead of making everything political and holding public festivals. The Eastern Order worships the cat goddess Sekhmet far out in the deserts of eastern Meristyian. Sekhmet is the sister of your former mistress in Haawiyah, Golda."

"I don't remember Basteh mentioning a sister. I don't remember many things from those days. The nectar took everything away."

"We should head back to the Redoubt," Ayelet said. "These high priestesses of Sekhmet were as strong as any of us. We shouldn't take any more risks than we already have. We've found some clues that will help Allyssia decipher the vampires' intent. We'll return to report what we've found and let the Lady decide how to proceed next. This hunt is at an end."

Ivanka shrugged. "These two were likely tired and unfed so far from their home. Maybe they were easy prey. I'll agree to Ayelet's plan of retreat if she believes that some of our group members are too weak."

Golda urged her mare towards the long, golden demi-lune polearm lying nearby, which lay across the exposed roots of a tree. "I'll get this."

"No, I will," Ivanka said. The witch waved her hand with a powerful desirous kin-hex. The weapon scraped from the ground and flitted through the air. Ivanka caught it easily with one hand. The weapon was longer than she was. Golda reined in her mare and stared at the old witch with a dangerous feeling in her throat.

"Let her have it, Golda," Ayelet said. "Please just lead us home."

Golda kicked her horse forward through the far side of the dark clearing and down a moonlit ravine, following a small track leading into a wide canyon bottom that rose towards the general direction of the Redoubt. The clatter of hooves on the exposed stones of the rocky banks told her that the others were following.

The existence of Jinni who worshiped a cat goddess made her head spin.

She'd never heard of such a thing unless Basteh had mentioned it in passing. Golda clenched her reins tightly in her fists. Why had Ayelet never told her about the Eastern Order—the existence of something potentially so amazing and important? Ayelet was certainly withholding knowledge from Boudi. Had the Lady also conspired to never mention a cat-goddess named Sekhmet who lived in Eastern Meristyian?

The walls of the ravine grew narrower, blotting out even the moon. The mist and shadows cast a deep gloom over the gravelly stream bed. Golda glanced back. The others were a short distance behind her, picking their way through a group of boulders in the light of Ivanka's lux. Golda felt a terrible feeling of dread roll over her shoulders and into the pit of her stomach. Something wasn't right. In fact, something was very wrong. Wrapped up in her tangle of intense emotions, she hadn't unfolded her tracking senses fully. She hadn't sensed the danger, and it was already too late.

She tried to cry out, but her chest heaved and a roar emerged from her throat instead. Her horse bucked under her as a second wave of sickening, paralyzing dread assaulted the forest. Shadows flitted through in the night. The chestnut mare squealed, shuddered, and buckled under a sudden impact.

Golda leapt. In the space of a few seconds that seemed like an eternity, she transformed. As her chestnut mare collapsed underneath her, she sprang onto the nearest shadow. The bonecage of the vampire pulverized under the impact of her paw, but the creature rolled away and recovered quickly, only to be joined by two more. The vampires were everywhere. The rocky ravine bottom was flooded with blood-suckers.

Chapter 20:

Tajee awoke to the sound of a knock. At first he thought he was dreaming. Golda had drained him twice that morning, and he'd slept away the day to recover his energy. He'd dreamt of Boudi, Phylicia, and even Trace, disturbingly. The bedchamber door opened. The stripe of light widened to reveal Trace's silhouette.

"Let's go, Tajee."

Tajee rubbed his eyes. "Where? Are we going to see Boudi?"

"Yes. Golda left the city with Herpessenia."

"Let me get dressed." Tajee slipped into his pants and shirt. He was finally going to see Boudi. His epic quest had reached the most important turning point, and once and for all Boudi-Ca would know how much he loved her—enough to jump from Heaven and serve a Jinn so he could save her from her terrible fate.

With Golda gone, he prayed that he'd have a chance to escape with Boudi-Ca that very night. He brushed his hair quickly at the vanity mirror, pulled the map and knife from Golda's drawer, and slipped them into an old leather satchel from Golda's wardrobe. He joined Trace where the Ahyehass waited in the hall. Trace put a finger to his lips.

"Quiet, Tajee. I don't want Phylicia to know about this, or she'll hold it over both of us. Why do you have Mareinah's old purse?"

"There's a big knife and a map of Meristyian in it."

Trace hesitated, wide-eyed. "Damn, Tajee. You've got even bigger balls than I thought. Fine, let's take this up a notch. We have free will, right? Just don't let a mistress catch you with that weapon, and don't even think of going at Ayelet."

"I hope I don't have to. I'm counting on you."

Trace nodded, and Tajee tiptoed down the stairs after him. The houseboy inserted a key in the front door, turned it until it clicked, and then undid the latches and levers. When the door opened, they slipped outside into the cool night. The sky was clear and moonlit. It was strange to see the street in front of Golda's house from an angle other than the second-floor bathroom window. The mossy street stones were uneven and surreal.

Trace was already hurrying up the street. Tajee padded after. The darkened streets of the Redoubt were silent and eerie at the late hour. Invisible things winged past. Trace looked back and laughed.

"Chasm bats. Hurry, Tajee. The faster we go the less chance we'll get caught by a prowling mistress who wants to fuck us. When I say 'us', I mean you."

Trace led the way up a long steep hill to a bend in the road, where the sky opened up to reveal a giant tapestry webbed with twinkling pink and purple lights. There was no time to admire the queer chromatic beauty. Tajee hurried after Trace, who had left him behind again to continue at pace up the road, which continued to a broad hilltop.

Tajee winced as he went. The stones hurt his bare feet, but he ignored the pain. Boudi-Ca was waiting for him. He'd imagined the meeting a thousand times. He'd imagined the happy, shocked smile on Boudi's face. He'd imagined the desperate kisses that she'd give him. He'd imagined her hugging him for long minutes, gratefully proclaiming him her knight and savior, with her head nestled sweetly on his shoulder, unwilling to let go.

What would Boudi-Ca say? The biggest question was what the Jinni had done to her. Was Boudi-Ca living in a cruel cage? Was she serving as a pathetic dressing-girl like Phylicia? The Jinni had surely ruined all of

Boudi's virtues. All of his fears over the previous months came crashing back into his head, leaving him shuddering, breathless, and enraged at the evil Jinni, especially Golda.

At length, Trace stopped at a low stone wall that rose along the right side of the stony road. "Your girlfriend's in that Villa, mate. Mistress Ayelet is a mean proper bitch, though."

Tajee looked over the wall. The sprawling bulk of a mansion rose on the far side of a broad lawn and a well-tended, tree-studded garden. The grand house sported sloping tiled roofs and multiple levels. A smaller structure rose behind the house—a detached building silhouetted against the moonlit mountainside behind it. The hilltop complex was dark except for a faint lamplight that came from a window in the upper level. Tajee grimaced.

"So where is Boudi, and how are we going to get in? The place is huge."

"Hold on to your pants, Tajee," Trace answered. "I have an inside connection. I was checking to see if Ayelet's gardener was around, but it looks like he's inside for the night, or maybe he went for a drink at the Pandocheion. He shows up there sometimes."

"What's the Pandocheion?"

Trace chuckled. "It's the city inn. The front half is a brothel and hotel for Gypsies, Kishi ambassadors, and whoever else. The back half is for Ahyehasi. On dies Lunae nights most of us in the city show up for drinking, dancing, and fun. As long as no one tosses their juice, we can have all the debauchery we want. If anyone goes over the edge, the worst that can happen is a spanking and a chastity belt. I wasn't supposed to tell you about the Pandocheion, but you should ask Golda if you can go. Actually, you should demand to go to the Pandocheion. It's the Lady's law that you can. Golda will love that."

"Let's just keep going."

Tajee followed Trace along the wall until they passed through an opening where the drive from the Villa connected to the road. Trace ambled along the drive and angled across the lawn. Tajee followed him to the side of the house, where thick vines climbed the bricks. The bulk of the Villa was a dark fortress, foreboding.

"Can you climb this?" Trace whispered. The male Ahyehass slowly climbed the vines up the side of the wall. In less than a minute, Trace had pulled himself over the lip of the roof tiles and was looking down. Tajee dropped his leather satchel and groped among the rough branches. The vines were thick and twisty. They ran vertically. He had no idea how to pull himself up.

"How?"

"Just wait there then. Maybe you won't have to. Wait."

"Alright. I'm waiting." Tajee fidgeted while Trace disappeared over the roof. He tried to climb the vines again, but he could only lift himself a few feet off the ground before the rough bark hurt his hands. He waited for long minutes in the blackness under the eaves. The night was eerily silent. He wanted to run and start pounding on any door he could find, shouting Boudi's name. After what seemed like an interminable length of time, he heard scuffles and Trace's head looked over the edge.

"Careful."

"What?" Tajee took a step back. Trace was whispering, but not to him. First a leg, and then a female form were silhouetted against the night sky. The girl gasped quietly, and then she was climbing down. Tajee felt his heart leap to his throat. He wanted to help Boudi-Ca in some way, but he was afraid to touch her. Her legs were long. Her rear end looked bigger than he remembered. Tears welled in his eyes as she dropped the last several feet.

The girl didn't look anything like Boudi-Ca in the moonlight. In fact, she wasn't Boudi-Ca at all. The girl was sturdy and well-figured, not wiry and tomboyish. Her breasts were big and lumpy in her worn linen nightgown, not small and pert. Her light hair was thick and curly around her shoulders, not fine and ebony. The girl stared at him, panting from her effort. Tajee stared back. Trace climbed down the vines and landed heavily on the ground.

"Boudi-Ca isn't here, Tajee. Yenta says she went out on a ride with Mistress Ayelet hours ago. They haven't come back, just like Golda. Yenta thinks they all went together."

"What? I can't believe this!"

"Sorry, Tajee." The Ahyehass named Yenta pushed her long hair over her shoulder. "Trace says you and Boudi-Ca were friends in Heaven."

"Who is Boudi-Ca? My friend's name is Boudi."

The female Ahyehass shrugged. "Boudi-Ca was her name when she first came. Everyone calls her Boudi-Ca now. The Lady made her into a Jinn fledgling, but I like to call her Mistress when she takes me. I know Mistress Ayelet wouldn't think it proper, but Boudi-Ca secretly likes me to call her Mistress."

Tajee swallowed. "Boudi-Ca takes you? Where does she take you?"

Trace chuckled. "Most of the New Order Jinni go both ways, mate. Tajee's jealous of you, Yenta. Just look at him."

Tajee felt hot. "Shut up, Trace. Can we wait for Boudi-Ca to come back, then? When is she coming back?"

Trace shook his head in the starlight. "Nay, because if they're together, then Golda will come back at the same time, and she'll catch us."

Tajee clenched his fists. "I hate Golda. She's keeping me from Boudi. She's the one who's probably jealous."

"Look Tajee, calm down. Yenta said she'll let us see Boudi-Ca's personal bedchamber. Do you want to see it, or not?"

"Yes. I want to know where it is."

"Follow me," the female Ahyehass said. Tajee fell in behind Yenta and Trace. He couldn't believe that he couldn't see Boudi. He'd gotten all worked up for nothing. They followed a stone walkway past garden plots around the house.

Tajee watched Yenta walk. She reminded him of the nimfa that he'd met in the Isandlwana jungle. Yenta's hips swayed like a nimfa when she walked. He tried to imagine Boudi-Ca taking the girl in a sexual way. He couldn't imagine such an impossible thing. Maybe 'Boudi-Ca' was just a wicked Jinn who happened to have the same name. Maybe it was all a big mistake.

They reached a heavy oak portal set into the side of the house beside a large glass window. Yenta turned the knob and pushed the door open into darkness. The air inside was warm and smelled of hearth ashes and linens.

A light flickered to life.

Yenta had lit an oil lamp that illuminated a modest bedchamber. A heavy low-slung bed sat along one wall, and next to it stood an antique side table. A cavernous wardrobe stood in the opposite corner of the room with its doors flung open. Dresses and robes hung in a jumbled row. Piles of undergarments lay heaped on a shelf at the bottom, and below the lingerie was a shelf laden with shoes.

Tajee approached the writing desk where Yenta and Trace stood with the oil lamp, watching him. A small backpack lay on the floor next to the desk. Tajee bent and picked it up. All doubts that he had about the identity of the room's resident were quickly dispelled. The rucksack was salty, smelly, and stiff, but it looked every inch like Boudi's college rucksack from Heaven. She'd sewn it herself. Tajee loosed it back to the floor from his nerve-wracked hands. On the desk sat a pair of silver pens next to a thick, leather-bound tome. He reached to open it.

"No," Yenta said quickly. "That's private. Boudi-Ca doesn't want anyone to read her diary."

"I'm going to look at it." Tajee flipped open the heavy cover and turned to the first page. His heart clutched again. Boudi's handwriting was as recognizable as his own. Her familiar stilted script was thicker and bolder than it had been in Heaven, but it was still the same handwriting with which Boudi-Ca had written him many a note in Earth History class.

My name is Boudi-Ca. I used to be an mimọ in Heaven.

Yenta's hand slammed the book shut. "You can't look. That's Boudi-Ca's private diary."

Tajee tried to pull the cover of the book back up, but Yenta held it firmly against the desk. The Ahyehass was very close to him. She smelled like soap. Tajee resisted the urge to shove her away. "Her name is Boudi, and she was my friend long before the evil Jinni ever brought her to this wicked place, and long before she ever met you."

Yenta stared dangerously at him in the low light of the oil lamp. "You can't. This is Mistress Ayelet's Villa, and I'm the house-girl. If the mistress isn't here, you have to do what I say."

"Just leave it alone, mate," Trace muttered. "You're just an Ahyehass. Yenta is risking punishment from old Mistress Ayelet just to let us in, which was really nice of her, by the way. You know, Boudi-Ca has a lot of pretty clothes in her wardrobe. She could show Golda a few things about how to dress sexy."

Tajee continued to tug on the book, but Yenta continued to pin it firmly on the desk with her hands. Tajee sighed, exasperated. "Just leave me alone. I want to read what Boudi-Ca is writing. Please?"

"No," Yenta retorted. The girl's face looked resolute in the lamplight. Tajee turned away from the book, but not before he slipped one of Boudi's silver pens off the desk and into his hand. Yenta grabbed his hand immediately. He wrestled with her again.

Trace tried to pry them apart. "Enough. What's gotten into you, Tajee?"

Tajee slipped away, still holding the pen. "So how does Boudi-Ca 'take' you, Yenta? What does she do?"

Yenta stuck out her tongue. "I'm Boudi-Ca's favorite Ahyehass. She does lots of things to me. You'll never know, and I'll never tell you."

"I don't believe you. Tell me."

"I said I'm not telling, you stupid mimọ boy! Are you deaf?"

"Calm down, Yenta," Trace said. "How can you be so upset, love? I'm here, and we're going to have some fun."

"Fine. Let's go the Pandocheion."

"Why? We're already next to a nice bed." Trace held onto the voluptuous Ahyehass and half-embraced her from behind. Trace's hand found her breast. Yenta tilted her head back, accepting Trace's inelegant attack.

Tajee stalked away from the desk and went to the wardrobe. He could feel Yenta's eyes on his backside. He ran his hands over Boudi's dresses. Some seemed formal, others informal. None were chaste and Mimọic. All were of a Jinn style—low-cut, lacy, and sensual, with lots of silk, leather, and velvet. The clothes looked newer and more expensive than any of Golda's well-worn, practical garments. Tajee leaned to smell the scent of them. His foot bumped a shoe—a heeled shoe with a pretty bow on the toe.

The folded garments in the bottom of the wardrobe were indeed underclothes. He ran his fingers over the top one, a blue corset with brown laces and delicate bows where he imagined Boudi's hips would go. He fingered smaller, more delicate things—stockings that were well-used, a slip, and a brassiere. The petite silk-lined breast cups were less than half the size of Golda's behemoths.

Yenta moaned softly. The Ahyehass had settled on the edge of the bed with Trace. His arm was buried under her raised nightgown. Yenta's hand rubbed the bulge in Trace's pants. Tajee glanced at the book on the desk, but Yenta's eyes were hooded like a viper ready to strike. Tajee sidled back towards the desk, testing Yenta.

"I told you to leave Boudi-Ca's things alone," she said immediately. "Do mimọ boys have hearing problems?"

"Hey Yenta!" Trace said animatedly, withdrawing his hand. "Do you think Ayelet's dressing-girl would want to have fun with us? What's her name again?"

"Herzl," Yenta murmured. "I don't know. Is the new boy going to go?"

"Tajee is a good man." Trace massaged the girl's shoulders. "He's just a little tense. He's in love with his mimọ friend, so he's jealous."

"I'm not jealous," Tajee said quickly. He rubbed his temples. The pounding in his heart had gravitated up to give him a headache. "I just want to see Boudi. I want her to know that I'm down here in this damned place with her. It's killing me."

Trace guffawed. "That's obvious, mate."

"I try to think of everything that could be happening to her, and I can't do anything about it. I just want to make sure that she's alright. Can you tell me anything more about her, Yenta? Please. You don't have to tell me what she does with you."

"What should I tell you?" said the Ahyehass indignantly. "Boudi-Ca is Mistress Ayelet's fledgling. Who are you?"

"How about this," Trace said. "Can you just tell Boudi-Ca about Tajee, Yenta? It would really make him happy. Just let her know that he was here to visit, that's all. Boudi-Ca can do the rest."

Yenta shrugged. "Does he want me to?"

Tajee nodded. "Yes! Can you tell her for me? Please, Yenta? Tell her about me as soon as she gets back. I'm sorry I tried to read Boudi's book. I didn't know it was so important."

"Fine. I'll tell Boudi-Ca about you the next time she takes me, if she lets me speak first. She's very strict. If not, I'll tell her after she takes me, if I can still make words. Sometimes I faint from the pleasure, and I don't wake up until the next day."

Trace clapped his hands together. "Excellent. Thanks, Yenta. Now let's get back to being bad Ahyehasi, shall we? Let's find Herzl. I don't want her. I want you, of course." Trace kissed Yenta on the cheek. "I was just thinking about Tajee."

Yenta sighed. "First he has to put the pen back."

Tajee replaced the silver Conclave pen on the desk, resisting the urge to grab the book. Yenta rose from the bed, went to the desk, and extinguished the lamp, plunging the bedroom into darkness again. Tajee followed Yenta and Trace out the door. Yenta shut it behind them, and they walked back around the house. Tajee tried to guess at Yenta's attitude. Had he pacified the girl enough that he could count on her? He wasn't sure.

Yenta led them to the front portal of the Villa. She pushed the massive door open. The entry hall was dark. The moonlight through the windows revealed polished marble columns and floors. Ayelet's extravagant stone foyer shamed Golda's entryway with its footworn wood floor and chipped moldings. "Upstairs," Yenta said in a low voice. "Don't wake Bola."

Tajee followed Yenta and Trace through the darkness of the foyer and up a steep curving stairway, and then down a lamplit hall to where Yenta knocked on a door. The door opened, and a voice emerged.

"Oui? C'est quoi?"

"Hey Herzl," Trace said smoothly. "How are you?"

A young brunette Ahyehass with a mousey round face poked her head out of the door. Her dark, kohl-lined eyes widened. Yenta whispered in the smaller girl's ear for long moments until Herzl motioned them all inside.

Herzl's bedchamber was warm and cozy. The floor was adorned with a soft patterned rug. A stick of incense burned on a gold-leafed table that was littered with books and picture cards. A worn armchair with flowered upholstery sat in one corner between a crammed wardrobe and a full-length gold-framed mirror. An odd bird perched its claws on the footboard of a messy, blanket-piled bed. The bird was a blue-green peacock—stuffed, motionless, and dead.

"Nice room, Herzl," Trace said. "My room in Golda's house is more like—let me think—yes, it really is a closet. Tajee, this is why I'm not so upset about getting another mistress, even if she isn't a hot Egyptian redhead." Trace reached down and petted the stuffed peacock.

"Merci, Master Trace," Herzl said. The girl spoke with a thick accent. "We have the best with Mistress Ayelet, yes?"

"Aye." Trace grinned. "You can keep calling me Master. I like that."

Yenta rolled her eyes. "Herzl, you're a horrible flirt. Trace is with me, not you."

Tajee ogled Herzl. Herzl pouted at Yenta, and then ogled him back. Herzl was dark-haired like Yenta, but there the comparison stopped. Yenta was full and womanly. Herzl was small and bony. Yenta wore a full-length nightgown. Herzl wore a leather collar and a black silk slip around her hips. Her puffy little breasts were on full display.

Herzl was about Boudi's age or a little older. Herzl could have been a junior student at the Crystal College of Sacred Moons, but she was far from any mimo. She was looking at him darkly, licking her pouty unpainted lips as if sizing up prey. Tajee felt his phallus stir, but he wondered if he should be afraid.

"Excellent," Trace said, rubbing his hands together. "I think Tajee and Herzl like each other enough. Do you girls want to play a game?"

Yenta looked skeptical. "What kind of game?"

"I have a bottle," Herzl said quickly. The Ahyehass pranced onto her bed and searched under the pile of blankets. After a few seconds, she extracted old wine bottle with its label worn off. "We can spin, yes?"

Trace chuckled. "That's wicked, Herzl."

Yenta shook her head. "No. I don't think so."

"Oh come on, love," Trace said. "It'll be fun. I brought some Blue Violet Beauty that I stole from Golda, too. Herzl? Where's a candle? I'll heat something up. Yenta and Tajee have to relax."

Yenta watched with interest when Trace pulled a small leather pouch from his pocket. Herzl produced a candle from a drawer, lit it with a match, and placed it on the floor next to the bedside table. Trace settled next to the candle with his back against the bed. Yenta joined him. Herzl sprawled and dropped the bottle in the center of the rug.

"Make a circle, yes?" the Ahyehass said.

Herzl motioned Sharply with her finger. Tajee blinked. Herzl had evidently been talking to him, and she wanted him to sit. He sat cross-legged on the floor with the others. Trace lifted a small spoonful of purple powder to the candle flame. It melted quickly. He turned with it to Yenta, who opened her mouth.

Trace inserted the spoon between Yenta's lips and upended it. The girl swallowed, moaned, and fell back. Her leg tensed and crawled across the carpet. Trace leaned and kissed her lips. Yenta pressed against him.

"There we go," Trace muttered. "That will do her."

"That was a big bunch, yes Master Trace?" Herzl said. The dark-haired girl was grinning like a jackal at Yenta. "I spin!"

Trace continued to embrace Yenta, who was mewing softly. Herzl picked up the bottle and flipped it. The bottle spun in circles on the floor. Tajee swallowed. It pointed more or less at him. Herzl wasted no time in crawling on all fours towards him across the carpet. She jumped on him and kissed him, pressing her lips and insinuating her tongue.

Herzl kissed like neither Herpessenia nor Golda. Her furtive tongue wriggled like a salamander. Her mouth tasted sour and fruity at the same time. Tajee hitched at the gentle tug at the drawstring of his pants. Before he knew it, Herzl's agile little fingers were inside. Tajee groped at her, rubbing her stomach with slow strokes, reaching low. Herzl's weight and smallness reminded him very much of Boudi, which unnerved him, as did the thought of touching the strange girl's forbidden womanhood. As

Herzl's hand stroked his phallus, however, he felt his resistance erode.

"Okay, enough you two." Trace had climbed off of Yenta. As quickly as she'd come, Herzl was backing away and re-taking her place on the carpet. Yenta slumped against the edge of the bed with a look of drowsy delirium on her face. Trace reached for the bottle. "My turn."

"Nooo," Herzl said. She wiggled her finger in the air. "Is time for Tajee!"

"No, those are Ukraine rules," Trace admonished. "We go counter-clockwise where I'm from."

"Mais non!" Herzl protested. "I don't hear of this thing."

Trace picked up the bottle and spun it. After three full turns it came to a rest. Tajee shrank. It was him again.

"Yes! The boys kissing!" Herzl clapped her hands excitedly.

"Okay, I'm coming for you Tajee." Trace grinned. "We need some nectar for Herzl first."

"Non, non."

"Oui, oui." Trace dipped the spoon in the pouch and warmed it over the flame. Herzl watched the spoon like an interested kitten. She didn't protest further. When the powder melted, Trace lifted it to Herzl's small lips. She opened and took the spoon in.

"Mmmph!" Herzl squeaked. She fell to the floor, rolled onto her stomach, and rubbed her face excitedly between her hands. Trace lowered his head to kiss and bite the curve of Herzl's bare shoulder.

"Stop!" Yenta's bark was querulous. She shifted her weight and fell onto Trace. Trace turned and wrestled playfully with the housemaid. He found leverage. He lifted Yenta body up and threw her up on top of Herzl's bed. He climbed on top of her.

"Non! pas sans moi!" Herzl jumped onto the bed too. Her excited words were indecipherable. She wrapped Trace from behind, giggled and gnawed at his back. Trace lifted Yenta's nightgown up over her breasts, but it only tangled with her limbs, blanketing her head. She struggled with it. Trace turned his head and pointed Sharply at the door. Tajee realized that Trace was looking directly at him. The Ahyehass mouthed words.

The book! The book!

Tajee rose slowly to his feet. Trace pointed again at the door. Tajee grabbed his leather satchel, stepped backwards, turned the door handle, and slipped into the hall before Yenta could spot him. He glanced once more into the bedroom at Trace, who had turned to wrestle with the befuddled and nightgown-blinded Yenta, and also with Herzl, who was wriggling crazily. Tajee closed the door.

"je crois que c'est dans!"

Herzl's muffled mania inside the room was drowned out by Yenta's loud moan. Tajee stood alone in the dark hallway. He stared at the closed door. Herzl was inside, and he kind of liked her. Herzl was one of those deeply flawed girls that he'd always been attracted to. He almost wished Trace hadn't distracted the girls, or at least had waited a lot longer. Tajee felt a slow burn of anger surge through him. No. His priority was Boudi.

Tajee crept back down the hall, down the stairs into the darkness of the dead silent foyer, and back out the ponderous front door of the Villa. Outside, the night was growing colder. He wrapped his arms around himself for warmth. From Ayelet's front lawn, he could see the rooftops of the little city down the hill and the glows of light from a few windows. He made his way back around the stone walk to Boudi's room at the side of the house. He pushed the unlocked door open and stepped inside Boudi's dark dormitorium. He stumbled against the desk and found the metal and glass of the lamp with his fingers, but he had no matches. He had no way to make a light to read Boudi's diary.

He searched with his hands across the expanse of the desk. He could feel the diary sitting there, but he couldn't see it. Boudi's silver pen skittered when his fingers hit it. He trapped it under his hand. He opened the desk drawer. He felt another pen, a few papers, and a couple of tumbled ink bottles, but nothing that would light a lamp. Exasperated, he picked up the book along with the pen and took them to the open door, where the moonlight shone grey across the frame. The dim light wasn't nearly enough to read by, even with Boudi's thick script. Did he dare take the book back into the Villa?"

No. It would take too long, and Yenta would soon realize that he'd gone missing. He probably didn't have much time, and he didn't want to anger the girl again. Tajee fingered the book. A bold plan came to his mind. Maybe he didn't need Yenta at all.

He went back into Boudi's bedroom and found her wardrobe in the blackness. He tucked her diary under his arm and slid her pen into his mouth. He knelt and picked up a pair of Boudi's shoes and what felt like a corset too. The corset smelled like Boudi, feminine somehow, although he honestly couldn't remember that she'd smelled like anything in Heaven. Everything seemed different about Boudi, and her bedroom felt like a sacred female precinct to which he wasn't privy. A cool fear came over his bones, like a dread of desecration.

Tajee pushed everything into his satchel. He slipped back out into the night, and then he was stealing across the yard as quickly as he could go. He'd read the entire diary while Golda was away. He'd learn everything about Boudi. He'd learn what had happened to her. He'd learn what he was up against. Boudi-Ca would notice her things missing when she got back. She'd want to know where they'd gone. If the Jinni figured out what had happened, perhaps he could hold the things for ransom.

Golda could punish him, but he wouldn't give back Boudi's things until he was allowed to see her. Now that he knew where the Jinni were keeping Boudi, he could keep running up that hill at every opportunity that presented itself. He had faith that he would see Boudi-Ca soon with the blessing of Lord Tuhan. He felt a sense of confidence that he hadn't felt since he'd left Heaven. Thanks to Trace, things were finally going his way. He was making things happen like a Conclave agent.

Chapter 21:

Boudi-Ca squeezed the reins in one hand and grabbed her horse's mane with the other as the animal stumbled across the rocky terrain. A clatter of rocks came from the darkness to her right. The roar of a big cat echoed up the dark ravine. The horse tossed its head and wrenched out of control, twisting to the left. Boudi-Ca tried to recover and stay close to Ayelet. Ayelet was advancing with her sword drawn. The polished steel gleamed in the light of Ivanka's tenebris lux.

"The vampires are here," the black witch hissed. "It's a trap."

Another feline roar sounded down the ravine. Boudi-Ca gasped. Her horse reared underneath her, and she tumbled off onto a sandy embankment. She sprawled onto her back. A jolt of pain shot through her shoulder, but she was otherwise unscathed. She saw movement out of the corner of her eye. As quickly as she tried to get up, the vampire was quicker. It leapt onto her, knocked her back, and planted its knee into her stomach. The creature pinned her with its dead weight. It gave off a stench like death.

Boudi-Ca felt a wave of fear grip her belly. She punched at the vampire's unprotected head and landed a solid blow. The vampire was unphased. She'd only managed to graze his skull and knock back the hood of his cloak to reveal a bald head, hooked nose, and swarthy visage. He held her like a ragdoll. The furrows at the corners of his mouth deepened as he looked down at her with a cruel smile.

A sun-like blue tenebris lux burst into the night then, illuminating Ivanka's raised hand and bathing the entire ravine in brightness. The vampire flinched and turned his eyes away from the light. Boudi-Ca twisted and kneed upwards. She pummeled the vampire's groin with her knee and swung again with her fist. A thud sounded. The vampire slumped off of her. Four inches of a crossbow quarrel shaft protruded from the creature's ribcage. Herpessenia bent nearby, also unhorsed, where she loaded another quarrel into her silver weapon.

Boudi-Ca scrambled quickly to her feet. She found the hilt of her Oya-blade and pulled it from its sheath. She swung with a beheading blow to finish the vampire. The tip of the Oya-blade clanged against the rocks, but the stroke had been accurate. She raised her blade in a defensive stance and ignored the spray of sickly blood against her leg.

The ravine echoed with the sounds of battle. Ayelet was on foot and surrounded by several of the dark creatures. Ayelet waved her hand, and another blast of magical light illuminated the scene. The pinkish light burned away the mist in Ayelet's vicinity and set the leaves of the trees aglow with a magical fire. The fire shed a red illumination across the tumbled, mossy stones in the ravine bottom.

Beyond Ayelet's fallen mount, the huge bulk of Ivanka's Hell horse loomed in the faint light. The old witch still sat atop, swinging right and left with wide sweeps of the golden demi-lune weapon that she'd taken from the dead Eastern Order Jinni. Magical flames poured down the shaft of the weapon to ignite the vampire assailants.

Beyond Ivanka, near Golda's fallen horse, the large form of a lioness was just visible. The great cat leapt onto a vampire. Boudi-Ca heard a stifled cry and a whimper. She whirled to see Herpessenia struggling against a large dark form that held her from behind with its head buried in her neck. A smaller, hooded vampire looked on.

"Mistress Ayelet!" Boudi-Ca yelled. Ayelet didn't seem to hear. Ayelet had waded into the thick of the vampires, and she was dancing like a whirlwind. Her blade was alive with a strange crackling pink energy, and every swing of the charged blade elicited a scream of pain from a dark assailant. Meanwhile, Herpessenia's silver crossbow lay useless at her feet while her pale hands clawed at the dark arm that was locked around her neck.

Boudi-Ca broke into a run with her blade, even as fear wracked her abdomen. The smaller, hooded vampire flitted to intervene, as quickly as a bat in the night. Boudi-Ca slipped to the side and twirled, bringing the Oya-blade down hard in a diagonal slash with all of the intensity of her passion. The small vampire blocked the blow competently with a short wooden staff. Boudi-Ca swung sidearm with a hard slash intended for the head. Her intensive blade training with Ayelet came to her instinctively, but her vampire opponent was fast.

The creature ducked under her attack with inhuman speed. It thrust its hand at the center of her chest. Boudi-Ca blinked. Five digits pressed into her skin above the rim of her corset. She shrank from the paralyzing coldness that shocked her sternum. The coldness spread through her body and rooted her feet to the ground underneath her.

With a tremendous effort she pushed herself away from the vampire's hand. She sent warmth from her inner Jinn reservoir to re-awaken her feet. She managed to kick, surprising the vampire, and landed a hard blow that staggered it. She swung the Oya-blade and scored another hit with the slash. The vampire reeled back.

Boudi-Ca brandished her Oya-blade and sprang for the figure holding Herpessenia, but apparently she was too late. The divine daughter collapsed limply into a jumbled heap. Herpessenia's eyes were glassy and wide under a shock of her mussed white-blonde hair. The tall vampire standing over Herpessenia was unlike the others. He was uncowled, and instead of a cloak, he wore a vest studded with shiny black stones. His long dark hair fell down each cheek to frame the triangle of his neatly trimmed beard. Under the beard a heavy golden chain glinted in the magical light.

Boudi-Ca summoned her courage and surged to attack, but the vampire held up his hand as if to indicate that she should wait. She met his dark gaze, which was pregnant with a fascinating, inchoate intelligence. Another discharge of pink light rocked the ravine, accompanied by howls of pain from the vampires in Ayelet's vicinity. Boudi-Ca dimly heard her Oya-blade hit the stones, and she followed it down. Her mind went strange and disconnected, and her legs folded like blades of grass. She fell to her knees.

Boudi-Ca turned her head vaguely to the left. Ivanka had joined Ayelet to battle the main mass of the attacking vampires. Ayelet smacked the creatures with her flashing sword, toppling them like black matchsticks. Some of the vampires got back up, and some did not. Ivanka pointed her hand and intoned a spell. A bolt of fire erupted to flash with a crack through the chest of a nearby vampire.

Ayelet had finally seen what was happening. The elder blade mistress leapt over the rocks with sword raised. Boudi-Ca looked back up at the male vampire standing before her. He smiled when he glanced down. He wiped his thin lips with his hand as nonchalantly as if he were eating a fig. He stepped forward to intercept Ayelet.

Boudi-Ca realized that she couldn't move, nor could she seem to will herself to do so. She was completely immobilized, and everything around her was moving in slow motion. Rough, papery hands grabbed her. Pain jolted her paralyzed neck. A serpentine rush of pleasure arose deep in her sex. The pleasure leapt to join with the intense pain in her neck. It felt like a sexual release, but it flowed upwards with her blood. Her life force was flowing out through the bite—unbidden and uncontrolled.

Boudi-Ca moaned viscerally, a moan that echoed through the confines of her shrinking consciousness. She tipped back into a comfortable and inarticulate oblivion.

~*~

Golda swatted the vampire, bashing it like a rag doll against the rock with her paw. Its curved blade clattered to the gravel, and the thing finally lay motionless. The vampire was a mess of dead flesh, blood, and bones.

Golda urged her tired limbs into motion. She trotted down the ravine towards the center of the melee. Several deep bleeding cuts were sapping her energy. Her feline fur was more durable than skin, but her human form with a sword would have been more effective than paws for fighting the vampires. Sometimes her passion left her no choice. Even if she paused and focused, she had no confidence that she could regain control.

A foul-smelling wind was rushing down the ravine, setting the pink-glowing leaves of the trees to fluttering madly. Golda bounded over flame-crisped vampire bodies, making her way towards the eerily illuminated figures ahead. Ivanka was still mounted, beating back three or four vampires with the golden demi-lune blade.

Several paces past the witch, Ayelet was locked against a bearded vampire. Pink light erupted from Ayelet's hands and flashed in great arcs into the air, borne into snakelike spirals on the stench that blew in a howling circle around the powerful male. The plague wind was evidently a spell. Ivanka glanced over her shoulder from atop her Hell horse.

"It's a vampire prince, Golda," she rasped. "Help Ayelet if you can."

Ivanka's demi-lune slashed through the back of an attacker, toppling him to the ground, where his still-squirming pieces bracketed the blood-spurting remnants of his shattered vertebrae. The witch muttered an incantation and a blast of flame followed, rendering the vampire into swirling ash. Ivanka hissed as a vampire seized her blood-drenched leg in its teeth. The witch hammered the vampire's head. Golda bounded past and moved closer to Ayelet.

Ayelet was grappling with the prince in the center of the storm. The man held onto Ayelet's left wrist, while Ayelet held his throat with her right hand. The whirlwind of dust and flying insects enveloped them. Golda crept forward. She squinted her eyes against the unholy storm. She stayed low, digging into the sand and stones for purchase with her sore and bloody paws.

Not far in front of her, a small vampire crouched at the outskirts of the hissing, twisting gale. The thin features and painted lips under the black cowl revealed a female visage. The vampiress produced a short staff, which she laid on the ground. The staff, instead of being blown aside, transformed magically into a viper that slithered through the stones towards Ayelet's feet.

Golda surged forward to position herself to lunge at the viper, but she could hardly advance over the rocks of the stream bottom. The force of the storm was overpowering, and it carried an odor of decay and death that sapped her strength. There was no physical way that she could reach the snake, and its sinuous shape was quickly closing the distance to Ayelet.

Golda roared with desperation. Perhaps if she killed the vampiress, or at least distracted her, it would break the spell. When she pawed through the gale towards the vampiress, however, the woman met her with a three-pronged dagger in her hand. Golda snarled and leapt.

The vampiress rolled away from the blow and slashed a counterattack with the dagger. Golda groaned as the pain washed through her chest. She snapped her jaws viciously onto a wrist. A sickly, ashen taste filled her mouth as bones broke between her teeth. The vampiress buffeted her with her free hand. Golda rolled heavily, dazed. The skeletal hand found her wide throat. Filed nails dug into her fur, piercing and finding a tendon.

Golda felt a cold, numbing chill spread through her throat, her chest, and her stomach. She flailed, scrabbling against the rocks as she tried to right herself on her paws. Weakness overtook her. She agonized to pull another breath into her lungs with frozen chest muscles. She heard the coarse, loud voice of Ivanka behind her.

"Enflammer les colonnes de feu!"

Golda felt another burst of pain as a jet of flame formed a column of greasy smoke. She pawed blindly backwards with her face and fur scorched, but the vampiress had gotten the worst of it. The woman shrieked and rolled away, engulfed in fire. The wind whipped the flaming shreds of her dress from her body, and she flitted pale and smoking into the black shelter of the forest.

Golda stumbled to her feet. She struggled to refocus. She'd been badly burned and half-blinded by Ivanka's fire column, and the acrid smell of her own charred fur was hot in her nostrils. Ayelet and the prince were still in a deadlock. The staff-turned-viper seemed to have disappeared, following its mistress.

Golda spotted for the first time the motionless, slumped form of Boudi, and a short distance beyond lay the body of Herpessenia. Golda's stomach lurched. Both Herpessenia and the mimo girl were as still as death. Meanwhile, the vampire prince was the only enemy still in the battle. Ayelet remained locked against the creature. Her dagger hand was pinned, while his throat was firmly in her grip.

Golda stiffened as weakness stole over her wounded limbs. She was turning back. Her passion was spent. She braced herself against a boulder with bleeding paws that transformed into shredded fingers. She shook locusts from her hair, cast-offs from the maelstrom. It was all she could manage just to hold on and not blow away. She watched Ivanka snap her crop against the hindquarters of the Hell horse. The horse snorted and thundered forward, but it couldn't enter the whirlwind. It reared with jets of flame erupting from its nostrils, and Ivanka was pitched off onto the rocks. The charge distracted the vampire, however. The whirlwind slackened for a second.

Ayelet let go of the vampire's throat. Her hand swept low to pull another hidden dagger from her boot. The vampire released her in turn. Its form dissolved into nothingness as Ayelet stabbed up through the air, forming an eddy in a thick mist that drifted on the final force of the extinguishing storm.

Silence fell over the forest. Ivanka's lux flickered as the witch climbed slowly to her feet, appearing weary. The odor of smoke mingled with the smell of death. Golda rubbed her shoulder, and her hand came away slippery with blood. Her cuts and burns were painful, but she would live if none of the vampire blades had been poisoned. Ivanka brushed grey ashes off of her black skin and peered into the surrounding forest.

"We've won the skirmish, but we need to stay wary," the witch muttered. "The vampire woman can move very quickly. Have all of them been sent properly to the void? All of mine had a run through the furnace."

"All of mine are decapitated," Ayelet answered.

Golda cleared her tight throat. "I'm afraid mine have had nothing. They might be reviving and escaping by now. I was using paws instead of a sword."

"We'll deal with them." Ayelet's voice caught as her eyes lingered on the still form of Boudi-Ca nearby. "It's imperative that you learn to control your emotions, Golda. You need to be the mistress of the animal within you, not vice versa."

"Sorry, Ayelet." Golda rose to her feet. Her whole body ached. Fortunately, her change had a way of healing her when her human shape reformed. She stumbled to her fallen chestnut mare, which appeared close to death. She opened her saddle bag and pulled out her spare riding shirt, which she used to staunch her chest wound. Her Hunger surged hard in her belly then. She was empty. Like Ivanka, she didn't have much left.

Golda watched Ayelet examine Boudi. The mimo's flounced white riding shirt was stark in the forest gloom. Ivanka lifted Herpessenia's body high over her head to drape the young divine unceremoniously over the back of the Hell horse. The black witch worked quickly to lash Herpessenia's body in place. Ivanka looked over her shoulder. "I understand little Herpessenia-Ca has bedded down with you recently, Mistress Golda."

"That's none of your business."

"Well, I'm only saying this because I care, but Herpessenia is an utter whore, unlike her older sisters, Harmoniah and Persephoneh."

"I'm a whore too. What's your point?"

Ivanka shrugged. "The girl gets around and doesn't nest in any one place for long. Hear the wisdom of an elder when she advises you not to take this one's attention too personally. Herpessenia is just using you for her own amusement like she does with everything."

In her upended position on the horse's rump, Herpessenia's blonde hair had fallen over her face. Ivanka stretched her gnarled finger to slide the fine white strands of Herpessenia's hair behind her ear. Herpessenia murmured something inaudible. The divine fledgling was still alive, if only barely. Golda felt a growl forming low in her throat. Such a conversation at that moment was completely inappropriate, and it was just like Ivanka to take the opportunity to sow chaos.

"You know nothing, Ivanka. How would you know the things Herpessenia and I have done together? We understand each other."

Ivanka's black lips widened into a smile that was just visible in the low light of her tenebris lux, which still floated feebly above her head. "And you think you know anything of Herpessenia's passions? You're a fool, Golda. As to how I know what you Share, my fledgling tells me herself. Everything."

"Not possible."

Ivanka's black face was inscrutable. "Herpessenia is independent from her mother, but she is still a divine at heart. As unique as you are, do you really imagine she'll be interested in you for long? You're a former slave and a beast-creature. This girl has bedded gods. She was once betrothed to Poseidon."

Golda sighed. "I've heard Poseidon has nasty, icky skin like a squid. You're just trying to provoke me, Ivanka. It's horrible timing and poor taste."

"Yes, I'm trying to provoke you, Golda. Didn't Ayelet ever tell you that adversity makes you stronger? Well, you need some work in that area, as well as in choosing lovers suitable for your station."

Golda took a deep breath. She felt a roil of emotions rising, sucking dregs of energy from her body that she didn't want to expend. "I suppose I'm all the stronger for having worked my way up from such a fate then. I trained and studied for over a hundred years with Ayelet. That's an eye blink to you, but that doesn't mean you shouldn't show others respect for their own accomplishments and perspectives."

"Oh, I do respect you Golda," Ivanka countered. "I respect the unlikely thread of fate that wove you into the fine servant of Lady Allyssia that you are today. On the other hand, respect should be given in the measure that it's due. If anyone should show more respect, it is you."

"If I may interject something here?" Ayelet had approached and stood with her arms crossed. "Firstly, Ivanka has good points, Golda. You should listen to her."

Golda shrugged. "Live and learn. Tell me something I don't know, Ayelet."

"Very well. Boudi-Ca is alive, although only barely. She needs Demetriah's healing, and she desperately needs to feed, like Herpessenia-Ca. We need to get them back to the Redoubt as quickly as possible."

Golda eyed her mare. "All of our horses besides Ivanka's look to be dead or crippled. We can steal the horses of the vampires though. I should be able to find them if I relax and open my mind."

Ayelet nodded. "Excellent plan. Let's go quickly. For Boudi's sake, we'll forget the vampire prince and the female who escaped."

"Well spoken, Ayelet," Ivanka said. "There's only one more matter." The black witch paced across the stones to the ashen shreds of fabric that had been the clothing of the female vampiress. The witch fished with her fingers and lifted a pair of objects. One was a wavy circlet made of gold that seemed to be in the form of two serpents, each swallowing the other. The second object was a silver cylinder engraved with designs like those on the clothes of the two dead Eastern Order Jinni. Ivanka pulled a rolled parchment from the metal cylinder and scanned it. "Egyptian."

"Let's be out of this place." Ayelet's voice was tense. "We'll take those things to the Lady. Golda, what happened here should be kept solely among us. There's no need to disturb the Spring Festival with news that we still have Disciples of Set on the loose."

"My lips are sealed. Who would I tell anyway?"

"Track the vampire horses and carry Boudi-Ca for me. Ivanka and I will need our hands free in case we're revisited by the enemy."

Golda went to Boudi-Ca and gently gathered her. She was very familiar with the weight of the pretty mimo. She struggled to re-open her senses and clear her head. The whole forest stank of vampires. She couldn't understand how she'd let the group get ambushed. The vampires had used powerful magic. She was grateful that neither Ayelet nor Ivanka had yet said anything.

Golda hefted Boudi-Ca and hiked along the upslope. She felt Ayelet and Ivanka following her. The moonlight had returned with the dispersal of the mist, and the trails of broken twigs and crushed earth were visible. She followed circuitously through the brush and back up the ravine, and then steeply around a knoll. Soon she arrived at a high flat where a herd of saddled horses grazed.

Golda opened her tracking senses fully, focused, and detected the faint red streak of the escaped female vampire, which was just visible in the Isandlwana tapestry. The vampiress was circling through the forest to her horse, but she was still a few minutes away. Golda worked quickly to tie Boudi-Ca over the back of a dusty Disciple steed. She felt pained sorrow for the wounded mimo, but she didn't feel bad for Herpessenia at all. She'd countered Ivanka's cruel comments, but only to defend her personal decisions in life.

She hated to admit it, but Mistress Ivanka was right. She'd have to look further than Herpessenia for true love, just like she'd have to look further than the ill-treated Disciple of Set horses to replace her loyal chestnut mare.

Chapter 22:

Boudi-Ca licked the pomegranate juice from her lips. Her body felt better, although her bones still felt hollow, and her arms were weak and leafy. Demetriah and Ayelet had removed her corset. She lay nude with the bedcovers folded down to her hips.

"How do you feel, chérie?" Ayelet looked over the shoulder of Mistress Demetriah, who sat on the edge of the bed. Beside Ayelet stood the housemaid Yenta, whose dark eyes looked grave under her curly black hair. Anders the gardener sat solemnly in the desk chair with his balding head bowed and his worn gardening hat turning this way and that in his calloused hands. Herzl perched birdlike next to Anders on the edge of the writing desk with her hands on her thighs above her dirty knees. Herzl looked across the room at Golda, whose long body was silhouetted by the late-day sunlight that fell across the gardens outside.

"My neck is still hurting." Boudi-Ca looked away from the light that hurt her eyes. If she'd had any warmth in her cheeks, she would have blushed at all of the attention. It seemed as if everyone had come to visit her. She'd awoken that morning from a deep deadness, and she'd struggled to stay awake. Mistress Demetriah had come and gone at intervals all day, re-applying herbs to the puncture wound and imparting a healing warmth. It was Demetriah's last visit of the day, and Ayelet had summoned everyone, including Golda.

Boudi-Ca felt a constriction of shyness in her chest. She was extra-conscious of being naked to the waist and exposed to Golda's gaze. Golda had come to visit five times that day—more than anyone else other than Ayelet. Demetriah touched her throat.

"Do you feel like you can swallow again without too much pain, fledgling? Eating will restore enough of your energy to help you to feed properly."

"Yes. I think so." Boudi-Ca lifted herself up slightly and turned her head to allow Demetriah to move another pillow behind it. Her neck only hurt when she moved her head. A warm, damp herb cloth covered the tender spot where she'd been bitten.

Demetriah bent to a tray on the bedside table and returned with a spoonful of pomegranate pulp. Boudi-Ca opened her mouth, and the mistress slid it in. The seeds felt good, but at the same time the Hunger awoke again in her belly, which was still clenched tight with emptiness. The spoon dipped and returned to her mouth. She swallowed another lump of pomegranate and licked her lips. Pleasant energy trickled into her limbs.

"Ah, that's working well," Demetriah murmured.

"I do feel better." Boudi-Ca sighed. "A hundred percent. I thought for a while that I was going to die."

Demetriah smiled softly. "The vampiress could have destroyed your desire-body with a few more drinks from you, but apparently she decided to spare your soul from the void. Maybe she wanted to make use of you later."

"She probably thought Boudi-Ca was an mimo slave and loved the taste." Golda said quietly. "If the rest of us had gone down, Boudi-Ca would be waking up right now with a new Mistress and a vampire feed collar locked around her neck."

Ayelet paced across the bedroom and fussed with the tangle of clothes in the open wardrobe. "I take full blame for what happened. I knew there might be danger, but I thought I could keep my fledgling safe. I thought the adventure would be good for her progress. Maybe I made a bad decision. I can only hope that she'll forgive me."

Boudi-Ca took a third spoonful of pomegranate. Her belly warmed still more. She quivered. She felt slightly sick. "It's not your fault, Mistress. I should have just flashed away. I don't know why I didn't. I just stopped thinking. I tried to fight, but I was afraid."

"You attacked a vampire prince," Mistress Demetriah said gently. "Your Jinn will is weak yet. He dominated you mentally."

"The Mimos put that fear into you," Ayelet added. "Your fear drains your energy. You must let your Jinn energy flow freely. Your will needs to be a channel for your passion, not a barrier that constricts it."

Demetriah rose from the bed. "Perhaps that's not how her flashing works. Her power is fueled by her passion, but her flashing is a gift from the mental realms. Only a balance will allow her to use her full powers. Well, I'm going to go. Boudi-Ca will need some time to heal from these punctures. Until then, her energy will leak. I'd recommend giving her a rest from any training or other fledgling duties, Ayelet. You'll soon have a healthy fledgling. If you need me for anything else, send a bird."

"Of course. Thank you so much, Mistress Demetriah."

"I have to go too," Golda said. "It's good to see that you're going to be fine, Boudi-Ca. You did great against those vampires. You were very brave."

Boudi-Ca winced. Her neck hurt when she turned to smile at Golda, and by the time she managed it, Golda had already disappeared out the door. Demetriah passed after her, followed by Herzl and Yenta. Anders ambled out last with a sympathetic tip of his hat. The bed creaked. Ayelet sat down in Demetriah's place. "There's almost a full spoonful of pink knuckle-bark left, fledgling. No sense in letting it go to waste."

Ayelet scraped up the seeds with the spoon and offered them. Boudi-Ca took them into her mouth and swallowed. Despite her nausea, she felt like she was coming around. The edges of things looked less fuzzy.

"Thank you so much, Mistress."

"I'm afraid I'm going to have to leave you now too, fledgling. There's an important meeting at the Lady's palace. We're discussing these vampires. I think you'll be fine without me for a little while."

"I'm feeling much better."

"Good. Mistress Demetriah can work healing miracles. I'll come and check on you as soon as I get back. If you feel up to it, perhaps you could take a bath. You smell like horses and vampire ash."

"Thank you for everything, Mistress Ayelet. Thank you for saving my life."

Ayelet grimaced. "Nonsense, fledgling. It was I who put you in danger in the first place. I hope you're not too angry with me."

"No. I wanted to go."

"You can take a full month off from your blades training. You've earned it. You can relax and catch up on your diary writing. The martial competitions at the festival are exciting, so you might like to go watch those."

Ayelet rose, strode out the door, and closed it behind her. Boudi-Ca listened to Ayelet's boots clack down the walkway. She rubbed her stomach. Months had passed since she'd last had a pomegranate, and already the seeds had awakened her belly down to her sex. She felt the wetness sluice through her, but she resisted the urge to touch herself and lose the wonderful energy provided by the wicked fruit.

She lay on the bed for long minutes and stared at the ceiling. She was relieved that her bite was going to heal. Ayelet had informed her that there was no risk of transforming into a vampire. Vampires were created by a blood infection that could only occur on Earth. She kept thinking about the events of the battle, and especially her glimpses of Golda's inner cat.

The memories disturbed her. She needed to distract herself. She pushed herself into a sitting position. Her head swam, and the pomegranate seeds inside her shifted. The hallway to the bath beckoned, but the heated pool was too far from her bed. She didn't trust herself not to fall over. She crept instead to her desk, carrying a bed pillow with her. Her pen was missing. Her diary was oddly placed too.

Boudi-Ca checked stiffly under the desk. She didn't see her best pen. She sat down and searched the desk drawers. Her best pen was missing. She drew forth her second Conclave pen, uncorked an ink bottle, and set to work. She wasn't sure of the date. She guessed.

4 March

I went outside the Redoubt yesterday with Ayelet. It was my first time out of the city. We were on a mission to track some vampires. Meristyian is a beautiful place of forests and flowers. Herpessenia-Ca said there were nimfas and fairies, but we didn't see any.

Golda tracked the vampires through the Isandlwana Heartland. I was excited to be on an adventure with Ayelet and Golda, even though my rear was hurting from the saddle. I was proud to be a part of the hunting party. I was impressed with how Golda led the group. She's so beautiful. Golda hardly seemed to notice me the entire trip, but after I was bitten, she came to visit me.

Boudi-Ca tapped her pen on the black lip of the ink bottle. The ink didn't flow well from her second pen. The inner surfaces of the nib were corroded from the salty waters of the Sea of Desire. She sifted through the drawer. She was sure that she'd left her best pen on top of the desk. The desk top was spotless and polished, so Yenta must have cleaned. Boudi-Ca summoned her messenger bird.

"Mistress, my best pen has disappeared. I think Yenta did something with it. If she isn't busy, could you please have her find it for me?"

Boudi-Ca sent the little blue bird aloft. It flitted out the horizontal slit above the window. The pomegranate was still thickening and roping through her core. She didn't feel like writing. She felt like feeding. She didn't feel like being alone. She wanted to talk with someone she could trust. She felt reluctant to confide her feelings to Ayelet for fear of being corrected and judged. She wondered if she really was angry at Ayelet for what had happened—for not protecting her better during the vampire attack. She couldn't really tell. The pomegranate was dominating her drifting emotions with its queer influence. She wasn't thinking straight.

She set her pen on the desk, rose from the chair, and moved stiffly back to the bed. Just as her head hit the pillow, Ayelet's messenger bird scrabbled at the slit above the window and flitted down. Boudi-Ca flinched. The bird's little talons pricked on her bare shoulder. The bird hopped up onto the pillow next to her ear and spoke with Ayelet's voice.

Yenta has confessed to borrowing your pen and then losing it, fledgling. Because of this turn of events, I'm skipping the palace meeting. I'll bring Yenta down and instruct you how to punish her.

Boudi-Ca felt a slow burn of indignation. She couldn't believe that Yenta had stolen her favorite pen from Heaven. It wasn't long before she heard footsteps and a knock on the door. Ayelet entered sternly with Yenta in tow. Yenta looked penitent with her eyes downcast.

"What do you say to the fledgling, Yenta?" Ayelet said.

"I'm sorry, fledgling," the girl murmured. "Please punish me."

Yenta pulled her dress up over her melon-shaped breasts, sloughed it from her body without hesitation, and then denuded her legs of her stockings. Ayelet held a two-foot crop with a handle wrapped in leather. Yenta, bare-buttocked and wearing only her under-bust corset, fell on all fours with her face to the desk and her rear to the bed. Ayelet swung the crop. It landed with a smack in the quiet room. Ayelet ran her fingers over the mark.

"The tip of the crop and the end of its shaft sting the most, chérie. You must vary your strokes, move them to different places, and spread out the punishment so as not to make them too unbearable. Take the crop."

"Mistress, I—"

"You're feeling well enough. The crop and whip are symbols of our Jinn rulership. I know I said you could take a month off from your blades, but this is something different, and opportunities like this don't come every day."

Boudi-Ca stood up slowly and took the crop. It was light in her hand. The leather grip was well-worn. She'd never heard Ayelet's voice sound so unbalanced and emotional. Ayelet's hair was unkempt, and the faint wrinkles around her eyes and lips made her look older and more tired than normal.

"Mistress, I don't—"

"Punish her, please." Ayelet's strained tone left no room for argument. Boudi-Ca examined the crop. She didn't want to hurt Yenta. It was just a pen after all, although it was her best Conclave pen. If she'd dared to steal a Conclave pen in Heaven, Professor Brown would have lifted her skirts and paddled her ferociously, or worse. Boudi-Ca swung the crop. Yenta yelped. Boudi-Ca moved and swung again so she could connect with the full of the girl's left buttock.

"Get more of the shaft onto her skin," Ayelet said. "Stay in control and slowly build up effort as her desire-body compensates for the pain."

"Yes, Mistress." Boudi-Ca swung. Yenta flinched. This time the crop left a red mark. She swung again. With each strike her anger was pacified slightly, only to be transformed into little rushes of pride that warmed her. Her vampire bite throbbed. She moved to Yenta's right buttock and struck again and again—five times, then ten.

"Good enough," Ayelet said. "Yenta, sit up on your knees and face Boudi-Ca."

"Yes, Mistress."

The Ahyehass turned and did as she was bid. The dark locks of Yenta's curly hair were pasted to her sweaty forehead. Her pale breasts moved up and down with her heavy breaths over her tight under-bust corset. Ayelet knelt next to the Ahyehass.

"You can also strike her breasts, fledgling." Ayelet slapped quickly with her hand and smacked Yenta's breasts. Yenta's breasts bounced up and down with every strike, slowly turning pink. "Now with the crop, chérie. This will sting her. Her breasts are sensitive. Just strike the tops of them. With your neck the way it is, don't try to bend. You can skip the undersides."

"Yes, Mistress."

Boudi-Ca stepped to the position that Ayelet indicated and steadied herself. Her neck no longer hurt, and instead she felt heated between her legs. Her sex warmed not only from pomegranate, but from the sounds of Yenta's gasps and her cries. Boudi-Ca tried to focus. The sensation of arousal mingled with the stimulation of the pomegranate was a heady mix that threatened to tip her from her feet.

"Hit her, fledgling," Ayelet repeated. "When Yenta took your pen, she disrespected you. She offended your personal pride, and that is unacceptable. Take command and act like a Jinn. Make sure Yenta never does this again."

"Yes, Mistress." Boudi-Ca felt her pride rise still higher. A rush of strength filled her body and limbs. She planted her feet and swung the crop. It caught Yenta's breast across her nipple. The Ahyehass cried out.

Boudi-Ca fingered the crop. She wanted to improvise and slap Yenta with her palm right across girl's sullen cheek. It felt good to stand over Yenta—to be in complete control of the naughty Ahyehass, doling punishment as she saw fit. She felt a surging strength born from the intensity of her Jinn sin. In that moment, her inner mimọ girl surfaced to register a pointed protest. Sadness swept over her, making her hand tremble.

"I'm too tired for this, Mistress. I've decided to forgive her. Yenta is a loyal Ahyehass, and she's my friend. Everyone makes mistakes. I love her even though she took my pen. I'm sure there's a good explanation for why she took it."

Ayelet cleared her throat. "The relationship between a New Order Jinn and her Ahyehass is not solely one of friendship. Our arrangements are sacred pacts of domination and submission in honor of the Ifreeta. You can do this, fledgling. Just rest a second and take a breath."

Boudi-Ca avoided those Sharp hazel eyes. In that moment a rustle sounded at the bird slit, and a grey dove flew to Ayelet's shoulder. Boudi-Ca dropped the crop. She wanted to pull Yenta to her feet and smother the girl with a big hug. "What does the Lady want, Mistress?"

Ayelet looked at the floor for a long moment. "Allyssia says that you're right. She says Yenta shouldn't suffer a second more, and that I should be the one apologizing. I'm sorry, fledgling. I'm sorry for everything. It's certainly your prerogative to forgive Yenta. You have your own unique wisdom, and so does the Mimọic Hierarchy, as the Lady just reminded me. Yenta will find your pen, chérie. Send me another bird if you need anything else. I'll be in the training hall meditating."

Ayelet turned quickly on her heel. A smirk played on Yenta's lips as she followed Ayelet from the bedchamber. Boudi-Ca took a deep breath. She felt a sudden intense happiness, and her inner mimo girl was almost singing in her head with joy. Until that moment, she'd never won an argument against Ayelet. The Lady had personally stepped in to defend her. For the first time in her young Jinn life, she offered a prayer of thanks to Allyssia.

Chapter 23:

Boudi's white dive suit was stark against a grey-green sky. Boudi-Ca flew on a witch's broom with its bush of kinky bristles under her fluttering robe. She shot back and forth. She dodged bolts of lightning. She spiraled lower and lower. The rotten hands of old gods reached down from black clouds to grab her. Tajee ran through the flowered plain below. He was trying his best to catch her.

"Boudi!" he called. Boudi-Ca didn't hear him. She was high above on her broom. She didn't see him. She didn't even know he was there. "Boudi!"

Boudi-Ca fluttered and tumbled to the ground like a dead bird. Tajee ran to the spot, forging his way through a thickening field of purple flowers that were taller than his head. The flowers loomed over him and made him feel small. Boudi-Ca was stuck deep in the middle amidst a thick clump of green stems.

"Tajee? Is that you?" It was Boudi's voice, just as he remembered it. The flowers stirred and a hand appeared, and then her face. Her eyes were large and liquid. Boudi's umber eyes looked vulnerable, as if she'd been crying.

Tajee breathed deeply with relief. "Yes. It's me. I've been so worried."

"Tajee, you're late again." Boudi-Ca looked at her Conclave wrist-watch. "Are you hurt? Let me help you."

"Tajee, don't be silly. Come here." Boudi's arms stretched out. A white choker encircled her throat. She wore a pale white mimǫ corset. A pink satin bow peeked from the swells of her imprisoned, smothered breasts. Boudi-Ca slipped back again into the darkness of the flowers. Her legs fell apart. Her underwear was a promising waterfall of thin white mimǫ fabric.

"So are we going to do it, or not?" Boudi's voice sounded far away. "Take off my panties, Tajee. Have a gander."

"No." Tajee took a step back. "No. You'd never do anything like this, Boudi."

"I'm lucky to be moving up in Heaven. I'm doing something important for the Conclave, and you've just got a bad case of envy."

Tajee felt Boudi's soft stockinged foot tickle his ankle. He bolted awake in Golda's bed amidst a muss of sweaty covers. Golda stood nude next to the bed with her strong arms crossed over her chest. She was looking down at him. The warm candlelight from the bedside table framed Golda's wild red-brown hair in gold and cast her eyes in deep shadow. Her bluish lips were taut and unsmiling.

"Time to wake up, Tajee. Phylicia drew us a bath."

Tajee slid out of bed and followed Golda down the hall. Steam rose from the heavy claw foot tub to mist the bath windows above it. Outside the windows, the cool sun had risen to light the triangular tiled rooftops of Allyssia's little city. The light caught the fresh buds on the trees across the street, which swayed in a morning breeze. Phylicia was on her knees on the cold bath floor with her bare ass up in the air. The Ahyehass was naked except for her apron. She was mopping up water from under the tub. The metal handle of the pump had been leaking in recent weeks.

Tajee lowered himself into the hot water. Golda climbed in and settled behind him with her legs around his hips. The water rose with the displaced volume of Golda's body. She grabbed a soapy sponge and scrubbed him. As always, Golda's touch on his skin felt wonderful.

"Thank you, Mistress," Tajee offered.

"Turn around in the tub and lie back," Golda commanded.

He swiveled awkwardly against her. His wet wings pressed against the wall of the tub and compressed against his shoulder blades. Golda scrunched forward and ran the sponge over his face and chest, and then down to his thighs. She moved the sponge deep between his legs under the soapy water.

"That feels good, Mistress."

Golda stared at him. She was so close that he could see the individual hairs of her red-brown eyebrows. "You're so beautiful, Tajee. A mistress doesn't normally attend to an Ahyehass like this, but I feel bad. I know that I didn't keep my promise to you, and that's why you misbehaved."

"Have you decided yet whether to punish me?"

Golda leaned back and rubbed her temples with wet fingers. "Ayelet said that I should, but Ayelet got us into this situation in the first place. She refused to let me take you to see Boudi. Ayelet was afraid it would ruin Boudi-Ca's training. I refuse to punish you just because of Ayelet's questionable decision-making."

"Thank you, Mistress."

"Ayelet taught me to think for myself and to escape from my slave mentality, yet I've been deferring to her in everything. I should have stood up to her and found a way to fulfill the promise I made to you. Instead, I was lazy. I promised to let you see Boudi. I need to live up to my end of the bargain."

"So Boudi-Ca still doesn't know about me?"

"Not that I know of. I gave Ayelet the diary, but Ayelet insisted that I continue to remain silent about this whole thing."

"Why didn't you stand up to her then, like you said?"

"This deception has been going on for months now, Tajee. If we trot you up to see Boudi-Ca at this point, it will be like Ayelet and I have been lying to her this entire time."

"You've been lying."

"Watch your tongue." Golda's eyebrows furrowed. "We meant the best, and everything was done for a reasonably good reason. But then you stole Boudi's diary, and now I just got a bird from Ayelet saying a pen is missing too. What all did you take, Tajee?"

"The diary and the pen. And a few other things."

"Don't you see, Tajee? On top of everything else, now Ayelet and I are working together to cover up this diary incident too. Once all of this comes out, and Boudi-Ca learns that we've been keeping you from her, she won't trust me or Ayelet any farther than she can throw us."

"So?"

"So she'll feel alone. She won't trust anyone. She'll collapse emotionally. All of Ayelet's work with her will be ruined. At least, that's what Ayelet said. As much as I'd like to say differently, Ayelet is probably right."

Tajee swallowed. "How is Ayelet working with her?"

"Ayelet is training Boudi-Ca in the ancient ways of the Jinni, just like she trained me. Maybe Ayelet thought you wouldn't last as my Ahyehass, and that the Lady would send you packing."

"I don't understand."

Golda stretched back in the tub and sighed. "Ayelet was sure that I'd fail with you one way or another, like I fail with a lot of things, and the Lady would eventually send you back to Heaven. Well, it hasn't happened. You're still here, and you still want to be here. Now it's Ayelet's problem to figure out how to deal with it, unless the Lady steps in and does something."

Golda lapsed into a strained silence. She reached up and made an idle circle on the steamed window pane with her finger. Tajee trembled inwardly. He felt angry, sad, and intensely frustrated. His plan to steal Boudi's diary, pen, corset, and shoes had accomplished almost nothing.

According to Trace, Yenta had discovered his disappearance and consequently his theft. According to Golda, Yenta had gone straight to Ayelet when the mistress came home, and Ayelet had gone straight to Golda to get the diary back. Golda had come to him and demanded that he surrender it.

He'd refused to divulge the diary's location. Golda had been furious at first. She'd slapped him with a hard blow on the cheek that had sent him reeling. Golda had immediately apologized, kissed his cheek, and insisted that she loved him. She'd turned the entire house upside down with the help of Trace and Phylicia.

Phylicia had found the diary where he'd hidden it in a deep, dusty crack between the stubby feet of Golda's wardrobe—a crack just a few inches wide between the boards of the bedroom floor and the wardrobe's chipped bottom edge. He'd further obscured the diary behind an old cobwebby stocking, but that hadn't deterred Phylicia from claiming her promised reward of pleasurable purple nectar.

Golda leaned forward and dunked her head to rinse her hair. The water crested and splashed. Golda rose up from the water to stand knee-deep in the tub, pulled her mane over her shoulder, and began to wring it with both hands as she looked out the window over the city.

Tajee gazed up at the dripping Jinn jungle that stirred him with its proximity. He didn't want to hate Golda. He wanted to love her and her sex, but the secret place inside of him—his secret resistance to her—reminded him of what she was. He hated himself for being so weak.

Golda arched and pushed her hips forward. "I actually like that you were bad."

"Why?"

"You remind me of myself. I was bad too when I was a slave. I just wanted someone to love me. I knew my Mistress couldn't love me if she did those things to me. I just wanted love, and now I'm alone again. I'm in that same loveless place where I've been for too many decades."

Golda stepped out of the tub. Tajee rose and followed her out of the water. Golda grabbed a towel and pressed her face into it. Golda's eyes glistened. Tajee felt his stomach quiver in sympathy.

"Don't cry, Mistress."

"I wanted you to be happy, Tajee. I brought you into this city, so you're my responsibility. I don't deny that. It's just that I want to be happy too. I envy your love of your mimo girl. You don't know how lucky you are to be in love."

"What about Herpessenia-Ca? I thought—"

"I dumped Herpessenia last night when I went to visit her. Ivanka is right. I was just a toy to her. You should have heard her. She was insulting me and calling me names. She said that she's the daughter of Allyssia, and no one leaves her, and the divines are the ones that do the leaving. I was so upset on my way home that I almost transformed and ruined more of my clothes."

"Please don't be sad, Mistress."

Golda turned away from him. "Come. I want you."

"Yes, Mistress." Tajee felt his phallus stir and thicken as it always did when he heard those words. He followed Golda back into her bedchamber. When he climbed onto the bed, he was ready—such was her intense power over him. Golda sat on the edge of the bed and fumbled in the side table drawer for her spoon.

"I love your long hair, Tajee. I want to do something with it. I want to do something with you in general. I hope you won't be too upset if we change the way you look and dress. I want to see how it makes me feel."

"I don't understand."

"Yes? Questions?" Golda opened her nectar box and spooned an unusually large heap of purple powder. She lifted it to the candle flame.

"How long have I been here in this place?" Tajee watched the silver spoon waver at the end of Golda's trembling fingertips. The purple nectar melted quickly into liquid in the heat of the candle. A strong flowery aroma filled the bedroom.

"You've been here in Meristyian for five moons or so." Golda lay back on the bed with her head on the pillow and carefully transferred the spoonful of liquid nectar down to her sex. She thrust the spoon into her pumpum with a practiced motion. Golda moaned, let the spoon go, and writhed with pleasure. She pulled the bed pillow over her face and held it there with both hands. Stray drops of nectar glistened wetly in the wild red hair on Golda's lower belly. The silver spoon handle glinted and twisted between her thighs. Tajee bent on impulse and licked.

A gentle pleasure pulsed through his mouth and down his throat, warming him to his chest before petering out. He licked Golda's pumpum hair clean, and then he moved up, searching for more drops of hot nectar on Golda's bath-warmed stomach. He found them and licked. More wonderful pleasure filled his tongue and mouth, chased by a curious numbness.

"What are you doing?" Golda murmured. "Silly boy." She reached and caressed his cheek. Tajee felt his head swim. The pleasure was spreading through his nose and made his eyes dry.

"I, um—"

Tajee fell onto Golda's heated skin and pressed his cheek against her breast. The heady sensuality warmed him down to his chest, and then to his belly. He felt an urge for more nectar—much more. He eyed the box on the side table.

"That's not for you, my beautiful boy. Not for you." Golda reached low and removed the spoon from her pumpum. She raised it to her mouth, licked it clean, and dropped it with a clatter off the side of the bed. "I don't want you to be like I was, don't you see? I can't afford it anyway since I might have a supply issue soon. Oh, Tajee. What should I do with you?"

"I don't know, Mistress."

"Just kiss me, and keep kissing me. I don't care where."

"Yes, Mistress."

Tajee felt his phallus pulse. His sexual response to Golda was automatic and unavoidable, and he knew that she'd wickedly made him that way. He dutifully kissed Golda's nipple. She insinuated her long fingers and puckered her breast for him. He sucked and licked gently around the tip.

"What do you want besides Boudi, Tajee?" Golda said softly. "Maybe I could find you a replacement for her—something to distract you from thinking about your old girlfriend. Is such a thing possible? Could you let Boudi-Ca go? Could you forget her? It would save us both a lot of headaches, you know."

"Mmmph." He didn't answer. The gentle pleasure of the nectar was still spreading softly in his body with a curious and happy sensation. He continued to engage Golda's nipple, licking and kissing until it was slippery.

"Lie on your back, Tajee."

"Yes, Mistress." Tajee rolled over onto his back. Golda climbed over him and straddled his hips. He pushed up, wanting the penetration. His phallus plunged into her hot, nectared interior. Tajee moaned. An intense wave of pleasure rushed through his groin and pressured his testicles. Golda rocked on top of him, back and forth. Her strong belly bounced on his own with her motions, rendering him breathless. Within a few minutes, he felt his release already rising inside him.

"Come into me, Tajee."

"Yes, Mistress," he gasped. He spasmed profoundly and obediently. Golda came to rest on top of him, still gripping his phallus with her intimate wet prison. She looked deeply into his eyes. She was so close that he could see the individual silvery flakes in her pale blue irises. She settled her powerful weight on top of him, pinning his body.

"Tajee, I've thought of a way that you can see Boudi-Ca soon."

"How?"

"Well, I'm speaking hypothetically of course, but you're going to have to be bad again. You're going to have to do more things behind my back. I know you've been good for months because I seduced you and made you venerate me, but you can do it."

"What do you mean?"

"Well, thanks to Trace, you know where Boudi-Ca lives in Ayelet's Villa, of course. It isn't a long walk. I'm not encouraging you to do this. I made a promise to you, but I also made a promise to Ayelet, and Boudi-Ca is much more important to this city than you are. She could be a major asset for the Lady someday. On the other hand, I can't stop you from escaping this house if you really want to, unless I cage you. I'm not going to do that."

"When would I escape the house?"

Golda rolled off of him and stretched on her back on the bed. She gazed up thoughtfully at the starry black bed canopy. "It will be the day after tomorrow on the last night of the Spring Festival. I'll be taking Trace to the palace to dismiss him and deliver him to the Lady. He wants to serve Herpessenia-Ca, if she'll agree to let him. You and Phylicia will be here in the house. You'll be my new houseboy then, so of course you'll have the keys to the doors. I'll expect you to behave while I'm gone, but sometimes new houseboys don't behave. They make mistakes."

"Thank you, Mistress."

"We'll go over this again when we look at your new duties as my houseboy. You remember the way to Ayelet's Villa, don't you? You know how to find Boudi's bedchamber across the flower gardens?"

"Yes."

"I only want one thing in return. Could you please remember put in a good word for me? That's important."

"A good word?"

"Tell Boudi-Ca that I was very good to you. Tell her I took good care of you, and that I wanted to let you see her, but Ayelet wouldn't let me. It was all Ayelet. Can you promise to do that? If Boudi-Ca doesn't hate me, then maybe we can save the situation."

"I suppose."

"Of course, if Ayelet discovers your intrusion, I won't know anything whatsoever about your rebellious escapade that happened while I was away."

Tajee bit his lip. "Understood, Mistress."

"Don't let Ayelet punish you or interrogate you, either. You're my boy, not hers. If Ayelet tries to make you squirm, you should tell her that she has no right, and she needs to come to me." Golda caressed his cheek. "You're so sweet, Tajee. I'm so glad I never let Herpessenia-Ca get her perverted little claws on you, not even for a minute."

"Thank you, Mistress. I'm glad I'll finally get to see Boudi."

"From the way Ayelet spoke, I think she has her own private strategy for damage control, and that's why I'm going on my own. If I know Ayelet, she'll twist things to her favor at my expense. Well, two can play that game." Golda turned and kissed him gently on his temple. "Do you really love your mimo girl? Do you really think she loves you back?"

"I know I love her, but I have no idea what she thinks of me anymore, or if she even does. She didn't say anything about me in her diary."

"I won't forbid you to fuck her. I owe you that much." Golda's eyes were hooded and shadowed in the candlelight. She splayed her long legs sensuously. "Please go down with your mouth now."

"Yes, Mistress." Tajee slithered low onto his stomach. Golda's pumpum was waiting wetly, and it was still sweet with nectar. Golda pulled his head forward with her fingertips. He took a deep breath and began to lick. He felt another wonderful tingle in his tongue that echoed and resonated with the warmth in his heart. His love for Golda had once again found the upper hand over his anger. The Mistress was not only encouraging him to be bad, but she was willing to be bad for him.

Chapter 24:

❦

It was a beautiful spring day in the Lady's city. Ayelet's gardens were damp from a morning rain that had left the air grassy and fresh. Patches of warm sunlight shone through the scudding clouds in the sky. Birds chirped in the cypresses. Boudi-Ca hurried along the Villa walkway. The Spring Festival was coming to an end, and she was going with Ayelet to the final-day festivities, where the Mistress would be sparring in a blade's exhibition. Her neck hardly bothered her. Three days had passed since the battle with the vampires in the Isandlwana Heartland. She'd spent most of that time in her bedchamber—sleeping, writing, and forgiving Yenta.

After the pen, she'd discovered a corset missing too. She'd told Ayelet, and the Mistress had brought Yenta down to confess and be forgiven again. After the corset, she'd discovered a pair of shoes missing. Again Ayelet had wrangled a confession from the Greek housemaid. The lost items hadn't yet turned up, despite Bola and the other Ahyehasi supposedly searching the entire Villa.

Ayelet had purchased gifts at the Festival to replace the missing items—a new silver pen with hellion-forged scrollwork on its grip, three expensive knuckle-bark pomegranates, a bottle of fine burgundy wine from the vineyards of Vegasis in Erebus, two new pairs of shoes, and a fresh bottle of the finest Merian writing ink.

Boudi-Ca traversed the walkway around the front of the house. Yenta's shocking thefts had tested her compassion. Her pen wasn't much, but the loss of her clothes was unacceptable. Although outwardly she'd held fast to her mimo girl virtues and her victory over Ayelet, inwardly she felt torn.

Ayelet had a point—the human Ahyehasi were not necessarily her friends. Yenta was required to obey and behave by the Lady's law, but what if the girl didn't? At some point, there had to be repercussions in the form of punishment, just like when Mimos disobeyed the commandments of Lord Tuhan. Ayelet was waiting in the rear Villa yard, directing Bola's preparation of the large, two-seated carriage. The elder mistress wore a faded grey training robe with a gold sash.

"Ready to go, fledgling?"

"Yes, Mistress. More than ready. I'm so happy to be out of my bedchamber and going someplace." Boudi-Ca climbed into the rear of the double-seater with Ayelet, who continued to seem tired, tense, and distracted. Bola snapped the reins from the front seat, and they rolled out of the Villa grounds and down the hillside towards the center of the city.

Boudi-Ca watched the houses of the Redoubt go past. She'd felt a strong bond with Ayelet during the previous two days. Without scheduled lessons, Ayelet had transformed into a sympathetic, honest friend than a constant taskmaster.

For the first time since she'd arrived in the Lady's city, she felt happy. She felt like someone cared for her. Lady Allyssia had never been a part of her daily life, but the bird that the Lady had sent to Ayelet had changed things. The mysterious and complicated goddess was not only watching—the Lady took an interest in her problems. Lord Tuhan had never paid any attention to her in Heaven, despite her thousands of prayers. Such personal attention was reserved for the important people—the arch-Mimos and the saints.

Boudi-Ca looked away from Ayelet as the carriage rolled through the grid of quaint streets and plazas in the lower central city. She'd dreamed twice again of Golda during her many hours in bed. In both of her erotic dreams, she'd been lying on a beach covered with bones, soaked and wet, and Golda was kissing her on the lips.

If she could summon the courage, she wanted to find and corner Golda at the festival. She kept dreaming of Golda. Maybe she only wanted a friend, but her dreams were telling her that she wanted something more. She tried to imagine herself boldly flirting with Golda, but she had no idea how such a thing was supposed to work.

Ayelet's feather-plumed horses pulled the carriage quickly past the city workshops. They arrived at the city amphitheaters on the northwest edge of the entry plaza within fifteen minutes. Bola drew the carriage to the end of several others. Ayelet gathered her sword, and they climbed the approach steps to the rim of the first of the three amphitheaters.

"I'm going to the warm-up area, fledgling. The last rounds of the blade contests should soon be underway. You can sit and study the techniques you see." Ayelet shielded her eyes with her hand and looked through the crowd. "I don't see the escort that I arranged for you. Perhaps she isn't here yet."

Boudi-Ca frowned. "An escort? Who?"

"Just sit down there, fledgling," Ayelet said, gesturing vaguely at an empty section of seats in the Amphitheatre. "You're waiting for Mistress Isabellah. You've met her, yes? She's extraordinarily pretty, chérie. Send me a messenger bird if anyone else comes along and bothers you overmuch."

"I will, Mistress. Good luck."

Boudi-Ca tried to hide her look of disappointment. Had Ayelet divined her rebellious mind yet again and arranged an escort to keep her from straying? She didn't want Ayelet to know how she felt about Golda. Those feelings were somehow special. Those feelings were her own. She didn't want Ayelet taking over and analyzing things, or worse yet insisting that she stay away from Golda for some reason or another.

The city amphitheaters consisted of three large pits formed by tiers of steps descending to flat stages, all linked together at the top rim like a three-leafed clover. The triple stages were marked as competition areas with swaths of red ribbon and multicolored pennants on high poles. The pennants fluttered in a breeze that blew down the mountainside.

At least a hundred spectators were sitting in the theatres—mistresses, fledglings, Gypsies, Kishi, and many other festival guests. Scents of leather and perfumes wafted on the air from the promanade, where the Gypsies had set up colorful tents and shops to hawk their hand-tooled wares. Boudi-Ca felt suddenly self-conscious. She was surely the only mimo at the festival that day, and many of the passers-by were staring at her with curiosity.

In the adjacent theater, a contest was underway. A line of archers faced a handful of tricolor targets. The contestants weren't all shouldering bows. One fledgling raised a long silver gun to her shoulder and sighted down the length of it. A gunshot cracked through the amphitheaters. The crowd cheered. Another fledgling with a bow stepped to the mark. All of the contestants were nude except for colored sashes around their waists.

Boudi-Ca stepped through the spectators and seated herself on an upper section of seating in the first Amphitheatre. She scanned the seats, but Golda and her wild ruddy hair were nowhere to be seen. Two fledglings came onto the stage. They were greeted by applause from the audience. The fledglings were nude except for black sashes. They carried stout wooden training blades. A pretty female Ahyehass pranced into the ring and waved a rod with a pale violet ribbon on the end.

"Introducing fledgling Jade Turtle, trained by Mistress Golden Gorila!" the Ahyehass announced. "Opposing her this afternoon will be fledgling Minnie-Ca, trained by Mistress Pyrinnah. This is the first semi-final of the blade's competition!"

The audience cheered, and the two fledglings circled each other with their practice swords. Minnie-Ca was young, sturdy, and fierce-eyed, while Jade Turtle was taller and muscled with white powder and black paint on her face. Jade Turtle attacked with a powerful cross-cut. Minnie executed a straight up-and-down block. She counterattacked fiercely. Jade Turtle ebbed against the assault. A scattering of applause came from the crowd.

"Well done, Minnie-Ca," cried Mistress Gallinah, who sat in the front row. Next to Gallinah, two other mistresses made marks on score cards. Minnie pressed the attack, but Jade Turtle, with a surprising move, swept the smaller fledgling's feet and toppled her headfirst to the dirt, and then

Minnie was on the defensive. She parried admirably, and the two fledglings circled again.

Boudi-Ca tried to follow Jade Turtle's impressive whirlwind technique. The technique looked like Ayelet's wild attack against the vampires. For several minutes Minnie was on the defensive and managed a stalemate, although the smaller fledgling was able to launch an occasional counterattack when Jade Turtle paused to rest.

"Time!" the announcer finally cried. The announcer consulted with the judges in the first row before raising her flag. "Victory on points to fledgling Jade Turtle. Congratulations! In the next semi-final, fledgling Katia-Ca will face the last non-fledgling competitor in this year's blades contest—the vampire Huesca!"

Minnie and Jade Turtle met in the center of the sand with a hug and pats on the back. The two fledglings exited together into a tunnel, from which emerged a swarthy, beak-nosed vampire and a willowy fledging with pert pointed breasts and an olive sash around her high, sleek hips. A chorus of catcalls greeted the vampire, who wore a plain black robe in contrast to the less clothed female contestants. Katia-Ca squared off against her vampire opponent. The purple flag waved. Katia-Ca attacked confidently. The vampire blocked and counter-attacked.

"Excuse me, may I take this seat?"

Boudi-Ca was startled by the smooth voice so close to her ear. The Jinn who stood next to her wore rubies and citrines braided with silver settings in her dark hair, which fell in long sweeps over her shoulders. Her pale jewels matched her cream-colored dress, which dazzled the eye with narrow burgundy stripes.

"Of course. I'm Mistress Ayelet's fledgling."

The Jinn smiled. "I know who you are, Boudi-Ca. I'm Mistress Isabellah. I don't think we've properly met." The Jinn extended a slender hand clad in a faded burgundy glove. Boudi-Ca took the hand briefly, nodded, and released it.

"I'd be delighted if you'd join me, Mistress Isabellah."

"I'd be delighted to accept, fledgling. You're well mannered, I must say, which is surprising for a student of Ayelet."

"Thank you, Mistress. I think I'm still an mimọ in my manners."

"I suppose that stands to reason, although all Jinni aren't ill-mannered." Isabellah winked and seated herself. She removed a folded fan from a hidden pocket in her dress.

"Have you seen Mistress Golda anywhere, Mistress Isabellah?" Boudi-Ca looked straight ahead and tried to sound nonchalant.

"Oh, no. I haven't seen Golda in weeks. She's either out in Meristyian at the behest of the Lady or cooped up in her little house, training a male Ahyehass that shall not be named. So what do you think of this vampire swordsman? What's your professional opinion, fledgling? Will he defeat Katia-Ca?"

"I think he's very good." Boudi-Ca returned her attention to the stage, where the vampire had cornered the fledgling Katia-Ca against the ivied rear wall. In a series of lightning-fast moves he disarmed her and pointed his practice sword at her throat. Katia-Ca spread her hands in a gesture of wide-eyed surrender.

"A quick victory to the vampire Huesca!" cried the announcer. "After a rest, Huesca will face Jade Turtle in the final!"

"Well, that answers that." Isabellah idly flipped open her fan and waved it back and forth. Small dark red birds flitted magically as if alive in the willow branches that were painted on the fan's surface. "You don't often see a vampire do well in our traditional Jinn competitions. We've had them before over the last century—the occasional ambassador from one of the peaceful clans who wanted to try his hand."

"Mistress Ayelet says vampires aren't that good at swords."

Isabellah nodded. "No vampire visitor has ever beaten our very best blade fledglings. Huesca isn't an ambassador or vampire royalty even, just a spy that we captured in Meristyian several months ago. It would be a scandal if the vampire won. I hope Jade Turtle can defeat him."

"I'm impressed by Jade Turtle. She's tall and strong. She has a long reach and good techniques. I'd be afraid to fight her."

"What about you, fledgling? You're Ayelet's protégée. Why aren't you down there on the gladiatorial sands showing us all what you've got?"

Boudi-Ca shrugged. "Mistress Ayelet probably thinks I'm not good enough to go against a fledgling like Jade Turtle or Minnie-Ca. My neck was hurt recently too."

"Oh, yes. Ayelet mentioned your injury. Well, there's always next year and the years after that. By tradition, you've got at least a few decades left until you pass your Mistress Test and become fully fledged."

"I suppose." Boudi-Ca felt a jolt go through her body when Isabellah patted her firmly on her knee with an elegant gloved hand. Boudi-Ca tried to calm her heart. For some reason, Isabellah's touch had been very tingly. She'd nearly jumped from her seat.

"Yes, I'm sure Ayelet knows best when it comes to blades. It's a shame that she keeps the most beautiful fledgling in the Redoubt hidden away and sweating with swords, though. It wouldn't hurt for you to socialize and go to parties with the rest of us."

Boudi-Ca felt a small flush of pride in her throat. "I like swords. I want to be strong so I can help fight the vampires." Boudi-Ca looked over at the beauty mistress, and Isabellah returned her brazen stare. Isabellah's oval face was almost perfect. Her eyebrows were neatly lined, and her nose was narrow. She wore a small beauty mark above the corner of her mouth.

"But you enjoy beauty too, I hope? I've rarely seen a more beautiful fledgling, although you could use some powder and paint, and your hair could do with a few smidgens of improvement."

Boudi-Ca felt another rush of pride—a warmth that spread downwards into her stomach. The pride gravitated to her vampire bite and pulsed there in a queer, uncomfortable rhythm. "Who is your fledgling, if you don't mind me asking, Mistress Isabellah?"

Isabellah waved her fan back and forth. "Oh, I don't have one right now, but I'm looking for one. I had my eye on Herpessenia-Ca some time ago, but the girl is stuck on Ivanka. Herpessenia is lazy, anyway. She has potential, but no discipline or ambition whatsoever. I'm firmly in the school of Ayelet on that. I'd get frustrated with a fledgling that never makes any effort to get better and improve herself. Ivanka never works with

Herpessenia-Ca's skills as far as I know." A cheer erupted from the archery Amphitheatre. A small group of smiling fledglings gathered, patting backs, and an announcer cried out.

"The winner of the archery competition is fledgling Lao-Ca, with Geraldina-Ca runner-up! An honorable mention goes to Herpessenia-Ca for a perfect score in the second round. Too bad she didn't get it when it counted!"

"I don't like Herpessenia-Ca." Boudi-Ca glanced at Isabellah to gauge her reaction. "She saved my life against the vampires, but I still don't like her."

Isabellah smiled. "You have strong opinions, Boudi-Ca. Good for you, but make as few enemies as necessary. This is a small city, and one day Herpessenia-Ca could be useful to you."

"I can't imagine for what."

"Divines are a breed apart, fledgling. They're special, just like you."

"I'm nothing special."

Isabellah clucked. "Nonsense. I can see straight away that Ayelet isn't nursing your pride as much as she should be. Do you enjoy studying with Mistress Ayelet?"

Boudi-Ca hesitated. "Is one supposed to enjoy one's teacher? I don't know. I guess I'm new to all of this. Mistress Ayelet is very wise. She teaches me well. She lectures me. I learn a lot from her."

"Does Ayelet ever talk to you about your posture and your bearing? You're slouching, Boudi-Ca. I can't help but remark on it. Such a beautiful, exotic fledgling should show herself off more. Your perfect young breasts are underemphasized by the slouching carriage of your shoulders, and your neck is half lost by the humble way you hold your chin. You have real assets, but you aren't using them as well as you could be."

Boudi-Ca felt a full-on blush coming to her cheeks. "I used to have a lot more discipline when I was an mimọ girl. I always kept proper posture, and I wore powder to cover up my imperfections. Since I've been living with Ayelet, I haven't paid attention to any of that. I'm not sure why."

"Your little wings are glorious, too. So unusual. One sees wings on devils down in the city of Mer, but those are batlike and ugly. Fallen Mimọs are normally snipped by their owners. You were very clever to throw those bottles over the edge of Heaven instead of just jumping and hoping for the best."

"I can't imagine any mimọ would jump from Heaven. They fall on accident, and then they have to be rescued."

"Oh no, I've heard it happens. They tell stories much like yours. They didn't like serving Lord Tuhan. They didn't like toeing the narrow lines of virtue and goodness, so they decided to commit mimọ suicide. I won't say more about those Mimọs, but I'm sure you understand your good fortune that the Lady took you instead of someone with coins as a motive."

The announcer down on the stage reappeared and waved the purple flag to get the attention of the audience again. "And now, fledgling Jade Turtle faces the vampire Huesca in the final of the blades competition!" The crowd cheered. Isabellah twisted her fan slowly back and forth on its axis as she gazed down at the stage.

"Oh, this should be interesting, fledgling. The Gypsies who participate in the competitions lack the endurance to go all the way. They always fade to our fledglings. The vampires are sometimes the same. I hope this one fades for Jade Turtle's sake. Huesca looks to be fed, though. I wonder who he's been feeding on. Maybe the Gypsies." Isabellah chuckled.

"Where do the Gypsies come from? Meristyian?"

"Oh, no. If they're from anywhere, it would be the region of Vegasis or the vicinity of Mer. They have camps in the outskirts of many of Hell's cities. You know Mer, don't you? It's the capital of Hell in the heart of Haawiyah. The best of everything comes from the capital city. It's the home of Hell's Court and the main body of Jinn and Djinnus society."

"I'd like to see it someday. Ayelet told me that the Old Order Jinni are our enemies, though."

Isabellah nodded. "I don't know where we stand with them anymore. I wish everyone could be friends. The New Order split off to protest the laws against lesbians, but now we're so far away from the capital and the luxuries that we once had. The Gypsy caravans still bring us some things—fine fabrics, nectars, and scents. The Gypsies are free from regulation by Hell's

Court thanks to their ancestral trade covenants. Smell this."

Isabellah pulled her glove from her right hand, revealing manicured nails painted in pale pink. Isabellah swiveled her wrist. Boudi-Ca bent and sniffed. The scent that arose from Isabellah's skin sent a queer pleasure filtering deep into her head.

"It's very nice."

"It's from a class of perfumes distilled from Haawiyah poppies. This particular one was mixed with other elements like the ground skulls of vultures. The exact composition is a secret. Down in the city of Mer, perfume-making for Jinni is a high art form. The best magicians of scents sit at the right hand of royalty in Hell's Court."

"Do we make perfumes here?"

Isabellah smiled faintly. "No. Fine arts require money to fund them. We don't have a Court here or any hierarchy of nobility besides Allyssia's divine family. Not that a society completely free of a patriarchy is meritless, or else no beauty mistress worth her shoes would even be here, least of all me."

"Is that why—"

"And so we have the imports. We do have some top-notch artisans here. I myself am a weaver. No one makes artisanal quality perfumes. The expense and difficulty of gathering all of the different materials by importing them would be prohibitive. Mer is a hub for those things, and so it's the center for perfume-making."

"That makes sense."

A Sharp crack sounded on the stage. Boudi-Ca turned back to the action. Huesca had blocked a ferocious blow from Jade Turtle. The fledgling bore down on the unbalanced vampire, who kicked and twirled. The strong fledgling blocked and executed a low sweep, which Huesca locked. The vampire stepped into Jade Turtle's guard and pommeled her in the stomach. Jade Turtle grunted under the thudding blow and slumped. Huesca toppled her. Silence fell over the Amphitheatre.

"The winner of this year's blades competition is the vampire Huesca," called the announcer. A smattering of polite applause was drowned out by a storm of hisses and boos. Even the announcer sounded disappointed. "And now a short break before a surprise exhibition from our two best resident blade mistresses."

Isabellah shook her head. "Shocking. And terrible, too, considering the recent events with the vampires outside our gates. I'll have to make some inquiries as to why this Huesca is even outside of the Lady's palace. I thought he was a prisoner."

"I feel sorry for Jade Turtle. She deserved to win, and vampires are dangerous. They should definitely be locked up."

"Boudi-Ca, would you care to go shopping with me?"

"Yes. I guess." Boudi-Ca rose and followed Mistress Isabellah up the amphitheater steps and into the market plaza, where rows of colorful tents punctuated a hodgepodge of sights, sounds, and smells. Isabellah raised her shapely nose as if sniffing the air.

"We're following the scents, fledgling. Look there—hippogryph feathers and eggs from the cliffs of the Trivium. It's a novelty the merchants have this year. I imagine come summertime we'll have baby hippogryphs running everywhere. According to the rumors, six mistresses in the city have already bought one or two eggs." Boudi-Ca felt the hand of Isabellah come to rest on her back as if to guide her through the crowd. The beauty mistress led her towards a small striped tent with a flap for an opening. A pudgy dwarf stood by the entrance. The diminutive man wore a pointed green hat. He puffed on a pipe and vigorously motioned to them.

"Step inside, step inside! Perfumes for the lovely ladies!"

Boudi-Ca followed Isabellah inside. Another Gypsy dwarf stood at a low table, which bore numerous boxes, bags, and displays of fine colored powders. Isabellah bent and smelled the scents at length with obvious pleasure.

"I noticed you weren't wearing any perfume, Boudi-Ca, so I thought I'd buy you some. Would you mind? You truly should wear perfume. It's a shame for you not to."

"I'm not sure what Mistress Ayelet would think."

"As far as I'm concerned, this is my civic duty. A young Jinn should be wearing perfume even if her only interest in life is beating on things mercilessly with swords. This is the city of Love, after all."

Mistress Isabellah beckoned to the dwarf behind the table. "Four drams of Lethian Velvet Light for the fledgling, Yaemus. Liquefied."

The man winked. "Right away, Mistress Isabellah. That will be two aurei and twenty."

"Boudi-Ca, in addition to perfume, they sell nectar here." Isabellah smiled sweetly. She opened a silk purse and extracted two gold coins and two silver coins. "Are you familiar with nectar?"

"No, not really."

"Traditionally, it's against divine law for anyone other than a divine to partake of nectar. Some gods and goddesses began gifting it to their favorites, and then those favorites gifted it to their human slaves, and today it's a part of Jinn society, especially down in Haawiyah, but also, to a lesser extent, here in the Lady's city. I don't partake. The expense is a bit extravagant if you're addicted. I'd rather have nice clothing."

Boudi-Ca watched the dwarf tip powder onto his scale, adjust the weights, and then tap the powder from the scale into the vial. The dwarf reached over the table for a flask of liquid and a small silver funnel.

"What is nectar, exactly? I don't understand."

"It's a powder made from Underworld flowers," Isabellah answered. "A number of varietals serve. Blue Violet Beauty is the most popular nectar and by far the cheapest for us since the flowers grow right here in the Isandlwana Fields." Isabellah leaned and whispered. "The black is the most wicked and powerful of all. It's distilled from poppies that grow on the banks of the river Lethe. The nectar makes you forget everything."

Boudi-Ca smiled and nodded politely. Isabellah kept hovering a bit too close to her, and the presence of the older Jinn was strangely intoxicating to her senses.

"Here you are, fledgling." The dwarf out stretched his hand. Boudi-Ca took the small bottle filled with liquid from the Gypsy's stubby, stained fingers. Isabellah reached forward and dropped the worn gold and silver coins into his palm. Boudi-Ca felt Isabellah's hip brush briefly and warmly against her own.

"Thank you, Yaemus," Isabellah said. "Out we go then, Boudi-Ca. Are you watching the hand-to-hand competition? It will be after Ayelet's exhibition, I suppose. Our young fledglings will be boxing, kicking, and wrestling in the nude against the Gypsy men and Freyah's battle-Ahyehasi. It's sometimes fun to watch. Personally, I'm not. I have an afternoon party to go to. I only came down for a bit as a favor for Ayelet."

Boudi-Ca studied the perfume bottle as she left the tent and walked alongside Isabellah. The bottle was made of clear crystal so as to show the rich red of the perfume inside. The bottle was capped with a black stopper in the elegant spiral shape of a lizard. She lifted the bottle and sniffed a perfume both sweet and intoxicating, just like Isabellah.

"Is this the same perfume that you're wearing, Mistress?"

"Mine is higher quality, but a red-nectar base nonetheless. It's a common grade staple of any self-respecting beauty mistress. Good perfume gives us an extra-special quality that enhances our attractiveness. Give it a try."

"Thank you very much for the gift."

"Well, it's time for me to be off." Isabellah folded up her fan when they reached the top edge of the steps that led down from the amphitheaters to the entry plaza. "It was a pleasure to meet you, Boudi-Ca."

"It was a pleasure for me too, Mistress Isabellah. I mean, you talk about a lot of things that Ayelet doesn't. I don't think she ever wears perfume. She tends to smell sweaty. You smell like beauty itself."

"Why thank you, fledgling. Flattery is an art form that we beauty mistresses cultivate to the highest levels, of course. You seem to have a knack for it. In fact, I would urge you to be cautious. Those of lesser abilities in the city might envy you. There are a number of fledglings in this city who dedicate themselves to blades, but only one gets to train with Ayelet."

Boudi-Ca felt a quick flush of pride. "I suppose."

Isabellah winked. "I'd really like to get to know you better, fledgling. Why don't you let me give you a few lessons? Perhaps, say, on Wednesday mornings? I can teach you things that Ayelet will not, and its high time you mingled with the rest of us instead of staying cooped up in Ayelet's Villa."

"That would be nice."

"Good. I'll arrange things. Take care, fledgling. We'll see each other soon." Isabellah slid her burgundy gloves back onto her hands to complete her picture of elegance. Isabellah's graceful female Ahyehass, who had appeared from nowhere, escorted her mistress down the steps to a parked carriage. Isabellah alighted in an extravagant carriage that was carved in the shape of a swan.

The Ahyehass snapped a whip. Large white wheels turned, and the carriage rolled away. Boudi-Ca walked in a daze back to the amphitheater. She slipped the lizard-stoppered perfume bottle in her pocket and re-took her seat. The announcer walked to the center of the fighting stage and waved her purple flag.

"We have another surprise exhibition before the hand-to-hand combatants begin. The vampire Huesca has agreed to a short spar with Mistress Golden Gorila, who wishes to avenge fledgling Jade Turtle. The first competitor to five points wins!"

Boudi-Ca bit her lip. Had she missed Ayelet's demonstration already? Wooden swords collided with a resounding crack on the theatre floor when Golden Gorila met Huesca. Golden Gorila kicked a plume of dust and straw from the stage floor into the air with a sweep of her foot. Huesca ducked. The quick, agitated mistress landed a painful-looking low blow into the vampire's thigh. The crowd erupted with cheers. Huesca recovered and the fighters circled each other.

"There you are, Boudi-Ca." Mistress Ayelet sat down on the stone Amphitheatre seat with her sword under her arm. Ayelet flipped her long braid over her shoulder and swiped a stray strand of greying hair behind her ear. Ayelet's eyes drifted down to the stage. "What do you think of this vampire, fledgling? He's a tremendous blade master. He'll beat Golden Gorila unless she conjures something special with her tricks and deceptions. There's much more to that vampire than meets the eye."

"He must be very good to have beaten Jade Turtle."

"Did you see my exhibition match with Freyah, fledgling? Did you notice the Bonetti defense I employed? I introduced you to it a few weeks ago."

"Yes, Mistress." Boudi-Ca looked away and pretended to be absorbed in the fight below, hoping Ayelet wouldn't realize that she'd missed the exhibition match entirely. Golden Gorila brought her sword down in an overhead smash that nearly brought the vampire to the dirt, but Huesca counterattacked brilliantly, striking Golden Gorila hard to her chest, and then sweeping her knee.

"Two points each for Golden Gorila and Huesca," cried the judge.

Ayelet gazed down at the battle. She restlessly tapped her knuckles on her knee. "The vampire is tiring, Boudi-Ca. Even the undead lack the tremendous energy reservoirs of a Jinn as old as Golden Gorila. She needs to be patient."

"That's what Mistress Isabellah said."

Ayelet cleared her throat. "So she actually showed. I thought I smelled expensive perfume, but I didn't think it would be coming from you."

"Yes. She sat with me." Boudi-Ca fingered the warm flask in her pocket. "She bought me some perfume, too."

Ayelet smiled. "Are you going to use it? Are you planning to seduce someone?"

"Maybe. Is Isabellah a friend of yours?"

"Not so much anymore. We've slept together on occasion over the decades, but we aren't a great fit. She's isn't my equal physically, and I'm no match for her wit. The golden ratio applies in love like everything else, fledgling. I like to be in control. Isabellah is a genius with knots. She likes to rope up her Ahyehasi, but she doesn't like being roped."

"I can't imagine you wooing a beauty mistress with flowers, gifts, and poetry."

Ayelet's smile widened. "The Old Order beauty mistresses down in Mer are the grand dames of Underworld high society. They are the critics and commentators for the arts and fashion scenes. They are the most celebrated mouths and faces of Hell's Court. They are matchmakers and fashion plates. Here in the Lady's city, the beauty mistresses are just small tokens of that obsession with wealth, beauty, aristocracy, and politics."

"Mistress Isabellah seemed impressive."

"Well, who else is she impressing besides you? Whose human slave will we assassinate in this city to avenge a minor insult? Whose husband will we ruin so we can elevate our own husband's position in Hell's Court? Whose fortune will we steal with an investment scheme, and who can we frame to be arrested by the devils while we take all the coins for ourselves? You've seen much of the Underworld's beauty, but not much of its ugliness yet, fledgling. We're all considered equals in the Lady's city. Isabellah's peacocking seem a bit silly to some. What else did Isabellah say?"

"A lot of things. She wants to give me lessons in beauty."

Ayelet nodded. "So do you want to go?"

"Isabellah wouldn't be as rude as Ivanka was with my magic lessons."

"Many say Isabellah is the most beautiful woman in the city aside from the Lady herself. She's sometimes called upon to greet and entertain important visitors, especially men. I'm sure she could teach you some things, chérie. I'll send her a bird. By the way, I received a bird a bit ago from the Lady. You're invited to come with me to a meeting of the mistresses tonight in the palace. Now that the Spring Festival is almost over, the Lady plans to make an announcement."

"What kind of announcement?"

"I'm afraid it's related to the vampires outside our gates."

A tremendous smack sounded across the Amphitheatre. A collective gasp rose from the crowd. The vampire Huesca had landed a tremendous blow against Golden Gorila, who crashed through the wooden side gate and careened out of sight into the adjacent archery ring. The announcer raised her flag dejectedly.

"That's another three points. Huesca wins again."

Chapter 25:

The evening gloom was falling over the city when Ayelet's carriage rolled across the palace plaza. The pillars, pediments, and facades of the palace were swathed in deepening shadows, while the remnants of the setting sun struck the highest cornices and crystal spires, setting them alight with a dying orange fire. Ayelet snapped the reins and turned the carriage towards the palace steps, where a stable boy directed her to fall in line with a dozen other carriages that had already arrived.

Boudi-Ca looked for Isabellah's swan carriage with white wheels, but she didn't see it. She'd asked Herzl for advice on how to use the potent Lethian Velvet perfume. Herzl had assisted with its application, but the dressing-girl had surely used too much. The perfume wasn't just wafting out into the air around her. It was intoxicating her own nostrils, making her feel light-headed and floaty.

Boudi-Ca breathed deep. It was worth it. If she ran into Golda at the palace, she'd have an extra-special attractive quality. The mere thought of attracting Golda made her feel like an mimo girl again—nervous and breathless like she'd felt around Makeda Deen. Deep down, she was skeptical that she could seduce Golda, however. She just didn't feel beautiful. She had a lot more beauty work to do.

Her lessons with Isabellah promised excitement. She'd be able to go places and do things she wanted. She was tired of being cooped up in Ayelet's Villa. She was ready for adventure, as long as the adventure had nothing to do with vicious, bloodthirsty vampires. The meeting at the Lady's palace was exciting too. It was her first official meeting at Ayelet's side, and it underscored her proud feeling of being accepted and respected by the other Jinni.

Boudi-Ca hopped down carefully from the carriage, balanced herself on the uneven flagstones, and scurried to climb the palace steps with Ayelet. Ayelet was striding at a speed that wasn't friendly to little three-inch heels with black bows on the toes. The elder blade mistress looked straight ahead as she climbed between the double lines of flickering candles that illuminated the marble steps.

They passed through the massive mother-of-pearl front doors and into the interior of the palace, which was thick with a comforting warmth on that cool March evening. A small line of palace Ahyehasi waited to escort the arriving visitors. A pretty Ahyehass wearing a pale pink skirt and a matching under-bust corset greeted them with a curtsey.

"Good evening, Pexa," murmured Ayelet. "Lead on."

"Thank you, Mistress," Pexa replied. "Please follow me." The girl kept her eyes properly lowered as she led them around a curving hallway, through an archway, and onto a wide stairway leading upwards.

Boudi-Ca strode with Ayelet through the palace behind the Ahyehass. Up and up she went alongside Ayelet, up the marble steps until the stair opened into an egg-shaped room that felt both grand and intimate. The high walls of the room were softly gilded, and the floor was like a cavernous honeycomb with several tiers of steep hexagonal seats around the sloping sides with a dais in the middle. Sixty or seventy mistresses and fledglings were seated and whispering quietly.

"Sit behind me, Boudi-Ca," Ayelet said in a low tone. "This is the spring meeting room. We call it the beehive."

"Yes, Mistress." Boudi-Ca occupied the seat that was above and to the left of where Ayelet sat. She knew only half of the Jinni in the room. Mistress

Cybelah was sitting down in the third row. Next to her were Mistress Elibah, Mistress Apolloniah, and the shoe-maker Mistress Mayah, with Mistress Gallinah on the aisle. Mistress Freyah sat in the first row next to the daughters of the Lady. Dour, pale, and dark-haired Persephoneh sat next to her sister, Harmoniah, who always wore a peaceable look on her amiable face.

Fledgling Jade Turtle and Golden Gorila sat next to each other in the second row. Both wore freshly applied white powder on their defeated faces. Jade Turtle looked gloomy and carried her arm in a sling, while Golden Gorila shot dangerous looks at the vampire Huesca, who sat alone in the uppermost row of the chamber next to masked Cupid.

Golda entered the beehive then from the far entrance. Boudi-Ca watched Golda saunter catlike down through the seats towards the blonde fledgling Herpessenia, who sat just behind the shrunken black form of Mistress Ivanka. Golda looked out of sorts. Her wild hair was disheveled, and her purplish lips bore a pensive overbite. Her silver-blue eyes darted under a ruddy rogue forelock. Golda was beautiful even when she was unkempt.

The numerous fluted oil lamps in the chamber dimmed at the moment that Golda seated herself. A magical light came to life from behind the highest row of seats. The light illuminated the top half of the egg-shaped chamber in such a way as to decorously display the rough golden texture of the sloping walls. The light climbed the walls to the apex of the curved ceiling, then collected and fell to illuminate the dais in the middle of the room. A hiss sounded as golden dust fell through the light and swirled towards the floor, where it coalesced into the golden-brown form of Allyssia. Boudi-Ca felt her skin prick. The presence of the Ifreeta was palpable. The texture of the air thickened with Her energy.

"Greetings, Jinni," the Lady began. "We are gathered here to speak of a grave situation that faces us all. A few days ago, a hunting party of our mistresses tracked a band of Disciples of Set that had struck against Patriarch Reik caravan on its way to the Spring Festival. The hunting party found the vampires. They also found the bodies of two Eastern Order Jinni who were sent to the void by the vampires not far from our gates. Those two Eastern Order Jinni were high priestesses of the goddess Sekhmet. They carried with them a message from Sekhmet—a message that asked for my help in defending Her secret enclave from a combined attacking force of Old Order Jinni and Disciples of Set."

"The Old Order attacked the Eastern Order?" Gallinah interrupted from the third row. Her voice sounded shocked. Golda also stiffened visibly in her seat. A susurrus of disbelief rushed through the meeting chamber.

"Yes, Mistress Gallinah," the Lady continued. "Mistress Artemisiah has independently investigated the matter, and she believes the message is at least three weeks old. The Eastern Order Jinni were delayed and unable to find my Redoubt due to the magical veils that hide it. They were apparently desperate to complete their appointed task, however, so they kept searching anyway. That is how they were overtaken by their pursuers, who did not want us to be forewarned."

"My Lady, forewarned of what?" Mistress Gallinah leaned forward in her seat with a frown on her normally jovial face.

"I have turned my eyes into the east, my Jinni," the Lady continued. "I see a threat that stirs in the desert even as we speak. The vampires gather under the guidance of the Old Order, which seeks to dismantle the rebel Jinn orders in Meristyian. I fear the ancient Eastern Order has fallen, and that the vampires intend to attack here next, at our home, with the purpose of either sending you all to the void or sending you all away in chains, to be punished and re-taken into the fold of Lady Allyssia and Lord Hades."

Boudi-Ca swallowed. She wasn't sure what was going on, but she could feel her skin pricking and her stomach clenching from the power of the emotional energy that swirled through the chamber in that moment. Golda looked aghast—an expression similar to that on the faces of the other Jinni. Even Herpessenia looked paler than usual. Jade Turtle sat open-mouthed in disbelief with her powdered face a frozen mask.

"Surely they cannot penetrate the Redoubt, my Lady," Freyah muttered. "If the high priestesses of the Eastern Order couldn't see through your protective veils, then how will the Disciple of Set sorceresses do it, even with the aid of the Old Order? I thought our Redoubt was almost invulnerable to attack by anyone from outside, even by a god."

Lady Allyssia inclined her head slightly under the soft beam of golden light. A shadow fell over her masked visage. "Sadly more than one god has tipped his hand in this matter. It's my belief that the vampires will attack with the aid of not only Lord Hades and the Old Order, but also with the help of Lord Tuhan and the Mimoic Hierarchy. Moreover, this attack on my city is imminent."

"But my Lady!" exclaimed Golden Gorila. "That's ridiculous. We've never seen such an alliance. The formal negotiations that would be required—"

"That is enough," Allyssia interrupted. "I shall continue."

"Please do," Ayelet said grimly. "How do they plan to attack?"

Allyssia lifted her hand for silence. "When our new fledgling Boudi-Ca came to us as an mimo, she carried a hidden trace inside her wrist-watch. It was an Mimoic dream beacon that enabled her mimo masters to track her through my and Ivanka's spells and thereby penetrate the dream-veils of this city. Ivanka and I have eliminated the dream beacon, but we cannot reverse the flow of time and repair the damage it has caused."

"What damage?" asked Mistress Cybelah.

Allyssia inclined her head further. "Lord Tuhan and the Mimoic Hierarchy, while not attacking directly, could have given the Old Order the means to breach the protective spells that took me centuries to fully strengthen. The message sent by the Eastern Order Jinni suggests that their own enclave was breached by a similar Trojan dream beacon just like fledgling Boudi-Ca's wrist-watch."

The room was dead silent. Boudi-Ca held her breath. The bottom had dropped out of her stomach. Every Jinn in the chamber was looking straight up at her, and many of the looks were wickedly venomous. She could feel the heavy weight of the harsh gazes on her face. Her heart thumped hard. She felt a melting feeling that she hadn't felt in a long time. She shrank and wished that she could turn invisible.

"Measures are already in place to defend us from a vampire attack," continued Allyssia. "There is no need yet for us to panic. Instead, we must act. A small contingent of mistresses will leave immediately to follow the

Eastern Order track back through Meristyian to the Eastern Desert. We do not know for certain if the Eastern Order and the cat goddess Sekhmet are wholly broken. If we don't follow the track of their messengers, any holdout or remnant of the Eastern Order may be lost to us forever. I would prefer to find them and offer an alliance, or at least a new home."

"What are we doing with the mimọ," Mistress Ivanka said coldly. "As I've said previously, she may still be dangerous. She's never been properly interrogated."

"Either send the stupid mimọ to the void, or send her packing back to where she came from," Golden Gorila added. "She's a liar and a spy."

Murmurs of agreement swelled in the chamber. Boudi-Ca gripped the edges of her chair with both hands. She felt terribly hot. A bead of sweat trickled between her breasts into her corset. The walls of the beehive seemed to constrict around her and crush her like a giant fist.

"Boudi-Ca will not be cast out of our society," Allyssia said. "The mimọ has shown no conscious desire to compromise this city. I've been watching Boudi-Ca closely. I've seen that she works hard to improve herself. She genuinely wishes to learn our ways. She's a promising young Jinn and a credit to the New Order."

"Well spoken." Ayelet said solemnly.

Allyssia raised her hand again for silence. "As a precaution, however, I've decided that Boudi-Ca must leave our city until this situation is resolved. Therefore, the fledgling will be a part of the small contingent that goes into the east on the track of the Eastern Order, and perforce, so must Mistress Ayelet."

Whispers and protests again erupted from the Jinni. Boudi-Ca blinked away her tears. Allyssia's and Ayelet's words of confidence filled her with pride, but the feeling didn't equal the burning shame of being fingered as a spy in front of all the New Order Jinni.

"Who else will go?" Freyah's voice rose above the din. "Will Mistress Artemisiah be the tracker?"

"And what of the two vampires that escaped the hunting party?" Ayelet added. "They might be tracked as well."

"Quiet," intoned Allyssia. "Quiet, please. I'm sorry, but in this special case the decisions will be mine, and there will be no debate. Golda will go as the tracker. The vampires that escaped into Meristyian will be ignored for now. It's telling enough that they were Disciples of Set."

"Disciple scum," hissed Golden Gorila, who craned her neck to direct her voice pointedly at the vampire Huesca. "May he and his blood be damned! Why in the hells is that vampire even in here?"

Allyssia raised both of her hands. "Your long-lost Eastern Order sisters are in need, my Jinni. If the time is not too late, we may still respond to their overture. If we can form any kind of alliance with Sekhmet and her people, we will be stronger to fight the powers that would see the rebel Jinn orders in Meristyian broken and destroyed. Ayelet, Golda and Boudi-Ca will be the core of the band that goes into the east. Who amongst you will join them? I ask for one more."

"I will." Mistress Cybelah raised her hand. "I've worked well with Golda in the past, and I can offer ranged support to Ayelet's sword."

"I'll go." Mistress Freyah raised her hand.

"No, Freyah," Allyssia murmured. "I eternally appreciate your bravery and service, but your expertise and that of Cybelah's will be needed for the material defense of the city. Again, this will not be a fighting group. Like the party that tracked the vampires here in Meristyian, this group will try to avoid direct confrontation."

"I'll go." A middle-aged blonde mistress in a long violet robe spoke. "I've always been a student of the east. If you recall, during the schism of the Jinni, I suggested the Eastern Desert as a place to locate the Redoubt. I'm not as skilled a magician as Ivanka, but my knowledge of eastern Meristyian and its people could be useful."

Allyssia nodded solemnly. "Mistress Gonorrheah, you will also travel to the east. Thank you for your service to the New Order."

"My Lady?" Golda raised her hand. "I don't know if I can track the Eastern Order Jinni. Their thread was almost nonexistent since they were trying to stay hidden. Nearly a week has passed on top of that. I never sensed a trace of those priestesses of Sekhmet until I was looking down at their bodies."

The Lady nodded. "I understand, but you must try, and you'll have help. Huesca will be going as well. He is familiar with the east, like Gonorrheah, and he's perhaps the best tracker I've ever known. Together, you and he will find a track in the tapestry, and you'll follow it to the Eastern Order." All eyes in the chamber turned to look up at the vampire Huesca, who still sat in the top row next to Cupid like a pale, expressionless ghost. Golda tilted her head to the side. Her face was a mask of surprise.

"So be it," Allyssia said. "Mistresses Ayelet, Gonorrheah, and Golda will leave at tomorrow's dawn with fledgling Boudi-Ca and the vampire Huesca. They will journey over the spine of Meristyian and into the wild lands of the Acheron River. The New Order will respond belatedly to the overture of the long-lost Eastern Order. The rest of us will prepare to defend the city. I will speak with all of you again as the situation unfolds. Good night." The column of light over the central dais consumed the form of Allyssia, and she was gone.

Boudi-Ca rose from her seat. She wanted more than anything to get out of the beehive. Her legs were trembling. Her heart was pounding. Sweat soaked her corset, and her ears were buzzing queerly. Her earlier sense of happiness and pride at being invited to the evening meeting had been replaced by horror. Her humiliation in front of everyone was apparently why she'd been invited in the first place. She looked at the floor to avoid meeting the eyes of the New Order Jinni.

"Chin up, fledgling," Ayelet said, patting her back. "They aren't really angry at you. Besides, almost everyone that matters has had an inkling about this for days, or even months, as far as the Hierarchy's trace."

Boudi-Ca gasped. "What? You mean all of this time—"

"All that I know is that you belong here with us, fledgling. I see no reason for that to change. When the situation is difficult, the warrior must look within for her true strength. Failure isn't in getting knocked down. Failure is staying down. Let's just go home, feed well from the girls, and pack our bags. We'll leave in the morning for the east."

"Why is that vampire going?" Mistress Golden Gorila stormed up and confronted Ayelet. "Allyssia can't be serious. Huesca is a Disciple of Set and a spy."

Ayelet arched her eyebrow. "If you had paid more attention to the beatings Huesca gave you and your fledgling at the blade's competition, you would have noticed that he expertly employed the Exquisite Form of the Smokeless Flames. No vampire would know that secret technique. Very few Jinni do. He also used the Courtly Form of Han Tsu in a style reminiscent of a few exclusive dojos in the Asian quarter in Mer."

Golden Gorila stared at her incredulously. "Then maybe you're mistaken, Ayelet. What are you saying?"

"I'm saying that he isn't really a vampire. I sent a bird to the lady earlier, and she confirmed my suspicion. Huesca is actually Masad, the son of Lord Hades, who has borrowed the body of our vampire guest."

"Prince Masad? You mean the Possessor?"

"Yes. The one and only. The Lady has contracted Prince Masad into Her service. Huesca has been imprisoned in the Palace for several months, as you know, and was a convenient body for Masad to possess. Now let me and my fledgling by, and do not question the Lady again in my presence."

Golden Gorila nodded. "Sorry, Ayelet."

Ayelet bowed curtly. "Boudi-Ca, why don't you head on out to the palace steps. I'll meet you there shortly. I want to speak for a moment with Golda, Gonorrheah, and Masad about our plans."

"Yes, Mistress. I'll wait for you."

Ayelet slipped away towards Golda. Boudi-Ca turned and quickly climbed out of the spring meeting room, acutely conscious of the accusing looks. She crossed her arms and hurried alone through the exit and down the long steps with the rest of the Jinni.

"Hierarchy spy."

Boudi-Ca glanced over her shoulder, but she wasn't sure who had said the words. It could have any of the cold-faced mistresses bustling down the hall right behind her. Boudi-Ca reached down, removed her heels, and quickened her pace to almost a barefoot run.

Apparently she'd carried a hidden magical trace in her Conclave wrist-watch without even knowing it. Pasteur and the Conclave Mimos hadn't even told her about such a thing. She felt a bit of anger rise in her chest to mingle with her embarrassment and hurt. Had the Conclave of Deviant Operations deceived her?

If everything the Lady said was true, that meant that Pasteur and the Conclave hadn't actually abandoned her. They'd actually planned in advance for her to be snatched so she could carry the dream-beacon. And that could mean, although it was almost impossible to believe, that after five months of living among the Jinni, the Conclave might still be planning to rescue her and take her back to Heaven as part of a master plan to destroy Ayelet, Golda, and all of the other New Order Jinni.

Boudi-Ca paced through the palace doors and down the front steps. The cold air of the evening felt good on her hot face. She walked laterally away from the line of carriages to a darker stretch of steps near the stables where she could wait for Ayelet away from everyone else. She sat and watched the Jinni slowly file out of the palace. In ones and twos, the elegantly dressed mistresses and fledglings descended the steps between twinkling lines of candles. They climbed into their carriages and drove away.

The stalls and pens around the plaza were being taken down by the Gypsies and other Spring Festival visitors, except for the long platform in the center. A crowd of festival guests was assembling for the final event of the festival, the Night Auction. A short line of humans wearing nothing but collars stood waiting to be sold for coins in the lurid light of a hundred burning torches. The Kishi owners of the humans were using combs and oils to primp and preen their property for sale. It was a truly sinful and decadent scene.

Boudi-Ca took a deep breath to try to calm herself. What would happen to her if the Conclave was still coming to rescue her? Could she still go back to Heaven? How could the Conclave find her and rescue her if Allyssia was sending her away? Perhaps that was why the Lady was sending her away in the first place.

A lone stable boy stood on the bottom step. He was watching the preparations for the Night Auction. He was handsome, slim, dark-haired, and brown-skinned, much like Tajee. From the bulge in his short skirt, the boy looked well-endowed in profile. Boudi-Ca looked away, suddenly conscious of herself thinking like a sinful Jinn. Her intense emotions had burned into her energy reserves, which in turn had awakened her need for feeding. She'd fallen so far from the mimǫ girl that she'd once been. She'd always scolded Tajee for his ignominiousness, yet she was the one drowning in sin.

Heels clicked on the marble steps. Golda and Ayelet were striding down towards her, both silhouetted in the soft glow of light from the open palace doors. Boudi-Ca quickly stood up and smoothed her dress.

"Hi, Golda."

"Hello, Boudi." Golda came straight at her with a hug. Boudi-Ca wrapped her hands around Golda's back. It was the most amazing hug ever. Golda's strong body was very warm, and her skin and hair were soft, just like when they'd fallen together so long ago from the Upper Allyssia Platform in the ruins of Chickasaw. Golda smelled exotic and sensual.

Boudi-Ca blinked away sudden tears. Allyssia had changed her, but in that moment, hugging against Golda, breast to breast, she was transported back to the atmospheres under Heaven, and she felt once again like an mimǫ girl, and not like a Jinn.

Golda finally released her and walked silently on towards the horses at the stable hitching posts. The intense warmth remained, echoing and dwelling in her whole body, even in her toes. Boudi-Ca took a deep breath. She felt somehow better. Her storm of emotions had gone queerly calm.

"Let's go, chérie." Ayelet's tone was horribly matter-of-fact.

"Are we leaving the Redoubt tonight, then?"

"No. We'll feed well from the Ahyehasi, pack our saddle bags, and leave first thing in the morning. We have a long road ahead of us. It will be a hard week's ride across the Isandlwana Fields and over the mountains just to reach the closest border of eastern Meristyian."

"What were you talking to Golda about?"

"Nothing. Well, actually we were talking about Prince Masad. He came out of nowhere, and now he's going with us. I'm impressed that the Lady has hired him for an ally, but it's suspicious."

"Who is he?"

"He's a possessor," Ayelet answered. "He is a discarnate hellion prince who borrows whatever body serves him in the moment. Now he occupies the body of the Disciple of Set vampire, Huesca."

"He sounds like an evil creature."

"Masad is the son of Lady Allyssia, the queen of the Old Order Jinni. His father is Lord Hades, the King of Hell himself in His dog-form of Set. Masad left Haawiyah shortly before the Jinn schism that brought the New Order to Meristyian. He went to work in Heaven for your Lord Tuhan, so he can't be all bad."

"I can't believe that. What was he doing in Heaven?"

"Masad is widely considered to be the best bounty hunter in all of the Underworld. He's a legend. He's a professional. He could be of great help, but I don't trust him. He's expecting to get something valuable from the Lady in return for his services. I don't want you speaking with Masad at all during our journey, fledgling. If he tries to engage you in conversation, you should politely decline."

Boudi-Ca silently followed Ayelet towards the carriage. She wasn't ready for another trip outside the Redoubt, even if Golda was going too. The bite on her neck no longer hurt, but her promising life as a young Jinn had just taken a dire turn for the worse.

III: Death In Mid-Spring

Chapter 26:

Boudi-Ca dumped an armload of wood next to the muddy steps of the mountain cabin. Her arms and legs were tired. Her belly felt Hunger-stretchy. Her buttocks were sore to the bone from three hard days of riding across the immense and beautiful flowered fields of western Meristyian, and then another day of riding slowly up the western slopes and valleys of the Alpacian mountains, which were still dusted with winter snow.

The afternoon shadows were lengthening and deepening. The last rays of sunlight streaked through alpine trees that still lacked the green buds of spring. Ayelet had described the Alpacians as the great spine of Meristyian—a snowy dividing line between the wet jungles, plains, and forests of western Meristyian and the bigger steppes, deserts, and plateaus in the east. They'd stopped in the heart of the Alpacians to hide and wait out the night. The mountains were serene except for the small army of Disciple vampires marching the same road in the opposite direction. According to Ayelet, the vampires could only be headed for one place—the city of Lady Allyssia.

Boudi-Ca brushed pieces of bark from her pants and shirt sleeves. She'd had plenty of time to think about her situation during the long ride. She'd been transformed into a Jinn, but she was still a Conclave agent. She had to be ready to act like one for her own self-preservation. If the Conclave tracked her down to take her back, they'd expect her to behave properly like an mimọ girl again.

The scale of everything that had happened—the planning by the Conclave and the distances involved—boggled her mind. The words from the Conclave recruitment flyer kept floating through her head like a twisting worm from an almost-forgotten void. Are you committed to suppressing sin and corruption wherever they may be found?

Boudi-Ca kicked mud and snow from her leather boots. She wondered if the Conclave of Deviant Operations would even be able to find her. She'd always thought of the Conclave was omnipotent. If the Conclave was coming to Meristyian to aid with the destruction of the New Order Jinni, they would probably find her even if Allyssia didn't want her to be found.

The hardest question was whether she wanted to go back. She'd finally been ready to accept her sinful Jinn life. Her inner mimọ girl had no equivocation. Her inner mimọ was in tears with joy at the thought of returning home to Heaven, where she'd be safe, sane, and comfortable again—away from all of the wicked Jinni, horrid vampires, and soul-corrupting lessons in taking and punishing Ahyehasi.

Boudi-Ca fiercely wiped her eyes. She couldn't let Ayelet and Golda see her mimọ doubts re-emerging. She pushed open the door to the old mountain cabin. The traveler's cabin was just a fireplace with a rough-hewn table, some worn chairs, and a half dozen old stacked bunks against one wall. It was far from comfortable, but it was a cozier place to spend the night than a camp in the forest.

Mistress Gonorrheah squatted in front of the black mouth of the stone fireplace. The wizardress hitched her faded purple robe over her knees and swept her blonde hair back over her shoulder. She piled the rusty iron grate with dry grass and twigs for kindling. Boudi-Ca silently removed her boots by the door. She avoided Gonorrheah's quick gaze. She prayed that she wouldn't be called upon to betray Ayelet and the New Order any more than she already had. She didn't want to be responsible for anything bad happening to them, especially Golda.

The warmth of Golda's big hug on the palace steps had stayed with her, along with the pleasant memory of Golda's arms. Golda had been unsmiling and detached during the trip, only chatting occasionally with Masad. The general mood of the group was grim except for Mistress Gonorrheah, who was in a perpetually good mood for no apparent reason. Gonorrheah waved her hand, and a gout of magical fire streamed from her fingers. The kindling in the fireplace blazed.

"Is there more wood outside, Boudi-Ca?"

Boudi-Ca nodded. "Yes. I collected bunches of it."

"Good. It's getting dark. The others will be coming back. We can huddle in here and stay warm until the war-column of Disciple vampires has passed through the gap."

"Is Golda safe down there spying on them?"

"None of us are very familiar with these mountains or with the scrying abilities of the vampire sorceresses, but I understand that Golda is very skilled. I figure she'll be safe if she's scouting with Masad."

Boudi-Ca looked into the flames of the fire. "A fire is going to be nice. It's so cold."

Gonorrheah smiled. "The wood is frozen, but I'm using a little pyromancy to heat it up. Ayelet tells me that you have a strong affinity for magic, fledgling. Have you learned fire magic yet or any general elementalism?"

"No. I don't think so. Mistress Ivanka taught me to cast a desirous kin-hex and to summon my magical messenger bird. I was working on the hateful kin-hex when I quit my lessons."

"Why did you quit?"

"I didn't like Mistress Ivanka. I used that as an excuse."

"So you can do a bit of mysticism and conjuration then," Gonorrheah said brightly. "I've heard that you have some Mimoic powers as well. As a student of all things magical, I'm interested. Can you show me anything?"

Boudi-Ca felt a slight flush of pride in her throat. "I can show you if you want."

"You don't have to."

"I'll cross the room." Boudi-Ca concentrated. She picked a spot on the far side of the cabin room near the single small window. She flashed. The room blackened and blurred, and the familiar ribbon stretched out beneath her feet. She ran down it six steps before she emerged. Gonorrheah's pale grey-silver eyes were wide.

"That's fantastic, Boudi-Ca! How far can you teleport like that?"

"I'm not sure. In Heaven I could go wherever I could think. Here flashing uses up a lot of my energy, and I'm scared to go anywhere that I can't see. Meristyian is so thick."

"You should always trust your instincts with magic."

"Mistress Ivanka told me not to rush my ability. She thinks that I somehow step through the dream-world with my desire-body like some types of vampires, but they can only do it while they sleep. She said that when I'm ready, she'll teach me dream magic. I don't think that will happen."

Mistress Gonorrheah bent and fed a couple more logs to the growing blaze. "If I could teach you to conjure fire, it would be useful against the Disciples of Set vampires. Fire is dangerous, though. This isn't the time or place for training."

"That's alright. I'm useless to the group anyway."

"Don't be silly, fledgling. You have a very useful ability, and Mistress Ayelet is a brilliant strategist. I imagine you have uses for our group that you don't even realize. On the other hand, Ayelet might be afraid to use you."

"Why? Because of what happened to me with the vampires?" Boudi-Ca looked out of the cabin window. Mistress Ayelet stood in the center of the snowy clearing outside. The elder mistress moved back and forth with her sword, practicing her forms.

"Maybe. I wasn't there. I know Ayelet loves you very much. You're her fledgling, and she doesn't want you in danger."

"She doesn't seem to worry too much about putting me in danger." Boudi-Ca rubbed her neck. Gonorrheah approached the cabin window and gazed out alongside her.

The wizardress pointed. "Golda came back."

Golda's cat form prowled through the silvery boles of the birches, slinking under the lowest boughs. Ayelet relaxed her fighting stance and raised her sword in greeting. Golda shifted in mid-stride, transforming from the big tawny cat to stand in human form on two legs.

Golda was beautiful in the full nude. She was long-limbed and muscular with full breasts like Yenta's but with pale nipples instead of dark ones. The thick reddish thatch on Golda's lower belly grew as untamed as her flowing mane. She strode barefoot with Ayelet towards the cabin through the snow. Boudi-Ca turned away and settled onto one of the rough-hewn chairs that sat at the worn wooden table by the cabin window.

Ayelet and Golda entered the cabin. Ayelet stowed her sword in the corner, sat down, and began to unlace her boots. Golda slipped into her pants, but left her shirt hanging from the worn brass handle of the fireplace poker. Golda slouched across the room and slumped into a chair. Her wild red-brown hair was more untamed than usual. A few twigs and burs were stuck in it.

"It's warm in here," Golda murmured.

Gonorrheah righted her saddle bags and pulled her smoking pipe from a side pocket. "Boudi-Ca did a nice job collecting the wood. What news from down in the gap?"

Golda shrugged gloomily. "I figure several hundred vampires are moving through. They're well-armed and armored. They have sorceresses too."

Ayelet's visage was grim. "Did you see any features or symbols? Anything to indicate what clans are involved?"

"The possessor decided he wanted a closer look. I warned him against it, but he didn't listen to me. I wouldn't be surprised if he brought them all down on our heads."

Ayelet looked concerned. "Are you serious, Golda?"

"No. I'm joking. He's a better tracker than I am. He was actually giving me advice on how to read the weave of the tapestry in this steep terrain."

"That poor vampire, Huesca." Gonorrheah chuckled. "He'll be in for a shock when the possessor lets him go, unless his soul isn't sent to the void at the very same moment."

"We shouldn't refer to Masad as 'the possessor,'" Ayelet said in a low tone.

"Just call him Masad, or even Prince Masad. I certainly don't trust him, and his methods are against our Lady's laws of free will, but he's still the son of Lord Hades, so he deserves our respect."

"Speak of the son of Set," Golda said, inclining her head towards the window.

Ayelet doubled over and massaged her calves through her pants, rubbing down to her ankles and scratching at her hooves. "We should have brought just one Ahyehass. It would have slowed us down, but Herzl could have fed us, groomed the horses, done our hair, and washed our clothes."

Golda scratched her cheek. "Why don't you ask your fledgling? Boudi-Ca already collected the wood for our fire, didn't she? What's the difference between—"

Ayelet sighed. "I'm not in the mood for this with you."

"I was happy to be able to help," Boudi-Ca said quickly.

The cabin door swung open, and Masad padded into the room. He'd clothed his borrowed vampire body in leather boots and pants with a black long-sleeved linen shirt. At his waist rode a belt bearing a sheathed sword and a dagger. "Greetings, mistresses and fledglings."

Boudi-Ca stared at the male vampire. She tried to see the hellion inside. She imagined that she could see the possessor peering out through the pits of the vampire's eyes like an uncanny black fire. Ayelet looked askance at Masad. "Did you discover anything more about the vampires or their clans?"

"Disciples and more Disciples," Masad answered. "Had I no idea there were so many in existence. Must be several hundred. Expect I they will skirt the Isandlwana Fields and approach the Redoubt through the Heartland."

Ayelet scowled. "The Disciples must have been doing nothing but making more of themselves in recent years. I feel sorry for the poor human souls in Esplanade and the other villages. I hope Allyssia warns them."

"Riding in front are twenty Jinni wearing red," Masad said. "They are Jinni of the Smokeless Flames—Allyssia's assassins. Wonder I what sort of terms Lord Hades and the Old Order struck with the Disciples for providing the foot soldiers for this operation with the Mimọs."

Ayelet shook her head. "Cybelah, Ivanka, Freyah, Artemisiah, and the others will have to be a match for the vampires if they can even find a way to cross the chasm and get into the city."

"Weak Ivanka is to death magic," Masad said. "The specialty of the Disciples. Avoid should she such an engagement."

Gonorrheah perked up from running her fingers over her pipe. "That's your specialty too, isn't it, Prince Masad?"

"Yes. Spent I many centuries in the east deciphering the mysteries of my father and the other elder Egyptian gods. Saw I the Disciple elders there, and met I with their ambassadors when still loyal I was to my father."

"Ivanka may be weak to death magic," Gonorrheah said with a grin. "But the Disciples are weak to fire, which is Ivanka's greatest gift. If a battle happened, it would be quite a spectacle, but I'd wager Ivanka would win."

Masad tilted his head. "If the battle is fought in the Merian Coliseum, would favor the odds the Disciple numbers."

"You sound like you enjoy this, Masad," Golda said darkly. "The vampires are marching on our home, and you're betting on the outcome. Well, I hate that old witch, but I'd give my life to see her win for the Lady."

"Hate is a well of darkness that belongs to the Old Order, Golda," Ayelet said. "We left that behind in the schism. Think of love even when you think of Mistress Ivanka, otherwise your hate will poison you."

"I'll save my love for my Ahyehasi."

"Ahem." Gonorrheah coughed. "Speaking of humans, how are we feeding tonight? Scavenging again?"

Ayelet leaned back against the stones of the hearth. "Golda found a small valley over the ridge. There's a farmhouse. We have a man, a wife, and two boys. They're mere shades of Meristyian and common folk of these mountains, but we have little choice."

"I'll find other arrangements," Golda said.

Ayelet looked at her Sharply. "You know that isn't healthy for you. You need to resist your animal impulses and control them. Didn't you learn anything from the skirmish with the vampires in Meristyian? Your paws didn't help much. What if frolicking in cat form tonight attunes you to your beast and makes you less effective if we get ambushed tomorrow? We don't have Ivanka's magic this time."

Gonorrheah cracked her fingers. "Thanks for the vote of confidence."

"I know I need to tame my animal impulses," Golda said. "But sometimes I need to indulge them. I'll feed from a few handsome mountain lion males that I smelled, and I'll be ready to go at sunrise."

Ayelet shrugged. "Suit yourself. Boudi-Ca will go to the farmhouse. Gonorrheah?"

Gonorrheah nodded with her eyes lowered. "I'm there. It isn't the way of the New Order, but like you said, it's necessary. Will you go, Masad?"

"No. Give the farm boys to your mimọ. Look she's pale."

Boudi-Ca ran her fingers over the pitted surface of the old cabin table, where prior visitors to the cabin had scratched designs, initials, and words in English text. She could feel everyone's eyes on her, especially Golda's. She wasn't sure anymore if she was an mimọ or a Jinn, but she felt the Hunger, and the Hunger was a curse that she had in common with every other woman in that room.

"I'm ready. When are we going?"

Ayelet reached for her boots. "Right now. The farm folk probably won't be in bed yet, but it's not like these people will have swords and death magic waiting for us. I brought a few sets of handcuffs." Ayelet went to the beds and searched in her pack. Boudi-Ca rose from the chair and found her cloak where she'd folded it over her saddle bags. Her Oya-blade rested there in its leather sheath. She hesitated.

"Mistress, should I—"

"Yes," Ayelet answered. "Strap it back on, fledgling. I know it's heavy, but you should never be without your weapon on this trip—not even for a minute."

Boudi-Ca buckled the Oya-blade to her waist. It was heavy, but she didn't really mind. It made her feel serious like the other Jinni. She followed Gonorrheah and Ayelet back out the cabin door into the cold evening and the snow. Her Hunger rose in her belly to stoke her with an energy of urgency.

Ayelet led the way through the snow for several minutes up a slope to an exposed ridge, which they followed for another half hour until the ground tipped down towards the bowl of a sheltered mountain valley. The last sunlight disappeared from the dark purple sky. Gonorrheah summoned a white tenebris lux that lit up the trees and sent eerie shadows over the snow.

Darkness had almost fallen when they reached the mountain farmhouse—a ramshackle affair of rough-cut logs on a fieldstone foundation. Firelight glowed from small high windows. Wood smoke hovered in a haze over small patches of cleared fields where an ancient family eked out their existence in the afterlife. The withered stalks of the previous fall's harvest poked from the frozen, snowy ground.

"What's the plan, Ayelet?" Gonorrheah said as they approached.

"We might be able to lure one outside, but I'm inclined to just go in and take them. I'm cold, and I'm tired of tramping through snow. Let's get this over with."

Ayelet crept up to the door of the house. Boudi-Ca felt her heart begin to pound. Her nerves were on alert. Her Hunger was quickening in her belly, sending a rushing intensity into her head. Ayelet tested the bronze lever handle of the farmhouse door. It wouldn't turn. Ayelet looked over her shoulder at Gonorrheah. The wizardress stepped up to the door and ran her fingers over the worn surface. She muttered an incantation and traced a slow circle around the handle with her finger until an audible clunk sounded inside. She gripped the handle and pushed the door open. Ayelet pressed into the house with Gonorrheah right behind. A woman shrieked.

"Vampires! Oh gods, din' ye bar the door, William?"

The main room of the house was a high-ceilinged kitchen and dining area bathed in the light of oil lamps and a low fire in the kitchen hearth. The room erupted into chaos. Two boys fled one after the other up a ladder that led to an upper level. A farm woman wearing a tired linen dress and a dirty apron grabbed a pot from the table, sending a dish skittering to the floor. She held the pot in front of her with both hands as she backed towards the hearth.

A rangy farmer with a grizzled beard jumped to a long gun that rested in the corner of the room. He reached it, raised it, and leveled it at Ayelet, who was striding towards him. Ayelet stretched her right hand with a desirous kin-hex. The farmer flew forwards and landed with a grunt on the floor. The gun went off. The slug slammed harmlessly into the logs of the wall next to the door. Ayelet descended on the farmer, who twisted and attempted to grapple with her.

"Oh, please be sparin' him. Please!" the woman cried.

"We aren't vampires," Gonorrheah said. The wizardress moved towards her. "Just put that down. We aren't going to hurt anyone."

The woman didn't lower her iron pot. Instead, she brandished it. Gonorrheah executed a kin-hex. The pot flew from the woman's fingers and clattered across the floor. The woman stumbled forward. Gonorrheah quickly gripped her arm and embraced her with a kiss. The woman gasped and grunted with surprise. Boudi-Ca advanced across the floor to where Ayelet had wrestled the farmer into submission. The elder mistress clipped a silver cuff onto one of his thick wrists, and then pulled his other wrist to the twin cuff until it clicked. Ayelet stood and gestured with a finger.

"Fledgling, follow me."

Boudi-Ca watched Ayelet climb the ladder after the boys. The farmer was looking up at her from the floor with a hateful terror on his face. Boudi-Ca bit her lip. "We aren't bad people. Don't be afraid."

"Coulda' fooled me. Who are ye, then? Lady brigands?"

"We're Jinni."

The man blanched and looked aghast towards his wife, who gave a soft moan in the arms of the wizardress. Gonorrheah had pinned her against the edge of the dining table with her plain linen skirt high on her sturdy hips.

"Come, fledgling." Ayelet was looking over the edge of the loft. Boudi-Ca felt suddenly queasy, but her Hunger was intense, urging her up the ladder towards a much-needed feeding. The two farm boys evidently slept upstairs. Two crude beds and a dresser sketched out a simple bedroom with a low slanting ceiling. The younger one huddled on the bed, obviously terrified, while the older one shrank as far as he could from Ayelet while looking over the railing at the scene below, wide-eyed. In his hand he held a long-curved knife.

Boudi-Ca slipped off her boots and shrugged her riding shirt over her head. Three days without feeding had left her ravenous. If she were still a Conclave agent, she needed to be chaste again, but her Jinn Hunger would accept no such silly argument. With the handsome young farm boys in arm's reach and Ayelet nodding silent approval, she allowed the Hunger to quicken her limbs.

Boudi-Ca grabbed the older boy's arm when he stabbed at her. She wrenched the knife easily from his weak human grip. She pulled him close. She could feel with her Jinn senses that the Isandlwana farm boy was weak and underdeveloped. His young male desires were flakes of thin ash compared to Yenta's well-stoked and cultivated passions. Boudi-Ca reached low and tugged at the boy's pants.

Chapter 27:

Tajee lay curled on his side in Golda's bed with his head on the threadbare pillow. He stared at the rectilinear shapes made by the open bedroom doorway where the far hall wall joined the wood floor at the juncture of painted molding. Based on his observations of the waxing and waning light that came down the hall from the bath window, Golda had been gone for four days.

The bedchamber and house were different without Golda's life-giving presence. The rooms and furniture felt drab and empty without her full-bodied feminine magic. Even the wood floor looked duller and dirtier, although Trace had waxed and polished it the previous week before he'd been dismissed.

Tajee rolled onto his back and looked up into the billowing sweeps of the faded starry black bed canopy. He listened to the soft breaths of Phylicia, who lay next to him. Before she'd left, Golda had instructed Phylicia to give him lessons in the techniques of pleasure. Phylicia and he had fucked several times since Golda had left. Phylicia had used his phallus whenever she could stir it for her puffy, greedy pumpum. At first Phylicia had seemed insatiable, but her enthusiasm had slowly waned after the three-day marathon.

Tajee lifted the pillow to his face, feeling the heat of his breath in the close darkness. Phylicia had changed the pillowcase, but it still smelled faintly like Golda's hair. He clenched the fabric in his angry fists. Golda's promise to let him see Boudi-Ca had fizzled yet again. The day before he was supposed to sneak up to Mistress Ayelet's Villa, Golda had come into the bedroom and told him that it would be impossible after all, for weeks at least, to go see his female friend.

An insane fury had consumed him. He'd yelled his objections until Golda had glared at him dangerously from under her mussed hair. She'd scolded him and told him that she had more important things to do than argue with a misbehaving, ungrateful Ahyehass.

As a result of their heated argument, Golda hadn't made him the houseboy after all. She'd hastily given Trace over to Herpessenia, and then she'd given the house keys to Phylicia along with full house-girl responsibilities. He'd refused to be defeated that easily. As soon as Golda had left on her trip, he'd left the house via the stable in broad daylight and hiked all the way up the long road to the fortress-like hill house of Mistress Ayelet.

Boudi-Ca hadn't been home. The heavy door to Boudi's room had been securely locked. He looked through the window at an empty bed and a diary-less writing desk. He'd headed for the front door to demand answers from Yenta, but then he'd run into the gardener. The old man had come at him with a shovel and chased him back to the road.

The inability to act was driving him mad. He was even considering giving up his quest. He was trying to decide whether to forget Boudi-Ca and attempt an escape from the Jinni all by himself. He could go back to Heaven, storm into the Conclave building, and demand that the elder Mimos do something about rescuing Boudi.

He found a sturdy leather travel bag on a shelf in the first-floor storage room. He'd put his spare clothes into it along with Golda's old knife, the compass, and the folded-up map that showed the stairway to Heaven. He'd hidden the bag under the bed. He was ready to go. The house keys were sitting on Golda's vanity where Phylicia had left them. On his daytime trek up the hill to try to see Boudi, he'd stopped at the railing. He'd looked for a long time at the view of the outer city wall.

It seemed easy to hike up the hill, bypass the road railing, and climb over the wall. The wall would be the hardest part, but it looked easier to climb than vines. If he could get past the wall, he could walk down the rugged mountain in the night and hide in the Isandlwana forests. Eventually he'd find his way west across the mountains to Mount Purgatory.

The idea of leaving Boudi-Ca behind tortured him, but he had to do it sooner or later to save his own soul. Unfortunately, the thought of leaving Golda tortured him just as much. She'd never delivered on her part of the bargain, but she'd delivered so much more.

His life with Golda was better than going to classes at the Crystal College, yet he hated her for taking Boudi-Ca away from him. He hated her for lying to him. A sound came from downstairs suddenly, disturbing the musty silence in Golda's house. A scuffle sounded, and then a thump. Tajee sat up on the bed and nudged Phylicia's shoulder.

"I think Golda might be home."

"What?" Phylicia rolled over and looked at the door. The stair steps creaked, then again. Phylicia's eyes went wide. "Tell her I was giving you a lesson. The Mistress didn't give me permission to sleep in her bed."

"Fine." Tajee listened more closely to the approaching footsteps. He didn't think it was Golda after all. Unlike Phylicia, who slept in the basement level, he was intimately familiar with Golda's footsteps. He'd even learned to guess the mood of the Mistress from the weight and cadence of her leather boots. The feet coming up at that moment were lighter than Golda's and more hesitant.

Phylicia climbed off the bed and went to the door. She peeked into the hallway and ducked back into the bedchamber. "It's fledgling Herpessenia."

Within moments, the blonde fledgling pushed through the doorway. She wore an elegant, near-transparent white dress that was tied tightly under her breasts. The dim light from the hall glowed through her dress to delineate the sleek curves of her hips and thighs. She held a black, silver-clasped satin purse that dangled from her pale fingers on a black leather strap.

Phylicia plopped nonchalantly onto the vanity chair. "What are you doing in here?"

Herpessenia looked startled. "Oh look, it's Golda's chubby little girl-slut. I didn't expect to find you in the bedchamber of your Mistress. I could ask you the same question."

"I'm the house-girl now," Phylicia said with an air of self-importance. "The Mistress wanted me to teach Tajee new things."

"Really?" Herpessenia said with a bored tone. "I'd love to hear about that, but I want to be alone with Tajee. So leave."

Phylicia didn't budge. "Does Mistress Golda know you're here?"

Herpessenia glowered at Phylicia. "Of course she does. She gave me a key. A bigger question is whether you are deaf. Didn't you hear me command you to leave?"

Phylicia glanced at the ring of house keys on the vanity. "I'm the house-girl now, so I don't have to leave."

Herpessenia stared at Phylicia. "You're quite an ill-mannered little glutton, aren't you? I get it. You're bored. Well, you're not my Ahyehass, remember? So I'm not going to punish you. What do you want? Gluttons always want something."

"Some nectar would be nice," Phylicia said breezily. "Golda took all of hers."

Herpessenia chortled and pulled a small bag from her purse. "You're as badly trained as your own mistress. This refined Blue Violet Beauty is probably worth more on the Merian market than you are. Open your hand, stupid." Herpessenia upended the pouch and dumped a small pile of powder on Phylicia's palm.

"That's all you're giving me?"

"It's enough, and it's too much. This is from specially bred flowers that don't grow wild. It's ten times better than the powder I sell to Golda."

"Thank you, Mistress." Phylicia slipped past Herpessenia and fled through the doorway with her hands tightly cupped together.

Herpessenia closed the door behind Phylicia and stepped to the bed. The room darkened without the light from the hall. The single candle burning low on the side table illuminated Herpessenia's face. The bed creaked when she seated herself. The fledgling sat her purse on the bed, rummaged in it, and removed a silver wand that was covered with jewels. She waved it above her head and murmured an incantation.

Tajee shifted to sit against the headboard. "What are you doing?"

"It's just a little spell that Ivanka taught me to give me some privacy from my mother. It probably isn't even needed. My mother has sequestered herself up in her bowers, and she isn't coming back out."

"Why?"

Herpessenia sighed. "How quickly your flaws are coming back to me. My mother is distracted right now by certain unfortunate events happening in the dream-world even as we speak. She is being mercilessly attacked day and night by Mimọic dream magic. It's nothing to concern yourself with, Tajee. My mother chose her fate when she betrayed Lord Hades and came here to form the New Order Jinni not far from the Mimọic Hierarchy's doorstep. We had everything in our old palace in Haawiyah, and she gave it all away."

Tajee frowned. He hardly understood what Herpessenia was talking about. "Did Golda really give you a key to get in to see me? She said that she was leaving me and Phylicia alone because she didn't trust anyone to look after us."

Herpessenia shook her head slowly back and forth. "Golda, Golda. You know your Mistress is tough on the outside, but inside she's fragile. She's has mood swings."

"That's true."

"In my opinion she isn't a good mistress for you, Tajee," Herpessenia continued. "Why would she leave you alone in her house with no one to take care of you? I'm never one to judge others, but Golda is neglectful, Tajee. You deserve better."

"I agree with you."

Herpessenia smiled sweetly at him. "How do you feel, my poor boy? Out of sorts?" The fledgling leaned over the bed and put her warm hand on his thigh. Tajee felt his phallus stir slightly. He shifted the bed sheet to cover himself.

"I feel fine."

"Don't be ashamed, and don't hide yourself from me." Herpessenia tugged the sheet from his fingers and pulled it back, re-exposing his phallus. "Your honesty, Tajee, is your second-best quality. Let's have an honest conversation. I came here because I care, and I was worried that Golda was neglecting you. Are you upset with her?"

"Why wouldn't I be? She keeps lying to me."

"I've been talking with Trace. He told me some interesting things. I know how you feel. I can feel your anger burning in you. It's silly for the most gifted male Ahyehass in this city to be sitting here alone with no mistress. You deserve so much more attention."

Tajee took a deep breath. "I don't know whether to love Golda or hate her. Just when I think she's finally being nice, she betrays me every time."

"Golda is unpredictable. She'll be one way one day and another way another day. She'll be your dedicated lover, and then nothing. Selfishness is her cat nature. She has trouble caring about anyone but herself."

"I don't really care anymore."

"Of course you do. What do you want? Usually when a Jinn is away from her trained slave, he has cravings." Herpessenia slid further onto the bed and lifted her hand to his forehead. "You're not flush at all, are you? Phylicia, on the other hand, was burning. She took a lot of your lovely bitter seed, didn't she? Maybe that explains her outrageously disrespectful attitude towards me."

"I'd rather sleep alone, but Golda wanted me to learn things from Phylicia. She's been sleeping with me since Golda left, except for when she got up to light the lamps and use the bath. She wanted me to soap her and scrub her too. She wanted to teach me to wash Golda better."

Herpessenia sighed. "Poor Tajee. You're such a good boy always doing what you're told. You're being taken advantage of by everyone. What do you want for yourself? Tell me."

"Well, I jumped from Heaven for my friend Boudi. I was trying to save her. Golda said I could see her, but then she wouldn't let me. Over and over. I think she's trying to torture me."

Tajee resisted the urge to shrink back. Herpessenia was leaning very close to him, and she seemed to exude a queer coolness instead of warmth. Her pale eyelids were almost closed as if she were deep in thought. Blue veins were just visible in the milky translucent skin of her cheeks and throat. Herpessenia's hair was beyond shoulder length—slightly longer than Boudi's and blonde to the point of ash grey. Up close Herpessenia seemed younger, although she was physically a little bigger than him. Herpessenia's lips parted for a moment, and when she spoke, her voice was slow and sultry. "I have to tell you something, Tajee, and I'm only telling you because I care."

"What is it?"

"Your beloved Boudi-Ca has been exiled from the Redoubt. She was banished recently from my mother's city. Boudi-Ca isn't within a thousand leagues of here, and she won't ever be coming back. Didn't Golda mention that?"

"No. She didn't even tell me!"

"Why would she? You'd get upset like you are now, and you'd be too much work for her to keep under control. Golda has been hiding the truth from you."

"What truth?"

"My mother discovered that Boudi-Ca is a sneaky little spy for the Mimọic Hierarchy. My mother punished your mimọ girl by sending her far away to a place of isolation in the desert. That poor mimọ. She's so traumatized by this whole thing. She must feel so alone and hopeless."

"Boudi-Ca isn't a spy!"

"You don't have to cover for your girlfriend, Tajee. The truth is out. The Mimọic Hierarchy used her. You told Golda all about it when you first arrived here. Of course Golda betrayed your trust and reported every word that you said."

"I told Golda about the Conclave. I never said Boudi-Ca was a spy." Tajee trembled. His anger was rising in his body, and he couldn't stop it. His anger boiled in his chest and pounded inside his skull. He clenched his fists. "You're right. Golda betrayed me. She lied to me. She's a selfish lying bitch."

Herpessenia nodded sagely. "Yes, Tajee. That's right. She's a bitch. You should be very angry at Golda. She stole your girlfriend away from you. She seduced you, betrayed you, and lied to you, just so she could control you and make you her own. Golda is just plain horrible."

"I can't never see Boudi-Ca again."

"Why not, Tajee?"

"I have to tell her how much I love her. I have to tell her how much she means to me no matter what you evil Jinni have done to her. Boudi-Ca has to know that I'm down here with her. She needs to know that she isn't alone. I'm here for her. It isn't hopeless."

"Tajee, you're truly bringing tears to my eyes."

"You have to tell me where I can find Boudi. Please. You know, right?"

Herpessenia's lips twisted into a small smile. "I do. In fact, I could take you to see Boudi-Ca right away. You'd have to be really good and do as you're told, though."

Tajee felt his heart pound still harder, and his lower lip trembled. "Of course. I should have known. It's always something with a damned Jinn."

"I'll take you to see Boudi, and that's a promise. The deal is that you won't be with Golda ever again. You'll be my Ahyehass from now on, not hers. Will that work?"

Tajee held his head in his hands. It was like déjà vu all over again. He felt afraid of Herpessenia, but if he ever wanted to see Boudi-Ca again, he had no choice. He couldn't keep waiting for Golda. "Fine, but if you don't take me to see Boudi, the deal is over."

"Good. Then it's settled. Aren't you glad that I was worried about you, my beautiful mimọ? Are you happy that I care?"

"Yes. So can we go now? I'm ready."

"Not tonight. The turning point hasn't tipped, and Boudi-Ca is still on her journey. We'll probably leave the night after tomorrow night. I'll come for you around sunset when things have arranged themselves. Until then, you mustn't tell a soul what we've talked about, especially not Golda's dumb house-girl. Can you promise me?"

"Sure. I'll do whatever you want as long as I can be with Boudi. So where is this 'place of isolation' you were talking about? Where is Boudi?"

"Boudi-Ca isn't there yet, but she's going. She's headed straight for a trap, and I expect that's where we'll find her." Herpessenia pursed her lips sensuously and slid her hand down to pinch her nipple, as if absentmindedly, through the thin fabric of her dress. Tajee stared at her fingers despite himself. Herpessenia batted her white eyelashes.

"I've wanted you since the first time I laid eyes on you, Tajee. I have a taste for the more bitter emotions, unlike the over-idealistic New Order."

"Trace is with you too, right?"

"I don't like Trace, although he was useful to acquire certain house key copies. With the depths of how much you've suffered for love, Tajee, and the intensity of your hate, you have so much more potential. I can feel it inside you. It excites me, boy."

Tajee swallowed. "Can this really happen, though? I mean, can you just take me from Golda like this and make me yours? Do I even have this choice to make?"

"Are you wearing Golda's brand on your backside? No. I don't think so. She's too nice. My mother doesn't have a branch of Hell's Court here, of course. That means the New Order Jinni don't file proper ownership papers for their girls and boys. Where we're going, Hell's Court is everything. You have no official papers, Tajee—not even a brand to establish ownership, so in the eyes of the Court, you have no mistress. I'll fix that. I'm going to make you mine. Isn't that delightful?"

"Fantastic."

"It is. It's exciting. I think I'm going to take you in Golda's bed. She doesn't own you anymore. Let's show that bitch what we both think of her."

"Yes." Tajee felt his anger surge with Herpessenia's words. Deep down he did hate Golda, and it felt good to hear someone echo the truth that he knew. Herpessenia edged off the bed, untied her dress, and let it slip over her hips to the floor. Whereas Golda was tan and muscled, Herpessenia was lithe and limp. The undersides of her breasts were oddly patterned in the candlelight. The patterning was more pronounced near her hairless sex, where the patterns formed diamond-shaped iridescent scales like the skin of a fish.

sat cross-legged on the bed again. She slipped her fingers into her purse and withdrew her nectar pouch again. From the pouch she pulled a nectar-coated implement—a bulb attached to a silver chain and pull-ring. Herpessenia lifted the contraption languorously to her lips. She popped it into her mouth, suckled it, and pulled it out. The bulb and chain emerged wet, silvery, and gleaming, just like Herpessenia's wicked eyes. Liquid purple nectar oozed from a hole in the metal bulb's pointed tip.

"Don't look me in the eyes unless I tell you, boy. Audacity like that won't pass down in Hell's capital. I'm going to teach you to behave."

"Yes, Mistress. As you wish, Mistress. Sorry."

Herpessenia gestured him closer. Tajee scrunched to the desired position, where Herpessenia pushed him onto the flat of his back. Her hand was queerly cool. She licked her lips. "Yes, I can feel it. Your mimǫ-sweet lust is mixed perfectly with the most pure and bitter anger. It's incredible. It might be the rarest delicacy that I've ever tasted. I'm so glad I finally have you. Your passions were totally wasted on Golda."

"I'm glad too. I hope."

Herpessenia bent between his legs. Her breast tickled over his hip. She pressed her lips to the tender skin of his abdomen. She bit. Tajee gasped at the pain that waved through his ribcage. The pain pulsed all the way down to his phallus, which stiffened against Herpessenia's cool belly. Her hand reached low and fished between his buttocks. Tajee arched on the bed, gasping from the sudden intense pain that split him. A queer sensation rushed through his soul, followed by a torrent of pleasure from the place that Herpessenia had penetrated. She'd somehow popped her metal bulb inside him. He could feel his anus clenching on the little chain, and then the sensation was overwhelmed with a pleasure that raced through his innards and down his legs.

"Off you go, boy," Herpessenia breathed. "Let's begin this. I'll sit you no more than an hour or two, so hopefully my mother won't notice. The flower bulb has enough nectar in it to keep you that long in ecstasy."

Herpessenia rose and hovered over him, smiling down like a goddess. Her white hair whipped when she swiveled. Tajee blinked his eyelids. The starry canopy above the bed had shifted into a spinning constellation. He was drifting like a boat on a wave of nectared pleasure, and Herpessenia was piloting him. She was his captain and navigator. Her thighs were the clamps that kept him from floating into infinity.

Herpessenia lowered her rear end over his face. Iridescent scales patterned the hills and valleys of her nethers. The scales were most pronounced near the puckered mouth of her pumpum. Tajee stuck his tongue out to lick. He was floating higher and higher, even as Herpessenia's pumpum sealed down, inundating him with her wet scaly flesh.

He tongued Herpessenia's rich fishy taste into himself. His face was burning hot, and Herpessenia's cool nethers delivered a pleasant relief to his forehead and cheeks. He felt little splinters of pain down his body, but he could scarcely pay attention to anything but the rising pleasure. The twin moons of Herpessenia's glorious buttocks eclipsed his personal universe.

Golda rode high in the saddle of the dusky Disciple horse. She led the group with her senses wide open to the weave of the Isandlwana tapestry. Upon leaving the Alpacians, they'd entered a region of Meristyian through which she'd rarely traveled before. The scents were different on the eastern side of the high mountains. The tapestry was bigger, more open, and woven with earthier colors. Olive, carmine, and rust replaced jade, aubergine, and vermilion.

The Sea of Desire was many leagues to the south. The smell of sea salt carried on the cross breeze. The road was still leveling down out of the mountains through the lightly forested Tuskan plain, which was dreary with the dampness of the Isandlwana spring season. The nearly non-existent tracks of the two Eastern Order priestesses had been obliterated by the chaotic energy of the passing vampire horde, even to the keen tracking senses of Masad. They'd given up re-finding the Eastern Order track. Instead, they were following the Disciple vampires back towards their origin, hoping the two trails would coincide.

Golda spit a strand of hair from her mouth. The Disciple horse labored underneath her. It was slathered in sweat from the long run across the plain. The vampire horde, headed by the warband of Old Order assassins, had stirred a despair the likes of which she'd never felt. She could only pray that the Lady and all of Her resources would be enough to hold the gates against the invaders, even if the enemy had the help of the Mimọic Hierarchy.

If the Redoubt fell, her life as she knew it would be over. She'd lose everything that she'd gained and worked for. She would once again be left with nothing. Her house wasn't very secure, and Tajee and Phylicia were alone. The doors and windows would hardly stop hungry Disciples of Set or Old Order mistresses looking for spoils.

Tajee had been furious with her when she'd told him yet again that he couldn't see Boudi. She'd argued heatedly with Ayelet to let Tajee see Boudi-Ca before they left, but predictably Ayelet had refused. Time had been short, and again she'd let the issue go. Golda leaned in the saddle to present a lower profile to the increasing wind. She felt sorry for Boudi. She could relate to the insecurity and alienation that the mimọ was surely experiencing.

Just because Boudi-Ca evoked sympathy, however, was no reason to start trusting her. Who could know whether Boudi-Ca wasn't still imbued with a Hierarchy tracking spell aside from her wrist-watch dream beacon? The Lady had seemed confident in Boudi's allegiances, but the mimọ's presence in the group was worrying. Boudi's presence was a liability to the greater mission, if not a danger to all of them.

"Someone ahead." Masad reined in his horse.

Golda frowned. She realized that yet again she'd lost her tracking concentration amidst her inner turmoil. She slowed her Disciple horse. She focused. She could see them in the tapestry then—small sparks of the faintest life, mere discolored bumps among the threads of the tapestry, unmoving. Ayelet drew alongside.

"Shall we rest, Golda?"

"Not yet. We have friends ahead."

"Sit they off the side of the road," added Masad.

Ayelet nodded. "Perhaps we should investigate. Dealing with a few vampire lookouts might be worth the effort in terms of information gained.

How many are there?"

"See I not vampires," Masad answered. "Old Order Jinni. Two. Hide they themselves. Has one some skill with the weave."

Gonorrheah drew up with Boudi. The wizardress shook her head. "I don't understand why Lord Hades is suddenly throwing the Old Order and his vampire lackeys at the Lady. Why not just order up a division of Hell's army into Meristyian with a contingent of Nankariders and be done with it?"

"It could be an agreement with the Mimoic Hierarchy," Ayelet said tensely. "Marching Hell's army across the foot of Mount Purgatory on the way to Meristyian would be provocative even if there is an alliance between the great powers to neutralize the Lady. The Mimos wouldn't like that sort of mobilization unless they moved likewise."

Masad nodded. "Fan the flames of war would any army in the demilitarized zone—even a foothold. Avoids my father that problem by giving Lady Allyssia and the Jinni the charge of closing the schism and re-uniting the Jinni."

Gonorrheah shook her head. "How do the vampires fit in? And the Mimoic Hierarchy? That's the question that I've been turning over and over in my mind. Why would the Mimos work with the Old Order to help the vampires take control of Meristyian?"

"Mimos wouldn't have anything to do with Old Order Jinni or vampires," Boudi-Ca said quietly.

"Be not so sure, young fledgling," Masad said.

"Polarity serves the purposes of the Hierarchy as well as Hell," Ayelet said grimly. "No one likes to see their monopolies compromised. Lord Tuhan was fond of Allyssia a few millennia ago before she betrayed him. This collusion is something that Allyssia might have engineered. We need more information."

Masad rested his pale vampire hand on the hilt of his sword. "Know I who might tell us, with enough persuasion."

Ayelet grimaced. "Whoever they are, they might well be old acquaintances from back in the day. We might take a few Isandlwana mountain folk against their will, but we won't torture our own, even Old Order."

"Know you that you would be tortured." Masad smiled thinly. "See I another way. A vampire am I. An ally am I."

"Yes," Ayelet said. "Golda, perhaps you can watch his back."

"Let's do it. What's the plan, Masad?"

"Ride I right down the road. Hide you in the bushes. Make you no move unless very ugly. Think a cask of blood, either mine or a Jinn."

Golda dismounted and shucked her shirt. She unclipped her riding corset and looped it over her saddle horn. She unfastened her sword belt, and then slipped out of her pants. She finished denuding herself by removing her hair clip. She felt intense umber mimọ eyes on her backside. She half-turned and verified them. Boudi-Ca was staring at her from under her off-ebony bangs. Golda turned and tucked the hair clip into her saddle bag. She nodded to Masad.

"After you."

Golda opened the gates of the beast. She let the fur envelop her. She transformed and flowed away from the road on all fours, padding over grass and dirt. She could still feel Boudi's eyes. What did the mimọ think of her inner nature? Did Boudi-Ca see her, like so many others, as a beast and a freak?

Golda bristled her whiskers. She knew she intimidated the mimọ, but there was a deeper emotion in Boudi's gaze. She remembered well the amazing hug that she'd had with Boudi-Ca on the palace steps. She'd felt a burst of love and compassion at that moment for the fallen mimọ and her pain. She didn't trust the mimọ, but she had an intimate understanding of Boudi's loneliness and suffering.

She heard Masad snap his reins behind her, and she slipped into the underbrush of the wild meadow through which the road ran. A pair of sulphury butterflies fluttered, and honeybees stirred up and buzzed around her, unhappy with her passing. Golda took a deep breath into her chest. It was a relief to run and stretch her legs. Whenever she felt unbalanced, four paws evened her out more than two feet.

She loped along, blending into the tapestry of Meristyian. She looked askance at Masad, who was only twenty meters away. The possessor rode parallel to her own course, but down the center of the road. He rode stiffly, as if he were pretending to be wounded. Masad turned his horse off into the meadow and headed for the corpse of trees where the enemy waited. Golda slipped under the shadowy shelter of a pair of low bushes. She could see and smell a few horses tethered in a grove of oaks. The coarse voice of Masad broke the silence.

"Is anyone here?"

A rustle of underbrush answered him. Two Old Order Jinni—one lanky and tanned and the other short and dark-skinned—interposed themselves in his path. The Jinni wore red sashes at their waists and red ornamentation on their sword scabbards. Golda felt her hackles rise. She knew the uniforms. The two Old Order Jinni were members of the Smokeless Flames. They were the same followers of Allyssia who were leading the vampire horde. Serpent Sisters were dangerous blade mistresses, trained in lethal combat. Masad allowed his Disciple horse to come to a stop in front of them. Golda inched closer so she could overhear the conversation.

"Huesca? Is that you?" The Flames mistress appeared to brighten in recognition, and then she frowned. "We thought your group was caught by Allyssia several months ago. You went into Meristyian and never reported back."

"I was captured," Masad said dully. "And tortured."

"Did you pass the horde?"

"I did. They gave me a horse and sent me this way."

"How did you escape from the Lady?" the mistress persisted.

"I did not escape. She released me. The others are dead. Allyssia has no idea of the horde. I tell her nothing."

The mistress looked nervous. "Would you like to come into our camp and rest for a spell?"

"Yes." Masad rode on into the camp, followed closely by the Jinni. Golda crept closer, stalking around the trees, sliding just under the texture of the eastern Isandlwana weave. She was downwind from the Old Order horses, fortunately. She padded to within twenty meters of the Jinni before she came to a stop. She settled onto her long belly and rested her chin on her paw.

She was unfamiliar with Masad' methods, but she felt a disturbing sensation that something wasn't right. A ring of stones surrounded a pile of ash from a campfire. A male slave slept nude on a mat in the sunlight. Masad was looking down from horseback at the younger Jinn, who was evidently a fledgling. "Help me dismount? I hunger so; I could fall and never move again."

The Flames fledgling moved to help him. He fell into her as he slipped heavily down over the stirrup. The fledgling reflexively steadied him. Masad caught the arm of the fledgling and hesitated for a second. Golda squinted. Either her cat eyes had deceived her, or the fledgling had twitched unnaturally.

"Where am I?" Huesca moaned. The vampire stumbled against a nearby olive tree. The fledgling backed away from him silently. The mistress tethered his horse next to three others and approached him.

"You're so weak that you've forgotten your journey, Huesca? Rest a spell. Tell us everything that happened."

"Journey?" Huesca shook his head and slumped into a sitting position against the base of a tree. He glanced at the sky and shielded his eyes from the sunlight. "Ah, I hunger so much. That damned witch put on a show of torturing me at my expense. I thought she was on our side. She wasn't supposed to enjoy it."

"You mean Ivanka?" The Flames mistress kneeled in front of Huesca, suddenly appearing interested. Golda crept still closer.

"Of course I mean Ivanka. Allyssia actually put her in charge of interrogating me." The vampire coughed and spat. "How in the hells did I get here? I can't remember a damned thing. My head is hurting. The sun is burning. Ivanka must have been responsible for letting me go. Some kind of transportation magic. How long was I gone? Is the attack underway?"

"The vampires are moving. You said you passed the horde."

Huesca scowled darkly. "No. What? I just don't remember how I got here, damn it. I was sitting in Allyssia's dungeon. I hadn't spoken with Ivanka in forever. Then Allyssia came in with her little cat friend. I swear that's the last damned thing I remember."

The long-curved blade was a blur from the belt of the Flames mistress to where it thwacked into the vampire's neck. The mistress danced away. The sword hilt quivered in the air with its blade buried horizontally in the trunk of the tree. The head of Huesca toppled to the dirt from the force of the sword blow. Dark blood spurted and soaked headless shoulders.

"That was him, fledgling!" exclaimed the Flames mistress. "That was Prince Masad! If Ivanka hadn't warned us, we'd probably both be dead. We need to get back to Memphis immediately. The others in his band are surely here. Hurry, fledgling. Hurry!"

"Yes, Mistress," the Flames fledgling answered.

The mistress stopped, stared, and backed away. "Wait. You already took her body, didn't you, you bastard? Damn me. Damn me for a fool!"

Golda stretched her claws into the dirt for purchase, readying herself for a sprint. Still, she waited. It looked like the ruse had somehow gone wrong, but Masad had insisted that she be patient. She wasn't sure whether a cask of blood had spurted yet from Huesca' severed neck. Masad drew the fledgling's sword and moved towards the mistress, whose sword was still buried deep in the tree.

"Surrender and kill you I will not. Masad indeed I am. Kill you your own fledging you will not, either. Ask I a few questions. Answer me."

"I don't think so. Let my fledgling go, damn you!" The mistress drew her whip from her belt. She circled slowly towards the horses, swinging her whip back and forth. Masad followed towards the horses, keeping a safe distance.

"Put down the whip and surrender. Have you no chance. Answer me. Received you a warning from Ivanka? Named Ivanka me?"

"You know how my superiors' frown on cowardice, Prince Masad. I'd rather take a chance at glory than certain punishment, even if you don't possess me or leave me dead."

"Involves this Ivanka how deeply? Communicates she directly with Lady

Allyssia? With the Flames?"

"That's for me to know and you to find out," the Sister snarled. "Continue to Memphis. Thanks to Ivanka, they're waiting for your group with reinforcements."

Masad lunged, but the mistress gave a hateful kin-hex with remarkable alacrity. The wave of magical force caught Masad in the chest. He staggered back and recovered in time to catch the whip around his leg. Masad swung and slashed the whip, but not before the Sister yanked and toppled him backwards.

The Sister leapt onto the back of her horse and spurred it. Masad hurled his blade, but it only glanced off of the Sister's shoulder. Golda sprang forward. It was her turn to negotiate. Her paws scrabbled on loose dirt until she found purchase and accelerated. The wind tickled the fur of her ears. She passed Masad, who was righting himself—or herself—gamely on one leg.

Golda pressed her legs to turn over faster. She was quicker at short distances than a horse, especially one burdened by a rider. She caught up, leapt, and planted her claws onto the running horse's haunch. She couldn't find a good grip. The Flames mistress kicked hard with her spurs. The horse accelerated.

Golda fell back, stumbled, and struggled to regain her speed. Ahead of her, the Flames mistress was turning in the saddle and unfurling her whip. The mistress swung. Golda dodged left. The whip nipped her. She felt a twinge in her hip, but she regained her stride. Again she closed on the horse, which had almost reached a full gallop. She prepared for another leap.

The Flames mistress swiveled in the saddle and threw the whip again. Golda dodged right, but she was too late. The tip of the whip clipped her shoulder. A thick numbness spread through her neck muscles, and with it came fear. She'd almost forgotten the narcabyss whips—those standard implements of control used by the Old Order. She'd felt them a few times as a slave, and they'd been her worst nightmare. The paralyzing numbness from the caress of the narcabyss whip had traveled halfway down her backbone.

Golda ignored the numbness and picked up her pace again. She was already a few hundred meters down the road, far from Masad and racing alone after the dangerous Flames mistress. The mistress twisted in the saddle again and flicked. The whip drifted back. Golda winced as it grazed her ear. She felt more numbness spread across the side of her head. The thin black-painted lips of the Flames mistress curled into a smile.

Golda grimaced. She had one more chance. She sprinted with all of her strength and sprang. This time she managed to dig her claws deep into the haunch of the galloping horse and lift herself up that last few feet. She vaulted and flurried with her free paw. She caught the robed arm of the Flames mistress. She rammed her paw through fabric into skin. She fish-hooked an arm bone. The Sister shrieked.

Golda dragged her quarry down from the back of the equine, and they bounced and rolled together, tumbling bodily over dirt and rocks. The fall stunned the mistress, but not enough. Golda felt the rubbery narcabyss whip loop over her head. She clawed, trying to tear the whip away, but she was too late. Numbness filled her paw and then closed over her throat like death.

She felt horror as she lost control of her limbs. Her head went cobwebby, and the world disappeared when her vision went blurry. She raked and thrashed blindly. She pawed with all of her remaining strength. The Sister's scream was close and blood-curdling.

Golda pushed energy forward from her belly to her neck. Somehow she bit, and then bit again. She couldn't see, but she could feel tendons ripping between her teeth. Hot blood sluiced down her tongue. Golda crawled away. The horrible whip slipped off of her head, leaving a trail of paralyzed muscles over most of her body. She circled, limping and dragging. She could barely stay on her paws. Her chest dipped and scraped the dirt. Within a minute she heard the thud of hooves as her eye muscles slowly refocused. Masad, still in the form of the Flames fledgling, rode up and dismounted.

Golda heaved herself to the side of the road. She was shifting back to her normal form. As her fur slowly left her arms, so did much of the numbness. When she was fully shifted and lying nude on the ground, she managed to summon her messenger bird.

It's over, Ayelet. She tried to run. I caught her on the road.

The bird flitted off. Golda raised herself into a sitting position with her elbows on her knees. She breathed deeply and watched Masad try to stop the flow of blood from the neck of the Flames mistress. The blood formed a wide crimson rivulet down the road, trickling along the old dry rut of a Gypsy wagon wheel.

Next to the Sister's hand lay a curved knife. Golda swallowed tightly. She'd narrowly missed getting gutted. Ayelet, Boudi, and Gonorrheah reached them within a few minutes. Masad greeted them. "Went the vampire Huesca to his final death, and goes to the void soon this Jinn. Unfortunately, forewarned she was of our presence."

"Masad? That's you?" Ayelet reined in and dismounted with her sword in hand. She surveyed the bloody scene.

"Of course me." Masad shrugged. "Turned I much younger, less undead, and changed my sex."

Ayelet didn't smile. "Do you often tell jokes over the body of a dead Jinn? What did you discover? How were they forewarned?"

Masad rose to his feet. "Turned Ivanka traitor to the Lady. Has re-aligned the black witch with Allyssia and the Old Order. Troubled is the Redoubt, more than already."

"Ivanka won't get away with this," Golda growled, trying to fight the wave of despair that threatened to overwhelm her. "I hope the Lady punishes Ivanka personally." She rose and went to her horse, which Gonorrheah had brought down the road on a tether. Golda clenched her throat to try to wash down the bitterness of the blood in her mouth. She really felt shaken.

"Calm down, Golda," Ayelet murmured. "Are you hurt?"

"She had that whip and a knife. She almost sent me to the void."

Ayelet's mouth twitched. "Did you learn anything else, Masad?"

"An Old Order presence is in Memphis. If dwelled in Memphis the Secret Eastern Order enclave, they may be no more. Warn we the Lady about

Ivanka if we can."

Gonorrheah frowned. "I brought all of the spell components needed to transfer messages through Ivanka's obsidian ball. The problem is that the ball is enchanted to send messages to Ivanka. That was Ivanka's idea, and I didn't bring any other way to communicate."

Ayelet nodded. "What would you need to send a long-distance bird that could reach the Lady directly instead?"

"A ritual circle. Parchment and a pen. A hawk feather and essence of Air. I have none of those things."

Ayelet looked down at the body of the Flames mistress. "It's a pity she won't live. She could have been useful to us."

"Sorry," Golda said shortly. "There's still a male slave back at the camp. He might have something to say."

"I can interrogate the slave," Mistress Gonorrheah offered.

Ayelet scanned the road, the hills, and the sparse corpses of trees that were interspersed with the surrounding meadows. "This area isn't safe. The Old Order were watching the road. It's too exposed."

Golda found the narcabyss whip where it lay on the ground. She picked it up by its handle. The magically poisoned leather strand was slick and pulpy. She touched it with her finger. Numbness spread into her hand. The whip was still functional. She threw it into the underbrush. "I could wait here by the road, Ayelet, and give some warning if someone is coming."

"So could I," Masad added.

Ayelet nodded. "That's a nice idea. Scout ahead and watch for anyone coming from the east, Golda. Masad, retrace our steps and keep a lookout to the west. You two will stand guard while we all rest. Golda, send a bird immediately if you see anything out of the ordinary."

"Sure, Ayelet. Good plan."

"Masad, can you summon a messenger bird by any chance now that you're in that fledgling's body?"

Masad smiled. "Can summon I many things, but dead things, and to kill they wish more than to carry messages. No. Take I the physical skills of my host, not so much the magical."

"No matter," Ayelet said. "You can handle any situation. Just make yourself comfortable. We will pass a five- or six-hour break, and then we will continue onwards into the east to investigate Memphis."

"Expect they that."

"We'll take a roundabout route. It's time we made use of the cover of darkness even if that means we're more likely to see vampires."

"It's frightening, but I agree." Gonorrheah flexed her fingers. "I'd prefer to fight blood suckers than the Old Order. I still haven't had a chance to incinerate anything, and vampires burn better."

Ayelet turned her horse back towards the Old Order camp. "Well, at least we know more about what we're up against. I just can't understand how Ivanka could have turned traitor against the Lady. I need to think about this news, assuming it's true. Boudi-Ca, chérie, can you collect wood again for a small campfire? I need some tea."

"Won't someone see the smoke?"

"It's near sunset, fledgling. I'll make the tea later."

"Yes, Mistress. I'm glad you're alright, Golda."

Golda turned away and unhooked her hair clip, riding corset, and clothes from her Disciple steed. Boudi's interest in her was obvious. From the look in Boudi's mimọ eyes, the girl was ready for a bed. Golda half-smiled, despite herself. Her big cat never mixed well with a small dog, or with Ayelet. If she made a move on the beautiful fledgling, Ayelet would surely have something to say about it. Ayelet kept the mimọ on a short leash, and Boudi-Ca still acted somewhat true to her mimọ nature—obediently.

At least the mimọ was finally opening to her own desires. It was beautiful to see a blooming desire in Boudi. It was also flattering. Golda drew her hair back and clipped it. She was growing calmer. She'd been shaken up. She'd won the hair-raising one-on-one encounter with the Smokeless Flames assassin, but she didn't feel triumphant. The fight to the death against the narcabyss whip had upset her too much.

It was one thing to play submissive games with Herpessenia, but it was another to come face to face with her former owners. Allyssia had changed her into a Jinn, but the contracts on her soul in Hell's Court would endure for an eternity. Her official slave papers would have additional stamps indicating that she was escaped, a criminal, and a wanted traitor. She likely had a sizeable bounty on her head in Hell's Court, just like Ayelet.

Boudi-Ca padded through a meadow that was lush with purple flowers and buzzing with honeybees. She skirted the bank of a burbling creek. She bent and picked up a dead branch. Ayelet had put her on wood-collecting duty again. The cool air of the Persium plateau pushed a pleasant chill through her riding shirt—pleasant because she badly needed a bath. She eyed the leafy creek. A soak would feel good on her sweaty skin and sore rump.

She would have given anything to be back in the Villa, where she could inundate herself in the warm pool in Ayelet's interior courtyard. Life in Meristyian was more pleasurable than Heaven, but it was also much more uncomfortable. Boudi-Ca jumped. A black serpent slithered away through the grass, startling her out of her reverie. She stopped and picked up another dead branch, and another, watching for serpents until she'd gathered up an armload. She made her way back to the campsite near the road.

Ayelet lounged on a large rock. She was deep in thought next to her copper teapot. Mistress Gonorrheah sat on top of the male Old Order slave with her long wizard dress splayed over him like the petals of a hungry purple flower. Gonorrheah moved slowly up and down. The slave's moans rose like the random pluckings of stringed instruments over the rustle of leaves in the trees. Boudi-Ca deposited the wood and looked askance at Ayelet. The Mistress raised a skeptical eyebrow.

"That wood is damp and muddy, chérie. It's no good even with Gonorrheah's skills. Get the wood from up there on the hillside. It will be drier than the branches by the creek. And try not to get so muddy. You're running low on clean clothes."

"Yes, Mistress." Boudi-Ca sighed and hiked back through the bushes to where the ground sloped upwards from the meadow flats. The sun was falling over the distant purple crests of the Alpacian mountains where they'd lodged two nights previously. Darkness was creeping quickly over Eastern Meristyian. Her stomach was tight. She was irritable, and she was tired of taking orders from Ayelet. She hungered, and the sight of Gonorrheah taking the Old Order slave boy made her want him for herself. She hadn't fed well from the Isandlwana farm boys.

She'd pounced on the first farm boy even as he'd backed away. She'd borne him to the hard planks of the bedroom floor and ripped through his patchwork clothes while his younger brother had looked on. Only when she'd encircled him with her legs and sucked his phallus into her needy pink had he stopped struggling. The anxious boy's protests had quickly turned to sighs of unbearable pleasure.

She'd ridden the farm boy for only a minute before he exploded into her. She'd left the boy drained while she pounced on his younger brother, who by then was less terrified. The second had been thin, supple and yielding, smaller than her. She'd ravished him as if in a trance. By the time she'd finished, Ayelet and Gonorrheah had been waiting for her down in the main room with the farmer and his wife huddling together silently in each other's arms. Ayelet had counted a small stack of coins onto the table before they'd left—surely a fortune for poor Isandlwana farm folk. Gonorrheah had offered an apology.

Boudi-Ca found a branch that appeared to be dry and picked it up. She found another. Her heart and sex were stirring from the recollection. She'd gone so far from the innocent mimọ that the Conclave had planted in the ruins of ancient Chickasaw, supposedly in order to capture a Jinn but instead for so much more. She was struggling to re-find her inner mimǫ. She kept wondering where she stood with the Conclave. Had they seen her as an mimǫ girl failure in the first place, and that was why they'd chosen her—because she was disposable?

She'd never heard of the Conclave giving up on bad Mimǫs. The Conclave reformed them and punished them, and apparently lied to them when necessary. At least Ayelet and the Jinni were honest. They wanted her to pick up a sword and fight for their cause—freedom to love the way they wanted, freedom to seduce and own humans, and to pounce on innocent farm boys and take them, no matter what the arch-Mimǫs or Lord Tuhan had to say about it.

Boudi-Ca picked up a long dry branch and snapped it in half. Her feelings for Golda had grown stronger during the long trip. She wanted to talk with Golda and get to know her better, but she needed to be with Golda alone. There was no privacy around Ayelet's watchful eyes. In the distance, down across the meadow, the Old Order slave moaned aloud with a note of finality. Boudi-Ca picked up another piece of wood. She had an acceptable armful that she hoped was dry enough. She could hardly find any more anyway. It was almost dark.

A twig snapped. She smelled an animal scent just before the beast grabbed her from behind. A massive hairy hand closed around her throat. Sharp fingernails dug into the soft parts of her neck under her jawbone. The hand pulled her head forcefully up and back. Boudi-Ca dropped the branches. They clattered over her semi-bent knees.

"Don't move," a guttural male voice growled in her ear. "And don't you dare cry out or I'll snap you in half."

Boudi-Ca crinkled her nose. The man's breath stank. More hairy men were creeping through the forest in the gathering gloom. A second hand reached around her cheek. A dirty cloth pressed hard against her mouth.

"Open," said the voice.

She didn't open. She turned her head Sharply to the side, kicked out her feet, and dropped straight towards the ground. Ayelet called the move

'The Falling Stone'. She'd practiced the escape move many times, and with the creature holding her throat, it came to her like a reflex. The man's hand tore painfully across her cheek as she fell. Boudi-Ca cried out. The hand didn't fully let go of her. She tried to roll away, but the man spun her around. He was humongous and hairy. There were several of the men, and they were all circling her. Boudi-Ca drew her Oya-blade quickly from its sheath and slashed just as a powerful hand exploded against the side of her head, sending her reeling.

"I told you not to move, little fool. What's a slave doing with a sword, anyway?"

"Boudi-Ca!" Ayelet's voice sounded distant. Boudi-Ca tasted blood in her mouth. She gritted her teeth. The man's hand on her forearm really hurt. He wouldn't let go, and he was circling her, leaving her no angle to properly bring her sword to bear against him.

"I'm not a slave, and I'm not a fool," she said. She kicked. The blow caught the man in his lower abdomen. She wrenched her arm out of his grip. She spun away, taking a defensive stance on the sloping ground. The men were not entirely men. Their heads were those of beasts—wolves with baleful yellow eyes, long furry ears, toothy snouts, and cheeks thick with tufts of hair. Their manes were long and wild like Golda's. Their tree-trunk thighs and arms bulged with strength. Boudi-Ca gripped her sword hilt tightly in both hands and slowly backed away.

"Boudi-Ca!"

To her relief, Boudi-Ca heard footsteps thudding up the slope behind her. The huge hairy man raised his hands in a gesture of surrender. "Score one for you. Touché."

Boudi-Ca blinked. The creature seemed to be grinning at her. Ayelet closed the distance with her sword drawn. Gonorrheah was right behind. A bright tenebris lux glowed over wizardress' head.

"You've chosen the wrong Jinni to attack, werewolves," Ayelet said. "You have no idea who you're dealing with."

"There are twelve of us and only three of you, old Jinn." The werewolf rubbed his knee and looked beady-eyed at Ayelet. "Are we supposed to be afraid? What kind of little friend do you have here, anyway? Is she a homicidal fairy?"

The werewolves guffawed, although nervously.

"She's an mimo̧," Ayelet said. "She's much tougher than a fairy. If you want a fight, you'll soon be wishing you had a lot more than twelve, even to us three."

"Make that four." Golda loped from the gloom. She was fully nude.

The werewolf grinned and cocked his head at Golda. "I smelled you coming, friend shifter. My count of three didn't include your so-called mimo̧. Nay, we didn't want a fight yet. I thought we'd grab your slave and see what happened. You know—make the confrontation a little easier on ourselves. Apparently she isn't who she appears. I see the Jinn silver in her eyes now. My name is Marcus. We need to talk."

Ayelet's hazel eyes were steady. "About what?"

"About where we're standing. These are our summer hunting grounds. My wolves just arrived a few nights ago from the eastern deserts, and we found the whole plain overrun by vampires and Jinni. We were looking to take out this little camp tonight, but evidently they're already dead, and so is a vampire, if I smell the blood right."

"We like dead vampires," added a werewolf with red hair. "Who are you and what are you doing here? You smell like Jinni, but you don't smell like Jinni."

"We are New Order Jinni," Ayelet said. "We are followers of Lady Allyssia. We come from Her hidden city on the far side of the Isandlwana Fields to the west. We're on our way to Memphis. I'm Mistress Ayelet. This is Mistress Gonorrheah. The shifter is Mistress Golda, and you've met fledgling Boudi-Ca."

"Memphis, you say?" said the werewolf with red hair. "You're allied with Allyssia's bitches then?" The werewolves visibly tensed.

"Easy, Elor," Marcus said. "I'll do the talking."

"No." Ayelet said Sharply. "We are enemies of the Allyssia's Jinni, although not by choice. We were heading to Memphis hoping to find the Eastern Order, not the Old. We're looking for Sekhmet's Jinni."

Marcus stroked his beard. "Well, I don't know how much you know and don't know, but be advised that Memphis has fallen to the daughters of Allyssia. They're helping the Disciples of Set take over key points in eastern Meristyian. They've overwhelmed the goddess Sekhmet there in Memphis."

"How do you know so much about it? You have spies?"

"We have more than our Share of trackers, yes," Marcus answered. "We've always been friends of the Eastern Order. It was a secret alliance, but there's no point in hiding it now. We normally spend four months of the year down there in the Acheron valley. Sekhmet's Jinni helped us maintain the balance of power in the region against the Disciples. Now everything has changed. The Disciples discovered the cat priestesses in Memphis, built an army, and took the city. We were too slow to react, and we didn't have the strength to respond to something that massive."

"What happened?"

"The Eastern Order is broken. Our beautiful rebel friends are mostly dead. We're still not sure how Allyssia's bitches defeated and imprisoned Sekhmet's avatar. After that, we wolves left our winter grounds early. We followed the vamp horde into the west to see where it was going. When they marched into the mountains, we let them go. We figured the Disciples of Set were either headed into western Meristyian or were creating a new stronghold in the Alpacians. We decided to retreat and try to clean up the Tuskan plain."

Ayelet nodded. "Those brutes are marching on the city of the Ifreeta Allyssia—our city. They intend to destroy the New Order Jinni just like they destroyed the Eastern Order out here."

The werewolf stroked his chin with a massive hairy hand. "So what in the hells are you doing out here then? Why aren't you back in western Meristyian defending your own?"

"We were sent by our Lady to find the Eastern Order and enlist their aid. If the vampires are gone from Memphis as you say, then we could try to take it back. What sort of force is defending it now?"

"Maybe a hundred Disciples," Marcus answered. "Maybe more. Jinni and vampire sorceresses hold Sekhmet's temple. Me and my brothers thought, like you, of the wisdom of attacking while the main vampire force was in the west, but Memphis is still crawling with them. It's impregnable for a werewolf clan and for you."

"Who is your clan?" Gonorrheah said. "How strong are you?"

Marcus sniffed. "I won't tell you our strength since I don't trust you, and I don't know the New Order as you call yourselves. But I will tell you that we are the ascended Clan of the Four Brothers. We range through eastern Meristyian from the slopes of the Alpacians to the moon-blessed deserts on the far Acheron shores."

Gonorrheah bowed. "It's a pleasure to meet you."

"Against a handful of vampires," Marcus continued. "We'd attack with bloodlust in our veins. But the vampires are many, and our shamans are no match for their sorcerers. The Disciples of Set are backed by the Jinni too, and they're worse than the vamps."

"What if we formed an alliance?" Ayelet said. "An alliance of your wolves and the New Order Jinni against the Disciples and Allyssia's bitches in Memphis."

The werewolves chuckled in chorus. Marcus shook his head. "The four of you with the warriors of our clan? Yes, that would be mighty. We might survive half an hour assaulting the city of Memphis."

"We are few, but we're a stronger group than you must imagine," Gonorrheah said. "Mistress Ayelet is one of the finest blade masters in all of the Underworld. I myself am a wizardress, more than a match for vampire magic. I have the fire spells that your shamans probably lack."

"And what does the mimo do," interjected the red-haired werewolf. "Besides standing there and looking pretty?"

"She can move like a ghost," Ayelet answered. "She can fly through the air, through walls, whenever and wherever she wants."

"Impressive," Marcus said. "I can move through walls too, but it takes a few hits to break up the stone. What's your story, cat-shifter? Only the high priestesses of Sekhmet are like you. Or at least they are if they haven't been sent to the void yet."

Golda shrugged. "It's just my gift."

"We'd like to talk with you and your brothers, Marcus," Ayelet said. "If there will ever be a time to strike back against the vampires, it's now. Imagine the Disciples returning home to find all of their kin dead and Memphis empty."

The werewolf licked his lips. His yellow eyes gleamed, but he shook his head in the negative. "I've heard Jinn persuasion before, Mistress Ayelet. I wasn't born yesterday. You'll use us like Allyssia's bitches are using the Disciples, and we'll be the ones to bleed. We don't know who all is holding the temple in Memphis, but they were strong enough to beat the priestesses of the Eastern Order and imprison their cat goddess. There is no way."

"There must be a way," Ayelet said. "The Eastern Order made us an offer of an alliance, but we received it too late. If we can still help Sekhmet, the cat goddess would be in our debt, and She might help us save our Lady."

"We're to make contact with the surviving Eastern Order," Gonorrheah said quietly. "The Lady didn't send us to take over Memphis by military force."

"If we don't try to liberate Sekhmet, or at least go into Memphis, then what are we going to do out here?" Ayelet countered. "Will we just go home, having accomplished nothing, and arrive too late to help the Lady? If there is anything we can do here, having come all this way, then we have to try."

The big werewolf shrugged. "I'm sorry, but it's impossible for the Four Brothers to help you. I suppose if the Greybeard Clan were to accept a peace offering, then maybe, just maybe, we would have enough wolves to go against all of those vamps."

"Know I Greybeard, although seen him I haven't for a while." Masad advanced from the shadows. The werewolves stepped back with a chorus of surprised growls.

"I didn't smell you," Marcus said warily. "You must be a very good tracker, whoever you are. But who are you, pretty Jinn, to even claim to know the great Greybeard?"

"Call me Prince Masad. Know you of me. Know I of the Clan of the Four

Brothers. Know I also the wolves of the Clan Greybeard, and speak they of the Brothers with respect. Reach an agreement we might for such an important reason."

Marcus took another step back. Gonorrheah cleared her throat. "Prince Masad has taken the form of an Old Order fledgling. He's the one responsible for the death of that vampire down in the meadow."

"I understand now." Marcus slowly nodded. "I can smell his great power. I know the Jackal can take the form of anyone he wishes. He's the son of the King."

"Met we once before," Masad said.

"Indeed," Marcus replied. "You helped my people." He bowed deeply, nearly to one knee. The other werewolves whispered among each other. Marcus rose and looked at Ayelet. His eyes gleamed. "The magic and exploits of the Jackal are legendary among my people. His victories against Hell's oppression are oft told to inspire young wolves."

"So what say you, Marcus?" Ayelet said. "Can we talk?"

Marcus eyed Masad. "Why are you helping these Jinni, great one?"

"Hired me their goddess did. Believe I in the cause of a free Meristyian. Benefits everyone peace. Believe too the werewolf clans. If can we, make a stand should we."

Marcus grinned at Ayelet. "If the Jackal wants the Four Brothers to attempt an assault on Memphis, and if he can negotiate a treaty with the Greybeard Clan for us in return, then the Brothers are at least willing to listen. We can go to our stronghold and discuss this."

Chapter 30:

Tajee sat on the top step in the silent second floor hallway. He put his elbows on his knees, rested his chin in his palm, and gazed into space. The light of the lamp above his head lit the oak steps down to the landing where the stairs bent left and descended to the entry hall. It was early evening in the city of Lady Allyssia. The sky glowed a deep purple outside the bath chamber windows. He was waiting for Herpessenia. She'd told him she would come.

The pale blonde divine had drained him twice on the night that she'd visited, and her facesitting and nectar had left him completely devastated. Herpessenia had stoked him, goaded him, and taken him to places he'd never known in order to please her. She'd consumed his body and mind with her salty, watery orifices. Herpessenia had praised his effort, and he'd spent two days in bed recovering. In all that time, Phylicia hadn't reappeared from the lower level.

Tajee rubbed his temples. He had to believe that Herpessenia would keep her word. He needed her to. For the millionth time, he wondered what Boudi-Ca would look like when he finally saw her. Would she still be surprised and delighted? When he considered Boudi's dark and disturbing Jinn diary, and the fact that she'd been exiled as a spy, worry gnawed at his mind. A sound like a loud thump suddenly shook the house and rattled the jewelry on Golda's vanity. Another thump sounded. Tajee turned and went to the bathroom, climbed into the claw-foot tub, and peered out of the glass panes of the second-floor window.

The last vestiges of sunset were falling across Allyssia's city. He didn't see a storm, but he saw a flash light up the tiled rooftops, followed by another thump. The window sill quivered under his fingertips. Another light flashed, and another thump rumbled. The light wasn't in the sky. It seemed to illuminate one side of the city. Tajee leaned his cheek against the glass to look through the windows at an angle. Another bright flash silhouetted a pair of spired towers.

Shouts sounded down below. The mistress Hatshepseh, who lived catty-corner across the street, was herding her three Ahyehasi out of her house and into a carriage. Another carriage was parked directly in front of Golda's house. Tajee whirled and ran out of the bath into the hallway. He faintly heard a knock on the front door. He grabbed the house keys from the vanity and dashed down to the entry hall.

Tajee fumbled with the wards. He turned the key, pulled a lever, and then another. He turned the latch. The door swung open. The visitor was Herpessenia. She was dressed in a long black overcoat that contrasted Sharply with her white hair. Her face looked impatient and annoyed. "Why did you take so long? I gave Trace to Mistress Cassandrah last night, and I only just now realized the misbehaving bastard stole back the key he gave me. Let's go, Tajee. Quickly, damn you."

"Wait. I have some things I wanted to bring."

Herpessenia blinked. "Things? Just know that you'll be carrying my things too, and they're a lot more important. Do know where Golda keeps her gold coins?"

"No, not really."

Herpessenia sighed. "You're so useless. Go. You have ten seconds."

Tajee turned and raced back up the stairs. The secret bag that he'd packed was hidden under Golda's bed. He could get in trouble if Herpessenia discovered the map, knife, and compass folded up under his clothes in the bottom of his bag, but it was worth the risk. He ran with the bag back downstairs. He left the house keys on the hall table and closed the door behind him. Herpessenia motioned him towards her carriage. He jumped in. Herpessenia slipped into the seat next to him.

Tajee clutched his bag to his lap. With luck, Herpessenia wouldn't take any interest in its contents. The fledgling seemed to be in a hurry. She snapped the reins, and the powerful black horses surged forward. The iron shod carriage wheels rang and clattered over the paving stones. Brilliant light limned the buildings along the street, and another thump sounded, loud in the evening stillness. Tajee looked over his shoulder, but he couldn't see anything through the trees at street level.

"What's that sound? Is a storm coming?"

"Yes," Herpessenia answered. "A storm like this little city has never seen."

Tajee looked askance at Herpessenia. She was looking straight ahead with her fists clenching the reins. Herpessenia definitely looked nervous. She was making him nervous too. She snapped the reins harder to hurry the horses to top speed. They gained a rise and rounded a Sharp corner, then rode straight through the city streets and plazas for long minutes until they reached the palace plaza. They turned right through a great silver gate. The carriage ascended a winding road between tall houses on a hill.

Another flash lit up the stone facades that lined the steep street. Another thump sounded, followed by a loud crack that split the growing night. A Jinn mistress scurried down the hill past them on foot, followed by two Ahyehasi carrying boxes and bundles. The Jinn hailed Herpessenia.

"Everyone is supposed to go to the palace! Where are you going, Herpessenia-Ca? Didn't you get a messenger bird?"

Herpessenia ignored the questions and cracked her whip on the haunches of the carriage horses. The carriage continued up the street, which soon became so steep that the horses struggled to keep the carriage from rolling backwards. The carriage stopped in front of a house. The flashes and thumps had stopped too, and a darkness descended over the city as the last vestiges of sunset disappeared over the edge of the mountainside. Faint screams came from far away. Herpessenia leapt out of the carriage.

"Get out, Tajee. You're carrying my bags."

"Yes, Mistress." Tajee slipped out of the carriage and threw his small bag over his shoulder. Herpessenia hopped around the carriage and procured her two bags from the back. She thrust them into his hands. The leather bags were crammed with Herpessenia's belongings. Tajee winced. The bags weighed his arms heavily. He struggled to lift them, but he did, and Herpessenia pulled him by his arm along a stone path towards the nearby house.

A bright light suddenly scattered the gloom. A mistress in white was running with long strides up the street behind them. The armor of the graceful mistress was polished ivory, and a brilliant glow hovered above her head. She held a massive white bow in her left hand. A sheaf of arrows poked over her shoulder.

"Let Tajee go, Herpessenia!"

Herpessenia's eyes widened when she looked over her shoulder. "Artemisiah!"

Tajee felt Herpessenia's strong hand tighten on his arm. She pulled him slowly backwards toward the open door of the nearby house, interposing his body between her and the white-armored mistress with the bow. Artemisiah drew an arrow, nocked it, and called out again.

"Tajee, drop the bags and come to me! She won't hurt you."

"Ignore her!" Herpessenia's voice sounded panicked. "She won't shoot."

With a Sharp motion, the mistress in white drew back her bow. Tajee's throat caught. The arrow shot forward and missed his head by two inches. Herpessenia dropped, pulling him to the ground on top of her. At that moment, a fierce wind sprang up. The carriage horses whinnied and stomped. From the dark house behind them strode a small mistress dressed all in black with black skin and black clothes, as if she collected the darkness of the street around her. She held a gnarled wooden staff high in her hand.

"Mistress Ivanka!" Herpessenia squeaked. "Help!"

"Tajee will go with Herpessenia, Artemisiah," croaked Ivanka. Liquid fire blazed from the end of the staff and streaked on the wind towards the mistress in white. The fire blasted the interloper, but Artemisiah appeared unphased. She released another arrow. The black mistress waved her hand, and a gust of wind blew the arrow aside.

"Betrayer!" shouted Artemisiah. The mistress in white drew her bow again and released another arrow. Again the black mistress waved her staff, and the diverted arrow transformed into a lightning bolt that thundered into the side of the house, shattering windows.

"The Redoubt will soon have new owners," Ivanka said. "This experiment has reached its end." The small black mistress raised her staff and barked a spell. A torrent of fire barraged the mistress in white, who retreated while letting another arrow fly. The arrow transformed mid-flight into another lightning bolt that screamed across the street. Again the black witch motioned with her hand, and a gust of wind blew the attack aside at the last second. The lightning bolt careened and bounced upwards into the sky. The witch countered with yet another spell. This time a ball of fire exploded, knocking back the mistress in white and setting the carriage and nearby bushes on fire.

"Hurry, Tajee!" shouted Herpessenia. "Now!"

Tajee struggled to his feet. Herpessenia was next to his ear, but her voice sounded distant. The blasts of magical energy had deafened him. Herpessenia snatched one of the bags that he'd dropped. He grabbed the other. She yanked him past the black witch towards the house even as another lightning bolt lit up the façade outside. Fire exploded again in the street and consumed the carriage. The horses whinnied, screamed, and reared in their harnesses. The flaming carriage began to roll backwards down the hill, dragging the burning horses with it.

"Faster, Tajee!" shouted Herpessenia. They gained the open door of the house, which resulted to be empty, dark, and unfurnished inside. Herpessenia led the way until the corridor ended in a round chamber. A rectangular hole gaped in the middle of the floor. Mistress Ivanka was suddenly between them with her black dress smoking. A burning smell filled the air. Tajee felt a powerful hand briefly on his back, and then he was launched bodily forward through the floor opening.

He tumbled headlong with Herpessenia and her bags down the flight of rough-hewn stone steps until he stopped on a stony dirt floor. He groaned in agony, but Herpessenia was back on her feet in seconds. She yanked him up. He staggered, trying to regain his senses. Above him on the stairs, the black witch waved her staff. The stone door that topped the passage shifted and grated into place, just as a lightning bolt exploded into the opening. Ivanka deflected the blast with a wave of her hand, and the massive stone closed the passage.

Ivanka waved her staff ferociously in the air. Bright sigils glowed into being across the rough surface of the stone. The low chamber at the foot of the stone stairs fell savagely still. Tajee rubbed his arm and stifled a groan. His elbow felt broken. His head felt fractured, and his body ached everywhere.

"Problems Ivanka?" A third Jinn stepped forward from the darkness. She was tall and wore a coiled whip at her waist. A small glow above her head cast a low violet light down a sloping underground passage. The withered black mistress hobbled down the stairs, patting at her smoking dress with a gold-ringed hand. She picked up a leather satchel from the ground and slung it over her shoulder.

"My spell should hold against Artemisiah," Ivanka hissed. "She has weakened me greatly, however. You shouldn't have gone for the Ahyehass, Herpessenia-Ca, even as much as you hate Golda. If you weren't Allyssia's daughter I would have sealed the door and left you for the vampires to ravage."

"I'm sorry, Mistress," Herpessenia whimpered. "Tajee took forever to open the door! I was pounding and pounding! I was getting ready to break it down. He must have been asleep or playing with himself or something. I tried to send a messenger bird, but Golda closed all of her bird slits."

"It's always a slave's fault, isn't it?" chuckled the tall mistress with the whip. "He's a fine mimọ boy, though. I can see why you had to have him. Have the Disciples of Set broken through the front gates yet?"

"Yes," Ivanka answered. "The defenses of the Redoubt have cracked."

"What of Mistress Persephoneh's insectarium?"

"Delivered as per the agreement," replied the black witch. "Allyssia's secure vault full of Haawiyah moths will be sealed until the Redoubt is fully under control. Persephoneh will not be able to break the ward I applied to the door. Commander Anaximah can then enter and raise the temperature when she is ready, causing the moths to be born."

The mistress with the whip smiled. "It's a brilliant plan to use the Lady's own defenses to betray and destroy our undead allies after they've served their usefulness to us. May the victory be swift and the Jinni once again be united. Now, there is only one more matter of official business to be done with here, as per our agreement—your trip to Memphis, and then your escort from there to Judecca."

"Yes." Ivanka glanced at the stone slab that blocked the stairs. "Let's be at it quickly. Allyssia's primary avatar is in a desperate position against the attacks of the arch-Mimos via the dream-world, but she's still far from surrendered."

The mistress with the whip chuckled, swiveled on her heel, and strode down the dark tunnel. "Our ride is waiting. Once in the air, we'll be safe. We should arrive in Memphis within ten or twelve hours."

Tajee hesitated. His arm ached painfully. He wasn't sure if he could even lift Herpessenia's bags. Herpessenia glanced back at him, then at her bags on the floor. She no longer looked terrified. Herpessenia's face glowed with an emotion that could only be described as ecstatic glee.

"Why are you just standing there, Tajee? Get my bags. Don't fall behind, or I'll make you suffer for it, slave."

Tajee grabbed the leather straps of Herpessenia's incredibly heavy bags. He hurried after the three Jinni as quickly as he could, ignoring his aches and pains. The passage floor was difficult and uneven, but at least it was sloping down, and he could see where to put his bare feet in the flickering light of the magical glowing balls cast by the Jinni. The passage curved and dropped steeply down sets of carved stone steps for several minutes. Tajee panted. He grimaced. His shoulders popped. His arms were killing him from the strain, and the bottoms of his feet were shredded by the Sharp edges of the stones. He didn't dare complain. The passage went on and on.

Finally, just as he was about to drop the bags, wipe the tears from his eyes, and beg for a rest, he smelled fresh air and saw stars. The tunnel ended, and the three Jinni clambered down a steep moonlit path into a chasm. Tajee hefted the bags with one last desperate effort. He followed Herpessenia down the gloomy sloping path for another minute, stumbling and tripping, but managing to keep the bags off the ground.

A gigantic shadow loomed in the night. At first it looked like a house-sized boulder in the darkness, and then it moved. It appeared to be an enormous, scaly, reptilian beast. It hopped, flexed its folded wings, and let out a roar that echoed in the chasm below. A riding basket was strapped on top of the thing, from which a rope ladder swayed.

Chapter 31:

The stronghold of the Clan of the Four Brothers was buried in a maze of hills in the Persium plateau. The warren of tunnels and chambers ran deep under the living cliffs. Round chiseled window-openings from the lower-level rooms gave views along the length of a deep gorge, while the highest chambers allowed views of the plateau over the opposing rim.

Boudi-Ca stood on tiptoe with her elbows resting on the sandy sculpted lip of an oval stone window. She watched the sunset cast a warm pink glow over the rugged landscape. A light evening breeze blew through the opening to stir her bangs and tickle her forehead.

Boudi-Ca wriggled down from the window and crossed the room to lie back on her blanket. She winced when her saddle-sore buttocks pressed against the hard stone through the layers of coarse woven fabric. She turned onto her hip instead and rested the side of her head on her saddlebag. She'd slept the entire day in the guest quarters while Ayelet, Gonorrheah, Masad and Golda had met with the werewolf leaders. She was tired of lying around. She needed to feed her Hunger.

Boudi-Ca eyed the cuffed male slave that they'd captured on the Tuskan plain. He'd been with her in the guest quarters all day, but she hadn't tried to seduce him. He was much bigger and surlier than Yenta or the

Alpacian farm boys. His dour face wore an angry scowl. His heavy collar was locked and bristled with metal rings intended for ropes and leashes. Two discolored brands marked his lower back. According to Ayelet, the humans who served the Old Order Jinni lived in a much different, much crueler world.

Boudi-Ca rolled onto her stomach and flopped her arms over her saddle bag. She pressed her nose into the leather and sniffed the pleasant smell that made her think of the day that she'd punished Yenta. She admonished herself. Her vague renewed vows to recoup her mimǫ girl virtue were constantly being tested.

As if to torture her, delicious erotic thoughts kept running through her head. On an emotional level, she was thinking of Golda. Her mind kept returning to Golda's wild spirit, feline beauty, and wonderful warm arms. No one else had ever hugged her like that.

Three days had passed since she'd fed from the boys in the farmhouse. Her Hunger had risen to a fierce intensity. She kept thinking of Yenta. What would happen to Yenta if the Lady's city were attacked? What would happen to Herzl? Herzl was perverse enough to almost like being ravaged by a vampire.

Boudi-Ca put her hand to her neck and rubbed. Her neck was tender in new places where the werewolf Marcus had mauled her. She thought she'd reacted well to the werewolf. Thanks to her months of training with Ayelet, she'd managed to escape. She felt a warmth of pride in her chest. She'd forgotten to flash again, however. She'd panicked, and in the intensity of her emotions, she hadn't been able to focus herself on the necessary mental level.

Ayelet had told the werewolves that she could move like a ghost through solid walls. She wasn't certain whether she could flash through walls, but after Ayelet had said those things, the werewolves had looked at her with respect. After the werewolves had learned that she was with Prince Masad, they'd treated her almost like royalty.

Boudi-Ca turned onto her hip again. She didn't feel like royalty. She hadn't rested well on the pile of thin, unwashed blankets laid over the unfinished stone floor. All of the werewolves in the Clan of the Four Brothers had converged on their stronghold for the big meeting, and the werewolves evidently had no decent beds to spare—not even for distinguished visitors.

She eyed her saddle bags, which contained her diary. She wasn't in the mood to write. The vampire attack on the Lady's city depressed her. Maybe none of it would even matter. If the Conclave found her and took her back to Heaven, she'd have to leave everything behind. When she tried to imagine living in Heaven again, she kept thinking of Tajee. Tajee's overtures towards her were a bit different from a Jinn perspective.

In fact, she'd be willing to grab him when she got back, drag him to his stupid dormitorium, and hit him with everything he'd always wanted, plus far more. She'd ride Tajee's cock so hard that he'd beg her to stop and let him do his math homework. Boudi-Ca groaned. Once again her Jinn Hunger was taking over her thought processes. It was almost impossible to think rationally with her Hunger bugging her.

"Boudi-Ca? Are you awake?" Ayelet strode into the room on her bare hooves. The mistress wore only a pair of dark leather riding pants that supported her sword belt and a white flounced long sleeve shirt with mother of pearl buttons. Ayelet seemed different in the werewolf stronghold—as if her normal air of invulnerability was tempered by not being in total control. Boudi-Ca sat up and watched Ayelet dig in her saddle bags, from which the Mistress produced a pair of pearl hairpins. Ayelet worked to put her greying hair up in a ponytail.

"Mistress? Are we leaving?"

"No," Ayelet mumbled past the pin in her mouth. She grabbed the pin and slipped it into her hair next to the other one. "Not tonight, at any rate."

"But we will?"

"Yes. Masad went to the Greybeard clan today with Brother Marcus. Marcus just returned an hour ago to announce an alliance between the Four Brothers and the Greybeards. Tonight Greybeard will marshal his wolves. Tomorrow we'll start traveling. In about three nights' time, we'll arrive at the ruins of Memphis on the banks of the Acheron and strike against the city to drive the vampires from the home of the Eastern Order."

"So that's good then?"

"Yes. That's good, fledgling. The Old Order and the Disciples won't see this coming. Hopefully we can make a difference for the Lady."

"Did Gonorrheah send a bird to the Lady?"

"No. She asked the werewolf shamans, but they didn't have the needed elements of air. The werewolves use mostly earth and animal magic. The Lady should be capable of contacting us from her end, but she hasn't. This worries me. One of us could try to travel through the dream-world across Meristyian back to the city, but it's a very far distance. I'm not a great sorceress, and I hesitate to ask Gonorrheah."

"I traveled across Meristyian in the night after my ritual."

"Such a trip would be very dangerous. Your wrist-watch pinpointed the city in the dream-world for the Mimoic Hierarchy, so the Mimos are certainly watching the city, maybe even preparing to attack the Lady's dream defenses."

"I don't like that everyone thinks that I'm a spy. I didn't know any of this was going to happen."

"Just forget about that, chérie. We trust you. There's no question in any of our minds that you belong with us."

Boudi-Ca accepted Ayelet's warm hug. The mistress smelled like wolves and garlic. "Why aren't you wearing your boots, Mistress? Do your hooves hurt?"

Ayelet leaned back and rubbed her ankle. "I'm chafed a bit, like everyone. None of us is used to so much riding. I didn't take my boots off for that. A big party has broken out downstairs. I was grabbed for some dancing, but I remembered my fledgling, so I came to see if you'd like to go down."

"Are Gonorrheah and Golda there?"

"Yes. I think both of them plan to have some fun, and they certainly plan to feed. We all hunger enough." Ayelet smiled softly. "You didn't take the Old Order slave?"

"He's full of anger, and I know he doesn't want me. I can't bring myself to even try. It isn't appetizing."

"I can understand not wanting to take his bitterness. It's good that your senses are Sharp enough to feel it. Anger is an acquired taste, and I don't want you to acquire it."

Boudi-Ca looked across the room at the sleeping slave. "I don't want another male anyway. I've had two farm boys already lately."

"That's just an excuse. You like males fine for feeding."

"I know, but that isn't what I want. I want someone to really love me."

"Chérie, everyone loves you." Ayelet hugged her again, this time even more warmly. Boudi-Ca wrapped her arms around Ayelet's hard, muscled back.

"Thank you, Mistress."

"I know what you mean, though," Ayelet continued, releasing her. "I was feeling the same way before all of this happened. In difficult times, we remember what's really important—the things that we fight for every day. Love is all that really matters. What kind of lover do you want, chérie?"

Boudi-Ca shrugged. "I want someone who understands me. I want someone who doesn't see me as a spy or as a homicidal fairy. And I want someone to love me for who I am, not just because they think I'm beautiful."

"Have you considered Golda? I see how you look at her sometimes. I think it's obvious to everyone."

Boudi-Ca bit her lip. "Is it? I admire her, but at the same time she intimidates me. She doesn't seem interested in me, either. I tried to sympathize after she killed that Old Order Jinn on the road, and she totally ignored me. She's hardly spoken with me during the entire trip. I don't think she finds me interesting."

"You're very interesting, fledgling. You need to open up and give the others a chance to know you better. Golda broke it off with Herpessenia, you know. She's probably on the prowl, but she's skittish, just like you. You should approach her."

"I...I don't know. I'd be terrified."

"She won't bite. You should at least come down to the lower level and join the party. You might have some fun. Golda is dancing down there right now. A few of the werewolves have asked about you, too."

"What about me?"

"What do you think?"

Boudi-Ca shivered. "I don't want anything to do with those werewolves! They're big, smelly, and rude, and they grabbed me by the throat."

"They thought you were a slave. They were rude because that's what shifters tend to do—act first and ask questions later. They're curious about you chérie, to say the least. It's not every day that werewolves socialize with Jinni, much less beautiful Mimos."

"I'm bored of being up here by myself, that's for sure. Are there any female werewolves, like Golda but, well, ugh—"

Ayelet chuckled. "I don't think so. They're all males that I've seen. Come, chérie. You can leave your shoes off. They have dried grass on the floor for dancing in bare feet."

"I don't want to dance."

"Let's dance. Put on one of the dresses you brought. If the werewolves see you wearing only your corset, they might go wild with animal desire."

"I can't see that happening."

"It's true. You could have three or four of them on top of you. Or ten at once. You probably couldn't handle all of those big, hairy cocks."

"You're right, Mistress. The more clothes I have on, the better. And what will the werewolves be attracted to less when it comes to my hair? Clean and mimo-straight, or messy and tangled? I can do both."

"I imagine they like wild hair like Golda's."

"Fine. I need to brush my hair before I go."

Ayelet smiled. "Get your dress on and forget the brush. You need to feed well tonight because we're leaving tomorrow to fight a battle."

Boudi-Ca felt her Hunger stir at the thought of a nice phallus to fill her—even a big hairy werewolf one. Her thoughts of Golda were stirring too. Could she find a way to get Golda alone in the werewolf stronghold? She found her dress in her pack and slipped into it while Ayelet watched. It was wrinkled and dirty, but it was still a barrier against unwanted werewolf paws. When she was ready, she followed Ayelet down the stair steps into the lower level.

The great hall of the werewolf stronghold was cylindrical. The walls tapered to a ceiling so high that it was almost invisible. Lamps in wall niches illuminated a hundred or more werewolves in various states of dance or relaxation. Musicians performed on a low stage, rattling out a rhythm with drums and stringed instruments. Dry grass covered an area of the stone floor in front of the stage.

As Ayelet had promised, Golda was dancing in the nude. Several werewolves were dancing with her. The hairy werewolves wore crude leather loincloths and vests as if in some semblance of formal attire. Gonorrheah sat near a wall with the long sleeves of her purple robe rolled back casually on her forearms. The wizardress lifted a long pipe to her mouth and puffed, sending a plume of smoke upwards. The odor of burning herbs scented the subterranean air.

"Come along, fledgling," Ayelet said. She gestured with her finger. Boudi-Ca followed Ayelet to the dance floor. Many of the werewolves turned their heads to stare at her.

"Mistress, I really don't—"

"Nonsense. There's much more to being a Jinn than swords and sorcery, fledgling. Let's have some fun for once. Move your feet and coordinate with your hips. That's it, chérie. Right and left, repeat. Once you have the hang of it, you can start to improvise. I can't teach you this half as well as Mistress Isabellah, but I'll try."

Boudi-Ca tried to imitate Ayelet. She ignored the watching werewolves. Despite her dark mood, she was almost having fun. Golda distracted her, however. Golda shook her naked buttocks and swayed, first with her arms above her head, then with her hands sliding down her hips to emphasize her gyrations. Her body was oiled from head to toe. Her full breasts and muscled torso glistened sensuously in the low lamplight.

Boudi-Ca drifted to watch Golda, but her view was increasingly blocked by werewolves. She was becoming a second epicenter of hairy dancing males. The man-wolves jostled each other to drift close to her, whereas Ayelet drifted away. A tall werewolf danced his way aggressively in front of her. He appeared to be the red-haired werewolf from the group that had grabbed her in the woods, although it was hard to tell them apart.

"Hey, beautiful. I'm Elor. Sorry. I forgot your name."

"I'm Boudi-Ca. Hello, Elor." Boudi-Ca glanced at Mistress Gonorrheah over by the wall. Gonorrheah was deep in conversation. The wizardress gesticulated at a werewolf who sat at the low table across from her. She underscored a point with the stem of her smoking pipe.

"Sorry about the misunderstanding out there on the Tuskan plain," the red-haired werewolf persisted. "Marcus didn't mean to hurt you."

Boudi-Ca struggled to dance and think of something to say at the same time. She lost the beat, re-found it with her hips, and attempted to match the werewolf's rhythm. "My neck and shoulder hurt a little, but I'm fine."

"What do you think of our stronghold? It's probably not what you're used to, eh? Do you have a nice place to live where you're from?"

"Yes. I have a proper bed. I have a bath. I have gardens of flowers just outside my window, although most of them haven't bloomed yet. Everything is beautiful, well-kept, and smells wonderful."

"Aw, this place doesn't smell that bad, does it?"

"Well, I don't mean to be rude, but it kind of does. You yourself could use some perfume or herbs or something."

"Me?" The wolf-man chuckled. His big yellow eyes pierced hers. "I could use a lot of things, I suppose."

"That's a little bit presumptuous, don't you think?"

Elor grinned. "Well, you're a Jinn, aren't you? I'm sorry if you think I'm rude. It's obvious you're a little different from Golda and the others."

"You're not really rude. I'm a Jinn."

"Well, that's good." Elor grinned again. "We don't have any she-wolves here, in case you haven't noticed."

"Why not?"

"Ah, they run in separate packs. They call themselves the Lobaness. Most of them go solitary when they're in heat though, and a lot of times you can hunt one down if you go alone. They say you don't have to hunt a Jinn. She comes to you. Is that true?"

Boudi-Ca pondered. "I suppose. We're definitely the hunters, not the hunted."

"Very nice." The red werewolf grinned again and moved closer. Boudi-Ca tried to match his movements and imitate the motions of his body. He was small compared to the other werewolves, but he still dwarfed her, taller at least by a head and twice as wide.

"Mind if I cut in?" A much larger werewolf sidled close to Elor and snapped his hairy fingers. His leather loincloth was ornately patterned, and a jewelled dagger hung on his belt. The muscles of his big hairy chest bulged from his vest. Boudi-Ca recognized him immediately as Brother Marcus albeit with more clothes on—the same werewolf who had grabbed her by the throat.

"Of course," Elor said. "See you later, Boudi-Ca." The red-furred werewolf backed away, and Marcus took his place. Marcus grinned. Werewolves evidently had a habit of grinning. Marcus' teeth were yellow and big.

"What do you think of our stronghold, Boudi-Ca? We didn't carve it out ourselves. It belonged to some ancient wizards. We had a dispute with them a long time ago about the ownership of this corner of the desire-world. Fortunately, we werewolves have resistances to fire and frost magic—"

"That's fascinating," Boudi-Ca said politely. She kept her eyes lowered and focused on her movements. Marcus droned on about werewolf history and politics, but she hardly listened. She shifted her position until she could glimpse Golda again past Marcus' brawny arm. A big werewolf was dancing close behind Golda with his hands on her hips and his belly against her back. Boudi-Ca felt her stomach quiver with envy. She could never dance with Golda like that. She wasn't tall enough for one thing. Could Golda have any interest in her as Ayelet had suggested? She wished that she'd asked Ayelet more questions.

"Are you listening?"

Boudi-Ca blinked. She was startled by the loud voice of Marcus in her ear. The werewolf's huge hand had wrapped around her arm. She shook her arm loose and looked him square in the eye.

"I'm sorry sir. I'm feeling a little faint. I really need to feed."

Marcus bowed and grinned imperiously. "Well, I might—"

She paced quickly away before he could finish his sentence. She didn't even politely look back. Marcus' rough hand around her arm had positively made her skin crawl. Boudi-Ca stalked off of the dance floor as the song came to end. She made her way to the table where Gonorrheah Shared her pipe with a grey-haired werewolf who had a light brown snout.

"Hello, Mistress Gonorrheah." Boudi-Ca sat on the stretch of worn wooden bench next to the wizardress. Her stomach felt a little sick. Her Hunger was complaining because she'd left the dance, which was increasingly charged with eroticism. A new song started, and the drumbeat deepened. Two werewolves pressed against Golda instead of just one. They'd stripped their dance clothes to match her nudity, and they were rudely groping her, one from the front and the other from behind.

Boudi-Ca looked away. She didn't want to witness Golda getting frisky with the horny werewolves. She watched Mistress Ayelet, who was dancing nearby with an older grey-furred werewolf who wore a patterned loincloth like Marcus. Gonorrheah reached across the table and tapped her arm with the stem of her pipe.

"Did Marcus bore you, fledgling?"

"Slightly."

"Try some herbs. Ayelet won't mind."

"Are you sure?"

"Of course. They're innocuous and relaxing—the perfect thing for your obviously frazzled nerves. Here. Take the pipe and give it a try."

"I didn't realize my frazzle was that obvious." Boudi-Ca took the pipe from Gonorrheah, who flicked her fingers and sent a spark of flame into the round bowl. Boudi-Ca puffed the mouthpiece and burst into a coughing fit. The werewolf next to Gonorrheah grinned. Boudi-Ca massaged her throat. The herbs relaxed her once she was done coughing. She puffed again and returned the pipe to Gonorrheah. She slumped in the chair and let out a deep smoky breath. She hadn't realized that she was so wound up. Gonorrheah puffed, then pulled the pipe from her lips and tapped the mouthpiece pensively on her chin.

"What about that other werewolf, fledgling? Did you fancy him?"

"The red one? He was alright. I mean, he was big and furry, and he didn't smell particularly good, but at least he was nice. What about you, Mistress Gonorrheah? Why aren't you out there dancing?"

Gonorrheah patted the hairy hand of the werewolf who sat across from her. "I've got my huckleberry, and he's enough. Looks like Golda is going for four and five. Why don't you talk to the red one, fledgling? He went over to those blankets to sit with his friends."

"I don't know."

"Have another smoke." Gonorrheah handed her the pipe. Boudi-Ca took it and managed to draw more smoke in. She felt more relaxation drift through her body all the way down to her toes.

"Thanks, Mistress Gonorrheah."

"You're welcome. Now go after him, fledgling! Attack!"

The brown-snouted werewolf chuckled. "Elor's a nice guy. He's kind of different. He's kind of like you, mimo."

Boudi-Ca shrugged. She decided she wasn't interested in any werewolves. She rose from her chair and walked quickly out of the great hall towards the stairs back to the upper levels. She stopped short in the middle of the stony corridor, however. She felt suddenly light-headed. Her Hunger protested viciously, rising up to constrict her throat. She couldn't ignore her Hunger, and if she went back to the guest room it would only grow worse.

She imagined a horrible scene like the opening night of the Spring Festival. She'd faint dead away while climbing the long stone stairways of the werewolf stronghold. Ayelet would find her, carry her back down and ask for volunteers. In no time, she'd have a long line of werewolves wanting to fill her up, and Ayelet would make her take them all.

Boudi-Ca steeled herself, turned on her heel, and went back to the dance. She simply needed to feed. It was a necessity. She walked over to the group of werewolves that lounged on blankets. Elor and his friends were drinking and talking animatedly, but they all stopped and stared at her as she approached.

"Hi Elor," she said. "I was wondering if you might want to show me around. I've been sleeping today, and I haven't really seen anything in this place."

"Sure, Boudi-Ca." Elor grinned, revealing his Sharp-looking yellow teeth. Predictably, all of the other werewolves grinned too. Elor stood up and led her from the great hall. They passed down a wide torchlit corridor and up a short flight of stairs. They walked down another hall that sported a row of arched openings. Elor ducked into one of the openings through a ragged cloth hanging. A pair of raised sleeping pallets sat against two walls with small tables and trunks in between them. An ancient feeble oil lamp offered a low glow of light. Elor sat down on a sunken but comfortable-looking bed.

"This is my room. I Share it with my mate."

"Your mate? You have a lover?"

Elor chuckled. "Nay. I don't go that way like some of the other guys, and I told you we don't have women here. I meant my partner. Everyone has a partner on patrol. You never know when you might run into a vamp or one of those hunting parties that come up sometimes from Haawiyah—rich and bored military types looking to shoot werewolves with guns for fun. The vamps are really a bigger threat. Their eyes can see us at night."

"You and the vampires must really be enemies, I guess."

Elor's furry ears pricked. "The vamps lord it over us here in Meristyian. The hatred goes way back. Things have gotten worse lately though. The balance is out of whack, what with the Disciples of Set bedding down with the damned Jinni. I mean Allyssia's bitches from Haawiyah, of course. No offense meant."

"None taken. I can't believe the vampires are marching on the Redoubt. It's such a beautiful place, and the vampires are so awful."

"The Redoubt is your home, right? It's in western Meristyian?"

"Yes. It's a beautiful little city, or at least it was the last time I saw it. We passed about a thousand vampires on the way out here, and they were all headed in that direction."

The werewolf shook his head. "Foul bastards. Not all of 'em are bad, mind you. There are a few clans out there that know how to get along with everyone else. Those aren't the Disciples of Set, though. We Brothers had a nice working relationship with the Eastern Order Jinni, but that's all over now. The vamps killed every last one of them as far as we know."

"I'm afraid they're going to do that to the Lady's city, too."

"So, are you excited?"

Boudi-Ca shrugged. "About my home being destroyed?"

"No. I mean the battle we're planning on the Acheron—taking a little revenge for our Eastern Order friends. The Clan of the Four Brothers, the Clan Greybeard, and the legendary Jackal are taking down a bunch of vamps and Jinni in Memphis under the full moon. This will be the biggest battle in Meristyian since a very long time."

"I suppose. I don't expect to have much of a role. I just want this to be over. I used to think that I was an adventurous mimọ girl, but lately I'm not so sure. I never realized how dangerous and difficult adventures could be."

The werewolf shook his head. "Aye. For all of this world's beauty, it's too bad powerful people feel the need to take over and control everything. And for what? Greed? Meristyian is big enough to just let everyone live in peace."

"I agree."

"On the other hand, how can you appreciate being happy unless someone comes along and shows you something unhappy? Right?"

Boudi-Ca ran her eyes over Elor's muscular, hairy arms and chest. "I suppose you've got a point. I appreciate my old, safe mimọ life in Heaven a lot more these days."

"Well, I was thinking about it a different way, but I guess that's true too. Some kind of romantic conversation we're having, eh? Do you want to go look around the place some more? My room was close, so I brought you here first."

"I don't really care." Boudi-Ca let her gaze drift lower to the bulge in Elor's shabby loincloth. Her Hunger was urging her to jump him. She turned and rested her hand on his thigh.

"That feels good, Boudi-Ca."

"You're nicer than the other werewolves, Elor. You're sweet and smart. You're not rude and boring like Marcus."

"Psht." Elor put his finger to his lips. I'm not saying I don't agree with you, but try to keep it down if you talk about one of our clan leaders, you know? We werewolves have very good ears, and there are a lot of us around tonight."

"Well, I do like you even though I might look and act like I don't. I haven't been in a good mood. I've had a lot of problems."

The werewolf touched her hair where it fell to her shoulder. "You're really beautiful, Boudi-Ca. A lot of the guys are crazy over Golda because she's a cat-shifter and everything, but I like you. You're feminine. You don't have anything really vicious inside you, but at the same time you aren't as wimpy as you look."

"Thanks. I think."

"You should get some healing herbs for your cheek. I think Marcus got you somehow in that little scuffle. I have a mirror if you want to see."

"You have a mirror? That's funny. I don't feel anything on my cheek."

Elor grinned and rummaged in the trunk next to his bed. He held up a small round mirror. Boudi-Ca looked into its dirty surface. It was true. A long, ugly red weal streaked her cheek. A spark of anger burned in her chest. "This is so embarrassing. I didn't even bring a mirror with me on the trip. Why didn't Mistress Ayelet warn me that I was disfigured before she invited me down to dance in front of everyone?"

"Maybe she didn't think it was serious." Elor reached and caressed her cheek gently. Boudi-Ca grabbed Elor's hand and pulled it away. She pressed her own fingertips to her cheek. Inexplicably, she felt like she was going to cry. She couldn't have a hideous scar on her face. It was unacceptable. Would she have it forever? Despite all of the beauty and pleasure in the desire-realm, everything seemed to involve pain and suffering. The mirror shook in her hand.

"I hate Marcus."

Elor looked concerned. "Boudi, are you alright? You seem a little out of kilter. I'm sure it will heal fine."

"No! I'm not alright! This is just what this world does. Whenever I think I'm almost about to be happy, something happens to make me sad. I just want to go back home. All of this isn't worth it."

"Boudi, you're beautiful. You don't have to be sad from that. I mean, you'll always be a hundred times prettier than me."

Boudi-Ca pursed her lips. Elor had a point. She covered the scar with her hand. Her fingertips warmed her cheek.

"You won't think I'm ugly even with my occasionally lazy eye, and my uneven wings, and my hair that isn't perfectly ebony?"

Elor stared at her, uncomprehending. "Of course not. You're beautiful, Boudi-Ca. I'll say it as many times as you want."

"My classmates in Heaven didn't think I was beautiful. They made fun of me. I'm really not that pretty of an mimọ girl, to be honest. I didn't have many friends in Heaven, and no female ones. No one really loved me."

"I'll love you, Boudi-Ca." Elor put his hairy hand to her cheek and closed it over hers. "You deserve to be loved."

Boudi-Ca felt tears coming to her eyes. Oddly, she could feel Elor's love in that moment. She felt Elor's love like an electric connection that zapped across the space between them. The feeling went down and touched her heart, and then spread out and filled her arms. Her cheek felt suddenly hot where she touched it. She wasn't sure if it was from Elor's warm hand over hers, or whether she was blushing. She smoothed her injured skin in a circular motion, as if loving herself, accepting herself as she was—a Jinn. She leaned and kissed Elor's cheek.

"Thank you for saying such nice things to me. You're sweet."

Elor blinked. "Whatcha? Your cheek looks healed already."

"We can pretend."

"No, really." The werewolf nodded at the mirror. "Look."

Boudi-Ca raised the mirror once more. Elor was right. The long red streak had disappeared, leaving only the slightest trace of pink on the surface of her skin. "I don't know how that just happened."

Elor grinned. "It's a blessing from your goddess maybe."

"Maybe." Boudi-Ca looked once more into the dirty mirror, and then put it down, puzzled. The scrape must have been a trick of the light in the first place. Elor's eyes, meanwhile, were roaming lower over her breasts under her dress. He wanted her, and she or her Hunger—she'd reached the tipping point where she couldn't discern which—wanted him just as much. She threw herself onto the bed and pulled Elor over her. His hairy thighs pressed against hers. The fur of his belly tickled when his leather vest fell open. Boudi-Ca bit her lip. She couldn't help but giggle. Elor stiffened.

"What's so funny? Werewolves aren't legendary lovers like Jinni, and I'm pretty rusty. You're going to have to forgive me."

"Oh, no. You're just furry, and I've been ticklish ever since I fell into Meristyian. It's true that I'm a Jinn, but I'm not very legendary myself."

"Well, you're still the expert. Do you want me to shave my chest and everything like that pretty slave boy up in the guest quarters? The whole pack would laugh at me, but I'd do it just for you."

"No, you're fine as you are." Boudi-Ca tugged on Elor's arm. She wanted him. Her Hunger wanted him. She wanted to lay claim to Elor's manly love. Elor moved over her on the bed. She wrapped her legs around his hips. His massive phallus rubbed against her inner thigh and bumped against the entrance of her sex. He caressed her shoulder and stroked softly down to her breast. Elor licked his lips.

"So, what's it like running with the Jackal, Boudi-Ca? Has he ever—I mean—have you and he ever—"

"No! Of course not. I don't know him very well. He's a bounty hunter. He's mysterious and kind of above everyone else."

"Kind of like you?" Elor bent his head for a kiss. Boudi-Ca met his lips, trying not to betray with her face how she felt about his breath. She turned her head away and scrunched low to tug his stiff and hairy phallus in her hand. She shifted her hips and rubbed him low. Thankfully he got the message, centered himself, and slowly penetrated her.

Boudi-Ca groaned. Elor was surely bigger than Bola. The werewolf began to thrust in a slow rhythm that matched the distant drumbeat in the central chamber of the stronghold. She held onto his massive hairy shoulder blades and relaxed through the ache. Elor's phallus stretched her and then kept going, plumbing her deepest depths. Her belly quivered and jumped. Waves of pleasure melted the splinters of pain away. The werewolf rocked faster and faster. He had impressive stamina. After long minutes Elor jerked and emptied into her. His love overflowed and filled her, more than she'd been filled since the opening night of the Spring Festival. Elor drew back and out. The weight of his body slumped heavily on top of her.

"Sorry," he said. "Like I said, there aren't any females around here."

"It's ok Elor. I loved it." Boudi-Ca stretched and reveled in the familiar aliveness of being full—that wonderful rush of power that had only begun when Lady Allyssia made her into a Jinn. Renewed energy flowed into her limbs. Her mind cleared, and Elor's little stone bedroom seemed to crystallize into crisp clarity around her. Elor's yellow eyes were close and bright. He was panting quietly.

"You really loved it?"

"Oh, yes. Thank you so much for inviting me to your bed."

"You're an incredible girl, Boudi. I can't believe I'm this lucky. I think I'm going to fall in love with you. All of the guys are going to be jealous. Will you let me adore you? Can I be your one and only?"

"That's sweet Elor, but I think I may be in love with someone else."

Elor grimaced. "Nuts. Whoever he is, he's a lucky guy. Is he handsome? Is he big? Does he tell you how beautiful you are?"

Boudi-Ca pondered. She was feeling really good. Surely it wouldn't hurt to confide her feelings about Golda to Elor. She really wanted someone to talk to. "She's bigger than me, actually, and she did tell me that I was beautiful once."

"Wait, you're into women?" Elor's jaw dropped. "I would never have guessed just from looking at you, Boudi-Ca. You seem so feminine. Gods, now I feel stupid. Who is it? What lucky girl are you in love with?"

Boudi-Ca smiled and caressed his cheek. "Don't worry about it. Tonight, I'm all yours. I really need to feed. The more you can give me, the more I can help at the battle in Memphis. Maybe if I can impress the woman I'm in love with, she'll pay more attention to me."

Chapter 32:

Silvery moonlight draped the Acheron river valley. Great dunes heaved against the stars that twinkled in the Isandlwana sky. The grey sands were like a magician's silk cloth hiding infinite mystery. The night air was pregnant with the bold hopes of the werewolves.

Boudi-Ca sat astride her horse between Ayelet and Gonorrheah. Ayelet had dressed regally for the battle. With her panniers, blooming skirts, dress gloves, and hair coiffed with pearls, Ayelet looked like a renaissance queen astride her steed. Ayelet wore both of the swords that she'd brought on the trip—one hanging over each of her hips. Vampire bodies were tough enough to break a blade.

Marcus and his brothers talked in low tones with the venerable Greybeard, who was a larger werewolf than any of them. He wore a braided mane and a thick beard that was true to his name. A force of nearly two hundred wolves had gathered around their leaders. Under the full moon, many of the werewolves had shifted form. They'd dropped down onto four legs and grown thick protective fur over their entire bodies, transforming fully into wolves instead of wolfish men.

In their shifted forms, the werewolves used a different language. The night was filled with syllables sounded out with growls. Boudi-Ca tried

353

to spot the red-furred form of Elor beyond the soft glow of Gonorrheah's low-floating tenebris lux. She wasn't sure what she would do if he bounded up to give her a slobbery good-luck kiss.

She'd spent the entire night with Elor at the werewolf stronghold. She'd taken him three times, then twice during the three-day ride across the deserts to Memphis. He'd sent her over the edge once, a waste of her love energy. She'd been strangely relaxed, and Elor's easygoing friendliness had been infectious. He'd proclaimed his love for her several times. He'd filled her with his seed as well as with pride from his flattering words.

Despite her prolonged enjoyment of Elor's phenomenal phallus, she continued to think of Golda. Was Golda enjoying her werewolf adorers? Was Golda falling in love with one of them? Boudi-Ca felt a queer queasiness in her belly. She needed to get Golda alone. She needed to say something before it was too late, even if the Conclave came to take her away the very next day.

Considering the situation, there were more important things to worry about. The battle was a tall task. The goal was to retake Memphis and liberate Sekhmet, the cat-goddess leader of the Eastern Order, from the Old Order Jinni and Disciple vampires. Even Gonorrheah, normally ever-cheerful, sat tight-lipped and unsmiling on her horse with her eye sockets shadowed by her tenebris lux. The wizardress looked straight ahead over the desert where the ranks of werewolves were readying themselves.

Prince Masad, still in the shape of the lissome Old Order fledgling, strode across the sand through the werewolf packs, accompanied by Golda in cat form. Golda's shape shortened and rose until she stood long and nude on two legs. All of the werewolf heads turned to watch her. Masad and Golda came into the light of the lux and closed the circle with Ayelet, Greybeard, and the four brothers.

"Dead are the three sentries on the southern perimeter of the city," Masad said. "As well as the roaming patrol."

"The way is clear," Golda added tersely. She wiped her bloody cheek with the back of her hand.

"Excellent," grunted Brother Marcus. "The Clan of the Four Brothers is ready to ride to glory at the side of the Greybeard Clan."

Greybeard nodded. "My wolves are ready. The Smokeless Flames and the Disciple sorceresses are yours, Mistress Ayelet."

"We'll strike first with a feint to draw the vampires onto the sands along the river," Ayelet said. "Masad and I will lead that charge. It's critical that your wolves obey the signals that we discussed. Once the vampires are in the open, Mistress Gonorrheah will hit them with fire storms from the cliff's edge. That should weaken them. The scattered vamps should be easier prey to take down in the chaos."

"Stay in your packs," Brother Marcus called. "Follow your leader."

"Victory to the Clan!" A smattering of cries echoed through the hills, followed by a chorus of wolf howls. Ayelet raised her voice again over the canine cries.

"Everyone should stay as far away as possible from the Sekhmet's hidden temple. If any vampires seek to flee there, do not follow them. We'll take command of the outer city first, and then we'll regroup to plan a more cautious attack on the inner compound."

"To Memphis!" Greybeard roared. He bounded away, followed by the brothers. The packs of werewolves fell into line. Boudi-Ca felt her heart start to pound. She nearly jumped from her saddle when she felt Sharp pricks on her neck. The pricks were only the little talons of Ayelet's messenger bird.

Remember, fledgling, your job is to help Golda protect Gonorrheah while she casts fire spells. They will defend you too. We all have to watch each other's backs in this battle.

"Yes, Mistress. I can do it." Boudi-Ca summoned her blue bird to her fingers and sent it aloft with her words on its wings. It flew through the moonlight towards Ayelet, who was pressing her horse forward to lead the werewolves. Boudi-Ca gripped her reins tightly. Gonorrheah had drawn alongside her.

"Just follow me, Boudi-Ca. We'll fall in behind the wolves."

"I'll watch your back, Mistress Gonorrheah." Boudi-Ca directed her horse to follow Gonorrheah over a dune. Golda was riding close by, just to the side. Golda looked over with a smile. Boudi-Ca returned the smile. Her heart leapt still harder in her chest. Golda had strapped her sword to her horse's harness instead of her hip. She was evidently going to fight in the nude. Her statuesque body was beautiful in the moonlight.

They rode for an hour until the faint firelights of a city gleamed in the hills ahead. The moon illuminated the dark forms of the werewolves coursing through the dunes. They topped a rise, and the ruined city of Memphis lay spread out before them. The column of wolves slowed to a cautious lope.

Golda snorted audibly. "I can smell the stench of those vampires. And to think this used to be a sacred place of peaceful Jinni. The thought of a vampire horde camping in the Redoubt like this fills me with disgust."

"Hopefully they won't be able to breach our gates," Boudi-Ca offered.

"If Ivanka betrays us, then she will get them through the gates," Golda muttered. A cry sounded in the night—a single note of agony in the blackness. The werewolves surged forward. A howl sounded, and more howls. Golda reached for her sword. "There are vampires everywhere in the tapestry, but I can't see them yet."

"You'll be able to see when the fire starts flying," Gonorrheah said. "Follow me." Gonorrheah prodded her horse along the base of a low cliff that looked over the sandy flats below. She ascended steep ground towards the cliff's edge.

Boudi-Ca followed Gonorrheah alongside Golda. Soon clashing blades rang below the cliffs, followed by cries and howls. Golda dismounted and readied her sword. Boudi-Ca imitated her. The Oya-blade felt heavier than normal in her hands, which were tired from so much riding. The blade glowed faintly in the dark. A feeble flicker ran along the steel, setting the magical engravings on the silvered guard to shimmer in circles around the socketed citrines.

"This is a good spot to both attack and defend," Golda said.

"I agree." Gonorrheah dismounted and brandished her staff. An arc of fire shot from the end and exploded in the air over the battle below, limning the combatants in a lurid glow. Gonorrheah waved her staff again, and another arc formed that showered elongated streaks of fire. Vampires hissed and smoked wherever the flames fell. The werewolves pressed the advantage and ripped into them.

Gonorrheah waved her staff again, and another, longer arc formed, followed by more streaks of fire and more screams. Golda gazed down over the edge of the cliff at the dark fleeing forms. Her smiling face was ruddy in the light of the fires. "The vamps are already retreating."

Boudi-Ca stood on tiptoe next to Golda to see over the cliff's edge. The dark forms were indeed scattering as the tide of the battle moved away. Gonorrheah twirled her staff as the fire faded and darkness descended again over the battlefield.

"They're out of my range now. We have to advance."

Golda shook her head. "Not yet. We have company coming."

Boudi-Ca followed Golda away from the cliff's edge. She took a practice swing to test the weight of the Oya-blade. She heard the footsteps first, and then a group of vampires burst from the darkness. They were running low, almost on all fours. The tip of Gonorrheah's staff flared to reveal four vampires. Their pale skin was patchworked with splotches of fur. Huge fangs sprouted from slavering jaws. Their faces were twisted into animal masks of rage.

"Ishologu!" shouted Gonorrheah. "They found us fast!"

Boudi-Ca side-stepped the first vampire. She landed a glancing blow with her sword against the creature's thick neck. The Ishologu's lunge for Gonorrheah went astray. The thing scrabbled to keep from sliding over the cliff. Gonorrheah lashed out. Flames streaked from her hand to engulf the vampire. It rolled away and over, but a second vampire quickly leapt onto the wizardress. Gonorrheah cried in pain. Boudi-Ca raised her hand and formed a fierce desirous kin-hex that dislodged the vampire temporarily. She intercepted the creature, which took the opportunity to change targets and leap straight at her.

Boudi-Ca switched to a defensive stance to divert the creature's path, but the bestial vampire was too heavy. It bowled straight through her defense, ignoring the blow to its head. It knocked her onto her back and caught her with its claws. A hard burn of pain shot down her leg. She rolled to her feet desperately, expecting another hit, but instead the creature whined with pain. Golda stood over it with her blade sunk deep into its body. Boudi-Ca delivered an executioner's strike that cracked the Ishologu's skull. The bone yielded in a satisfying way under the weight of her blade.

With Golda engaging the third vampire, Boudi-Ca found herself face to face with the last. She avoided a flurry of wicked claws, but with a sudden leap it bounded into her, and she was knocked over yet again. The vampire lunged at her a second time, but she anticipated the move and rolled away. As fast as the creature moved, it attacked mainly straight ahead. Boudi-Ca tried a contretemps that Ayelet had taught her, but she missed the thrust. The difficult footing had thrown off a move that needed perfect timing.

The vampire went for the throat. Boudi-Ca flashed just in time. The ribbon unfurled through the still grey space. The vampire's claws remained frozen in midair. She passed bodily through the bestial vampire and emerged behind it. She twirled and caught the surprised creature with a hard shot to the head. A crack sounded. The vampire let out a howl.

A fiery burst exploded. Boudi-Ca closed her eyes to a squint. The blast of Gonorrheah's spell knocked the creature from its feet. It rolled away across the sand and down the hill in a ball of smoke and flame. Boudi-Ca grabbed her painful leg. Her fingers were blood-slippery. She felt weak and nauseated. Golda finished off her vampire and leaned on her sword. Gonorrheah swung her staff and unleashed two more fireballs off the edge of the cliff. Shrieks of vampire agony rose from the battle below, which ebbed again.

"The vamps are heading back into Memphis," Golda said as she looked over the edge of the cliff. "I can see the red threads in full retreat in the weave. I think we can advance and help Ayelet and the werewolves. Are you alright to ride, Boudi?"

"I think I'll be fine." Boudi-Ca mounted alongside Golda and Gonorrheah. She urged her horse to follow them at a canter. They doubled back and rode around the end of the cliff, then across the battlefield towards the dark walls and toppled columns of the ruins of Memphis.

Boudi-Ca followed closely. She didn't want to lose Gonorrheah and

Golda in the dark. The hooves of the two horses ahead of her stirred up burned vampires. She spat ashes from her lips—warm flakes that tasted like death. She spurred her horse to draw even with the two mistresses as they entered the streets. She reached down and rubbed her leg again, willing warmth under her skin. The bleeding seemed to have ceased. The fact that she was well-fed seemed to help her Jinn healing.

As the pain in her leg subsided, her nervousness increased. The vampires were far from defeated. The maze-like streets of Memphis were in chaos. Dark forms ran in all directions. Vampires and werewolves chased each other in and out of charcoal shadows. Cries of pain split the night. Boudi-Ca silently offered a prayer to Lady Allyssia. Golda led them down a narrow alleyway, and then into a wider thoroughfare on the outskirts of the small city.

"I don't like this," Golda said suddenly. "I feel the presence of Jinni, and they're close."

Gonorrheah hefted her staff. "Everything's going to be fine. Where are they, Golda?"

"I don't know, damn it. They're right here, but this tapestry is crazy. Threads are running everywhere. I've got a splitting headache already."

"We need to find Ayelet," Gonorrheah said. "Can you see her?"

"I don't need her track," Golda answered. "I can hear—"

Golda's voice was cut short by a snapping sound. More snapping sounds sounded in the darkness. Boudi-Ca felt a twisting line of pain snap across her back. Numbness spread into her buttocks and neck. Her horse reared. Pain licked again. A cord wrapped around her forearm and yanked. She fell hard to the sandy ground. The impact stunned her.

"Help—"

Mistress Gonorrheah's high voice went silent.

"Foul bitch—" Golda grunted. Her voice broke into a feline hiss.

Boudi-Ca felt numbness spread over her shoulder, throat, and the side of her head. The numbness came from the rubbery cord that was wrapped around her upper arm. She tried to rise, but her arm failed her. A dark figure blotted out the night sky. Sounds of struggle and scuffles were all around. Boudi-Ca succeeded in rolling, but the whip stopped her motion. The dark figure, satisfied with her inability to escape, dragged her by her arm over the sand and pebbles of the Memphis street.

Boudi-Ca reached for the hilt of her Oya-blade with her left hand, but she couldn't pull it from its sheath. She gripped the whip instead, which was a mistake. The numbness spread through her left hand and wrist. More dark shapes loomed. A whip struck hard at her chest, rendering her breathless. Another whip wrapped around her leg. The whips tugged, helping the first one. Boudi-Ca felt tears coming to her eyes.

Pain and numbness shot down to her foot and up into her buttocks, then higher to join the numbness that filled her shoulders, her stomach, and her spine. The additional whips took over, and she was dragged by her legs into the yawning black rectangle of a nearby open doorway. When the tension of the cords relaxed, she lay in the pitch-dark interior of what seemed to be a small stone hut.

Boudi-Ca struggled to move her numbed limbs. She reached slowly over her body and thumped her numb arm with her numb hand, trying to drive feeling into either of them. She closed her eyes, focused, and angrily moved flushes of Jinn energy from her belly to her limbs. Warmth flowed into the cold and dissipated it. She wiggled her fingers. She urged more of her energy there. She finally managed to grip the hilt of her backup dagger and pull it slowly from its sheath.

More dark figures appeared in the moonlit triangle of the doorway. Boudi-Ca felt another long body being deposited next to her. She caught the furry scent of Golda, who was motionless. She finally had her dagger in hand, but she was afraid to attempt a swing in the narrow space. Metal screeched. A hatch opened in the floor. Yellow light poured out across a low ceiling. The dark silhouette of an unknown Jinn bent over her. The woman wore silver earrings and a black leather corset and skirt. She was surely Old Order. Boudi-Ca rocked her body to get leverage.

"She has a blade!" a voice warned.

Boudi-Ca thrust. The dagger found yielding flesh. Her captor groaned and fell backwards. Boudi-Ca raised the blade and struck again, but she missed. Another figure flitted across her field of vision. Whip coils smacked hard against her arm—once, twice, three times as she tried to fight. Numbness racked her again, and the dagger clattered from her useless fingers. Boudi-Ca gasped. The whip coils snapped hard against her cheek.

"Nasty little viper," said an enraged voice. "I'll have her head for that."

"Perhaps," said another voice. "Quickly now. Is that constriction collar tight enough around Gonorrheah's neck? I think she got a bird off."

"Don't fight them, Boudi," came Gonorrheah's choked, whispery voice. "No use."

Boudi-Ca let her head loll. Gonorrheah was right. Resistance was hopeless against the whips. Gloved hands were on her shoulders, lifting her body. Dark silhouettes crowded around her. They wrenched her arms behind her. She felt the dull presence of metal against her wrists. She heard clicks.

"This one has wings," said a voice. "She looks like the mimo. Yes. I think we've found her. The Grand Auditor will be pleased."

"Who cares about the Auditor," said another voice. "This creature is vicious. She needs to eat a whip." Boudi-Ca felt the hard curves of a coiled whip rub against her forehead. The whip sent tingles over her scalp and defocused her eyes. A blurry woman hovered over her with black-painted lips.

"She's under control," said a voice.

Boudi-Ca felt the whip lower to caress her nose. The whip didn't smell like leather—it smelled like dung and death. The coil snapped down hard on her nose. She felt the whip wedge between her thickened, tingling lips. She pressed with her numbed tongue, but she couldn't push the rubbery coil from between her teeth. Coldness spread through her mouth and tongue. Boudi-Ca shuddered viscerally. The numbness in her tongue crept deeper into her swollen face, then into her brain. She gazed at the pool of light on the ceiling as it slowly faded away.

Chapter 33:

Golda straddled the stone floor with her wrists chained to her cuffed ankles. She held her head low while the Smokeless Flames mistress entered the chamber again and paced in slow, patient circles around her. Captain Kriteh's boots were dusty black leather with spiral copper buckles in the shapes of coiled vipers—Allyssia's sacred snakes. The hem of Kriteh's red wool skirt was woven with an entwined serpent motif. She smelled like black poppy and mastic incense—a mixture both heady and poisonous.

"We have news, Golda. I'm happy to tell you that the hidden city of Love has fallen as planned. Allyssia has been imprisoned like Sekhmet. Her cult of pathetic rebels has been crushed. The New Order Jinni have surrendered. They are all chained and caged. Soon they'll be going back to Haawiyah to stand trial for their crimes."

"I don't believe your lies, Kriteh. Even if they are true, the New Order will survive and rebuild itself. You can't kill Love."

Captain Kriteh spat. "The New Order does not exist, and it never existed in any official history. The only question is whether you'll be erased as well."

Golda edged up to shift more weight onto her toes. The pebbly grit on the floor of the small cell was biting painfully into her knees—almost enough to make her weep. She'd been chained kneeling and nude for hours. Kriteh's abuse was intended to break her mentally. She needed to resist. She also needed to stay calm and avoid shifting into cat form, which could break her bones.

"What is your offer then? Get on with it."

"Mistress Ivanka says you shouldn't be given to the devils like the other lesbian bitches," Kriteh answered. "You're too skilled to be broken and imprisoned. Ivanka says you should be turned to serve our Lord in a military capacity. She suggested a certain medicine to make you forget your misbegotten loyalty to Allyssia."

"That evil witch." Golda curled her lip. "I don't need her charity any more than I need medicine to cure me."

"We can make you forget everything, and then perhaps we can forget about your crimes too. That's the deal. You'll serve Lord Hades properly as a Jinn. You'll go to the chapel and worship our Lord. If you're a good girl, maybe you can join us in the Smokeless Flames and serve in Hell's army. We need talented trackers to fight Heaven and the other rebels."

"I only serve Love."

"Love?" Kriteh laughed. "Is that Allyssia's nonsense? Love doesn't exist. A Jinn serves her Lord and her husband, and her husband fucks her and fills her Hunger. After you're reformed and married, your empty head will only crave your husband's seed. He will own you, and then you'll know your true purpose."

"I'll make a note to kill him before that happens."

"Oh, yes. I'm told you were the ruler of Egypt centuries ago, but you murdered someone, so Heaven rejected you. Your violent nature might hurt your prospects for finding a decent man. At least you've got a decent pair of milk bags for him to play with."

Golda winced when Kriteh gripped her nipple. She felt pain splinter in her breast when Kriteh applied the clip. She felt more pain when her other breast received equal treatment. The clips were heavy, military-grade things. Golda wrenched her head down as the captain squatted like a toad and tried to kiss her. Her belly quivered with Hunger. She felt terribly empty and stretched. Kriteh's face leaned close.

"You hunger, Golda. If I don't break you, your Hunger will do it for me. A few hours from now, you'll be consumed by desperate lust and need, begging me pathetically for anything that I deign to give you."

"I don't think so."

"In the meanwhile, we'll start the first step of your reformation, yes?"

Golda clenched her throat. "Don't do this."

"I thought you said you weren't afraid. Are you confused inside? I'm trying to be nice. The official punishment for treason against our Lord is eternal imprisonment or the void. Gonorrheah appreciated my overtures, or at least she made an effort to pretend."

"Go back to Haawiyah where you belong."

"Gladly. I've earned two moons of off-duty with my husband. Unfortunately, I've been given the burden of dragging you back to Mer with me on a leash, and I've reached the limits of my patience with the gentle negotiations that Ivanka requested. Witches love their cats, I suppose." The Flames mistress rose, strode to the cell door, and opened it. "Come inside now, Master Kelneth."

"Thank you, Captain Kriteh." A tall and muscled Djinnus entered the room. He had long dark hair that curled over his shoulders and a herculean bulge in his tight leather pants. He bent and deposited a silver tray on the stone floor. Golda eyed the tray. Her captor hadn't been bluffing. A mortar full of aromatic black nectar sat next to a small candle, a spoon, a pair of silk gloves, and a variety of metal implements, including a thick phallus clad in polished copper.

"Get me something to sit on, please," Kriteh muttered. "I want to be comfortable."

"Of course, Captain," the Djinnus replied.

Golda tried again to slip her aching hands through the thick manacles that bound her wrists to her ankles, but both iron bands were adequately tight. She arched, pressing her fingertips against the backs of her ankles to relieve the painful pressure on her knees. Kriteh's narcabyss whip smacked across her shoulder blades.

"Get back down."

Kriteh's whip cracked again, and a third time, each time harder. Golda slumped as the numbness re-invaded her back muscles. The whip slid slowly along her spine to the nape of her neck. The numbness followed. Her stomach muscles gave way, unable to support her weight, until her arms strained again against the limits of the iron chains. Kriteh chuckled.

"Isn't my bondage nice?"

"I hope you die over a bed of coals." Golda groaned when the whip snapped hard across her buttocks. Three strokes fell across her right arm, and then the whip moved to her left. The whip returned to her back, plying harder with loud cracks. Kriteh was an expert with the narcabyss whip, increasing the intensity of the blows to keep thrusting pain through the numbness. The deeper the unfeeling, the harder the blows fell. The whip stopped, and Golda felt fingers probe the folds of her exposed pumpum, the only still-sensitive part of her hindquarters. Kriteh pinched with filed fingernails.

"You're wet, you whore. Your old slave training comes back quickly. That's why you might be better off sold as an exotic Jinn slave, but no. Ivanka had to champion you. You can blame her for your black nectar reformation, but you won't remember her when it's over. We'll make sure you love the Lady and the Lord, and that's all you'll know."

Golda felt a sob welling up inside her, but she managed to stifle it. Kriteh's hand left her rear end. The tray rattled. Golda felt the length of the cold metal phallus slide deep inside her pumpum. Footsteps sounded in the hall. The Djinnus dropped a pair of heavy wooden cubes to the floor.

"Wonderful, Master Kelneth," Kriteh said. "Would you mind working the dildo for me? I want this bitch weak for transport back to Haawiyah."

"Of course, Captain. I'd be delighted."

Golda felt thicker, rougher fingers pulling on the cheek of her buttock, and then the phallus in her pumpum slid deeply in and out with a steady rhythm. She moaned when the pleasure trickled into her belly despite her best efforts to resist. Kriteh gripped her hair and pulled her head back with one hand. Golda wrenched her head away. Kriteh's free hand slapped her.

Her head jerked under the impact.

"None of that," Kriteh admonished. "You know better. Present yourself."

"You're a damned hypocrite." Golda kept her head averted with her lips pressed tightly together. Kriteh's coiled whip caressed her throat until her head lolled. Kriteh pulled her limp head back, doubled over, and sealed with a kiss. Golda tried to press her lips against the assault, but her chin muscles were useless. Her jaw was slack, her mouth was kissed, and the familiar whirlpool of suction seized her soul.

She resisted having an orgasm with all of her strength. She held her stomach tight. Meanwhile, the Djinnus increased the speed of his thrusts, bumping skillfully against her clitoris with every stroke. She still held fast. Captain Kriteh wasn't strong enough to take an orgasm from her. Golda allowed herself a measure of grim satisfaction. The Flames captain finally broke the kiss.

"You're a stupid little fool."

Golda snorted her disagreement, but Kriteh locked her lips again and reached under her. She felt the narcabyss whip patter and slap against her abdomen—once, twice, three times. Golda hitched. The numbness of the whip inundated her stomach then, disabling the diaphragm muscles that had enabled her to hold. She felt her soul opening, and the pleasure waved up through her throat. Kriteh drained her orgasm in long draughts.

Golda felt the phallus rock harder in and out of her pumpum. It felt like a fist. With every thrust the Djinnus hit the right spots. The whip continued to slap and numb her belly to erode the return of any resistance. The clips dangling from her thick nipples sent waves of distracting pain into her breasts and ribcage. Soon she came again and a third time in quick succession under Kriteh's intense suction. She couldn't remember the last time she'd been so drained, not even by Herpessenia's attentions. When Kriteh let her go, even her bones felt hollow.

"I'm good, am I not?" The Flames captain chuckled. "Now that you're more receptive, Golda, it's time for you to meet an old friend of yours. Soon you'll forget your current allegiances completely, and you'll be a drooling servant of Allyssia. I'm giving you a new name, too. The reformation is more effective that way."

"I need to talk to Ivanka."

Kriteh didn't answer. She slid the wooden cube across the floor and slipped the silk gloves onto her hands. She picked up the largest needle. Golda breathed in the scent of the wicked black nectar—the odor of the sweet lotuses from the banks of the river Lethe. It made her head tingle. She almost wanted it. It would make her pain go away. When she floated in the black, she would forget everything except pleasure. Nothing else would matter.

"You want it, don't you?" Kriteh said. "Tell me what I want to hear."

"No."

"Your heart whispers yes. Good girl. Now lower your head forward as far as it will go. We're doing a permanent insertion for you, Golda. You'll have a silver socket and screw cap in the back of your neck for easy and measured nectar treatments. Where did that cat come from, Master Kelneth? Did you let it in the door?"

"No. I think it jumped down the light shaft, Captain. Apparently our Hell hounds still haven't killed all of Sekhmet's little pets."

Golda relaxed completely. She heard a cat's meow. She could smell the needle heating. She was ready to surrender. She felt Kriteh's fingers on the back of her neck as if from a distance. Kriteh pressed her head down further. Golda felt the metal pressing on the back of her numbed neck, and then a pinch. The smooth pressure turned to a burning pain as the drill grated against her spine. She felt a rattle in the depths of her being. Her head felt airy as if a cool breeze were blowing through her soul.

Kriteh shifted and reached for the tray. "Now for the insertion. Put that down, Kelneth. What are you doing?"

"This," the Djinnus answered. Kriteh jerked and rose upwards from where she sat. The wooden block rocked, and the candle fell with a clatter across the tray. Kriteh screamed and kicked. The room filled with a sickly odor. Golda lowered her eyes and listened to the struggle with disinterest. Her remaining energy swirled sweetly like cinnamon in melted butter, all draining towards the little hole on the back of her neck.

"Need you to wake, Golda." The male's voice was distant like a god in her consciousness. Golda felt fingers again on her neck. The Djinnus knelt and dropped a bloody cloth. Kriteh lay motionless on the floor.

"What are you doing?"

"Trying to get you out of here." The Djinnus reached for her chest and removed the clips from her nipples. He worked at her wrists. In moments the manacles came free. Golda toppled over onto the cold floor. Her soul felt like a boat loosed from its moorings, only to sink into a bottomless whirlpool.

"Masad? Is that you?"

"Yes. Found I some keys. Have we a chance to get you free."

Golda rolled onto her back. She tried to work life into her numb throat with her fingers and thumbs. "I'm glad you're on our side, Masad. Unless you can find me a slave though, I can barely move. What's happening? How long have I been here? Did we win or lose?"

"Won the werewolves the battle, but scatter they into the shelter of the hills to rest in this afternoon. Made they never into the temple. Sealed and warded the temple gates are from the inside. Open them no one can from outside, not even I. Happened what to you, Golda?"

"The Old Order ambushed us. They hit us with whips. Gonorrheah, Boudi-Ca, and I were captured. I guess you figured that out."

"Yes. Thought I that stayed back on the cliff had you, but when the battle was over, found I your threads in the tapestry. Received Ayelet a bird from Gonorrheah, but could not locate her to come to her aid. Realized we together what must have happened."

Golda sighed. "I've been in here for hours. You arrived just in time. That Smokeless Flames bitch was finally getting down to the business. We're in Sekhmet's temple?"

"Yes."

Golda gazed at Masad. "I'm going to have to get used to you being in yet another body, Prince. This one seems more like you. You are a male, right?"

"Yes. My father's son am I."

"So where is Ayelet?"

"Saw I her last, standing was she in the plaza outside the front gate in the middle of a hundred dead vampires. Demands she that the Old Order either come out and fight her, or release Boudi-Ca."

"That would be like her." Golda rubbed her forehead. "I'm so empty, Masad. She took everything I had."

"Have I something. Give I it to you."

"That might be strange, but good thinking." Golda bent and let Masad lift her leg. He slid his Djinnus cock into her wet pumpum. Her Hunger reached down of its own accord, wrapped around the phallus, and pulled. Masad held her in a warm embrace. He fucked acceptably until he came in a flood. Golda absorbed the hot Djinnus lust. She wasn't sure if the lust had come from the Djinnus or from the son of Lord Hades himself, but it was a jolt of incredible energy into her depleted body. Her numbness continued to dissipate.

"Masad. You may have saved my life."

Masad caressed her gently. "Lose I not the most beautiful tracker in Meristyian."

"So what's our plan?"

Masad rose slowly and re-fastened his pants. "Find we Gonorrheah first, if can we. Then Boudi-Ca. If get we to the front of the temple without notice, try we can to open the doors and re-unite with Ayelet. Use you can a narcabyss whip?"

"I've had lots of experience, but all on the wrong end of them. I'm not touching that thing. Do you want it?"

"No. Throw I spells."

Golda looked over at the crumpled corpse of the Flames mistress on the floor. Kriteh's skin looked wrinkled and withered, especially around her eyes and mouth, as if the mistress had been dead for five moons instead of five minutes. "What in the hells did you do to her, Masad?"

"Death magic."

"I've never seen anything like that. Do you think you've got the power to send more Old Order to the void?"

"Learn we only one way." Masad pulled the cell door open. Golda climbed to her feet, suppressing a feeling of queasiness as she looked down at the chains that had held her. The torture had devastated her physically and emotionally, and worse yet the little hole in the back of her neck was steadily leaking her energy. She could feel her emptiness slowly returning, along with a weight on her heart. Sekhmet's temple felt dark and oppressive. She was still inside a trap, and another whip would be enough to send her again to her knees.

Golda followed the possessor out into the narrow hall, which gave onto a number of other cell doors. The cell area seemed quiet and unoccupied. Masad peered through each door window until he stopped at a door and unlocked it. Gonorrheah was inside. Masad knelt over the wizardress and worked with the keys until the manacles and collar came free. Gonorrheah climbed warily to her feet.

"Where are we going?"

"Out," Golda said. "Our friend here is Masad. Thank you again, Prince Masad. We owe you our lives. I was worried about you, Gonorrheah. The mistress who tortured me told me lies. She said you'd agreed to serve Allyssia."

"They talked to me. I wasn't very cooperative, so they left. Where is Ayelet? Was the battle lost?"

Destroyed were most the vampires holding Memphis," Masad answered. "Returned the werewolf clans to the safety of the hills. Had the werewolves many casualties. Need we still to find Boudi-Ca. Thought I she would be here, but see her not I."

Gonorrheah stretched her fingers and cracked her knuckles. "I'm so weak. I've got next to nothing. I really need to feed."

"There's little we can do about that now," Golda said shortly. "We have to find Boudi-Ca and get out of here." Golda led the way back down the hall past her former cell. She searched around a corner and looked into more cells. The doors all stood open. The rest of the cells were empty. Masad shook his head.

"Golda? Feel you Boudi-Ca?"

Golda opened her tracking senses to Sekhmet's proprietary tapestry. She couldn't see any thread for the mimo fledgling, but she saw other threads—the threads of the enemy. She needed to escape from that place. Her desire to flee Sekhmet's temple was overwhelming her rational thought as well as her emotions. She couldn't cope. As Kriteh had cruelly reminded her, she was afraid of the Old Order.

"No. Boudi-Ca isn't down here, so we need to go up. Let's get those front doors open for Ayelet. I want to save Boudi-Ca as much as anyone, but now is not the time. We need more help. We need the werewolves. We need—"

"I think Ayelet's fledgling is around the other corner," Gonorrheah interrupted. "If I remember correctly from when they brought us in—"

A growl interrupted the wizardress. At the end of the hall from where they'd come, a shocked-looking Flames fledgling held two dogs at the ends of leather leashes. The dogs were huge and black with small red eyes and heads that were little more than casings for slavering maws that dripped three-inch teeth. The dogs snarled. The Old Order fledgling released the hounds. Gonorrheah raised her hand and released a fire bolt. The dogs skittered. The bolt hit a door frame. The fledgling disappeared, and the dogs bounded forward.

"Hell hounds already," Gonorrheah groaned. "I'm too naked for those teeth." The hellion hounds headed straight for the wizardress. Masad leapt forward to intercept them. Golda focused and allowed the change to come to her. She felt tears coming to her eyes. She tried to steel herself, but she was trembling. The fur on her arms and legs thickened, and she went to four paws. The first Hell hound lunged. Masad lifted his knee and connected. He gripped the dog's thick neck with both of his strong hands. Claws rent his chest as he drained the life from the dog. Its shiny black eyes bulged.

Golda crouched. The second Hell hound was gathering itself. She leapt and met the dark creature in midair. She rolled in a heap with the foul, sulfur-smelling beast. She was the more desperate fighter. She found the dog's throat and ripped deep. The dog thrashed, quivered, and stilled. She licked and spat sulfuric blood that burned at her lips.

Thank you, Mistress Golda.

The voice of Masad came wavering but clear, similar but deeper and more resonant than the voice of the Djinnus. Golda scratched her damp, bloody cheek. Her cat form made her feel a little better. Had the voice of the possessor really been inside her head, or had she only imagined it?

"Coming will be more," Masad muttered. "Need we a plan."

"Yes, and fast," Gonorrheah added. "She sent a messenger bird."

Masad led through an open doorway into what appeared to be a guard room for the cell area. An array of blades glinted on a massive weapon rack. Masad grabbed two scimitars. Gonorrheah snatched a robe from the back of a chair and slipped it over her shoulders. The wizardress drew a sword and hefted it.

"This is Boudi's magical sword. She must be here somewhere."

Masad nodded. "Take the blade. Find we the mimo, perhaps."

Golda hardly listened to the conversation. She paced back and forth at the doorway in cat form, watching the hall behind them. She tried to maintain the lust of battle in her blood—the heat and intensity that kept her senses heightened and her muscles ready. She heard the voice of Masad again in her head.

Golda, remain you as a cat? Speak you can to me.

Masad? Yes, I'll stay a cat as long as we're fighting Old Order and not vampires. As a cat I'm more resistant to the whips and magical attacks. Can you really hear me?

Yes. You can speak to me. Conceived from my father's dog form, have I an affinity for the beast. Call me the werewolves the Jackal for this. Call me the werewolves a friend for this.

I'll call you a friend too if we survive.

A chilling skitter of paws sounded again in the hall. Two more black dogs from Haawiyah skidded past the doorway, reversed, and accelerated through the opening. Masad raised his blades and stepped to meet them. "Save power, Gonorrheah. See we more soon."

Golda squared off against one of the dogs, which emitted a guttural growl.

Masad met the other dog with a blade in each hand. One sword cleaved its snout vertically in twain, and the other split its skull. The report of the sword meeting bone cracked in the small room like a gun shot. The dog retched a blast of fire in its agony. Masad dodged to the side.

The first dog appeared shaken by the death of its mate. Golda attacked. She took the dog down by its black scruff, but it was bigger and tougher than the previous one. She couldn't get into its neck. It seized her shoulder with its teeth and spun her around. She spotted the Old Order fledgling, who shadowed the doorway and raised a whip.

Watch out, Masad!

The fledgling snapped the narcabyss whip around the wrist of Masad. Masad dropped his sword, but raised his other arm and hacked with his second scimitar, severing the pulpy cord. The fledgling retreated. Golda wrenched free of the Hell hound that tangled with her. She circled, trying to get the advantage. It snapped at her leg with its maw. She pulled away just in time and went on the defensive. She felt a wash of pain in her leg.

The hound leapt at her again, but she leapt higher. She scored long gashes down its back with her claws. Masad moved in behind the hound, aiming a killing blow with his remaining sword. One of his arms hung at his side, limp and paralyzed. Down the hall, two Smokeless Flames mistresses in red uniforms had joined the fledgling. They unfurled their whips in their red-gloved hands. Three more Hell hounds raced forward with a chorus of low growls.

Chapter 34:

"Boudi-Ca Marcus?" A timid voice whispered. "Are you awake?"

Boudi-Ca opened her eyes and focused on a low stone chamber with a silver door. Three rays of sunlight came from stone shafts in the sloping ceiling. A row of three beds—thick woven mats on blocks of stone—lined the wall across from the door. Boudi-Ca sat up on the bed. A wide-eyed blonde girl stood over her. The Ahyehass was young and pretty, and a faint tarnished halo glowed above her head. Boudi-Ca stared into the girl's eyes. "You're an mimọ."

"Boudi?" The girl offered a bright smile. "It's really you, but you're older-looking. Don't you remember me? I'm Makeda Deen."

Boudi-Ca sat up on the edge of the bed in disbelief. The girl was Makeda, but without her perfectly-pressed robe. Instead, she wore only a leather collar around her neck. Boudi-Ca looked down at her own bared breasts and legs. The Old Order Jinni had stripped her completely, including her corset. Ugly red lines still crossed her leg and arm where the wicked whips had hit her.

"What are you doing here, Makeda?"

"I didn't think you were you at first, Boudi, because you looked so different. I'd never seen you in the nude. The Grand Auditor insisted that you were you, and then I saw it was true. We both applied for the special project at the Conclave of Deviant Operations, and we were both accepted. I think we went on different missions."

"Who is this 'Grand Auditor'? Is he with the Conclave of Deviant Operations?"

Makeda nodded. "Yes. The Grand Auditor fell on purpose like we did. It was all part of the plan, you know—for the secret Conclave project."

Boudi-Ca rubbed her temple. She felt sore all over. Her right arm was still slightly numb. She felt weak, as if she hadn't fed for days. She wondered how long she'd been unconscious. It was obviously daylight outside the narrow stone light shafts, so several hours must have passed. She leveled her gaze at Makeda. She realized that she felt no shyness anymore around the star senior student from the Crystal College.

"They didn't tell me the plan. Did the Conclave trick you too?"

"Trick?" Makeda looked puzzled. "Well, I forgot about a lot of things for a long time, but then the Grand Auditor made all of my memories come back. He said there was another one just like me, another spy for the Hierarchy. He wouldn't tell me who it was, though. He said I might be surprised. Now here you are! It's Boudi-Ca Marcus!"

"So it's true that I'm a spy, then."

"Yes. The Grand Auditor said that soon the battle will be over, and the Conclave will have won. We're going to be heroes in Heaven!" Makeda grinned happily. "I'm so excited to see you, Boudi. I know we weren't the best of friends, but I hope we can patch things up. We have so much in common now, don't you think? I've been really lonely, to be honest. You're the only mimọ I've seen except the Grand Auditor."

"What's happening? Are they taking us back?"

Makeda beamed. "Yes! I don't understand how it will work. The Grand Auditor wouldn't tell me. He's so proud of me, though, and he's proud of you too, Boudi! He said we'll be rewarded soon."

Boudi-Ca looked around the room. The lone silver door offered the only possible egress. She stood up from the edge of the bed. Her legs trembled for a second, but she managed to make her way to the door. She tested the handle. The door was locked. She peered through the small barred window. Outside, a hallway ran perpendicular to the door. A band of hieroglyphic Egyptian paintings decorated the stone wall. Beyond that, she could see nothing. She could flash out of the room easily, but she was in the heart of the enemy camp, and she wasn't eager to get whipped again.

"What kind of reward are we getting, Makeda?"

"I don't know. He wouldn't tell me. The Grand Auditor is very busy. Whenever I ask questions, he just pats me on the head and tells me not to worry, and that everything will be fine. We're both just simple mimọ girls, right Boudi? We can't expect to know what's going on with important politics."

"Where are my friends? Are they here somewhere?"

Makeda frowned. "I don't know who you're talking about. I heard a lot of screaming. There was a lot of commotion last night."

Makeda moved to sit on the edge of one of the beds. Makeda's small white wings almost glowed in the dim light that filtered through the ceiling shaft above her. The Eastern Order Jinni had apparently used Makeda as a slave. Her lips and eyes showed traces of tired paint. Her eyes were slightly vacant, and the old tarnished D-ring at the front of her leather collar showed worn metal where a leash had rubbed. Boudi-Ca crossed her arms over her chest.

"So what have you been doing here? Did you agree to serve as an Ahyehass for the Eastern Order, or did they just snatch you and make you into a slave like the Old Order mistresses do with Mimọs?"

Makeda winced. "Boudi, I thought you'd be more fun. You were always the class rebel, you know? You did bad things with Tajee. I was kind of a bad mimọ girl too."

"How were you bad?"

Makeda blushed. "I flirted with the Grand Auditor during my interview. I don't remember what I did, exactly. I was feeling faint, and then I remember holding his hand and kissing it. I begged him shamelessly to give me a position. I wanted it so much."

"That's enough. I get the picture."

"I really thought you and I would get along now, Boudi. I was looking forward to talking to you. I don't understand. Why are you acting so angry?"

"I'm sorry, Makeda. I'm trying to figure out what's happening. So we're both really going back to Heaven?"

"Yes. That's what the Grand Auditor said. He said he was going to get some things ready. He wanted to leave as soon as you're awake."

Boudi-Ca slumped back on the bed. It was unbelievable that she was going back to Heaven, but the reality was hitting her. She touched the ugly red-purple marks on her arm. The whip-wounds reminded her of the flesh of a pomegranate. They were sore and ugly. The pain of them felt deep, as if the scars were not only on her physical skin, but also on the skin of her inner mimọ.

She continued to touch the whip-wounds with her fingers. Somehow she could feel the taint under her skin with her Jinn senses. The darkness of the Old Order dwelled in the discolored stripes. She didn't want that taint inside of her. She didn't want the scars. The Old Order mistresses and their whips disgusted her.

She felt love pour from her heart suddenly like molten metal from a crucible. She wrapped her hand fully around her arm. She could feel the heat of her love. It was the warmth of Golda's wonderful hug, gaining strength and flowing like liquid through her fingers. It was a spark that she'd somehow received from Golda and kept aflame so she could rekindle it.

She could feel with her Jinn senses the special warmth flooding the whip-wounds. She could feel the ugliness diminishing. She pushed more heat to her fingertips for a minute, pushing the warmth until she couldn't push more. She pulled her hand away. Incredibly, the wounds were almost completely gone. Makeda stared at her from the next bed.

"Boudi? What are you doing?"

"I don't know. I thought it was a mistake when I made the scrape on my cheek go away, but I just did the exact same thing."

"What thing?"

"Makeda, please be quiet. Stop pestering me."

Makeda's lower lip trembled, and she began to quietly sob. "I've been so lonely, Boudi. Please talk to me. The cat women treated me nice except for the disgusting things that they made me do for them. The women in red came, and they were cruel, and I wanted to die, but the Grand Auditor apologized and made everything alright. I miss Heaven so much. I just want to go home. I miss Ashanti and my friends."

"I'm sure everything will be fine, Makeda. I'm sorry I'm not happier, but I'm really confused. I don't know what I'm doing. I'm still an mimǫ, but I also hate the Old Order and the vampires. I can't believe the Conclave would be friends with them."

"The Old who? I don't even know what you're talking about."

Boudi-Ca shivered. "I guess I have to talk to this Grand Auditor."

"When he came and talked to me, I was so happy." Makeda's eyes widened. "Oh. I think I hear him coming now!"

Footsteps sounded in the hall. A key turned in the door lock. It swung open. The elder mimǫ was even taller than a werewolf. His tired-looking face was long, and his full beard was white. A tarnished halo shone dully some distance above his head, almost scraping the ceiling. He wore a pale grey robe with oversized sleeves that swayed when he opened his arms wide. His body looked bigger, wider, and bonier, but he was surely a denser, more solidified version of Pasteur.

"Hello, Boudi-Ca Marcus! It's been a long time since I trained you at the Conclave for your mission. It's surprising that you showed up here! You've turned into quite the little traveler." Pasteur chuckled and blotted a sheen of sweat from his forehead with a dirty white cloth.

"So you're the 'Grand Auditor'?"

"One of them, yes. I received a promotion from our Lord! He blessed me recently with an honorary clearance seven rank in the Sin-Watch Conclave to go with my guardianship duties and administrative duties, plus an extra week of vacation per annum."

Boudi-Ca gritted her teeth. "So what's my rank in the Conclave? What rank is allowed to be taken prisoner by the enemy? Or does bait even count as a rank?"

Pasteur tilted his head. "My, you've developed a shocking bit of pride in your time among the Jinni, haven't you, Boudi? Well, we all have our little gifts to give to the greater good, and you can be proud that you've given yours."

"How exactly did I do that?"

"You enabled us to pinpoint the hidden location of Allyssia's city in Meristyian and strike at her, just like Makeda-mouse was instrumental in dream-locating this evil lair of the cat-goddess Sekhmet in the desert. Meristyian will soon have a calculated ninety-five percent fewer Jinni and vampires running around causing trouble—a great improvement, I'd say."

"How does that improve things?"

Pasteur reached to pat her on the head. "You don't need to worry about any of this, young mimo. You're going home."

"I want to know what's going to happen. I deserve that much. I did my part in the plan, didn't I? What will happen to Lady Allyssia?"

Pasteur nodded tiredly. "I suppose there's no harm since it's over. Allyssia's primary avatar is imprisoned in Her city by the power of our Lord, as channeled through the dream-world by Azrail, who is another Grand Auditor just like I am. We suspect Allyssia has already severed one or more of her lesser avatars to conserve her strength, but severing her primary avatar and starting over in the desire-world might take Her centuries. Until then, things will be like they used to be."

"What way did things used to be?"

"Up or down, Boudi-Ca Marcus!" Pasteur said cheerfully. "Heaven or Hell! Souls must dedicate themselves to our Lord with the proper devotion, or the devil will take them. It's the way things should be. We can't abide a wiffly-waffly everything-is-acceptable zone down here in Meristyian. Our Lord and his brother created kingdoms, not democracies."

"So Ayelet was right. You're just trying to eliminate the competition."

Pasteur chuckled. "You can't understand, Boudi. You've been too misled. Your mind is too clouded by your corruption. I see your halo is missing. Very interesting."

"Yes. The Jinni made me into one of them. So what's going to happen to me, then? Can I still go back to Heaven?"

"You've been changed far more than Makeda, and in a very unexpected way. Allyssia turned you into an evil creature of lust, and it's horrible. I'm still your guardian, however, and I'm going to help. You did your best for Heaven, so now let Heaven do its best for you."

"If you're my guardian, then why didn't you try to save me? Why weren't you looking for me in Allyssia's city months ago before I was corrupted?"

Pasteur's eyes darkened and shifted towards the beams of light that came from the ceiling shafts. "Our ambassadorial delegations have shown that elder Mimos can develop feelings of fondness for their underlings in this realm. Sinful feelings can compromise logic and endanger the Conclave's mission. To minimize those complications, the Conclave sent me here to complete the mission with Makeda, and Grand Auditor Azrail was sent to Allyssia's enclave to collect you, Miss Marcus. Apparently I will take you both back to Heaven instead. Are you ready, then? You know in your mimo soul that this is for the best."

Boudi-Ca sighed. "I suppose."

"Have faith, Boudi. Have faith in Lord Tuhan. Have faith in the Conclave of Deviant Operations. Young Mimos need more faith these days. So let's be off, ladies. We're on our way back to the higher paradise, Makeda Deen!"

Makeda jumped from the bed and hurried happily into the hallway with Pasteur. Boudi-Ca followed them. It was time. It was time for her to become an mimo girl again, although she wasn't sure how. She was still a Jinn. Even in that moment, her Hunger was crouching in her stomach, and she was looking at Makeda's tight, attractive backside.

Pasteur shouldered a rucksack that he'd left sitting on the hall, and then they were striding along. It was dark and foreboding inside Sekhmet's temple. The hallways were dimly lit by flickering torches at intervals. From a distance could be heard faint barks and growls of unknown beasts. Pasteur clasped a large hand over Makeda's bare shoulder as if to calm her down. Makeda was so excited that she was skipping.

"Can Boudi-Ca and I go to the Crystal College when we get back, Mr.

Grand Auditor? Can I see Ashanti and all of my friends?"

Pasteur shook his head. His tarnished halo skittered back and forth along the ceiling as he walked. "I'm afraid not, Makeda. You need to be decontaminated for quite a while."

"I can still see Ashanti, right?"

"No, no. You wouldn't want to do Ashanti mental harm, would you? Of course not. Even the slightest contact with you or Boudi-Ca could have the gravest consequences for the morality and well-being of any mimọ in Heaven."

Makeda sighed. "I suppose you're right."

"You've done very naughty things, haven't you, Makeda? You did them for the Conclave and the glory of all Mimọs, but you and Boudi-Ca must start new journeys of penance, purification, and humble prayer."

Boudi-Ca felt a warmth of anger in her chest, and an old fear filled her belly. "Makeda said you'd reward us, not lock us up for our sins."

Pasteur glanced back at her as he walked. He patted his forehead again with his cloth. "Makeda's job experience will be valuable in the Conclave Sin-Watch Conclave. Your situation is a little different, Boudi. Your manner of induction into Jinn society was unexpected. We'll find a way to help you. Even though you did this for the Conclave, you should still be ashamed of what you've done. The first step on your road to recovery is admitting your sin and feeling guilty. We'll get this done."

Boudi-Ca bit her lip. "What about my friends?"

Pasteur looked over his shoulder again. He seemed annoyed. "You mean Tajee?"

"No. I mean Golda and Mistress Gonorrheah. What have you done with them? What has the Old Order done with them?"

"Well, your friends are rebels," Pasteur answered. "They've broken various laws related to how Jinni should behave with proper evil and so forth, and therefore they are traitors in the eyes of Hell's Court. Perhaps they'll be reformed from their side just as you'll be reformed from ours. I couldn't know or care."

"I care."

"As I said, your friends went against the establishment of Hell, and thus they will suffer whatever justice that Hell hands down upon them." Pasteur cleared his throat. "All the more reason for you to be more grateful that I'm taking you back to Heaven, actually."

"I can't wait to get back to Heaven," Makeda said. "Even if I can't see my friends right away, it's going to be great."

"Here we are," Pasteur muttered. "I keep getting lost in this heathen temple." They turned a corner and arrived at an open doorway that gave onto a large gloomy storage room filled with wardrobes, trunks and tables, all laden with what appeared to be piles of personal belongings. Clothes, shoes, hairbrushes, perfume bottles, vases, statuary, and other knick-knacks were strewn across the floor. Pasteur stepped to a large wardrobe and opened it to reveal an interior stuffed with robes.

"Are those for us?" Makeda said.

Pasteur nodded. "Yes. It's agnostic ceremonial garb, but it will be good enough to cover you up until we get proper robes at the Conclave. I see some nice modest robes here. Some shoes might be useful. We've got a lot of stair steps to climb!"

Boudi-Ca looked over the musty robes for one that would fit. She reached past Makeda to select a red robe with gold trim. It was too big for her. She tried another. "So do we have to travel on horses to get to the stairway? Will the trip be cold?"

Pasteur forced a smile. "No. The stairway has a single fixed terminus here in Purgatory, but its core function is a thought-structure in the mental realm, so its coordinates can be temporarily modified at a high vibration to translate through dream-space to exist at any time when a high-vibration mimo requires it. That would be me."

"What do you think, Boudi?" Makeda twirled a red chemise that reached her mid-thigh.

"That's too risqué, Makeda Deen," Pasteur said Sharply. "Both of you put on those simple white linen robes, please."

Boudi-Ca picked a white robe and drew it on. She tied a linen sash above her hips to lift the excess material. The shoes strewn around the floor were exotic and leathery. She slid her left foot into a soft, ruby-jeweled slipper with a red ribbon and a shallow heel. It was beautiful and new. She glanced at Pasteur out of the corner of her eye. He looked disapproving, but he didn't say anything. She scanned the room for the slipper's mate.

"Are we ready?" Pasteur glanced at his wrist-watch. "Where's your other shoe, Boudi? There's a plain shoe right in front of you that will fit your other foot. Put it on."

"That one doesn't match."

"Put on the shoe!" Pasteur boomed.

Boudi-Ca quickly slid her right foot into the old woven monk's sandal. It was a functional shoe, but it was ugly compared to the red slipper on her left foot. Boudi-Ca tried to suppress her anger. Pasteur was right. She wasn't in her right mind. Her Jinn-self was protesting the return to Heaven with an urge to wear sparkly, un-Mimoic slippers. She just had to shut up and go. Even if she were punished and reformed by the Conclave, it was better than living in Hell. Was there any good reason for staying in Hell forever?

Pasteur led her and Makeda back into the hall. They turned a corner, passed through a large chamber, and then turned another corner. A wider hallway rose towards a pair of tremendous open golden doors. They passed through the doors and entered a grand vaulted chamber that was painted with hieroglyphs. A sarcophagus dominated the end of the room nearest the doors. The burning torches threw a feeble light over its golden surface, revealing the engraved shapes of cats. Pasteur ran his fingers over the top of the locked sarcophagus as they passed.

They crossed the huge room and climbed a set of steps to a dais, where a Jinn stood in a circle of burning candelabra. The Old Order mistress was tall and slender like a reed with a coif of black hair piled high on her head. Her elegant black dress sheathed her body like a tightly buttoned sleeve.

"Mistress Enneamiah," Pasteur said. "It was thoughtful of you to see me out."

"Goodbye, Mistress." Makeda's voice quavered timidly.

Enneamiah winked. "Goodbye, Makeda. I'll miss you, and parts of you will also miss me. Auditor, it's been a pleasure working with the Mimos. Your gifts for espionage and offensive dream magic are admired even by the powers of Hell."

Pasteur nodded. "There were equal contributions from both sides. Have you received any word about the status of Lady Allyssia?"

"I received word from Commander Anaximah an hour or so ago. Allyssia's city is fully under the control of the Smokeless Flames. There was chaos for a while due to Cupid's crafty love magics, but they've managed to trap Allyssia and her son in separate sealed rooms in the highest levels of the palace bowers. The first imprisonment spells were already placed by the vampires. The next wards are now being placed by Grand Auditor Azrail."

"What of Allyssia's Jinni?"

"I'm told the New Order Jinni are mostly chained, caged, and ready for transport to Hell's Court, where they'll stand trial for treason against our Lord and Lady Allyssia. The first caravan of chained prisoners is already heading out, including Mistress Demetriah. She is bound magically to separate her from Allyssia's other avatars. The caravan is escorted by General Astaarteh."

"What of the Disciples of Set?"

Enneamiah's black-painted lips curled into a wicked smile. "The Haawiyah moths that Allyssia retained for her own personal defense of her city were released yesterday afternoon while the vampires were sleeping inside the homes of the New Order."

"They were all infected?"

"Mostly. Commander Anaximah said that the swarming of the newborn moths through the city was truly a sight to behold. The New Order houses were all equipped with proper messenger bird slits, of course, so the moths flew right in. Trapped by the sunlight and hordes of moths, there was no escape for the Disciple vampires even if they were awake. When night fell, we think only a few vampires were able to survive and escape without the moths nesting in them."

Pasteur smiled widely. "Excellent."

"Of course, we'll officially deny any foreknowledge of the existence of Allyssia's plague of undead-eating moths. We'll apologize to the vampire lords and swear that it was a complete surprise, a brilliant and unexpected last-gasp effort by Allyssia."

"Wonderful." Pasteur rubbed his hands together. "Please don't forget that we expect Hell to honor the new geographical boundaries of the treaty."

"We will. You have my word as a Jinn." Enneamiah smirked.

Pasteur patted his forehead. "Then let the games between Heaven and Hell begin again with less interference. Could you politely step aside, or is this going to get ugly?"

"Of course, Pasteur. My apologies." The mistress in black bowed and stretched her hands magnanimously. "This ritual altar has been kept pristine as promised since you cleansed it yesterday. You may summon your silly stairway at your leisure."

"Once I leave, I expect you'll be finished here?"

"Yes. We still need to lower the entombment block on this room, which will put the fifth and final seal on Sekhmet's sarcophagus prison, and then we'll all return to Haawiyah. I'll escort Mistress Ivanka. Lady Allyssia doesn't trust her, of course, despite her apparent defection to our fold."

Boudi-Ca felt sudden anger burn through her body at the thought of Ivanka's treachery. "I definitely don't trust Ivanka."

Enneamiah arched her eyebrow. "Ivanka spoke of you, mimo girl. She says you have potential. She says it would be worth the effort to turn you and Golda to serve our great Lord Hades, but alas the Grand Auditor insists on taking you with him. It's part of the contract. Sorry."

"Boudi-Ca will be a great asset," Pasteur interjected. "We'll find ways for her to aid the Conclave and serve our Lord Tuhan."

Enneamiah rolled her eyes. "How many Jinni are you holding prisoner up there now, Pasteur? Do you really need another one? What exactly do you do with them, anyway? Do you visit their bedchambers on your lunch breaks? Do you take them on holy pleasure trips to Italy? I've always wondered how your holy men keep our women fed."

"We study Jinni to understand their corruption, of course," Pasteur answered. "The goddess of lust created a perversion from this innocent mimo girl. Perhaps we can lift her curse. Certainly we can't let such a thing happen again."

"Nonsense. Boudi-Ca may have gone down the wrong path with the rebel lesbians, but as a Jinn, she's a thing of beauty. Allyssia created a masterpiece. You're so naive, Boudi-Ca. You're a complete fool to let him take you away from this place."

Boudi-Ca felt her cheeks heat. "I'm not naïve, and I'm not foolish. I'm an mimo girl, and I'm proud to be one."

"Isn't pride a dire sin?"

"That's quite enough, foul temptress," Pasteur said sternly. "You'll cease this immediately and leave us."

"Ivanka was right," Enneamiah continued. "I can feel the potential in you, mimo. You might have actually amounted to something one day. It's a pity you won't join us, but maybe they'll find a way to cure your jinnism if not your insecurities."

Boudi-Ca felt her stomach twist. Her Hunger turned over like slick red leaves under dry brown ones. She looked down at her mismatched shoes. She felt sick. A tremendous thump suddenly sounded through the temple of Sekhmet. The stone floor shivered. The faint howls of dogs could be heard in the distance. A shower of sand pattered across the lid of the golden sarcophagus in the center of the chamber.

Enneamiah glanced quickly towards the sarcophagus. She glowered at Pasteur. "By the balls of Cerberus, what was that? This better not be a last-minute trick from Heaven."

"No," Pasteur answered. "Maybe your local beast-men are trying to break down the temple doors. Whatever the problem is, the physical defense of this temple is the job of your people, not mine. Please leave and lower Sekhmet's entombment block. I need to perform my ritual immediately."

Chapter 35:

Golda ripped into the Hell hound's throat. Burning blood sluiced between her teeth. The beast quivered and went limp underneath her. The hounds were ferocious, but Masad had given her enough strength to match them. Gonorrheah had created an effective barrier against the attackers by kine-hexing the heavy weapon rack into the corridor archway, which offered Masad a convenient array of blades to use for attack and defense.

Masad pointed his sword and uttered words of power. The floor of the temple hallway shuddered yet again on the far side of the weapon rack. This time the foundation buckled, and cracks splintered up the stone walls. A second tremendous boom shook the temple of Sekhmet. The arms of creatures emerged, and the rotting monsters climbed forth.

The hallway breathed with the stench of worms and decay as the dog-headed undead creatures assailed the Old Order Jinni. The two Smokeless Flames mistresses swung their whips, but the cruel cords had no effect on the walking corpses. The Hell hounds scattered and howled, and the howls sounded frightened. The Jinni retreated under the onslaught.

"That's wicked death magic, Masad," Gonorrheah said tensely. "I'm impressed. Are those things really going to stop the Serpent Sisters?"

"Not for long," Masad answered. "Keep moving we. Out must we go from this trap." He flexed his numbed hand and bent to retrieve his second blade, even as two more Flames mistresses came running around the far corner of the hallway to join their allies. One was small and black. She pressed to the fore and pointed her staff. Gouts of flame engulfed the dog-headed corpses. A choking smoke rose. The burning dog things still interposed themselves, but the Flames mistresses began to knock over the walking charcoal with kin-hexes.

Gonorrheah paled. "By the Lady, that's Mistress Ivanka! I can't even beat her at my best, and I've got no power left!"

"Run we must." Masad ducked into the corridor and ran away from the chaos. Golda loped after Masad and Gonorrheah. She struggled to keep her head from entering a frenzy. If Ivanka caught up with them, she and Gonorrheah were possibly dead. The corridor opened into a high-ceiling hall with steps leading up to a pair of large golden doors. The doors were blocked by a massive beam attached to ropes and pulleys.

Golda sniffed a trace of fresh air—air that suggested the front entrance to the temple. Two more Old Order Jinni were moving to cut off their escape, however, emerging from a hallway at the side of the temple entry hall. A third Old Order mistress in a long black button-down dress ran from yet another, bigger passage entrance.

"Kill them!" the mistress snarled.

"That's Mistress Enneamiah," Gonorrheah groaned. "She's an elder elementalist, and Ivanka is right behind us."

The elder mistress trotted like the others to block their path to the temple doors. She stretched out a long arm, and a lightning bolt blasted from her fingertips across the intervening space, forking as it flowed. One prong of the bolt caught Masad in his shoulder, spun him hard, and pattered across the wall with an ear-splitting crack.

Golda shook her head and twitched her ears. The lightning bolt had bounced close to her, too. She smelled smoking fur. Pain washed over her shoulder blade. Enneamiah uttered another spell, but Gonorrheah barked Sharp words and a gust of wind blew through the chamber, disrupting the incantation.

"Follow me quickly." Masad turned and sprinted to the right past Enneamiah, dodging into the hall the elder mistress had come from—a wider tiled passage that sloped upwards. Golda loped with long strides after Masad with Gonorrheah at her shoulder. She could hear the footsteps of the Old Order coming, and from farther behind came the bays of the Hell hounds. The pressured voice of Masad intruded on her fear.

Are you hurt, Golda?

Where are we going? The outer doors of the temple are back there!

No way can we open them with the mistresses defending. Go we to the inner sanctuary for defense instead, perhaps something else.

You know where it is?

Know I the center of Sekhmet's weave, yes.

A long sloping hall ended at a pair of open golden doors that marked the entrance to an immense room. In the near end of the room sat a long, low sarcophagus decorated with golden engravings. A brilliant white column of light rose from a raised dais beyond the sarcophagus at the far end of the room. The form of a robed figure stood with his hands raised in supplication. Two smaller figures dressed in white stood on either side.

Golda glanced over her shoulder. The Old Order were in close pursuit. A lightning bolt flew up the hall and glanced past Gonorrheah's head. Golda felt the fur on her back stand on end. Gonorrheah cried out, stumbled, and rolled across the floor with her hands raised to her ears in pain. Masad grabbed one of the leaves of the gold doors.

Golda, need I you.

Golda leapt to the other door. She regained human form and rose to two feet, shifting almost instantly. She wished Ayelet had been there to witness her quick transformation—a feat that she'd rarely managed before. She was inches from death, yet she was totally focused. She put a shoulder into one of the sanctuary doors while Masad grabbed the other in his meaty Djinnus hands. The Jinni were just behind. An incantation pierced the air. Another blast of lightning stroked up the hall, bouncing between the doors and through.

Golda flinched. Stars shot through her vision. The pain of the bolt coursed through the door into her shoulder, but she managed to slam the door home a second after Masad closed his own panel. Exasperation registered on Masad' normally implacable face. There was no latch or bolt visible on the interior surface of the doors, which opened inward.

"Gonorrheah, do something you can?"

The wizardress was back on her feet. Her hand sketched an arcane symbol in the air, and a glowing glyph sparked across the etched metal surface of the closed portal just before the dull metallic thuds and scrapes of the Hell hounds came from the far side. Gonorrheah shook her head.

"It won't hold. Ivanka taught me that glyph of sealing. I'm sure she can break it easily. I can't do anything better. I'm too empty. I have no energy left."

Golda gazed again at the far end of the central chamber of the temple, where the tall figure on the dais had raised his intonations to a crescendo with his robed arms outstretched. The white marble steps of a stairway appeared, shimmering and resolving in the air, stretching from the top of the dais to extend through the high ceiling. The two smaller figures in white closed ranks and climbed the stairway.

"I think that's Boudi-Ca. We have to get her." Golda surged forward, but she felt the strong hand of Masad clamp over her wrist.

"No. Need we Sekhmet." Masad nodded at the sarcophagus. "Her prison. See I four wards to break. Do this we must now, and quickly."

A boom shook the sanctuary doors on their massive hinges. Gonorrheah's glyph flickered. Gonorrheah circled the great golden sarcophagus, running her fingers along the edge. She examined the glyphs. "The north and south wards on the sarcophagus were placed by the Disciples of Set. They're immune to magical effects, but can be broken with tremendous physical force. Try your swords, Masad. Do your best."

Masad strode to the northern lock and aimed his blade with a tremendous blow. The steel sword shattered with the force, but so did the ward. He circled to the south side of the sarcophagus and swung with his second blade. The sword shattered, but so did the second ward. Masad examined the remaining two wards with Gonorrheah.

Golda licked her lips and looked at the shivering doors. She could feel her inner calm slipping. She was ready to die, but she prayed to the Lady for a chance to take Ivanka with her. If she shifted back to cat form, she could leap clean over the dogs. She might have one small chance, if the Fates wished it, to get her claws into the black witch's throat.

"Please hurry," she growled.

Gonorrheah shook her head. "I think the third ward on the east is a trick. It will hit you with lightning if you strike it. The fourth ward, on the other hand, has a sigil inscribed in the language of the Mimọs. I think it says, 'One Who Is Not Damned.'"

Another boom rocked the double doors. A crack appeared between them. Sparks sprayed and bounced across the floor. Masad paced back and forth. "If break they the door, need we surrender. Talk I will with the mistresses. Break can you the east ward or not, Gonorrheah, with your alteration magic?"

"I may be able to neutralize it, but it will take more power than I have right now. I hunger too much, and then what?"

"Then try can I to break the fourth ward. Divine blood am I. Consider the Mimọs the divines to be not damned."

"Then place your hand on the ward, and it should open." Gonorrheah sighed. "Alright. I'll try." Gonorrheah bent over the east ward and traced the magical glyphs with her fingertips. She muttered arcane syllables. Her fingers glowed softly pink. The moon-silver in her eyes blazed, and then winked out. The wizardress slipped to the floor in an unconscious heap.

"Broke it she did," Masad murmured. Another boom rocked the doors to the inner sanctum. They opened further. The snout of a Hell hound wriggled through the opening with a growl. Golda felt the remnants of her energy flooding into her arms and legs, readying her body for a battle to the death. Her heart was thumping with the pent-up fury of her inner feline beast.

"Open the last ward, Masad. Release Sekhmet."

Masad placed his hand on the ward. He wrenched it away. An acrid odor of burning flesh filled the air. His face was a frozen mask when he looked down at his smoking hand.

"Damned am I."

A final boom shattered the doors open. Golda pivoted. A mortal fear tingled over her skin. A bright shower of sparks sprayed through the room and bounced down the top of Sekhmet's sarcophagus. A half dozen Hell hounds streamed into the chamber with a chorus of roars. A cadre of Old Order mistresses strode behind them. Two fledglings in black dresses led the way, followed by four Serpent Sisters in their red military regalia. Lastly Mistress Enneamiah walked side by side with the shrunken black figure of Ivanka.

Golda let her passion flow and her form thicken. Fur raced down her forearms as she changed back into her cat. She skirted Gonorrheah's body and drew alongside Masad. She took one last look over her furred shoulder at the stairway. Boudi-Ca was stepping upwards through the air. Her small white wings glowed in the light. The stairway flickered and dimmed, and so did Boudi. Golda heard the voice of Masad in her head.

Stop. Fight you will not!

She ignored the warning. She refused to let them put her back in a cage, and she had nothing left to live for anyway. She surged forward to face the oncoming dogs.

~*~

The light that streamed down the stairway held a curious enchanted quality, just like the familiar marble steps. Boudi-Ca could see the light with her inner eyes as well as her outer ones, like a double vision. Pasteur tugged her hand, and she took another step. A terrible pain was splitting down the center of her chest, but her heart and mind felt light. She felt fine except for the horrible scene playing out behind her.

While the Grand Auditor had been finishing his ritual, she'd surreptitiously watched over her shoulder. She'd seen the efforts of Gonorrheah to open the sarcophagus. She'd seen the blonde wizardress slump unconscious to the ground. She'd seen Masad, as Golda had called the handsome male, recoil from the last stubborn ward. She'd seen the fatigue and desperation on Golda's face.

Boudi-Ca frowned. Pasteur was tugging her harder, and the pain split open her chest again, leaving her breathless. She looked over her shoulder once more at the dark world that she was leaving behind. Her picture view into Meristyian had become a tunnel, just like when she flashed. Golda attempted to leap over the huge black dogs. The dogs leapt and met her in midair. Golda's tawny body twisted and fell into a snarling sea of black fur.

Boudi-Ca felt wet tears overflow her eyes and cascade down her cheeks. Her love for Golda exploded in her heart. She felt a profound echo of the hug-spark that Golda had created inside her. Her hand slipped from Pasteur's. The bright light of the stairway flickered away. The high dais at the end of the room descended into darkness, and so did she. She was lying on uncomfortable stone, and the reality of Meristyian came back around her like waking from a dream.

Pasteur lay motionless and withered nearby. Makeda lay next to him. Her blonde hair and skin were dry and lifeless as if aged. Her eyes were desiccated and glazed like a dead fish. Boudi-Ca recoiled in horror from the bodies. The group of Old Order Jinni at the other end of the room hadn't yet noticed her, nor had the dogs. They all stood around Golda, who was bleeding and broken on the floor.

Gonorrheah lay unmoving at the nearer end of the huge golden sarcophagus. A sword glinted at Gonorrheah's hip. The citrines of the Oya-blade shone dully in the low light. Boudi-Ca focused and flashed. She ran along the twisting ribbon and emerged from her flash next to Gonorrheah's body. She pressed into the end of the sarcophagus, where the torches on either side of the entry doors cast a shadow. She reached and slid her sword quietly from its sheath. She could hear the pained male voice of Masad.

"Won this round you have, Enneamiah."

"This round?" Enneamiah laughed at him. "This is the end of the fight, Prince Masad. Allyssia is trapped in her bower, soon to be imprisoned like Sekhmet. Everyone should celebrate this effort between Hell and Heaven. The Eastern Order and the New Order Jinni are extinguished, gone forever from history. Meristyian will no longer be a free haven for organizations of miscreants who dare to reject our Lord's dominion over His realm."

Golda groaned. "You toadies make me sick. Just kill me."

"Your wounds look like they hurt, cat-shifter," Enneamiah said, looking down. "You should definitely bleed out while regretting your poor choices."

"Turn her to serve, Enneamiah," Ivanka rasped.

"No. The rebels in this room have proved themselves to be too dangerous again and again, especially Masad. It's a pity that he persists in going against our Lord, his father. Well if you wanted to lock yourself in this chamber with your new rebel friends, then so be it. I have a better seal for these doors than Mistress Gonorrheah's pathetically weak warding glyph. It's a six-foot-thick granite entombment block. It's ready to lower and hold all of you in here for a long time with Sekhmet."

"Congratulations," Masad said. "Imagine I that my father will reward you when learns he of this event."

Enneamiah chuckled. "A Jinn can only pray for such beneficence from our great Lord. I see you've broken one of the seals on Sekhmet's sarcophagus, however. That doesn't please me in the least."

"Broke we three."

Enneamiah's voice Sharpened. "Damn you for being a pain in everyone's ass, Masad. Which one couldn't you break, pray tell?"

"'The one that says 'One Who Is Not Damned'. Think I only an mimo can break it, correct?"

"Yes. The Grand Auditor was clever with that one. Goodbye, Masad. I suppose your father might come to visit you at some point. We'll be sure to let Him know. Everyone exit the room one by one, and take care lest Masad trick us by jumping into another warm body. Are you still there, Masad?"

"Yes." Masad chuckled. "Although hope I soon you will not be."

"Exactly. I'll leave last and pull the entombment lever."

Boudi-Ca summoned her courage. She knew what she needed to do. She slipped around the end of the sarcophagus, staying low until she found the ward. She reached up and pressed with her hand. The ward glowed and warmed under her fingers. She willed the magical lock to dissolve even as the Old Order mistresses spotted her. The sarcophagus lid trembled under her fingers. Enneamiah paced forward.

"You! You shouldn't still be here!"

Boudi-Ca ducked back around to the end of the sarcophagus even as a lightning bolt sprang from the hand of the mistress in black, crashed along the side of the sarcophagus, and bounced into the far wall. The bolt was followed by a low rumbling sound that pulsed through the stone floor. A hot wind picked up with a hiss, building speed and gathering loose sand as it rushed through the open doors. Enneamiah retreated.

"Everyone out now! Lower the entombment block! Quickly!"

Boudi-Ca peeked around the corner of the sarcophagus. The horrible black dogs had advanced to stare at her hungrily with their beady eyes, but high-pitched whistles split the air, and the dogs ran back towards the outer hallway with Enneamiah, Ivanka, and the Old Order Jinni. Enneamiah stopped short on the other side of the entry doors. She grabbed a lever. Metal gears creaked and echoed.

With a rumbling sound, a massive stone wall slowly descended from the hall ceiling. The black dogs growled and milled amidst the crowd of Jinni beyond, all of whom held their whips and blades at the ready. Boudi-Ca gripped her sword. She had only seconds before the entombment block reached the floor and sealed the room. There was no time to think about her fear, which felt like a fist in her stomach.

She flashed. The ribbon uncoiled. She tiptoed through time past the sarcophagus and Masad, who sat crippled and bleeding on the floor. She went straight through the entombment block and emerged from her flash right in front of Enneamiah. She thrust with the Oya-blade, burying the steel into the ribcage of the Old Order mistress. It was a finishing move that she'd practiced a thousand times.

Boudi-Ca wrenched the blade down and away. Warm blood spurted onto her leg through the gash in Enneamiah's black dress. The life melted from Enneamiah's face like a dying candle. The raven-haired mistress slumped to the floor. Her hands slipped from the block lever. The lever creaked up, and the entombment block stopped less than a metre from the floor.

Boudi-Ca turned her back to the wall and readied her sword to defend the entombment lever. She'd stopped the block, but she was surrounded by a crowd of black hounds with big teeth, as well as several Old Order mistresses. Ivanka was standing closest. The witch raised her staff. Boudi-Ca focused and flashed. She emerged and backhanded with her sword, but only hit Ivanka with a glancing blow to the shoulder. The witch skittered. A hound leapt. Boudi-Ca met it with a cleaving down-stroke to its snout.

A pair of Old Order whips snaked through space. Boudi-Ca flashed behind one of the red-robed mistresses. She plunged her Oya-blade into a spinal column. She drew the blade and twisted it into another strike that cut the arm of another mistress holding a whip. Both Jinni screamed in pain and toppled from their feet.

Out of the corner of her eye Boudi-Ca saw Ivanka's quick flick of the wrist, but her flash came too late. The hateful kin-hex caught her on the chest and threw backwards into the air, hard into the stone hallway wall. She groaned and slumped. Her head went dizzy, and the corridor spun. The hounds and the Old Order were blurry shadows swimming around her. When her vision resolved, Ivanka stood over her, flanked by drooling hounds.

"You little fool," Ivanka muttered.

The dogs suddenly turned their heads and growled in unison. Their beady eyes turned to the entombment block, where a hot sandy wind howled through the space between the block and the floor. An enormous lion-headed woman darted through and snatched a black dog in her massive cat jaws. The dog whined as its body crumpled. Another dog leapt to the attack, but the goddess swung a gold scepter that sent the dog reeling back. In that moment, all of the dogs burst into flames, filling the hallway with intense heat and canine death-screams.

The goddess Sekhmet rose tall to disperse the gloom with shards of divine fire. She leveled her gaze down at the remaining Old Order Jinni, who turned and fled. A sheet of flame poured down the hall on an increasing gale, engulfing Ivanka and the Jinni. All caught on flame except the black witch, who emerged from the chaos unscathed. Ivanka flitted away. Sekhmet pursued with another blast.

Boudi-Ca rose quickly to her feet as the smoke and screams flowed down into the temple entry hall. She was bruised from Ivanka's hateful kin-hex, but she was seeing straight enough to finish off the Old Order Jinni that she'd felled. She lifted her Oya-blade and severed their throats with finishing strikes like Ayelet had taught her. She crouched and slithered back under the entombment block into the great vaulted tomb. Golda and Masad still lay where they'd been mauled and whipped. Golda's nude body was covered with gashes that oozed blood. Tears streaked Golda's bruised cheeks as her lips cracked a smile.

"We did it, Boudi. You did it."

"Yes," Masad said with an odd grin. "Damned perhaps we are not."

Boudi-Ca grimaced. It hurt her to see Golda in so much pain. "Gonorrheah is over there on the floor. Is she—"

"She's completely empty." Golda's voice was weak. "If a male feeds her, she might survive."

Masad propped up his battered body. "Alive is she. See her can I in the tapestry. Can do it when this numbness passes from me. Happened what, Boudi-Ca? Went you not back to Heaven why?"

Boudi-Ca frowned. "We started to climb into the light, and Pasteur pulled me up, but I slipped out of his hand. I was thinking about you, Golda. I saw what was happening to you, and I was thinking about you. I couldn't abandon you. I think I love you."

"Me?" Golda blinked and lowered her eyes. "I'm humbled, Boudi-Ca. I don't know what to say. I need bandages. I'm bleeding."

"Let me try to help. I have a new spell." Boudi-Ca knelt. Ugly wounds striped Golda's breast, and her right arm was purple and torn to the bone in multiple places. A line of punctures in Golda's thigh drooled blood freely. Boudi-Ca wrapped her hands gently around Golda's strong forearm.

"What are you doing, Boudi-Ca?"

"Just breathe." Boudi-Ca willed her energy to flow. Her love bloomed and poured forth like a river into her shoulders and down her arms. Her hands warmed, and her fingertips turned burning hot.

She could feel the taint in Golda—the poisons of the dogs' teeth and the Old Order whips. She could feel the love flowing from her hands into Golda's wounds, dispelling and counteracting the damage and agony. She slid her hands over Golda's warming skin.

Her Hunger grumbled at the energy loss, but she focused with all of her will for long minutes until the darkness in Golda was somewhat dissipated. When she pulled away her hands, Golda's arm was still purplish, but the wounds on her arm were pink, healed, and no longer bleeding. Golda blinked with a look of amazement.

"How did you do that?"

"I don't know. It tires me so much, though." Boudi-Ca inched closer and turned her attention to Golda's bleeding thigh. She pressed with her palm. She could feel the pain. The taint ran deep into the muscles underneath, all the way to the hot arteries that ran close to the bone. She let her love flow for a minute, and then bent and kissed the punctures that no longer leaked blood. She tried to rise up, but Golda's hand grabbed her shoulder and pulled her close.

Boudi-Ca met Golda's kiss with a magical passion, stoked by the Hunger that had grown intense in her belly. She sealed her lips and fenced her smaller tongue with Golda's big, thick one. She wanted the kiss to last forever. She straddled Golda and embraced her breast to breast—just like the hug on the palace steps. She didn't care if Masad was watching them. Finally Golda broke away from the kiss, eyes shy, with her mottled bluish lips forming a wide smile.

"I love you too, Boudi-Ca. You're beautiful."

Boudi-Ca felt heat come unbidden to her cheeks, and a rush of pride rose high in her throat. She was glad she hadn't gone back to Heaven. She was a Jinn. She was learning amazing magical powers, and she'd saved Golda's life with them. Best of all, she was in love, and Golda loved her too. She'd never been so happy—not in Heaven or ever.

"I'm happy I could heal you. The Old Order Jinni are just awful. What do we do now? Don't we need to leave?"

"Destroy will Sekhmet the Smokeless Flames without the vampire sorcerers or arch-mimo to contain her," Masad said. "Help we must, convince Sekhmet to help Allyssia we must. Sekhmet can help fight the vampires in the Lady's city."

"The vampires are all dead," Boudi-Ca said. "Mistress Enneamiah said so."

Masad' eyes opened wide with surprise. "How is this?"

"She said something about a plague and moths. They were a secret defense of the Lady. Yes, I think all the vampires are dead." Boudi-Ca bit her lip. "Enneamiah also said that all of the New Order Jinni are chained and locked in cages. The Old Order holds the city. Where is Mistress Ayelet? Is she alright?"

"Think I she is fine," Masad said. "Walk you can, Golda?"

"It's incredible, but I think I can—thanks to Boudi-Ca's healing magic. She might have saved my life. I've made a lot of mistakes lately, so I guess I've needed a lot of saving. Thank you both."

Masad nodded. "Go you two back down the passage quickly. Try to get the door open for Ayelet. Stay I and help Gonorrheah."

Boudi-Ca helped Golda to her feet. Golda was taller and heavier than her, but she offered her shoulder as best she could. The temple had fallen dead silent. They walked together down the still-hot, body-strewn corridor to the great entry chamber of the temple, where they climbed the wide, timeworn steps to the gilded front doors.

"Help me, Boudi. You get the other side." Golda limped to a geared metal wheel that was attached to a pulley, which in turn was fastened to a massive rune-inscribed beam that was barring the doors. Boudi-Ca grasped the wheel on the opposite side of the door. She and Golda cranked the beam up inch by inch. When the heavy beam was above the doors, they locked the wheels and grasped the heavy golden handles together. They pulled the massive portal open.

Boudi-Ca shielded her face from the sunlight that poured through the temple entry. She breathed the mid-day air from the sandy Acheron plain. Ayelet strode quickly towards them across the temple plaza, which was littered with vampire bodies. Ayelet's dress was drenched with blood. Her silvered eyes were manic and bright, and her taut lips widened into a werewolf-sized grin as she closed the distance. She walked with her sword in one hand, and with her other hand she guided a half-nude, brown-skinned male Ahyehass.

"Masad actually did it!" Ayelet exclaimed. "He's unbelievable. I can't wait to hear the story of what happened in there."

Golda gazed across the plaza. "You slaughtered all of these vampires? There must be almost a hundred, Ayelet."

"Of course. They needed slaughtering." Ayelet straightened and pushed her hair over her shoulder. She took a deep breath. Her shoulders relaxed, and her greying eyebrows softened their angles on her blood-spattered forehead. "What's the status? Where is Gonorrheah? Have you found Sekhmet?"

"How did he get here?" Golda pointed at the boy next to Ayelet. Boudi-Ca squinted in the sunlight and met the boy's chocolate brown eyes. Strangely, the boy was staring straight at her with a glazed look of shock on his handsome face. He looked familiar. His smooth chest and hair were the same as Tajee's, although his hair was down to his shoulders.

"Herpessenia-Ca had him," Ayelet answered. "The werewolves found a couple Flames-Sisterhood Nanka parked behind the temple last night. Herpessenia-Ca must have flown in with her mistress. I caught that little schemer trying to get to the Nanka a bit ago."

Golda nodded. "Yes. It makes sense that Herpessenia would go with Ivanka. She was never very loyal to her mother. So Herpessenia stole Tajee from me, but maybe she saved him. Where is she now, Ayelet?"

"I told her to run as fast as she could if she didn't want to get caught and ravaged by a werewolf patrol. She was dressed from head to toe in traditional Old Order blacks. If Herpessenia wants to go back to the old ways so badly, I wasn't going to stop her. I wasn't going to let her take your Ahyehass either."

"Thank you so much," Golda murmured. "I feel sorry for Herpessenia. She didn't even have a horse?"

"No." Ayelet shrugged. "Perhaps I was cruel, but I had other things to do. I was trying to find a secret passage into the temple. I'll send a bird to Marcus and tell him the temple is open. The werewolves can help clear the place out, and then we'll hope Sekhmet is willing to help us. As for Tajee, I think it's time Boudi-Ca knows the truth."

Boudi-Ca blinked. She couldn't believe what she was seeing. "It's really him? How is he even here? Were you a spy too, Tajee?"

"No," Tajee answered.

Golda cleared her throat. "He jumped from Heaven to try to save you, Boudi. He jumped to save you from me, actually. I tracked him and dragged him into the Lady's city several moons ago, and he's been serving as my loyal Ahyehass ever since."

Chapter 36:

"I love you, Boudi," Tajee pleaded. "That's why I jumped. I wanted to save you."

Boudi-Ca rubbed the remnants of dried blood from her Oya-blade with an oiled linen cloth. It was mid-afternoon in Meristyian. She sat next to Tajee on a low stone wall that banked the plaza in front of Sekhmet's temple. A Nanka, as Ayelet called it, squatted with its wings folded in the center of the plaza.

The huge dragon-like creature dwarfed Ayelet, who stood in its shadow. Ayelet was overseeing a werewolf, who was helping her load saddle bags into a riding basket perched high on the Nanka's scaly back. The basket was reached by a precarious metal-ranged ladder. Boudi-Ca eyed the Nanka skeptically. She didn't want to ride on that thing any more than she wanted to deal with Tajee's love for her. He did love her. She could feel it in a Jinn way. She turned and looked into his brown eyes.

"I can't believe all of this time you've been Golda's Ahyehass, Tajee. You willingly surrendered your body so she could use you and make you hers. You love her too, don't you? She seduced you."

Tajee gave a pained sigh. "All I wanted was to save you from the Jinni, so I made a deal with Golda. I had to, or the Lady was going to send me back to Heaven."

"Oh, right. I'm sure your love for me was the only reason you pledged to serve Golda as her devoted Ahyehass. You lusted for her, Tajee. You wanted her as your mistress. Just admit it."

"Alright, so what if I did. That doesn't change—"

"It changes everything! All of this time, Golda has been keeping you a secret from me. Ayelet knew about you too."

Tajee leaned close. "Listen, Boudi. We can still try to get out of here. Golda told me how to go back. We just have to take the stairway. It starts at the top of Mount Purgatory. I even have a map and a knife."

"Golda would track us down. She's a tracker, Tajee."

Tajee clenched his fists. "You sound like you want to stay with the Jinni! They're evil! I've seen your diary, Boudi. I know you've done horribly perverted things. I'm not blaming you though, and I'm not accusing you. You were seduced just like I was."

"At least I'm not an Ahyehass doing everything I'm told."

"You're a Jinn, and that's even worse. An Ahyehass can at least have a few noble virtues, and I'm still an mimọ, unlike you. You're not thinking straight. Try to remember who you used to be, Boudi. Try hard for me, please. Deep down inside, you're still a chaste and virtuous mimọ girl. It's not too late. I can save you if you just listen to me."

"Let me see that map, Tajee. It really shows how to get to Heaven?"

"I'm keeping it hidden from Mistress Ayelet."

"Ayelet trusts me more than Golda trusts you after you ran off with fledgling Herpessenia. Show me the map, Tajee."

Tajee opened his pack and groped. He surreptitiously handed her a folded map. It was a detailed ink map of western Meristyian. The Redoubt was marked, and so was the Sea of Desire where she'd fallen with Golda so long ago. Tajee leaned close and pointed.

"There's the Trivium. There's Mount Purgatory. Golda said the stairway is on the top of that big mountain."

"Where is your knife?" Boudi-Ca reached over Tajee's thigh into his bag. She felt his body stiffen when she pressed against him. She found the knife hilt. Tajee grabbed her wrist. He tried to stop her, but she pulled the knife easily from his bag. Tajee had been stronger than her in Heaven, but he was no match for her Jinn strength. She used the intimate moment to turn her lips and offer a kiss. Tajee met her lips tentatively. His body stiffened.

"What are you doing, Boudi?"

"Isn't this what every bad mimo boy wants? I'm not going to have sex with you, if that's what you're hoping." Boudi-Ca retreated and licked her lips. Tajee tasted sweeter than Yenta. She could smell Herpessenia's red nectar perfume on his skin. "Thanks, Tajee. You were really brave to jump after me. I don't think I would have done the same. You're truly the bold and adventurous one, and I admit that you deserve to be the Conclave agent, not me."

"That's why it hurts so much to give up on you, Boudi. Maybe I could petition in Heaven for them to send a rescue party. Keep the map if you want, but give me the knife back. I need it to defend myself in case Mistress Ayelet catches me."

Boudi-Ca sighed. "Ayelet could kill you before you could even blink. I hope you're joking. Why would she try to catch you anyway? You're an Ahyehass. You're allowed to leave. You're not a prisoner of the New Order."

"Ayelet grabbed me and took me from Herpessenia, and then she threatened Herpessenia with her sword. Ayelet held my arm and refused to let me go. She told me to behave and stop fighting her. I don't like her. I don't like the things she did to you either—the things you wrote in your diary. She kept seducing you and changing you so you wouldn't run away." Tajee clenched his fists, and his chin trembled.

"You won't run away either if you love me like you say. I'm staying with the New Order Jinni. I'm on their side. You should stay too, unless you want to be imprisoned by the Conclave for your sins."

Boudi-Ca examined Tajee's eight-inch blade. The tang was notched just above the hilt and serrated for three inches before tapering to a honed point. It was a real hunting knife like the ones in Ayelet's training hall. Ayelet was striding across the temple plaza, looking regal again in a fresh dress. She'd changed out of her blood-drenched garments. Ayelet's voice had re-assumed its tone of confidence and authority.

"We're ready to go. If we leave now, chérie, we might reach the Alpacian cabin by nightfall and be back at the Redoubt by tomorrow afternoon. You're certain Enneamiah said that all of the vampires are dead?"

"Yes. She said almost every single vampire is dead, and the Redoubt is now under full Old Order control."

Ayelet smiled grimly. "Not for long. Sekhmet is very angry at everything that happened. She's traveling there right now in feline form to help us. Hopefully with luck and an element of surprise, we'll only have to deal with Commander Anaximah and a tired Old Order garrison. I can't have any more sympathy for my sisters after this. If they've got no vampires or mimo ambassadors left to help them, Sekhmet will give us a big advantage in a battle."

Boudi-Ca slid her cleaned Oya-blade back into its sheath. "I'm ready. Are we just waiting for Golda?"

"Golda is staying here."

"What?"

Ayelet lowered her eyes. "Your healing helped her, but her deep injuries will take more time. She's rattled emotionally from the torture. I've never seen her quite like this. I insisted that she stay and rest herself. Prince Masad has also offered to take her as an apprentice when this is over. Golda agreed. She can serve as the Lady's ambassador here in the east. Now that we've made these allies, we need to keep them."

"I can't believe this. Is Tajee staying here with her then?"

"No. He's going back with us. I don't blame Golda for that decision after everything that happened. She has werewolf boyfriends to keep her company."

"I need to talk to her. Now."

Ayelet gestured. "She's over there supervising the cleanup of the temple, which involves a lot of charred bodies. Greybeard's wolves are making a small pile of dead Jinni outside the temple doors. We need to be flying to make the Alpacian mountains before dark, fledgling. You have ten minutes to say goodbye."

Boudi-Ca folded Tajee's map of Meristyian and handed it to Ayelet without a backward glance. She kept his knife in her hand. She crossed the plaza towards the temple. The bodies of several Old Order Jinni lay in a row just outside the temple doors. Most had been badly burned by Sekhmet, except for Mistress Enneamiah in her blood-soaked black robe. Boudi-Ca felt her stomach tighten further at the sight of so much death. Golda was standing in the shadows just inside the temple doors.

"You're leaving now, Boudi?"

Boudi-Ca steeled herself. "Yes, but Ayelet said you're staying here. I need to know why. I mean, I feel so much for you. Don't you feel anything for me too?"

Golda smiled. "I do, but I've realized that since Allyssia made me into a Jinn, I've been a lost soul. Masad is going to help me find myself. Sekhmet might have answers for me as well. I'm different from the other New Order Jinni, Boudi. I need to find who I am. You can relate to that."

"So Masad is going to teach you things, then?"

"He says I'm a great tracker, and I can be one of the best if he helps me. I just need to focus and work harder at it. Have you ever wanted to be the best at something?"

Boudi-Ca shrugged. "Not really. I don't think so."

"I'm sorry, but I have to do this. Masad wants a protégé. He says that's why he helped the Lady." Golda shook her head. "I know something happened between you and me, and I do feel it. We'll have our time. Right now this is what I want, and it's my duty."

"You know what, Golda? You shouldn't have to explain, but you should know one thing. I love you more than I've ever loved anyone. I think I always have from the moment you first put your arms around me." Boudi-Ca felt tears coming to her eyes. She felt like a wimpy, vulnerable mimo girl in that moment, and she couldn't help herself.

"You're wonderful, Boudi-Ca." Golda stepped forward and hugged her with that big, wonderful hug full of warmth. "I love you too."

"Then why can't we be together?"

"We can, and we will. I need to do this first. I feel sure that you, Ayelet, and Sekhmet will take the Old Order by surprise and find a way to save the Lady. When I'm done with my personal journey, I'll hunt you at the Redoubt. We can spend time together then."

Golda leaned close. Boudi-Ca raised her chin and opened to the kiss. Her whole body tingled with the pleasure of Golda's strong lips. She met Golda's tongue with her own, fencing wetly for a few seconds. She crushed hard against Golda's long body. She shivered when she felt Golda's hand dip low to cup her buttock. She grabbed Golda's muscled ass with her own hand. Her sex turned warm and wanting, and her thighs tingled wherever they touched those stronger, muscled legs. She wanted to be with Golda so much, and she wanted that moment to last forever, but after a minute Golda broke the kiss and edged away.

Boudi-Ca sighed. "Fine. I can wait. I have to ask you one more question before I go. Did Ayelet know all along about Tajee? Did she keep him from me on purpose just like you did?"

"I wasn't keeping Tajee from you. It was Ayelet. Ayelet forbade me all winter from telling you about him. She thought it would upset you and your training as a young Jinn. Ayelet did what she thought was best. I disagreed, but she's your mistress. She used to be mine as well. I wasn't going to disrespect her wishes."

"I don't trust her anymore. I can't."

"You don't have to be Ayelet's fledgling, you know. Ayelet doesn't own you. You can study with whoever you want, like Mistress Isabellah for example."

"I want to be with you then. I want you to teach me things."

Golda chuckled heartily. "That would be nice, but I need to get my own head straight before I'm ready for the responsibility of training a fledgling. A beautiful and talented fledgling like you deserves the best. I keep looking at your lips and wanting to kiss you again. You should go, Boudi. This good-bye is sappy enough already."

"No, it's not. When I was an mimọ girl, I didn't know who I was or anything that I wanted. I did my schoolwork like I was told, and I didn't know anything different. I finally want something for myself. I'm on a journey to understand Love."

"Our threads will meet again in the tapestry. With the Lady's blessing, they might even coincide for a time."

Boudi-Ca crashed into Golda again, and Golda held her in a tight warm hug for long minutes more. Boudi-Ca winced when she felt the pointy claws of Ayelet's messenger bird scrabble on her shoulder and peck at her earlobe.

Let's go, fledgling. It's time to fly.

Boudi-Ca felt a tiny quiver of anger when she broke from Golda. She was tired of taking orders from Ayelet. "I have to—"

Golda's faded purple lips curled into a smile. "I know. Go. We'll see each other again before you know it, I hope."

"Is this your knife?" Boudi-Ca hefted Tajee's knife.

"Yes. I think so." Golda looked pained. "Tajee is a beautiful boy, but he's a handful. He loves you more than me. Will you take care of him?"

"I'll try. Here's your knife. Goodbye." Boudi-Ca pressed the knife into Golda's fingers and forced herself to turn away. She walked alone, but she still carried Golda's wonderful warmth under her skin. She strode from the shadow of Sekhmet's temple into the bright sunlight.

Tajee was climbing the rope ladder up the side of the scaly Nanka. He grabbed the high edge of the riding basket and pulled himself over. Tajee's brown skin glistened in the sun. Ayelet reached to take Tajee's bag and help him into the rear basket seat next to Gonorrheah.

Boudi-Ca quickened her pace across the sandy plaza. Everyone was waiting for her. She wasn't looking forward to riding on the Nanka. The creature was dangerous and toothy-looking. On the other hand, she hadn't looked forward to a lot of things in Meristyian, and she'd survived it all just fine. Several werewolves had gathered by the side of the Nanka for the occasion of the departure, including Greybeard, Marcus, and Elor. Elor grinned. He started clapping as she approached, and the other werewolves joined in the applause. Greybeard raised his hand with a respectful salute.

"All hail fledgling Boudi-Ca," Greybeard rumbled. "Werewolf-friend and liberator of Lady Sekhmet."

"Come back and see us again someday," Marcus added. The big werewolf bowed solemnly without a trace of rudeness. Elor stepped forward and extended a small object in his hairy hand.

"It's for you, Boudi. It's a werewolf-friend whistle. If you ever come out this way again, you can use it to find us."

"Thank you, Elor." Boudi-Ca took the whistle from Elor's thick fingers. She felt pride bloom in her chest until she thought she would burst. At the same time, a blush stole over her cheeks. She could feel Elor's intense desire for her, yet he kept a respectful distance.

She tiptoed to give him two quick kisses on his cheek and snout, and then she grabbed the warm metal rungs of the ladder. She climbed up the side of the Nanka and into the woven riding basket. She settled into the front seat next to Ayelet and pulled the ladder up. Ayelet was clapping for her along with the werewolves. The great scaly Nanka, as if sensing they were ready, unfurled its massive green wings and took a short hop, sending the werewolves scattering. Ayelet grabbed the leather reins in her gloved hands.

"Are you ready for the ride of your life, fledgling? I promise you'll survive."

"Where is Masad?"

Ayelet winked. "We're riding him. Mother Oya down in Cocytus trains these Nanka from birth to serve in Hell's army. This one is tame, but Masad assures me that he can make it angry enough to cause real damage. We'll reclaim my Villa first and hold my hill as our base of operations. Don't worry, fledgling. We'll win this with Sekhmet's help."

"I don't want to be your fledgling any more, Mistress Ayelet. I've made up my mind. I've decided that fighting isn't the way I want to live my Jinn life."

Ayelet arched an eyebrow. "There are people out there who want to take away who we are, chérie. They want to control Love with their laws. That's wrong. Love is Her own law. Love should never be subjected to lawyers and legalities. Love should never be persecuted, prosecuted, or imprisoned. She should only be cherished."

"You can't have love when you're killing people. Violence can't lead to love. It can only lead to more blood and suffering."

"You have time to think, fledgling. You've seen why the Lady needs your fighting abilities. We might drive the Old Order off this time with the help of Masad and Sekhmet, but they could be back again, or the Mimoic Hierarchy could return. Things can only get worse. We're fighting for the Lady. We're fighting for the ones we love, so they don't suffer. You don't understand the evil of Lord Hades and the Hell's Court devils. I hope you'll grow into wisdom with Lady Allyssia's guidance."

Boudi-Ca crossed her arms. "I hope so too, but I wasn't meant to be a blade fledgling. I'm not like you. I don't like violence."

Ayelet shook her head. "You're more like me than you think. You're officially a murderess now as well as a rebel. Mistress Enneamiah was a high-ranking ambassador of Hell's Court, and there was a witness to her death. Ivanka escaped to tell the tale. Your bounty in Hell's Court might be as high as mine. Both the devils and the Smokeless Flames will want to bring you to justice, dead or alive."

"I've already made my decision. I don't trust you, Mistress. You've been hiding things from me. If the Lady and the Redoubt are saved, then I want to learn from Mistress Isabellah. I want to be her fledgling if she'll have me."

Ayelet's lips sketched a small smile. "If that's your real desire, chérie, then we'll make it happen. I want you to be happy."

"I'd be happier to stay with Golda."

Ayelet hauled on the thick leather reins. The impatient Nanka, or rather Masad, hopped again and stretched his great wings to full width, as if testing the weight on his back. "Golda might not be so innocent in all of this, fledgling. Heaven is a very long trip. Golda must have been desperate with Hunger when she dragged you onto the shores of the Sea of Desire so many moons ago. It was only you and her on that lonely beach covered with bones. Were you a virgin when you fell from Heaven, fledgling?"

"Yes. Of course, I was, without any question."

"Golda said your wet clothes were heavy," Ayelet continued. "How heavy are mimo clothes compared to Golda's strength? Not very."

"I'll have to ask Golda. Her story is usually different from yours." Boudi-Ca felt her heart flutter. She tried to imagine Golda taking her like that—hungrily stripping off her white robe, ripping open her chaste mimo girl underthings, sealing her lips in a desperate kiss, and ravishing her as a matter of Jinn survival.

Boudi-Ca slowly smiled as her embarrassment changed to a more pleasant sensation. She'd come so far from that innocent, helpless mimo on the beach. She secretly hoped that someday Golda would ravish her again while she was awake to enjoy it. Ayelet's attempt to discredit Golda had resulted in the opposite effect than intended. Such was the power of Love.

Ayelet snapped the reins, and the Nanka thrashed its massive scaly wings. The Nanka climbed into the air amidst swirling dust and blowing trees. The Nanka rose higher into the sky, then pitched forward and gained momentum. The riding basket swayed frighteningly, but the stout reinforced straps held. The wind rushed faster. The distant purple saw of the Alpacian mountains tipped into view on the horizon.

Boudi-Ca looked askance at Ayelet. She couldn't know what the future would hold, but she knew a few things. She was a Jinn, and she'd never go back to Heaven. She'd killed to protect the lives of her rebel friends, and she was proud of it. She'd fallen in love with another woman, and she was unrepentant. She'd fucked men that she'd never before met, and she'd enjoyed it.

Desires were wonderful, but they could also be painful. She loved Golda. Tajee loved her. None of it could be, at least not yet. She'd been cruel to take Tajee's map from him, but if she was staying with the Jinni, then so should he.

Boudi-Ca looked over her shoulder. Her heart clutched. Tajee wasn't sitting idly in the back seat of the riding basket. He was engaged in a passionate lip lock with Gonorrheah, who pinched his brown chin between her magical fingers. Tajee's dark hair blew in the fierce Isandlwana winds, mingling with the long blonde strands of the smiling wizardress.

~*~

~*~

MESAI Global Edition, License Notes:

Thank you for buying this Book. This book remains the copyrighted property of the author, and may not be redistributed to others for commercial or non-commercial purposes. If you enjoyed this book, please encourage your friends to buy their own copy from their favorite authorized retailer. Thank you for your support.

About the Author

I am Arnett Hartwell, Born on July 7th, 1952 in London, England. My Parents are Rupert and Wilma Hartwell. I Studied at Oxford. I have overcome Alcohol, Shyness, Debt, Dancing, ADHD, Smoking Kush (well not really, but I am working on it. That's not true either, I love it and I'm never giving that up). I worked as a bartender where I drank too much, and as a commercial window installer. I am told that I am a great listener, a great storyteller, and a great lover. I am always dancing, singing, and drinking lots of coffee. I never eat my veggies. I am famous for breaking my toe while break-dancing at a company Christmas party.